The Bogman

WALTER
MACKEN
The Bogman

BRANDON

Published in 1994 by
Brandon Book Publishers
Dingle, Co. Kerry, Ireland.

British Library Cataloguing in Publication Data is
available for this book.

ISBN 0 86322 184 6

Cover Illustration: Steven Hope
Typesetting: Brandon
Printed by Guernsey Press, Channel Islands

Chapter One

The silver birches grow,
  O hóró, o hóró!
The silver birches grow
  Near Caherlo, Caherlo.
The road, they say, is grey,
  Long and grey –
So they say, so they say –
  But I am free to go,
O hóró, o hóró!
  Where the silver birches grow
Near Caherlo, Caherlo!

THERE WAS NOBODY at the station to meet him, nobody at all.

It wasn't lonely there.

It seemed to be in the heart of nowhere. He could see the spires of the churches away about half a mile from the level crossing. That was on the far side. And this side the green and brown land stretched away to the horizon bisected by the grey road that he remembered. On one side of the road the river and the green pasture land licking its banks. And on the other side of the road the brown boglands.

He stayed there until the Dublin train had puffed importantly away. He saw the people in the carriages smoking pipes or smoking cigarettes or looking out superciliously at the little country station. It passed by the white and red level-crossing gates. They closed then with a clatter, releasing from bondage a few horses and carts, whose iron-shod wheels rattled on the rails. He watched the train until he could see the tail of it no more. Then he went to the exit. There was only himself and two greyhounds on leashes, four boxes of fish smelling to the heavens, and the porter. The porter was old and soiled and his moustaches drooped.

"Where are you away to now, boy?" he asked as he took the grey pasteboard. "Where are you away to now?"

"I go to Caherlo," said the boy.

"Begod a long way now, a long way," said the porter looking at him closely. "You are off to work for some man no doubt, now?"

"I'm going back to my grandfather," said the boy.

"Is that so now?" he asked, stepping back a bit to look at him. "Let me see, now. Let me see. You mustn't tell me, now."

"Devil a tell," said the boy, smiling, because to tell the truth he felt good that anybody at all should take an interest in him.

He looked into the blue eyes that peeked inquisitively at him from the low-hanging grey eyebrows. The porter's hands, soiled and encrusted, were up, one of them hitting his forehead and the other scratching his unshaven chin. He saw that the boy was as tall as himself, which didn't make him too tall. About sixteen now, he would be, wearing the short pants too. A kind of red-brown suit, awkwardly cut, long stockings and thick heavy black boots. He knew where he was from anyhow. The Industrial School. He wasn't the first to come to the station here to be apprenticed to the surrounding farmers or town cobblers or tailors. Well built. Hard to tell about the hair because they always had it cut short like that, almost bare to the bone with a fringe in front. Black hair, as black as the back of a bee. With black eyebrows and bright eyes. Sloped his eyebrows were like the devil. But the cut of his jib? What now? Where now? Black, with the straight nose and the full lips and the powerful chin.

"For God's sake," he said then, pointing his finger, "you're one of the Kinsellas from Caherlo."

"That's right," said the boy, very pleased and reaching a hard hand to meet the other's. They shook hands solemnly.

"Who'd ever?" the porter asked. "I know oul Barney well. I knew your mother too. Knew her well. You'd be Cahal now, that was away in the school in Galway? Am I right now?"

"You're right," said Cahal, thinking that it was nice of the old fellow to put it like that.

"I remember her well," he went on, lifting his peaked cap and scratching grey hair with his free fingers. "Well. Tell me now, you are free of the school. That's it?"

"Yes," said Cahal, "I am free of the school." Just like that as if it wasn't a great paean of a song that was swamping his whole head inside. I am free, free.

"And you're going home, now, is that it?"

"Yes, I'm going home now." Home, home, home!

"Bejay there's great doin's in Ireland!" ejaculated the porter. "I'm Tim Sheean."

They shook hands again on that.

Tim Sheean and Cahal Kinsella. Two names. The names of free men. Cahal felt like dancing a jig on the concrete platform.

"You'll see me again, no doubt. I'm part a the building here. I am that. How long have you been here? they ask me. Me is it? I say. Listen, I say, they planted me with the foundations. That's true."

"Do you welcome everyone like that, everyone coming home?" asked Cahal.

"Only our own, amac," said Tim. "Only our own. To hell with the foreigners. Eh, lad?" cackling and poking him in the ribs with a bony elbow.

"That's right," said Cahal, "to hell with the foreigners. We spit on them."

They laughed again.

"And they were to meet you?" Tim asked.

"I thought they were," said Cahal.

He tsk-tsk'ed.

"The hay," he said cryptically. "The hay, or the turf. It's a terrible bloody country. It's always weeping. It must be the angels weepin' at all the badness of us. If they get a fine day like today they must be at it. That's what happened, you'll find."

"I don't mind," said Cahal. "I'll walk home."

"It's a long trot," said Tim. "It's all of ten miles."

They were down the steps outside, on the gravel of the parking space. Nothing there now, but the post-car horse tied to the iron railing and drooping his head.

"And not a lift going the road," said Tim after going to the level crossing and looking at the long half-mile road to the town. "Not a lift. It's a bad day. The middle of the week. And the fine day. Keeps them at home so it does. God bless you, you are strong. Your legs are stretching your trousers. It'll give you an appetite so it will."

"That's right," said Cahal. "It'll give me an appetite." And I dying with the hunger this very minute. But it didn't matter. It mattered to be free. You could suffer a slack stomach if you were free.

"Take the road, so," said Tim, pointing down. "Four miles down till you come to the cross with the big house and then turn in towards the flow of the river."

"I remember it," said Cahal.

"Ah, so you do, so you do," said Tim. "Is it long now that you are away?"

"Ten years, now," said Cahal, "ten years."

"A year for every mile," said Tim. "That's it. You were young when you left, lad. Will your memory take you home?"

"I was six," said Cahal, "and my memory will take me home." He said it in a very determined way, so that the other looked at him, went to say something, changed his mind, and then said: "I remember your mother well. She was a fine woman. She was tall and straight and as black as yourself. I left her off at this station, time she went."

"I'll go, now," said Cahal. To hell with his mother. Imagine that! That was ten years alone now, bottled up with all the generations of boys, her image fading. What did she matter? Nothing mattered except waiting for freedom and the sight of the silver birches by the side of the road.

He swung away, his back to the half-brick station. A funny sight; a station out of sight of the town it served, near a bog, near nowhere. Red brick in the middle of nowhere, but it held Tim who shook his hand and remembered. He turned and waved a hand at the bent old man. Then he was on his own, and the grey road stretched its four miles in front of him. His feet walked faster. Way down over the hump of a bridge he could see the birch trees by the side of the road. That was what he had remembered all those years. Singing in him. The only visible thing to remain with him outside the narrow walls of the school where he had lived his ten years. He hummed the air in his head. With the words that were crowding him. His eyes were bright. The sun warm in his face. What had he now, starting his life? A suit of clothes and a hungry heart and a few ould airs hammering in his head. That's all. And freedom, friend. Don't forget.

The road was quite broad and in sound condition. The grey gravel gave it its colour. He could smell the river on his right, a broad lazy meandering river that wound its weary length past Caherlo. He remembered the bridge there, vaguely. When he got to the bridge he could say he would be home. The birches first and then the bridge over the wide river. That was home.

Smell of rushes and fat lands on the right. Great land. There were cattle grazing in the long fields. Sleek cattle; fat rounded cattle; contented cattle; bulging with milk and beef. On his left the bogs were stretching miles away until they were stopped by the birch trees below. There the land got good again. Big brown stacks of turf saved and dried in the sun. Good turf. As brown as the leaves of the copper beech tree.

He was alone in the world.

The sky was blue over his head. He felt he could walk a thousand miles if he had to, not to mind ten. Not a soul to be seen on the long road, in front or behind. Not a soul on the bogs; not a soul on the river. The smell of rushes and the purple heather and the dust of the road. That was all until, his journey down the long road half done, he heard the cart on the road behind him. A steady trot from the iron shoes of a horse pulling a cart with the turf creels erected. He looked behind him. It was a horse and a cart and a man in the cart, standing up, swaying. He walked on. He heard the sound closing on him. I wonder would I get a lift now, he was thinking. Hoping he would, and hoping he wouldn't. To get there faster would be good; to walk by the birch trees alone would be better, to savour them.

Hush, the man was singing. The man was drunk if you ask me.

Most unmusically he was singing, but on the calm air the words were clear, even above the sounds of the iron on the gravel.

"Oh, the mare she is goin',
She's goin' in great sthyle,
The mare she's behind you an English
  half-mile,
But if you run these rounds as you've run
  them before,
There's not in England nor Ireland can do
  any more."

Cahal grinned, listening close to the noise overtaking and passing him.

"When Skyball he drew near to the winning post
He cried, 'Gentlemen, gentlemen, drink a brave toast,
Drink to Miss Grizzle, that bonny grey mare,
That emptied yeer purses on the plains of Kildare.'"

That was it, and as he passed he flicked the old horse with a whip, crying "Hup, y'oul bitch ye!" jerked the reins, and passed Cahal by, raising his voice again in song.

He wore a tall hat with the crown flat on it, and a cut-away coat of bréidín cloth, and a stiff front with no tie on it. It was curling out of his waistcoat a bit. He had grey whiskers clipped close all round with a scissors, and they were brown with porter. Tiny little eyes over a pug nose that were like two candles in the dark. All that Cahal saw, as the equipage passed him by.

He could have given me a lift, he thought, and then saw the man pulling the horse to a standstill. "Whoa, whoa, whoa, y'oul bitch yeh." The horse stopped and raised a tired hoof and left the tip of it on the ground, and the old man in the cart turned to the side of it, and proceeded to urinate through the creel, singing away at his song about Skyball. Cahal passed slowly by on the far side, discreetly, as if he didn't notice anything at all. The man called him.

"Here, man, here, man!" he shouted, breaking off his song but proceeding with the function of nature. "Whoa-up, will yeh! Isn't it goin' my way you are now, or are yeh going the other way? What kind of a stranger are yeh, that'll let a man pass by and not bid him the time of the day?"

"How are you?" asked Cahal, standing the far side and looking through the bars of the creel at him. The old man was screwing up his eyes to peer at him, his head turned back over his shoulder.

"Wait a minute now," he said then, turning back to fix himself up. "The curse a God on that fella and his black porter. Laced he does have it, I tell yeh, so that you can't go ten minutes without havin' to get rid of it. Step up on the cart now, man, and I'll give you a lift wherever you're going. Where are you bound for?"

Cahal climbed into the creel. "Caherlo," he said.

"Caherlo? Indeed now? A good place. A noble village, but a dunghill when you have seen Ballybla, the village of the flowers. That's where I live. I'll be driving you near all the way, man. I'm Peder Clancy."

Cahal was about to give his own name when the old gentleman burst again into the song about Skyball. He stopped in the middle of his song to peer again at the youth.

"Caherlo? Caherlo?" he repeated, screwing up his eyes. He focused them eventually. "Be the cross of God," he shouted then, "you're Nan Kinsella's bastard!"

Cahal first felt his face going cold and then red and finally the whole complex burst its way out of him in a shout of laughter. Think of the years. Think of the fairy tales in the school, accounting for the fact that you had parents so uninterested in you to fire you into an Industrial School at the age of six. There could be only two reasons, the main ones, poverty or illegitimacy. Think of the romantic tales that you had concocted to cover the yearning and the puzzlement. Think of all that and see it soar away on the wings of a loud laugh at the voice of a drunken old man.

"That's right," said Cahal then, "I'm Nan Kinsella's bastard!"

Peder freed one hand from the reins and struck him a great blow on the back.

"Well, Jaysus Christians, boy," he roared, "you're a credit to your mother!"

Cahal felt good.

"She was as beautiful as a black lamb," said Peder. "Her hair was as long and as black as a night in November. Oh, a grand girl. And oul Barney is bringing you home, you tell me."

"That's right," said Cahal. "I'm let out now and he wants me back the way home."

"You'll be needed, son," said Peder. "How many did he rear? Twelve, thirteen, fourteen, and they away like young crows out of the nest when they are all fed. Away on the wind, boy. All the brave childer he had and not one of them left to him. You'll be a help to him. And your name is Cahal."

"That's right," said Cahal, "me name is Cahal." He wished the old man to be quiet. They were passing into the avenue of the birches. The branches closed over their heads, shutting out the sun. You could see between the trunks the meadows of waving hay, nearly ripe for the cutting. The road ran between the trees for a few hundred yards. Cahal felt a little disappointed. Surely the trees should have been taller and more luxuriant and greater than they were? The barbed-wire fences shutting off the trees from the road were rusted and sagging. But they were nice all the same, the trees, and the bottoms of them were clothed in blackberry bushes and green ferns with fresh fronds uncurling.

"You must come and see us below in Ballybla," said Peder. "We'll have a great welcome for you below in Ballybla. There will be great doings now. It's good to see a young man coming among us. We are all nearly dead old, so we are. Can you sing, now, Cahal Kinsella?"

"I can sing a bit," said Cahal.

"Rattle up an oul song there now, Cahal," said Peder. "The oul mare does be liking a bit of a song. Raise it now and watch her cock her ears."

Cahal sang the song about the silver birches. He had a deep voice that was breaking from a boy soprano. His voice rose up to the roof of the trees and came back again. The old man listened. The ears of the mare rose on her head and she trotted a little faster. His song took them clear of the birches.

"That's powerful," said Peder, a hand on his shoulder. "That's bloody miraculous, boy. Where did you get that now, tell me? Where did you get it?"

"I med it up meself at school," said Cahal. "Med it meself, time I was lonely and it rose up in me, like."

"Med it yourself! Begod, if I ever heard the like," said Peder. "A great thing. Sing it again now. It has a powerful refrain. Off with you, boy."

Cahal sang it again. And he sang it again. And Peder applauded and moved his feet on the turf mould of the cart floor. He was so liking it that he rattled up Skyball again. He insisted on Cahal learning the words of Skyball. He insisted on Cahal singing Skyball with him. It brought them to the forking of the roads.

There was a big house there at the fork. You could see the tall chimneys of it. The good road went off left and the other road, rough and flinty and pot-holed, went right. They took the right road.

"Sons of donkeys," shouted Peder, waving his whip at the house as they passed it by. "Look at that!" waving his other hand to the left where great long fruitful fields stretched away to the horizon behind the low stone walls.

"That's good land," said Cahal.

"That's the best land in Ireland," said Peder. "That's the land that should belong to us now, Cahal. We fought a war for that land. And what happened? When the war was over and we went in to take it we had a battalion of Free Staters down poking bayonets at our ahs. I must tell you. I have tales, boy. You have songs. We'll talk. You'll come to Ballybla. We'll kill a hen. Eh, man?"

"I'd love to visit ye," said Cahal.

"Only meself and the old woman," said Peder. "That's all that's left to us. Our seed and breed, boy, are scattered over the face of the earth. That's the young for you. They must be off."

The road before them was as straight as a good potato drill. Away at the end of it he could see the hump of the bridge that crossed the river Ree.

"Near to the bridge I take you," said Peder, "and then you can hoof it for two mile and you will be home."

"It was good of you to give me the lift," said Cahal.

"Push me down to hell," said Peder. "Stop your ravin'. Listen, oul Barney is a cross oul man. Do you know that?"

"No," said Cahal, "I do not. I have no memory of him at all."

"He is a stern man," said Peder. "But a just man. Some say this and some say that, but I like a man myself that can laugh. You'll be welcome there. He wants someone badly. You will answer him. But take him aisy, hear now?"

"I'll take him as he stands," said Cahal. "Isn't he giving me a home?"

"He is," said Peder, "and I let you down now. You cross the bridge and you walk there on the road and your house is two mile. You will pass by Mark Murphy's and you will pass by Tom Creel's and you will pass by Mary Cassidy's and then you will come into your own. Good luck to you now, and God bless you, and you must visit us beyant."

He pulled the mare to a halt at a gate on his left that led away from the road.

"This is my short cut home. Sometimes I come out from the town the other way and pass by your door. Sometimes I come this way. It all depends what pub I finish the last pint in."

"I'm glad you finished it in the right one today," said Cahal, climbing down from the cart.

"Open the gate, boy, now, do me the turn and close it after us."

Cahal caught the wooden gate in his hands and creaked it open. The horse and cart passed through, the wheels grazing the wooden pillars, and Peder drove on. "God bless you, now, Cahal, God bless you," waving his whip and his fist. The way was deeply rutted and the cart swayed like a ship at sea. But Peder kept his feet and raised his voice in song. Cahal closed the gate and leaned on it a while as he followed the cart with his eyes. He saw it pull to a halt and he saw old Peder performing again, so he grinned and turned away and climbed the road to the bridge.

He leaned on the bridge, a grey four-arched one, and looked at the deep smooth water flowing below in the broad river. He liked the look of it. I am home now, he thought. It wound away from him and it wound behind him. On either side of it meadows sloped down to it, and on his right he could see the cultivated fields, turnip-tops waving and the straight drills of the potatoes and the mangolds dipping down towards the banks.

The world smelled fresh. Over his head there was a fluttering lark piping away. He heard the plop of a fish in the water behind him, and then he turned and headed for home.

On either side of the road there were trees or bushes. You smelled them and the smell that came from cleaned stables. Three houses he passed. Long white-washed houses with thatched roofs set back from the road with cobble-stoned yards in front of them. The first one was the biggest. Who was that? Murphy's, Peder said. A tall red tin shed behind the house, holding hay. The next house the same. White lace curtains on the small-mouthed windows. A dog running out to bark at him threateningly. Hens picking at the grass growing between the stones. No people to be seen. Not a sinner. The big front doors closed on the half-doors in front of them.

He passed the third house and his heart started to pound.

I'm coming in home now, he thought, as he saw where the yard of the house swept down from the road. He could see the yellow thatch of his own house through the branches of tall plane trees that surrounded it. The road before it was arched with trees too, so that the showers that had fallen yesterday had left a residue of rain in the ruts. He got closer and closer and he heard a dog. The dog was crying. Why is the dog crying, he wondered? The dog yelped and cried and whined. He heard dull thumps.

He came free of the trees and stood in front of the opening of the house. It was long and white and there were four windows. The white stables with the corrugated-iron roof came away from it in a right angle. There was a dunghill there, rectangularly spread, and right near this the man was beating the dog with a blackthorn stick.

He was a tall man. He had a beard that was iron grey. It had once been black. His shirt sleeves were rolled, and although the flesh was old the tendons on his arms were strong. They bunched now as he grasped the stick in his right hand. In his left he had the dog held up by the loose fur of the neck. He was holding it high and thumping its ribs with the black stick.

Cahal halted, petrified.

It was a light-brown collie dog with white fur under its

neck. Its legs were waving in the air. Its teeth were bared in anguish. The stick rose and fell as regularly as the tick of a clock.

The man paused then. He held the dog high but let the stick low. He turned his head. He saw the startled eyes of the boy looking at him. His eyebrows were thick and almost hid his eyes. His face was deeply tanned by the sun. His eyes were cold.

"Oh," he said, "it's you."

"Yes," said Cahal, "it's me."

"Well, away into the house with you," said Barney Kinsella, "I'll be in after you."

He turned away then, raised the stick again and went on with the terrible methodical beating of the dog.

Cahal made his way over the stones and the grass and the droppings of geese, past the horse-cart with its shafts on the ground, and the green and yellow mowing machine and he opened the half-door into the dark kitchen and as he went in he thought, a little wryly, So I am free to go where the silver birches grow, near Caherlo.

The crying of the dog followed him.

Chapter Two

There is an alder grove that grows
Forninst the River Ree;
O there I saw her one fine day
Is moladh go deo le Dia!
My sowl forsake me
And Oul Nick take me
To hell or Purgat'ry
If there's an angel
In heaven her aqual,
O moladh go deo le Dia.

THE POLLY'S TEATS were as soft and pliable as rolled silk in his fingers. The milk was a white rain of music as it was squeezed rhythmically into the canted can between his knees.

He liked the polly. She was placid and he liked the feel of the down of her udder on the backs of his hands. The chain, polished almost to silver from the rubbing of her coat, jingled as she pulled the hay from the stall in front of her. Right behind him he could feel the bulk of the black cow as she leaned against him or flicked his hair with her tail. On the other side of the polly he could hear the busy milking of Bridie who was doing the Friesian.

Only one difference in the stable this morning. They weren't singing and they weren't talking. There was just the sound of the milk making a froth in the almost-filled cans. That and the coming and going of the one sparrow family that had built its nest up near the tin roof where the air-hole was. It was a roomy stable. After two years he no longer smelled it. An odd mixture; of baled hay and the manure of the cattle and up above their heads the wooden platform where the hens roosted, it bowing with the weight of their accumulations. The stable was divided into two. On the other side the jennet slept in the winter and there you could smell him and the polished harnesses hanging on the walls, and the light glinting on the cold steel of the hayforks and the pitchforks and the scythe and the blades of the mowing machine.

The flow of milk became scanty, so he moved from teat to teat, extracting the last drops, then he dipped his fingers into the milk and put the sign of the cross on the cow's hip. He rose then, stretching his back.

"Are you nearly finished, Bridie?" he asked, going around the cow's end to peer at her.

She didn't answer. Her head was buried in the cow's side, and her fingers were mechanically pulling away at the teats.

"Bridie!" he called again.

"I'll be in in a minute," said the muffled voice of Bridie.

"What the hell is wrong with you?" he wanted to know, coming closer to her.

He soon knew.

He saw her hand coming up and crossing the cow's hip with the mark and then she rose and her eyes were as red as boiled beetroot.

"Oh, Cahal," she said then, and wrapped her free arm around his neck. He could feel her tears on his skin and her black coarse curly hair on the side of his face.

"Bridie! Bridie!" he said, lifting his free hand to pat her back. He was astonished. "Sure you don't have to go at all," he said. "Nobody is forcing you to go if you don't want to."

"I'm all right now," said Bridie, pulling away from him and raising an edge of her dress to rub her eyes. She was up to his shoulder. Her face was big and burned by the sun. She wore the single garment only, as he could feel with his hand, and when she raised her dress he could see her thigh as white as an egg. He dropped his can and moved close to her. He put his hand on her arm.

"What would you be crying for, Bridie?" he asked.

"Oh, I don't know," said Bridie. "It's foolish of me, I suppose, but I'll miss ye, and what are ye going to do when I'm gone? Tell me that?" she demanded, turning her face full to him. He liked Bridie. She had been there in the kitchen the first night he came. A solid kind young girl with the strength of a man and a big heart.

"I don't know what in the name of God we'll do," said Cahal, "and that's a fact. But there's no need to be crying about it."

"No indeed," she said, "no indeed. It's just that I got soft. It's the last day I'll be milkin' that oul cow and now you'll have to do it all on yeer own, and how'll ye get on with nobody to bake a cake for ye or boil a kettle! What's to become of ye at all?"

"We'll probably poison one of us," said Cahal, "but God save us, if we're hungry we'll do it and that's all that's to it, and we might be able to get another girl someplace, but nobody like Bridie."

"I never thought," said Bridie. "It's excitin' to the time. I am goin' to America. That's what your mind says. Me poor sister savin' up like that to send me the fare. That's all you think of. And now when the time is up, I feel the stomach fallin' out of me. And I look at me poor father at home and I say what is to become of him when I'm gone. And me mother is gettin' old. And what's to become of her and then I'm walkin' away from you and oul Barney and lavin' ye with nobody to look after ye. All that came over me."

"Poor oul Bridie," said Cahal and put an arm around her. He liked the feel of Bridie. It was like the comforting feeling he had sitting down beside the polly. Bridie was bulky. Her chest was swelling her dress. She wasn't handsome. Her nose was small in a big face and her teeth were prominent and strong, but it came over him now – Bridie will go and I am left alone with oul Barney. Think of the bright kitchen with Bridie out of it.

"Why are ye all going to America?" he asked then. "The whole village of Caherlo is denuded of young people. Why can't ye stay at home for God's sake?"

"I don't know," said Bridie. "What's the use of talkin'? What good am I anyhow to me father? Let me go away and I will be of real use to him. Even if I only send him five shillings a week. Oh, I don't know. Here, come on out of this. All I have to do yet before I go. You'll come over to the house tonight, won't you? Don't forget now."

"I will," said Cahal, "if Barney lets me."

She went into the sun with her can. She grumbled back at him.

"If Barney lets me! I never seen anyone like you. You let oul Barney ride you, Cahal Kinsella. There's only one way to treat him. You have to stand up to him. Like me. Do you think I could have stuck the house athin for over two years if I hadn't stood up to him?"

She was out in the sun waiting for him. He joined her and they turned their steps towards the small dairy in the shaded side of the yard under the shelter of the tall chesnut tree.

"What does it matter, Bridie?" he said. "Life is short. He is old. Everything passes. What's the use of forcing it?"

She looked at him, her legs spread. She saw him confronting her, his thick black hair falling over his forehead, his striped shirt sleeves rolled on thick arms, hairy arms. His shirt open in front, a big chest pushing through. He was a head taller than she, and she wasn't small. A piece of light cart-rope holding up his trousers, old discoloured trousers, patched and darned by her own hands. Working trousers with a great slack behind on them. His teeth were very white in the middle of his dark face. She liked Cahal. He was as quiet as his grandfather was unquiet. But he could be too quiet.

"It worries me," she said, "to see you lying down under

him. You are big enough now to be different. You are eighteen, aren't you? I don't like to think of you going about for him as if you were his collie dog. What way will he treat you when I amn't here?"

He took her arm and ushered her towards the dairy.

"Don't be worrying about me, Bridie," he said. "I'm all right. I like life. Honest to God I do. If you were cooped up in a school as long as I was, you would feel like I do, what a wonderful thing it is to be out in the world and see it turning."

They unlatched the dairy and went in. It was small and clean. They poured some of the milk into the tall churns and the rest of it into the great stone jar. Then they came out.

Barney was in the middle of the yard.

"What's delaying yeh?" he asked. "It'll be night time alone before you have the cows down and the turnips not even started. Be off with you fast now, for the love of God. There are enough idlers in Caherlo without you becoming one of them."

He turned on his heel to go then and Bridie stopped him.

"Mister Kinsella," she said, "I hope you're coming over to the house tonight for the farewell."

He stopped.

"Tonight is it?" he said. "Maybe I will, if I have time. What the hell you are going to America for I don't know. Isn't there enough eejits in America already without increasin' the number a them?"

"That's the way," said Bridie. "But if you don't want to come, Cahal is coming."

He was wearing an old hat, the brim pulled down over his eyes. His grey brows were jutting out of the shade.

"He can go," he said then after a pause, "but let him be back in time here. He doesn't want to end up like his mother."

He turned away then, passed by the stable through the wooden gate and turned left to the kitchen field at the back of the house where he was planting young cabbages.

"The dirty oul thing," said Bridie.

Cahal was amused.

Taunts about his mother had always failed to hurt him. They were many. The old man was becoming crustier each month. What was Cahal expected to feel? He never knew his mother. For all he knew Barney might be right.

"Well, I'll see you tonight so, Bridie," he said, moving to the stable again.

"Now you see what I mean," she called after him. "Won't that be going on all the time? Why do you stand there and take it like you were a saint?"

Cahal laughed. He turned.

"I'll sing a song at your wake, Bridie," he said.

"You will!" she said. "That's great. Sing the song about the races of Caherlo. You know the one you gev me last night. I nearly died laughing. Won't you now?"

"I will," he said.

He went into the stable, put his arms around the necks of the cows and freed them from their chains. They made their way into the yard and climbed heavily up on to the road. He picked up an empty sack, threw it over his shoulder, and followed them. He was humming. Smiling. The corners of his eyes crinkling. About the races of Caherlo. That adventure he had heard from Peder Clancy the last time he had been to visit them. And he made a song of it.

The cattle picked their way knowingly on to the road and turned left at the first fork, on to the flint road that led to the bog below and the river meadows. He ambled along behind them, flicking at them with the sack and saying "Hup! Hup!" but they weren't in the least afraid of him and waddled along calmly. The road went down an incline. On each side there were tall hedges of ivy and mountain ash and the sides of the ditches were sprinkled with wild parsley. The cows would stop to pick a few mouthfuls of the green grass. He would clap them on the hip and off they would go again. He passed the Jordans' house. The old man was sitting out in front on a chair in the sun. His frock coat green with age and his bowler hat nearly the same colour. A dirty pipe in his mouth, he drooling on it. The stick between his knees and his old neck stringy and yellow. Nodding. You could see the black warts on his hands from here. Poor old bastard. He wasn't long for the world. His son and himself lived there. Not very clean. But a devoted son in a way. Growing old in the service of a doting father. For what? One of the ones that didn't go away.

"Good-day, Mr Jordan," he roared. The old head came up and the eyes squeezed their way around to him.

"Ho! Ho!" he said peering. "Ho! Ho! Cahal! The blight is on the spuds. Spray your potatoes. Hear me now! Spray your potatoes. Any day. Jamesey is out in the back at them!"

"They're done," said Cahal. "We have them done."

"That's right," nodded the other. "Spray the spuds. Terrible times, lad, terrible times. How is your mother?"

"She's well, thanks," said Cahal. He tried one time to tell pour oul Spray that his mother was no longer there. What did it matter? The old fellow was probably too deaf to hear. Certainly the old brain was no longer spry. All that was left to him was spray the spuds. Why? Because he was very old. Because when he was young he had lived with the terror of the Famine at his heels. Was that it? Let me grow old clean, Cahal thought, and passed on.

They cleared the lane of the tall hedges and came down into the plain. It stretched away from him as far as the eye could see. A great plain of bog bisected by the grey road, stopped on the left by the river and on the right by the horizon.

He followed the road for a few yards and climbed a little hump-backed bridge over a small stream that made its way to the river. It was a brown bog stream that came gurgling from the great breadth of the boglands. It was quiet now under the sun. He leaned over the bridge to see the small trout darting to the shadows as his own shade was thrown on the water. Then he passed on. The cows were waiting patiently at the wooden gate. He opened it. It creaked loudly. He hooshed the cows in there and locked the gate after them. They nuzzled the rough bog grass.

He turned then whistling and went back the way he had come until he reached the gate that led to the fields sloping down to the river.

There was one great common field here where the people of Caherlo grew their potatoes and mangolds and turnips. It was shared by six of them. Cahal walked on to his own piece. It was the one nearest the river. He admired the earth as he walked. It was black earth and it was steaming now as the hot sun raised the dew from it. There was a rough path bisecting the great field, formed from the stones that had been lifted from the plots to make a rough and ready path for the wheels of the carts.

There was a horse and cart on it now. Sonny Murphy was standing up in the cart as it joggled. He supported himself by usage and the rope reins leading to the horse's bridle. It was a brown horse, who was glad of the pause as Sonny pulled him up. He swung his head and aimed his mouth at the green stalks of the growing oats nearby. Caught two of them and pulled them into his mouth before Sonny dragged his head back with a chuck on the reins.

"It's a great day, Cahal," said Sonny.

"It is," said Cahal. "It's no day at all for working. We should all have free days whenever the sun comes out."

Sonny laughed.

He was a well-set-up young man with red hair bunching out from under a cap. The sun was glinting off the buckle of a brass belt holding up soiled blue trousers. His house was the one back there of the trees. They were well set up and somehow Cahal always thought that Sonny looked that way. Like his father, Mark. From dawn to dusk, a quiet man with little to say for himself except to get up and get out and work, hard, and work his children hard. No going to America for Mark Murphy's children. Mark didn't drink and he didn't smoke and kept to himself, but if he did, he had a grand horse trap for going to Mass on Sundays in the town, and he had a costly hayshed at the back of his house, and he brought home his hay in real hay-lorries that took the toil out of it all, and he had a reaper and binder for his corn; and in his long white house with two rooms added on to the back with slates on them he had a room where you just went in and sat down. A proper parlour. Not that anyone ever went in and sat down in it, but it was there if you wanted to. Currant cake twice a week and fresh meat on Tuesdays, Thursdays, and Sundays. That was Mark Murphy. Solid, dependable, successful.

And that was his son Sonny with the red hair and the confident laugh from a narrow face. Cahal always felt like a bastard when Sonny talked to him. He often smiled at that. But it was true. Sonny was all that was hardworking and respectable, and althought it was never said, Cahal always had the feeling that he was as he was when he talked to Sonny.

"It's great weather," Sonny said. "It'll give 's a chance at the hay. Three or four days of this and we'll have the back broke of it."

"Aye and your own backs too," said Cahal. "Whenever I see a day like this I feel like getting under a hedge and going to sleep."

"Faith," said Sonny, "that's no way to be a farmer around here. You work or you go to the wall. There's a lot a lazy men in this village, and that's what'll happen to them. You mark my words. It'll end up be us all havin' to go and give them a hand at the butt-end of the year when we will have to make up for their idleness."

"Ah, well, maybe they'll live longer that way," said Cahal.

"Aye," said Sonny, "or die of starvation. Are you going over to Bridie's hooley tonight?"

"With the help of God," said Cahal. "Are you?"

"If we get done in time I might," said Sonny. "What are they giving a hooley for? Where'll the oul fella Foxy get the money to give a hooley? Wouldn't he be better off not to be runnin' into debt but buying some lime to put into his land?

He has a field over beyant that's growing nothing but this-tles and dock for the want of a bit of care. What can make men so feckless at all, I'm asking you?"

"What age are you, Sonny?" Cahal asked.

"I'm twenty. Why?" Sonny asked.

"Well, if I were you," said Cahal, "I'd go home and tell me oul fella you were going to take the day off and then I'd hop into town and I'd get blind drunk, and if he asked you why, you could say, 'So that I won't be old before me time, father'."

"Are yeh coddin' or jokin'?" Sonny wanted to know.

"Neither," said Cahal. "You wouldn't know. I'll be leavin' you now, Sonny. I have to thin the turnips."

He passed by.

"You're a quare wan," Sonny shouted after him.

"I know," said Cahal. "I'm a bastard."

He left Sonny with his mouth open.

What the devil came over me at all, he wondered? Just that. Why shouldn't old Foxy Killeen mortgage the old home, if necessary, to see his daughter off to America? Why should men be smug about the failings of others? He bet there wasn't a laugh in the long body of Sonny Murphy or his oul fella either.

He cursed when he looked at the long lines of turnips.

Miles they seemed to stretch, each row of them. There were twenty rows. Two hours a row made forty hours. He thought of the school. Of a hundred boys being sent out into the long field. Given a section each and in an hour an acre would be thinned or weeded or whatever you wanted. He got down on his knees with a sigh and started at the first row. Pulling the weeds, thinning the sturdy plants, leaving the six inches between. The earth under his nails. The crushed snails slimy in his palms. And the sun getting hotter and hotter. Beating the sweat out of him. Nothing cool but his knees from the embrace of the black soil. He groaned and sighed and finally hummed. He liked it really. The smell of pulled weeds and the coarse feel of the young turnip leaves. Like the feel of Bridie's hair. Poor Bridie. Big and rough and awkward. But willing. Like a plough horse. With a trusting faith in everything. What would happen to her in the fabulous land of America? He tried to fit her in there. To see her with a suitcase staring up at the big big buildings you saw in papers. Would America digest Bridie or would it regurgitate her? Or what would happen to her? Probably manage. Be better off.

He wiped the sweat away with his hand, leaving a smudge of earth on him. He had been working for three hours when he straightened up to lick his dry lips. He saw the river glinting below him then. It wound away just below. Tempting. This big field and the ditch and a cool green field below where the river licked at the grass. On this side the reeds rising, silent today because there was no breeze, and then there at the turn the grove of alder bushes where the bog stream came into the broad flow of the river.

It was too cool. The very look of it tortured him with thirst.

He rose from his knees, walked the ridges, leaped over the ditch and walked in the grass field. It was a cool carpet cushioning the heavy hobnailed boots that were like ovens on his feet.

He went down near the reeds and threw himself on his belly and leaned over to drink the flowing water. Like a cow. He saw his red face before he broke up the smooth flow. A red face. Even now, the black hair was strong on his jaws. He had to shave once a week and looked bad in between.

He dipped his face into the stream. The water wasn't cold, but it was nice on his face. He opened his eyes in the water. He could see the gravel on the bed of the river under him and the small crawfish darting with their flat tails high. Burrowing and then they were gone. He saw where the gravel gave way to brown bottom and then black black as the river deepened to the great depths where the big pike would lurk. He raised his face, spluttering. He rubbed the wet on his face with his hand; saw his hand was dirty brown; washed that and then washed his face, with his two hands. He felt relieved. Felt the shirt on his back wet with sweat. He was right beside the alder grove. It was on his right, screened by the rushes. He was about to lever himself up when he saw the girl.

She had come from the road by the little humped bridge. She had crossed the intervening fields on the far side of the small stream. Through the rushes he saw her. A girl with red hair, not red, sort of copper and green under the sun. A tall girl, with the rhythm of youth in her walk and her body. Her feet were bare. She came right to the mouth of the little stream where it met the river. That side the river was beached. Yellow gravel that shelved gently away. Piled up at the meeting of the waters. She came into the grove, paused there, and in front of Cahal's petrified eyes she reached down with her brown arms, caught the hem of her light dress and drew it over her head. For the first time in his life outside his fevered dreams he was looking at the body of a girl. She threw her dress on to the grass, sat on the bank and walked into the river. No shiver. Just in until it covered her up to her waist. Then she took the soap that was in her hand, splashed herself and rubbed it on her body.

Cahal's mouth was dry and he felt a cold breeze in his head. What will I do now? Will I try and creep away?

He raised his hands on the bank to lever himself up. His hands slid on the wet clay and before he quite knew what had happened, his body followed his hands and he went gently head first into the river. He couldn't believe it as the water closed over him. Over the gravel and over the brown ground and into the black black. He became frightened then, because he felt a terrible pull from the flow of the river. So deceptive, so calm and yet it was hauling him along at a fast pace. He kicked out wildly, and kicked out again with his heavy boots. His head broke water, and he pushed at it with his arms and kicked with his legs and found to his surprise that he was being swept along with it, so that when his head emerged and the water cleared from his eyes he found himself looking straight into the eyes of the red-headed girl.

Her eyes were startled as she met his own, and her arms were up covering her small white breasts.

He felt terrible.

He waved a hand.

"Hello," said Cahal. "It's a nice day, isn't it?"

Holy God, his mind said, did I say that? What kind of an eejit are you at all? What will she think?

"I fell in," he added then as the water swept him past her.

She still remained looking at him with her eyes wide.

His heavy boots dragged him under then again, so it saved her from seeing the red of his face.

He set about landing. He was a good swimmer. Shades of the sea in the town of the school. In the summer the long line of the boys marching in twos to the big rocks near the shore that men called the Counsellors, they were so stolid and unloquacious and eternal.

He hauled himself up on the bank well past the alder grove and sat there to recover his breath. Would it be best for me now just to pretend nothing had happened at all and go creep away to the road, or would I wait until she might be gone and creep in there to the grove and strip and try and squeeze the wet out of my clothes or what?

He heard her calling.

"Come here," she said.

He turned his head.

She was standing there beside the bushes, the dress pulled on her again. It was a blue dress and there were dark patches on it where it was touching her wet body.

He rose stiffly to his feet and walked towards her as if he had two wooden legs, to try and keep the wet clothes from his flesh.

He stopped in front of her. It was all right. There was a tremble at her lips. Her eyes were crinkling. She's a very nice girl, he thought. Her features were very regular. A square sort of a chin and narrow eyebrows, that weren't the same colour as her hair at all but kind of black.

"What in the name of God brought you into the river in your clothes?" she wanted to know. "Do you do that often, or what?"

Cahal laughed. He laughed very loudly. Because it was funny. Damn it, it was, now that it was over. He had a picture of him passing by and waving a hand and saying Hello.

"You don't live in the river, do you?" she asked.

"No," said Cahal, "I don't. I was down having a drink and I slipped in." Don't say why. Let that be unspoken.

"I thought I was seeing things," she said. "What are you going to do now? You can't stand there like that."

"No," said Cahal. "And I can't go home like this either. 'Twould take a great deal of explainin' at home."

"Go in there to the grove and squeeze them," she said. Practical girl too, isn't she, Cahal thought. "I'll turn me back on you," she added then. "I won't peep."

Cahal looked at her closely. Was that a blow under the belt now, he wondered? Then he laughed again.

"Don't go away, please," he said. "I want to talk to you."

"Me too," she said, shaping her mouth grimly. They both laughed. Cahal felt good.

"I won't be long," he said and left her. She sat on the grass and shook the water from her hair. She listened. She heard just the dull sucking of the wet clothes leaving him.

Cahal removed them and wrung them as dry as he could with his hands. Crouching low. My God, if anybody could see me like I saw her. Laughing at the thought. He squeezed and squeezed at his old trousers and then put them on again and came out of the grove. He sat beside her, wringing his shirt. It didn't feel queer, that was the odd thing. It warmed him up, the thought. Here I am and never saw this girl in my life before and it's quite the accepted thing to be squeezing me shirt under her nose.

"You're Barney Kinsella's grandson," she said.

"That's right, I am," said Cahal. Now he should be able to

say, You are such a one. But he couldn't.

"You don't know me," she said for him. "I'm Máire Brodel. I live below there in Grange."

"Why haven't I seen you before?" he asked.

"We're new. We're not here long," she said. "You are very black." She was nodding at the black hair of his chest.

The change startled him.

"Oh, yes," he said, bringing up his hairy arms to cover himself. That gesture. Where had he seen it before? Her eyes were laughing. She fell back on the grass laughing. He felt a little foolish.

"Ah, we'll forget that," she said then.

"What brought you over here?" he asked her.

"Och, just walking," she said. "You know the Jordans up the road."

"Aye," he said, "I do," wondering what affinity there could be between her and Old Spray.

"They're sort of related," she said. "I come up to give them a hand. They have no woman in the house. My father is the new herd over on the estate beyond," nodding her head at the great land on the other side of the river. "We come from Roscommon."

"Do you like it here?" he asked.

"I don't know yet," she said. "It seems all right."

"I wasn't spying on you," said Cahal earnestly, "don't think that now. I was just there and you came and I didn't know what to do."

"That's all right," she said. "Don't worry. I don't mind. I knew about you. You were black, they said. Over there. We are near Peder Clancy. He passes us by and tells us things. We know nearly everything now."

"Oh," said Cahal.

"Are you going to the hooley tonight?" she asked then.

"You know about that too?" he asked.

"Oh yes," she said. "I know everything. Foxy's daughter is working for Barney Kinsella and she's going to America and Foxy is giving a hooley and everybody in the four parishes is wondering where he's going to get the money for it, but what matter? It's a hooley. Goodbye now. I have to go. I'll see you again." And she rose to her feet and went away, just as abruptly as that.

He stood and looked after her. She didn't turn her head. Great God, what kind of a girl is she at all?

Then he thought of the turnips. What would Barney say when he came down later with the can of buttermilk? What's this? Where were you? What kind of an idler are you? What have you done since you came?

He grimaced his way into his wet shirt and boots and ran for the field of turnips.

Chapter Three

Stars will gleam on the river stream;
Wee swallows build in the stable wall:
Wind will blow on the fields below;
The leaf will come and the leaf will fall.
   But uch, ochón – misfortunes grieve me!
Ten thousand blights on the foreign shore
That bears the bright one I love sincerely
And binds her from me for ever more.

PEDER HUSHED THE clamour in the kitchen by raising his voice roughly above the din.

"All right! All right! I will so!" he roared.

They quietened down a bit then. "Hear, hear!" Peder was called, sincerely from the older people and a trifle ironically from the younger ones. They had been "pursuading" Peder for the last twenty minutes. Everyone knew he was only panting to do his turn, but it was ritual that he be reluctant. That he had a sore throat; that his voice was gone back on him; that he had forgotten the whole incident. The last was a little incredible since he had been telling it at every gathering in Caherlo for the past twenty years nearly. So he was plied with porter and clapped on the back, and cosseted generally, until in a great glow of the fire and the porter working in his head, he cleared his mouth, spat expertly into the ashes of the open fire and commenced.

"'Twas a night in November," said Peder, and paused dramatically.

"That's right, Peder, it was surely," said Foxy, who was sitting over from him, dressed in his Sunday best and his eyes red from the smoke and the weeping. "I remember it well."

"There were peculiar goings-on all over the country at this time," said Peder, "with which we had little to do at all. Be times it was in us to put a bit of black on our kissers and go be the light of the moon back to the Grange there, and we'd drive your man's cows half into Offaly. But of this particular crime we were as innocent as if we was babies in cradles. As true as God. This was how it happened."

He launched into the preliminaries of the tale.

I suppose, thought Cahal, who was standing squeezed against the dresser, that there isn't a soul here who couldn't tell every word of the story and not miss out a comma or an exclamation mark. He saw, when the thronged bodies in front of him parted, Máire Brodel, over near the alcove beside the fire, where they kept the bag of flour on the box. She was there leaning against Sonny Murphy. He was talking into her ear, his white teeth gleaming in the lamplight. One red hand was on her shoulder. She had a blue ribbon in her hair, and a flowered dress on her, and when she had been on the floor a few minutes ago doing a half-set he had admired her legs in silk stockings. She hadn't regarded him at all since the evening started. Just raised her eyebrows and gave him a cool hello, as if they were meeting for the first time. It set him back but he didn't mind. He was caressing a glass of stout now in his hand, bending his black head to smell at it. It was a novelty to him. He didn't like the first one. It tasted just like the quinine they got at the school when they got a fever. But after he drank it, there was a sort of tang on his tongue that made him long for more.

"I was just finished rakin' the fire and scratchin' meself," Peder was saying, "and hangin' me socks on the crook, and there was herself above in the room and she complainin' down at me. What ails you? she is saying. Look at the hour of the night it is. Will you stop scratchin' yourself down there and come up to bed?"

"You were always a good man in a bed, Peder," said an anonymous voice from the great throng around the settle-bed. They laughed and shushed the interloper, and said: Don't mind him, Peder. Go on with you.

Peder spat accurately at the ashes again.

He glared at the young man.

"Any time I went to bed, me man," he said, "I turned out better than you anyhow, and if I'm not to have peace, why, then there's no more to be said and I'll be off home with me."

This nearly caused calamity, as he half rose from his chair. Foxy came forward and placated him. And poor Bridie went over to the young man and read him. He was an outsider anyhow, somewhere from the back of beyond.

"I'm sorry, I'm sorry," he said when they tackled him. "I was oney sayin'."

Bridie turns to Peder.

"Me last night, Peder Clancy," she says then, "and would you be lettin' a thick lug like me man be takin' the pleasure away from me, and it never again maybe I will be hearin' you at your yarns? Please mind me, Peder, and go on."

Cahal thought Bridie was looking very well, except that her eyes were as raw as freshly cut vegetables. She had a coloured dress on her that seemed to give her a shape, and her hair was brushed and curling, and she wore silk stockings and nice shoes. Very well she looked indeed. So did everyone else for that matter because they were all dressed in their best. Even himself. He could smell the tailor's chalk on his suit nearly. Hand that to oul Barney. He dressed him anyhow and filled his stomach. He wasn't mean in material things. He felt sorry for Bridie's mother. She was a small woman, sitting in on the hob seat over the fire with her head in her apron and she weaving from side to side and everybody pretending not to notice anything at all. Foxy was hugging the half barrel of porter, sitting beside it on a stool, and rising at times to take an empty glass and fill it, silencing the insincere protestations of the potationer. There was a terrible fug in the kitchen. There must be about half a hundred people there, he thought. They came from ten miles away. All were welcome. All you wanted was the word. There's a hooley over beyond on Saturday night. That was enough. Cahal didn't know a third of the people who were there.

"All right," said Peder subsiding, "but let that fella keep a spit in his gullet and gurgle it. Where was I?"

"You were goin' into bed with the wife, Peder," said Jamesey Jordan obligingly. A few titters. Peder looked suspiciously at Jamesey's face. It was a big honest face with no guile so he didn't take umbrage. Cahal was laughing in his stomach. He was enjoying it. Máire Bodel's eyes flashed over at him, saw him secretly laughing, his black hair falling over his forehead. She felt herself getting red. With anger. Placid, she was thinking, like a black bull. Negative he is. She wanted to go over and slap his face and shake him, and say: Wake up, you. Become vital. What didn't grow inside you? What had it to do with her?

"That's right," said Peder. "I took off me oul britches there in front of the fire and hung it over the back of the chair. It was as wet as water, because there had been great rain and the river was rising and we had been abroad savin' cattle from the meadow fields and getting them up to high ground. So I blow out the lamp in the kitchen and up I goes and pull into bed be herself. That was near midnight, they reckon."

"It was that, Peder," said Foxy. "It was about that time sure enough."

"So," said Peder, "I fell asleep like a baby and I had great dreams. It's queer now, I should remember the dreams. They were very pleasant. I thought I was over in the big house in Grange, that your man was dead and I was the owner of all that beautiful sweep of land on the other side of the river. Up at a window I was, lookin' out at it, with me thumbs in me waistcoat, and I sayin', Well, if any a them bees from Caherlo put a foot on me land or drive one a me thousand cows, I'll crucify them. That's true. And then, right at that I heard a sound like the heavens fallin' apart. A great bangin' and thunderin' and I feel herself shakin' me awake. 'Peder,' she is sayin'. 'Below, below. There's somebody beatin' the dure.' I came awake then, and I listened. It was true for her. Who could that be now, I wondered, at this hour a the night, and the curse a hell on them whoever they are to be wakin' a man from his wonderful dreams.

"'Go down,' she says, 'and see who it is. Maybe somebody is dyin' or they want you to pull a calf in Jordans'.' So I rose grumbling from me bed and I lit the candle and I went down in me shirt and I was a mad man, I can tell ye, and to this day I can feel the concrete of the floor cold to me feet. I got to the kitchen and the bangin' at the door was terrible. It was an oak door and it was resistin' but they were bendin' it with the power of the blows. 'Open up, there! Open up there!' they were shoutin' in funny sort of accents. 'Hould on, ye pagans,' I shouted back at them and I tuggin' the bolts. 'Hould on now, or I'll cripple ye. Do ye want to take the hinges away with ye?" And then the door opened."

He paused there and looked around him. He has them all right, Cahal was thinking. He was a good storyteller. He told it with his body as well as the cadences of his voice.

"'The cross a Christ about us,' I said then, and they put a rifle up to me throat. They seemed to fill the kitchen and there was oney three of them. All black tops and tan britches and guns swinging and tied to their thighs. They shouted at me. I stood there petrified in me shift and me mouth open. 'Who are you?' they roar. 'What's your name? Did you cut a trench in the road over? Come on, talk up, if you don't want a bullet in your guts.' I got mad. I pushed away the gun. 'I'll talk when you take that yoke outa me gullet,' I said. 'What the hell do ye want with me? I never done nothin',' I said. 'What are ye talkin' about?' 'Who else is in the house?' they ask, and then one fella lights a torch and off with him up the oul wan's room. 'Here, come back our that,' I shouted. 'Shut up!' says the other fella and digs me in the stomach with the butt of the gun.

"I heard herself screaming. It nearly raised the roof of the house, I can tell you, and before I can say more, your man comes running out of the room like he was scalded. 'Oney an oul hag up there,' he says. 'Come on out with you!' they say, clearin' the door. 'Here,' I say, 'where are ye takin' me? What have I done?' 'Out with you, you old bastard!' they say, 'and no more talkin',' and out I go into the night in me bare bum and I steppin' into a puddle in me bare feet. 'Herc,' I say, 'for the love a Christ let me put on me britches. How can a man meet his Maker without a britches?' 'On with you,' they say, and push me from behind, up to the road where I see the lorry with the lights on it. I'm a dead duck now, I say, and for no reason at all that I can think of, and isn't it a terrible thing that a man should be kilt in oney his shirt and thanks be to the great God it is dark so that no one can see me in me shame. Then I heard herself behind and she was roaring, and she running after, and one of the bucks pushing her back with the flat of the gun. 'Peder! Peder!' she is roaring, 'come back to me!' And all I can say is, 'I wish to the Lord God I could, Maggie!' when they push me on. 'Up with you now,' they say when we come to the tail-board of the lorry, and up I am flung and look around me and what do I see?"

He gave them the dramatic pause again.

"Seven citizens of Caherlo and Ballybla I see, and they trying to hold down the tails of their shirts to the lift of the wind. Is that true, Foxy Killeen?"

"It's as true as God," said Foxy. "It was a terrible thing to do to Christian men."

"Now!" said Peder. "There was me and Foxy and Barney Kinsella and his son John that is now in Boston, America, and Tom Creel and Mark Murphy and Mary Cassidy's man, Mike, God rest him. There we were, a lorry-load of skhin and bone on the road to nowhere. Two of me men climb in behind and the lorry roars away and we are off, and we trying to hold the side of it to keep from being kilt with the bouncing, and trying to hold our shirts down from the shame. I can tell you there was never a lorryload of human beings in the world before like we were that night.

"And where do we end up? Over on the road to the town. Over there when the silver birches grow. Ye know it well. We couldn't talk. We hadn't time. We were too mad and too ashamed. Oh, well the cripples knew what they were doing when they took us in our shirts. They took away our strength be exposin' our manhood, that's what they did, or we wouldn't have gone so quiet, or we'd ha' done somethin' of note to the villains.

"They halt there and we got down and they put shovels into our hands. 'Shovel now,' they shout, 'and we'll plug the first one that draws his breath.' Somebody had dug a ten-foot trench right across the road, and there was a lorry drawn out of it that had run into it. The whole front of the lorry was crumbled and the glass was splintered and you could see gobbets of human flesh hangin' to the splinters and right in front of the trench there was a great pool of blood like as if a bullock had been slaughtered. That cheered us up. Some of them had been kilt. There. The boys had dug the trench for the lorry and got it. It cheered us up at a great rate and God knows we needed it, with the November wind blowing on our tonsils.

"We didn't renege on the work. We filled that trench very fast. It was tiring work and very degrading for free men like us. But we did it. And they stamped around there, and they saying what they were going to do to us as soon as we had finished. The dawn was cold in the sky before we had it levelled and flattened out. If an angel of God had peeked outa heaven he'd ha' seen a sight that night, the seven men in their shirts working at the trench in the lights of the lorry. We were tired when we finished. We didn't give a damn be that time if they stuck bayonets in us. But they didn't. They did worse. They took the shovels from our hands and spat at our feet and mounted the lorry and off with them.

"Well, we could ha' cried. We ran after them a bit shouting. 'Here, ye bastards, what are ye doin' to us? Take us home, will ye? How are we expected to face home like we are now?' They made rude signs to us, that I can't tell ye about on account of the ladies, and then they were gone and we were left there.

"We walked home, men. We didn't go the roads. We went home be the fields. And when we saw an early morning car abroad, we dived into the grass and we went the lonely way to our homes, dodgin' and twistin' be the back boreens and the bushes.

"The wives were at home for us, holding wakes. Herself was bent over the fire and the apron over her head and she like a dog crying for the moon. She was glad to see me. Was she? For a while. Then what does she do? She starts laughing. As true as God. And I there like a stray dog with me legs a mass of bleeding scratches from the bloody bushes. I never et blackberries since that day. There was loud laughing in the sky that morning. There was. And then there was loud bewailin'. Because many men raised their hands to their wives that mornin', men. Oh, God, yes! Can ye blame them? No! So. You go to any house in the two villages now, when men are sleeping, and creep up on them in their beds and pull back the blankets from the bodies. And what'll you find? Answer me now? You'll find every single man of that seven, with the exception of the dead, wears his trousers in bed."

They laughed. Peder was pleased. He opened his mouth and laughed. He had only three firm teeth in his head, but what did he want them for when you didn't need them for drinking? They clapped him and applauded him and he was happy and drank more porter and since he was going strong then they got him to sing Skyball, and he did and you'd hear the roaring over in the city of Galway.

"The melodeon boy!" they shouted then at Cahal, and he took it from its resting-place on the dresser and leaned there and dragged out its length and caressed the buttons and then let it dance. They hit the concrete with their hobnailed boots and they hurrooed and swung the girls until their feet left the floor and they screamed in the breathlessness of their flying. Cahal was animated. He loved that melodeon. It made music for him. The happiest thing he could remember at school was the smell of the bandroom, the loosened pigskin on the drumheads; the blare of the brass and the note from the harmonium. Marching up the town with their polished instruments and they blowing their lungs out. How far did he get? He got to playing the triangle and he packed the instruments and sometimes he even played the cymbals. Because he was to be a farmer. Fill his head with no ideas, said Barney to them, when he threw him in there, like a pup you'd be throwing into a dogs' home. Make a farmer out of him because that's what he'll be. But the little black dots on the square of cardboard that fitted in front of the instruments. The little black dots that went up and the little black dots that went down with small tails on them and double tails and treble tails. All that. He got to know them. They were the best friends he had. He looked at them and they ran up and down in his head in time to the tunes he was playing.

He bent lovingly over the squeezebox and looked at it and tapped his heavy boot in time. A lively tune that danced in his head. There was sweat on his forehead. A lively tune, but behind it like all the Irish tunes there was that incalculable note of sadness. Lovely. He raised his head, his teeth free of his lips, and he found her looking him full in the face as Sonny swung her in a turn.

That look on his face. He likes playing an old melodeon. She pulled her eyes away from him. She doesn't like me much, he thought, as it went through his head; Diddle-ee, diddle-ee, diddle-ee, diddle-dee! Diddle-ee, diddle-ee, diddle-ee dum! Wom! And he ran his fingers up and down with a brand of variations of his own that brought a roar from the men and a shrill scream from the women, like as if somebody had run a finger up and down their funny-bones. Hah! That got them! Did you see that now?

He finished in a flurry of sweat and a lightning pull and the kitchen collapsed. They clapped and laughed and shouted: Good man, Cahal Kinsella! Begod, the boy's a marvel so he is! Here have a glass of porter now, man. You must be dead. He sank his face in it.

"And now," said Foxy, "Gob Creel will perform for us."

They cheered that. Gob drew back. He nearly walked up the walls with shyness and his face as red as a petticoat. Ah, listen now, let ye, no getting out of it. They propelled him to the middle of the floor and left him there squirming. Cahal laughed. He liked Gob Creel. He was a neighbour, wasn't he? He was tall and thin and he had a short upper lip that seemed to be always pulled back from big white teeth, like when the sun is shining in your face and you screw up your eyes and haul your lips off your teeth. Like that. Well, Gob was that way always. But quiet enough. And cheerful and always good for a laugh. He cleared his throat, then flexed his lips and started in on the gobsinging for them. It was a great do. The things Cahal could do with his fingers on the melodeon. Well, Gob could do those with his lips and mouth and throat. A dance tune gobbed. That's gobsinging. A very funny performance. He kept the rhythm going first standing and then he got down on one elbow and kept it going there, then he sat on the floor and gave it to them from there. Then he stood on his head and gave it to them between his legs and from every conceivable angle you could twist the body. I tell you you haven't seen or heard or watched rhythm if you haven't seen or heard a good gobsinger.

He brought the house down, Gob did, and they gave him a great hand so that he pulled the speck of his cap all the way down until it covered his eyes and his blushing face and then he hid himself away in a corner.

Bridie came over to Cahal.

"You will now, Cahal, won't you?" she asked. She didn't wait for his permission then. She turned on them. "Cahal will sing the *Races of Caherlo*," she said. "Aw, wait'll ye hear it. It'll kill ye! Go on now, Cahal. Sing it."

He sang it.

It was funny. It was good. Peder nearly passed out. He nearly wore away his thigh slapping at the episodes. All their names he brought into it. It even cheered up Foxy.

Like the story Peder told about the time they blacked their faces and had a cattle drive of your man's cows in Grange. One of them cut the tail off a bullock. He hit them with that. Nearly made them cry for the poor bullock roaring with its tail bleeding. The Free Staters surrounding them and digging at them with the bayonets. The Court after too. What was said to them. It was great stuff. It went down like a house on fire. He brought it to a close, and they clapped him and applauded him and he felt nice under it, until the door was darkened and Barney walked in, tall and straight with his stern countenance, and the clapping died away as if they had mufflers on their hands. He always had that effect. You felt obscene if you were laughing or enjoying yourself.

Foxy rose.

"You're welcome, Barney Kinsella," he said. "Will you drink a glass of porter?"

"I will," said Barney, taking it and knocking it back.

Foxy's wife came out of her apron.

"Won't you sit down, Barney boy?" she asked him.

"No," said Barney. "I won't. I came to say goodbye to Bridie like I said I would." He held out his hand to Bridie. "Goodbye, girl. I think you're a fool, but I have them in my own family." Then he turned on his heel and went to the door. He saw Cahal over at the dresser. He paused. "Come on home, you now," he said. "It's gettin' late." And then he went out.

You'd hear a pin drop in the kitchen.

Cahal felt his face flaming. So what? Máire was looking at him. He felt her. He didn't look the way she was at all. If he goes out that door now, the spineless bodach, she thought, I'll never speak to him again. Cahal went out the door, saying as he went, "Goodnight all. Come out here to me, Bridie, until I talk to you." Then he was gone and Bridie followed him. Bridie and the raised voice of Sonny Murphy. Saying clearly and piercingly, "Bring him a dummy-tit with you, Bridie." They laughed. He heard them. He heard Sonny. He heard the laugh of Máire Brodel. It's like the tinkle of the stream over the stones. I'll plaster that Sonny Murphy some day. I'll plaster him so that his own mother won't know him.

Bridie was squeezing his elbow.

"Don't go, Cahal. Don't be following after him like oul Prince. Waggin' his tail at the beast even when he is after breaking a rib of him with a blackthorn stick."

He put his hands on her shoulders and pulled her to him and kissed her.

"Goodbye, Bridie. I like you very much. I will miss you very much when you are gone. You are the very first that ever liked me because I was somebody. A person. I won't ever forget you, Bridie. For that. You were all that. The feel of a mother and the anxiety of a father. I love you, Bridie. Come back home some day, before you get too old. There's no happiness in going away from your own place. You'll be like a piece of dust hovering between the earth and the sky. Goodbye."

"Oh, Cahal," she said.

"All right," he said, feeling the coarse black hair of hers under his hard palms. For the last time. "Stop it now. I'm off. Or you'll have me bawling too, in a minute."

"You might look in on Foxy and ma for me. Sometimes. When you are passing by. Will you do that? And when he gets a little older, you might go over and fire some hay for him or cut a bit of turf. You'll keep an eye on them maybe, Cahal, will you?"

"I will that, Bridie," he said and turned away.

It was a fine night. There was a brave moon in a clear sky, blackening the green leaves of the trees, and reflecting on the calm water of the insinuating river that encompassed the land. He felt the sweat cold now under his arms and on his chest. He put his hands in his pockets and whistled. He could hear the steps of Barney, steady, methodical, around the bend of the road. He matched his own steps to the sound of them and thought of the ballad at school. That one: *Little Dog Tray*.

He laughed at the moon.

Chapter Four

The soil is black;
The grass is green;
The gorse is golden like the sheen
Of moonlight on the brave bog stream.
The earth and sky are painted fair,
The like no man sees anywhere –
Yet, sacred God, I love the hue
You gev the head of Máire Rua.

IT WAS ONLY a rueful laugh inside him. He halted when he heard the voice calling and the grating sound of hurrying hobnails on the flinty road.

"Hey, Cahal, wait! Wait!" the young man called.

"All right, Gob," he answered, recognizing him and wondering. The other slowed his run when he saw him waiting. The moon was very bright in front of them. It even lighted the dry ditches at the side of the road, and in the fields you could see the cattle with their front legs tucked under them, and their lower jaws chewing and the white horns of their heads glinting greenly. He could see the gleam on Gob's brass shirt-stud.

"What's up with you?" he asked. "What do you want me for? It isn't running away from the hooley you are, is it?"

Gob matched his pace with Cahal's.

"I'm goin' home too," said Gob.

"Aren't you a foolish man?" Cahal asked. "Only God knows when there will be another hooley in Caherlo."

"I'm goin' home," said Gob, woodenly, his hands in his pockets and his toecaps kicking at the road.

Cahal stopped asking questions.

They were silent for some time. He could hear a nightjar away in the trees, and the terrible song of about ten corncrakes, and off by the river the plaintive call of a curlew, lost and lonely; and once he ducked the sweeping approach of a bat that swerved up when it seemed to be only inches from his face. He tried to follow its erratic flight with his eyes but failed.

"What's up?" he asked then, quietly.

"Ah, nothin'," said Gob morosely, "nothin' at all."

"That's good," said Cahal, and whistled the tune of the *Races of Caherlo*.

"Did you really make that song up yourself?" Gob asked then.

"I did," said Cahal.

They rounded a bend and he could see the tall figure of Barney away turning a corner ahead of them. He was thinking about Gob. Sometimes if there was something wrong with people you could feel a tension from them almost like a hot wave of steam from a kettle. What do I know about Gob? What could be troubling Gob? Nothing. Son of Tom Creel, eldest son. Mother and father living and several brothers and sisters one just heard about scattered like seed over the world. What could be inside that head? Nothing much. Eat, sleep and work, and if you go to a hooley bring down the house with a bit of gobsinging for which you were specially talented, mainly on account of the protruding teeth. He knew his face. These big white teeth and a very prominent Adam's apple in a thin but tough-looking neck. That was Gob Creel.

He turned to look at him, and stopped his whistling and pulled his hands from his pockets. Gob's face was up, the cap was on the back of his head and the moon was shining bitterly on the tears that were flowing out of his eyes. Unrestrained.

Cahal felt terrible. What do I say? Great God, what's this? He put his hand on his arm. It was tense and taut.

"What's up, Gob?" he asked. It was barely a whisper.

"It's Bridie," said Gob.

Cahal nearly laughed. He had to pull in the muscles of his stomach so that he wouldn't let a shout out of him.

"What did Bridie do to you?" he asked, smothering his amazement.

"She's goin' away," said Gob. "I wanted her to stay. Me and Bridie have known, have known for a long time. She wouldn't stay. Nothin' would make Bridie stay."

Cahal was wordless. How little we know! He thought of Bridie. Was she just so what he had her made out to be? Here's an ordinary young man walking on a road crying because Bridie is going away. Bridie!

"Long ago, I knew her," Gob was saying. "All my long life, when we were back in the school beyant, up to sixth class the two of us. Kind of paired away, we did, because the two of us were so stupid at school. Nothin' could be put into our heads."

His voice was soft on the night. Cahal walked carefully so that his hobnails would not din his ears.

"We'd be kept in after school for not knowin' sums, so we would, and then we'd come the long way round be the river, and sometimes in summer we'd go swimming there, holding on to the branch of an ash tree because we couldn't swim. And other nights we'd be in Mary Cassidy's place, and old Mike'd let me fill his pipe and he'd let Bridie light it up for him. Aye."

Cahal was silent. He couldn't think of anything to say. The pictures Gob was creating for him left him cold. Just that. He didn't really care. Why is that? He felt that Gob sensed it. Gob didn't go on. Cahal thought, Well I'll have to say something.

"If you were like that," he said, "for why is she going away? Let you wed and go into your father's house."

"She wouldn't do that," said Gob. "She says it's oney exchanging one poor place for another poor place, that's all. There's money over beyant and she thinks she has to go after it. I'm sorry for telling you all this. I don't know what kem over me. Just her there in her new dress and she lookin' well. Wasn't she lookin' very well now?"

"She was," said Cahal, "she was looking very well." And then he shut up, and there was nothing to be heard except the pound of their boots on the road. I wish he hadn't come after me, Cahal thought. I wish I had kept me feeling to meself, Gob thought, and what med me do it at all, and nobody knowin' about it but me and her?

"Don't say about that to anybody, will you?" he asked then.

"No," said Cahal, "I won't." Don't add, who cares? What's coming over me? "It's your own life, Gob," he went on then, valiantly he thought: "Nobody can fix your life but yourself. Maybe something would happen. Maybe she wouldn't go at all. Or maybe she would come back."

"Maybe so," said Gob, closing up. There was heard behind them the swish and bump of bicycle tyres on the road. They swerved instinctively to the grass verge as the two cyclists passed. They were talking and paused to send them a brief "Goodnight, men," and they passed by. It was Sonny Murphy and Máire Brodel. They were cycling close together and one of his hands was resting on her shoulder. No lights on the bicycles, but they could be seen clearly in the light of the moon. Cahal felt himself tensing as he recognized her. He heard her voice. Raised so that there seemed to be a gibe in it. Her waist was very narrow and there was a sheen on her legs from the silk. Then she was gone.

Gob didn't say anything more. Neither did Cahal. Cahal had been trained so well. Speak when you are spoken to. Express opinions only when you are asked for them if you don't want a butt in the lug. He preferred other people to make the talking. He had his thoughts. That's what he always had. They couldn't train those, or get at them or beat discipline into them.

He saw the polly cropping grass in the laneway this side of his house.

"Well, the curshe a hell on that polly," he said, "she opened the gate below again."

"Tha's a smart cow," said Gob. "Drive her into the stable for the night."

"I will not," said Cahal. "What would himself say? That I left the gate open on purpose. I'll drive her down again and tie the gate. Goodnight, Gob. I'll see you again."

"Goodnight," said Gob and passed on. Cahal watched after him for a little. Well, I couldn't help him anyhow, he thought. It's nothing to do with me. And yet he felt a bit in the wrong. "Go on our that, or I'll hamstring you," he said to the cow, beating her on the hide with his clenched fist. She turned away. He caught her round the neck and forced her head back down the lane. "Off with you now, you renegade," he said and followed her. The Jordans' dog came barking furiously at him from the shadow of the doorway. Barked and smelled and then wagged his tail and Cahal bent and patted him and he returned again.

They came to the plain below. The moon was bright on the ribbon of the stream. He crossed the bridge, drove the cow in through the gate. The top of the gate was held to the post by the hoop of galvanized iron from a decayed bucket. She had raised this gently with her head and swung the gate open. A cute oul cow. She stood inside looking out at him now as he bent and tightened the hoop and tied the gate further down with a length of rope that trailed from it. Then he waved her away and turned back on the road and halted at the little humped bridge.

It's a brave night.

The bog away was black as coal in the light of the moon, and the green grass was an odd black colour too. But down here you could see the sky nearly all around the horizon. The stars were really out. They were shouldering at one another in the sky. He lowered his head then and spat into the tinkling stream. Is there something wrong with me, he wondered, that I can't feel sorry for Gob and Bridie? Two very nice people, but they don't mean anything at all to me. Should I be able to cry because an ordinary country girl of no particular appearance is going off to America and leaving behind her a nice ugly young country boy with a gap in his chest? Strange.

And then the bicycle came down the lane behind him. He was leaning on the stones of the bridge resting his chest on his arms. He didn't turn. He knew it was she without turning, from a sort of empty feeling that came in his stomach. He waited for her to pass him by. If she thought he was going to stop her up and ask her why she looked at him as if she hated the sight of him when he had done nothing at all to her, then she had another think coming, so she had.

The bicycle stopped. He heard her shoe scuffling the dust.

"Is that you?" asked her voice.

"Yes," he said turning, his elbows now supporting his body. "It's me."

"Will you tell me something?" she asked then.

"I will if I can," he said.

"What's wrong with you?" she asked.

"Nothing wrong with me," said Cahal, "that I know of except what's wrong with all men."

"Isn't it ambitious you are now," her voice jeered at him, "to be calling yourself a man!" He couldn't see her face. She had her back to the moon. He just saw her hands clenched on the handlebars of the bicycle. It was a new bicycle. He could see the green stripe of paint on the mudguards. The chain rattled hollowly in the case and green threads ran from all around the guard to the hub. Wavering like the strings on a harp.

"Why are you getting after me?" Cahal wanted to know.

"You're flattering yourself again," she said.

"No," he said. "Just why? You were looking at me tonight as if I was some kind of a worm crawling on your cabbage."

"I wasn't even thinking of you," she said. "Not until your grandfather came in and ordered you home and you went off with your tail between your legs. Did you feel no shame at all?"

"No," said Cahal. "I felt no shame at all. Only a little embarrassed."

"And you call yourself a man then," she said, sweeping the hair back from one side of her face. The moon shone on it. And on the glint in her eye.

"Why are you so mad with me?" Cahal asked then, coming out from the bridge. "What does it matter to you what I am or what I don't do?"

"Because you look like a man from the front and the back," she said, biting the words out. "And yet when you speak or do, there's nothing inside you at all, only maybe something small and puny."

"You had better go on home now," he said.

"Running away from you, is it, or you want to run away from me? Which is it?"

A vague anger stirred in him.

"What's come over you?" he asked her. "This morning I met you. I was nothing to you. You were nothing to me. What could I have done to you in such a short time to be making you want to wound me?"

"Nobody could wound you," she said.

"This whole place," he went on, "is dying for me to stand up to Barney. Why? What's it got to do with them or you or anybody else?"

"They're only interested in you," she said, "like they'd be interested in the training of a collie dog. Watching to see what way he'll turn out, that's all."

"What do they want me to do?" he asked. "Try and beat old Barney with me fists, is it? For what? What has he ever done against me?"

"Nothing much," said Máire. "He only took you away from your mother and threw her out on the side of the road, and cast you into a school like you had nobody belonging to you, and when he decides to have you back when all his family has run away from him, he orders you around

- 52 -

like a dog. Come here, Prince. Go there, Prince. And you come and you go, and tomorrow or the next day he'll take the blackthorn stick at you and break your ribs. Just to stand up and be a man, that's all they want to see of you."

"Listen," said Cahal. "All me life I have lived at the orders of impersonal men in a tight place. There was rules to keep. We kep' them. If we didn't we were punished, impersonally, coldbloodedly, without malice. All right. All my life. I like Barney to say, Come, and I come, and go, and I go. For why. Because he is somebody belonging to me. That's why. You don't know what it is to live among hundreds and have none of your own, to be comin' and goin' at the call of strangers to whom you mean nothin' but so many shillin's subsidy a week from the Government. I don't care what ye think of Barney. He feeds me and clothes me and he can order me around until he is blue in the face. I like it and it's none of yeer business. He's a oul lonely man that reared up a family of fifteen, and not one of them around now at the end of his life to give him a hand."

"Why aren't they around?" she asked.

"What does that matter?" he flared at her.

"You'll find out," she said. "I can maybe see what's wrong with you. You are nothin' but a statue. You have no real guts inside you at all. Nothin', only a big hole surrounded by machinery. You don't tick at all. Whose fault is it? Isn't it the fault of Barney that you don't? Can't you see it's him has made you empty by taking away a family from you and a way of life? There was no need for him to fire you into that place like you were a cuddy dog. There was room here and food and all the rest of it. There was no need. And now God knows what'll happen to you, or how you will wake up some day and begin to feel, and what the cramps of feeling will do with you when they start coming."

"You talk," he said. "Who are you? You come into the village shortly and now you know all. Are you God Almighty? What right have you to be going around trying to cut people open to see what they're like? Who made you that way?

Isn't it you should be the priest of the parish? What the hell has it got to do with you? Or who ever gave you a certificate that you had a right to be the probe of Caherlo."

He was over on top of her with his hands clenched.

"Feeling stirring in you already, is there?" she asked. "I don't know. I'm a fool. I don't know what I'm doing here now, talking to you. I don't know what made me pause up to talk to a stupid eejit like you. I would have been as well pleased to have gone on and talked in the night to the black bull up in Grange."

He reached for her arms and squeezed them in his hands. He felt her shrinking under his clutch. Then he pulled her in to him, the opening of the bicycle between them, and he crushed her face into his own. His hard mouth was squeezed tightly on her lips. He was sorry then. He didn't know why he did it. Like having a fight at school with one of the others. You weren't satisfied with kicking or scratching. You had to get your teeth into them. Just that. Only it wasn't his teeth. His clenched teeth with lips over them. And her face was smooth under his own. He could feel that and the soft lips and the smell of her and her taut breast pushed against his chest. Then he was defeated. What have I done? He felt her hand pushing at him and he went back against the wall of the bridge and his big boots slid on the stones and he sat in the dust.

She wiped her lips with the back of her hand. She spat on the road.

"Filthy! Filthy!" she said, throwing the words at him distastefully.

She stamped her foot. If there had been a stone she would have reached for it and flung it in his face. She bent there speechless and then turned away. She walked a little with the bicycle and then she got up and pedalled furiously away, bent over the handlebars, her legs twinkling, and she was not long on the road until her form was lost in the bedevilling light.

He got to his feet. He wiped the dust off his clothes. Was

all this a dream, he wondered? Since today. Life was all right until today. Until she came. Why did she pick on him? Why did he have to leave the field of the turnips and drink in the river like a black bull? Ugh! The thought of her there was nauseating. Why did he have to feel like getting his hands on her and soiling her with his teeth?

He felt small and ashamed and he walked back up the boreen with his head bent, hoping that below was hell, that the road would open and swallow him in and that he would be burned clean.

He opened the latch of the door very softly.

No light in the kitchen.

Just the moon shining in through the narrow window with the lace curtains and an odd spark from the white ashes of the banked fire.

He went into the kitchen and felt his way towards the fire and the brown bedroom door beyond it. He had the brass knob of the door in his hand when the other bedroom near the dresser opened wide and he heard Barney's voice. He turned. The old man was spewing talk at him. His false teeth were out and his mouth had caved in. Standing there holding the candlestick in his hand, the candle slanted and throwing grease all over the floor. Illuminating himself. The doorway was a frame for him standing there in nothing but his shirt. His legs were very thin and white and the skin hung loosely on them.

"I told you to come home. I won't have you creeping around the village bringing disgrace on me. You are the last one, and by God you'll be decent if I have to scald you. You hear me! You hear me!"

Cahal heard but he didn't say anything. A long explanation about the black cow lifting the hoop off the gate.

"None left but you. Let them all go. I held me head high in this village until she lowered it. But you won't. By the sacred cross of God you won't. You hear! You hear!" and in the excess of a trembling and senile fury he raised his hand and flung the candlestick at his grandson.

Cahal saw it coming. The flame of the candle went out half-way in its flight across the kitchen. Cahal didn't move. The candlestick crashed into the wall beside his head. He heard it falling to the floor. And then he heard the door slamming as the old man went and he heard the creaking of the old wire springs as he heaved his body angrily into the bed.

He bent and groped for the candlestick.

He picked it up, and felt for the candle and found it and stuck it back into the holder. It was broken in the middle and hanging on the white string. He squeezed it together with his hot fingers and then bent and groped for the red coal in the fire, extracted it and blew it into a flame and lighted the candle.

He went up to the bedroom.

I can see why his fifteen children left him all right, he thought, and why his wife may have sought the embrace of the grave, as they say, in preference to him. He recognized the old feeling of the head man about to punish him for a misdemeanour. Just the same. The first time you stood and your knees trembled before punishment descended on you, and you wet your trousers. That was the first time, but you became used to it. You ran over in your mind what it would be. The searing pain in the palms of your hands, or the dull agony on your buttocks. But you got used to it. You were obedient to the beating.

I don't care, he thought then. Maybe there is something wrong with me. Maybe I am lacking in something, but I think it's great to have one of your own cursing you and firing things at you. As long as it isn't a stranger.

He slept well.

Chapter Five

Like the driven clouds of heaven,
Wavin' weary to and fro,
Silken fronds do hold the cotton
On the bogs of Caherlo.

Faded gorse and rusty heather
Whisht to bitther winds that blow;
Curlew, snipe, and cunny kestril
Guard the bogs of Caherlo.

IT WAS THE following spring that they named him; the time of the turfcutting.

As you know, the face of Ireland is very beautiful when it is green. It is shaped like a saucer with the mountains all around the edges and the great plains in the dip. The plains are not all fertile. Many of them are bogs laid down thousands of years ago, quivering quaking bog that is hundreds of feet deep in places. These bogs have been very useful to the people since the first one put his foot in the country. They have provided fuel for fires, and hiding-places for men pursued by implacable enemies, who gained a measure of safety by travelling the lonely places on pathways they alone knew. Men have died in them and have never been heard of again until one day a turfcutter may disclose their bodies to the gaze of the sky. Generally they will have been well preserved and will only crumble at the kiss of the air. And butter has been preserved in bogs, and all sorts of things have come to light from them, but they can be frightening places, so expansive and treacherous, in their own big way somewhat like the sea, that can be placid and beautiful until it turns on you, or until you have learned to know its ways.

The fertile places in the village of Caherlo were those fields that bounded the great bends of the river. Inside the bends for about half a mile, the land was good but it became less good as the foetid breath of the bogs withered it. It was a great stretch of bog, reaching as far as the eye could see until it joined itself with the unfathomable Bog of Allen in the middle of the country.

Cahal came clattering down towards the bog on a spring morning.

He was driving the jennet and standing up in the cart, swaying and balancing to its leaping like a sailor on a ship at sea. The jennet didn't like Cahal. Cahal liked the jennet, mainly because he was sorry for him. Barney had asserted himself over the jennet. It was an amazing thing to see. Anybody else in the world could drive that jennet, and he would be sluggish and recalcitrant and as lazy as possible, avoiding work just as if he was a hired hand, but as soon as old Barney put the tackle on him and climbed on the cart, that jennet always set off as if he had the devil on his back, and he would never slacken until the journey was done.

It was fear drove him. Barney had beaten him into fear with the knobbly stick he owned. It was as old as the jennet. The jennet was fourteen years of age, and when he got him young Barney had beaten him for six months, every time he drove him. Now all he had to do was raise the stick in the air, and the jennet responded. But if Cahal beat him it did no good. Maybe because he sensed that Cahal's heart wasn't in the beating. So the animal was master of the man. Cahal smiled ruefully at the thought.

They came out of the lane into the plain and crossed over the little bridge. Cahal frowned as he looked away to his left to your man's acres where they stretched away for four miles, the river this side a wider barrier to their luscious fertility. Up away he could see the chilly sun shining on the white cottage of the herd. He hadn't seen Máire Brodel since. Once or twice they passed on the road and she raised a lip at him. What had he done to her anyway? He felt resentful still over their last meeting even though it had been months ago now. What had got into her to be driving needles of resentment into him? He would never have the courage or thought to tackle a complete stranger about vaporous things, hard to grasp. Yet she had made him think. About what he was and why he couldn't feel things. He knew it was partly the school was to blame, where you had been taught by instinct to look after yourself and if you saw another person crying to feel nothing but gratitude that it wasn't yourself; the fear at the back of your mind that tomorrow would be your turn to cry.

He was deaf to the sound of the cart behind him, until it swept past on his right almost driving him into the ditch.

"Out of the way, man," yelled Sonny Murphy at him as he passed by, the animal straining at its collar and foam on its lips, and Sonny leaning forward to beat its back with a switch.

Cahal pulled up the jennet, as Sonny swept by in a cloud of dust. He saw the jennet's ears going back, and he gave him his head. He laughed and galloped into Sonny's track. Barney's jennet went like fair hell. He didn't have to give him the whip. They closed up on the man in front. He turned back, his eyes gleaming and his big teeth white, and then he beat his own animal again. This was a dangerous road they were on. It was narrow and metalled and on either side there was a very deep ditch to take away the overflow from the seeping bog on their right. There was barely room for two carts to pass together, but Cahal's jennet made for an opening beside the other and went to pass him by. It was exciting. The left wheel was on the road and the right was on the grass verge that topped the ditch. Cahal's jennet took the bit and edged his way. It was like a chariot race, Cahal thought.

They drew level with the other cart and Sonny and himself looked at one another. Their faces were fierce and red with excitement. Cahal couldn't stop his jennet anyhow, and he didn't care if the whole outfit toppled, except the wonder in his stomach at what Barney would say. He looked his fearlessness at Sonny. One of us will have to give way now. The heavy hubs of the wheels were almost touching. The two animals were on a level, and Sonny's jennet was throwing its head up with fear and flecking foam in the air. Cahal's jennet was snapping its teeth and trying to bite at the other's neck. One of them had to give way and it was Sonny. He pulled the head of the jennet up and he came to a stop, turned into the ditch with the cart right angled on the road.

Cahal turned back and waved at him.

"Up the Kinsellas!" Cahal shouted.

"Go on, you madman!" Sonny shouted after him. "What are you trying to do? You nearly had me in the ditch!"

Cahal laughed and threw back the taunt of youth at him.

"Eggs and rasher for the Kinsella dashers! The lick of the pan for the Murphy clan!" then he felt a bit ashamed of himself, and pulled his jennet to a trot by nearly pulling the head off its shoulders with the reins.

"Here, are you all right, Sonny?" he asked.

Sonny dismounted and carefully got his jennet's legs on to the road and got the wheels of the cart into the ruts.

I don't like him because he is successful, Cahal thought, and because his father is successful and because they have about three times the amount of land that Barney has, and because they are good workers and careful husbandmen, and because he shows his teeth so much and because he seems to spend a lot of his little free time with Máire Brodel. Apart from that he is all right, but one should have better reasons for disliking people.

"You shouldn't do things like that," Sonny said as he caught up and followed behind, the two jennets making up for their exertions walking carefully and slowly. "Suppose I went into the ditch, I might have broken the shafts a the cart. And it's a new cart."

"You startled me," said Cahal. "I never heard you comin' behind me."

"You must be dreamin'," said Sonny. "A cart makes enough noise. Is it makin' more songs you were? What's the latest? You know everybody in seven parishes near knows the *Races of Caherlo* by this time."

"Do they, really?" Cahal asked. "Is that so?"

"Yeh," said Sonny. "But that won't dig spuds for yeh, nor yet save the turf. Have ye no help in the house at home yet?"

"No," said Cahal, "we haven't. But oul Barney can bake a cake. He's a great hand at bakin' a cake."

Sonny laughed.

"God, that's something I'd like to see, oul Barney Kinsella makin' a cake."

"It's not to see it at all," said Cahal, "but to taste it. It's like honey." Honey all right, but that's all Barney did. Cahal did everything else. Chicken's mash twice a day and chopping cabbage and boiling huge iron pots of spuds for the pigs. Feeding the cattle, cleaning the stables. He was getting sick of house work.

"Oul Barney will have to get married again," said Sonny. "Ye'll have to have a woman in the house. Why don't you get an oul haybag yourself, Cahal? A nice lump of a woman for the winter?"

"You're not moving much yourself," said Cahal.

"Maybe. You never know." Sonny smirked. "I'm on to something now. Pass the nights in great sthyle, man. It was a short winter."

Cahal felt like getting out and hitting him so he clicked his tongue at the jennet and turned him off the road towards the wooden gate that led into the heart of the bogland.

From there the road deteriorated sadly. It wasn't a proper road, but a cutting made in the bog by collective labour, branches of trees laid down on the raw bog, and thick scraws thrown over them so that they barely supported the heavy carts. They were terribly rutted so that sometimes one wheel went in to the axle while the other remained solid, and you had to be part acrobat to remain aboard. It was hard on the animals. They had to use every muscle they possessed, straining mightily against the harness, so that their eyes became wild. It was much worse on them coming back with a load. The bog road stretched away half a mile in front of them until it petered out in the heavy virgin bog that had been uncut for generations. On their right was reclaimed bog, that had been cut over and after that drained and sprinkled with coarse pasture seed and clover. This was divided up by drains and ash poles with wire strung on them; and the cattle were driven here sometimes to graze. They took a sad view of it all. They had to graze twice as hard as a real field, and no matter how much they ate, it only took the edge off their hunger. On their right were the turf banks, and already Cahal could see the small figures high up against the sky, pausing to look at the approaching carts, and then going back to work, the blades of the sleans shining and glinting in the dull sunshine.

There was a cold cutting wind across the bog, so he pulled his tattered coat across his shirt. He wore very old clothes, as did everyone else, because the brown bog seemed to be part acid and would eat its way through iron. Old, old trousers, patched behind so that they hung slackly down, tied with twine below the knee to keep the ends of them out of the eternal water. So as the two carts went on with the men high on them, clucking their tongues at the animals, they looked like two scarecrows that had miraculously acquired flesh-and-blood bodies. It was odd driving a cart on the bog. There was no noise of the iron shod wheels grating on the stones. Silenced they were and the only noise was the dull club-club of the wooden hubs of the wheels hitting against the powerful iron axle, or if a man had neglected to put car-grease on it squeaked as well.

Cahal waved a hand at Mary Cassidy and her daughter Jennie and her son Tommy. They were cutting the first bank. Mary Cassidy was a tall greyhaired woman with a flat stomach and strong tendons standing out on her arms like a man's. She was cutting and she leaned on the slean, her heavy-shod foot resting on the nub. Her two children were fetching for her, catching the wet sods as she cut them and flung them and placing them symmetrically on the wooden wheelbarrow with the heavy thick wheel. They were no light weight. A barrow could hold twelve or twenty of those sods, but if a grown man could push a barrow with twelve he was fine and strong.

Cahal liked Mary Cassidy. She was a silent woman. She minded her own business, and worked very hard, ever since her husband had died, leaving her the place and two young children. They were ten and eleven now and nearly finished school so that they would be a help to her. But she needed help from none, though she took it if it was offered. Cahal liked their house and he liked the children, who seemed to be older than they should be, and he often thought that they should be put in a glass case and put on display because as far as he knew they were the only children in the village of Caherlo.

The next bank was being cut by Jamesey Jordan. A big tall block of stupidity, amiable and unthinking, and there was oul Spray trying to fetch for him, Jamesey throwing the heavy sods at him carefully and the old fellow collapsing under the weight of each sod, so that Jamesey had to cut slowly and carefully, and all wondered why the hell he didn't get a woman for himself if it was only to keep the house clean, or like now to come and give them a hand on the bog. Cahal visited them an odd night or two. The house was very "upset" as Jamesey would say, apologizing. It was a soft word for it. The fowls made the kitchen their own and would land up on your saucer sometimes when you'd be drinkin' a cup of tea. And Jamesey was a poor hand at making a cake. It always ended up sort of doughy and half cooked so that you would feel your stomach protesting even before it received it at all. He had heard that Miss Máire Brodel had done a job on the house for them of late, but he avoided the house when he heard she was a caller. He always felt a slow burning of resentment when he thought of Miss Máire Brodel.

He waved his hand and turned the jennet's head off this road into the cutaway that faced their own bank.

"Don't work too hard now, Sonny," he said, and he swung away. "Lave a little for next year."

"I'll cut more in two hours," said Sonny, "than you'd cut in a month a Sundays."

"That's what I mean," said Cahal.

Sonny clucked his tongue and went past towards his own bank. There was his father Mark and his two brothers Piddler and Dipper. They were working hard, the old man cutting and the two brothers fetching, cheerless souls, Cahal thought, who didn't even raise their heads to see who might be coming the road. The brothers were twins, two years younger than Sonny, and they were sometimes called The Spits on account of the resemblance they bore to their father. Short and stocky, and all they wanted off him was the grey-sandy moustache.

He took the cart as close as he could to the bank, but then the ground became very soggy, so he dismounted, untackled the jennet, let the shafts of the cart rest on the ground, tied the jennet to one of the wheels with the rope reins and threw it a bag of hay from the cart.

Then he mounted his own bank. It was raised about eight foot off the ground below, from the years of cutting. As you approached the ground became wetter and wetter, like an eternal sponge, until at the foot of the bank there was a rectangular bog-hole from last year. Brown dirty water, inhabited by nothing except the water spiders who ran backwards and forwards over it, making a peculiarly broken wake, or occasionally the small yellow and gold bog-lizards. These intrigued Cahal. He often bent over one of them for some time, taking one into the palm of his hand, watching the belly in and out, in and out, and if you lay down and got it on an eye level you could believe all those things you read in the geography books about the strange animals that peopled the bogs of Ireland, incredible monsters of great size and ferocity, and all that remained of them was this tiny two-inch lizard that one time might have been as big as the whole village.

He didn't take off his coat. It was too bitter, the wind from behind him. He had already prepared the bank for cutting, having been two days with the spade clearing away the top of it to a depth of two feet, two feet of heather and gorse and the tangled roots of the ferns. A hard job, dragging away at nature like that, and she only doing a good job of covering the top of the bog, trying desperately to make it into good land.

He spat on his hands and started to dig with the slean. He liked the way it cut into the bog. Cut and thrust and lift with the knee and you had a grand-shaped sod of bog like jelly, only firmer, and you threw this away on the dry parts one side you and it rested there and you cut again and pitched so that it lay beside the other, and it was part white and part brown and the deeper you dug into the layer of the bog the browner and blacker it became. Poor turf on top, brown cooking turf in the middle and the black brittle coal turf below.

All right at first, but you got tired of it. It was hard work. He soon had the spaces within reach of his throw well covered with the sods. Then he had to slow up, because every sod he dug, he had to walk away with it in order to place it on the ground. Oul Barney should be here by this with the barrow to catch them and spread them on the dry ground.

He wiped his forehead, leaving a big brown streak across it, and looked over towards the road. The sky was grey, veiling the sun. He saw the figure of Barney then turning off the road by the bridge and crossing into the by-road of the bog pastures. He could even see the glint of the sun on the can he was carrying. Good job too. He tightened the belt holding up his ragged trousers. He was as hungry as a hawk. That's what the bog did to you. It blew an appetite into you.

Hungry as a hawk. He saw one over his head, hardly visible against the peculiar spring sky. Hovering. They were always there. You were always flushing the larks and watching the curlews away from you flying low and the snipe zig-zagging as if there was a gun eternally behind them. Not that you would be bothered here shooting snipe. They were too bloody small. There wasn't the fill of a tooth in one.

Another cart coming now and that was Tom Creel and his son Gob. They were his neighbours at home and his neighbours on the bog. Tom Creel, tall and lanky, seeming to be thin, but very strong. He had a harelip and wore a moustache and he looked like a rabbit with the split right in the middle of his mouth, outlined by the greying bushy moustache. Cahal would have liked Tom Creel terribly only for one thing.

People rambled in the villages. When the work was over or when it was winter it was the custom to ramble at night into a house, where you sat and talked or didn't talk, or played twenty-five for geese if it was near Christmas or if it wasn't near Christmas, but Tom Creel never failed any night to ramble into Kinsella's. Even if they were working late in summer and he couldn't get there until eleven at night, he came in for half an hour, to sit and smoke a pipe and talk or not talk and – spit. That is what Cahal found hard to forgive him for, now that he had become the housewife himself. After all, there was the big open fire with all the ashes, and even a fairly poor shot could plump a spit into the ashes. Not Tom. Tom spat all around where he was sitting, and when he would rise abruptly and go to the door, pause there to look at the sky and say about what it would do tomorrow, Cahal would be looking at the floor with all the spits, and he would be thinking what a distasteful task it was to go get the twig and sweep up those spits after Mister Tom Creel, the decent man.

"Ha, ye lazy bees!" he shouted at them now. "It's the middle of the day yeer comin' on the bog. Have ye no shame in ye?"

"The devil a bit," Gob shouted at him.

"Aren't we being after taunted be every scarecrow on the bog?" Tom Creel said. "And we cut more in two hours than the whole lot of them put together."

"Includin' yerself," added Gob.

"What's the need to be talkin' to us now?" Tom asked. "Isn't it oney dodgin' the work you are? Look at the brave Murphys beyant. You don't get honest men like them raising their heads and jeerin' at Christians passin' by."

"Hup our that," said Gob, hitting the jennet and turning her into the cutaway.

Cahal laughed and spat on his hands and went back to work.

Old Barney reached him after crossing the bog. It was high noon by this so they sat in the shelter of the seat they had cut on the away wind side of the bank and ate their lunch. It tasted very sweet to Cahal. A pint bottle of tea with the sugar and milk in it, wrapped in a cloth to keep the heat in it. And thick sandwiches with fried eggs and scallions in them. The grease had congealed but it was nourishing and the bread was fresh, and Barney could make a cake.

They didn't talk. They rarely talked. He wondered what went on in Barney's mind or if anything at all went on in it. He had a big nose and his cheeks were deeply engraved with lines. It made him look like something that was carved out of granite. The collie dog hunched in front of them with his head on one side, watching every bit that went into their mouths. Sometimes Barney bit into a sandwich and then threw the crust to the collie, and he would grab it and wag his silky tail. If Cahal threw him a bit, he accepted it, but had no thanks for it. Only Barney's bit seemed to give him complete satisfaction. Cahal wondered again at Barney's power over animals. He could make any animal come to him. Cahal trying to catch the horse and jennet in the pasture of a morning with a tin basin with oats in it. It was the only way he could get his hands on them. Barney just went into the field and whistled and they came to him and he would catch a clump of mane in his big hand and walk the animal back to the stable. Even with the oats Cahal had to get the blinkers on them and strap them before he could lead them home. Was it because they felt dominated, as he himself sometimes felt? Dominated by what. By unconscious ruthlessness. How had all his children succeeded in getting away from him? Maybe because they had half of himself in them. Cahal had only a quarter, and he felt sorry for oul Barney. Even when he flung candlesticks at him. He could see why Barney was left alone, but he could feel sorry for him.

They went to work.

Cahal cut and Barney fetched and filled the barrow and went away and spread the sods and came back for more. It went on all day. Mechanically. Unfailing. Nothing to break the monotony. Except Peder coming in his creel cart, and waving at them all and shouting as he passed to his bog. They jeered at him too. What an hour of the day to be coming on the bog! Oh, ye whores, ye, and me after going the long road to the town with a load of turf this very day. Up at six I was and on the way at seven without a bite in the belly. Ha, Mary, how about an oul cuddle? Go on, you randy lecher, you, and your wife waitin' up beyond. Begod, Jamesey Jordan, you'll never be as good a man as your oul fella. That's right, Spray, you have him worked to a standstill, the lout. Lo, Barney. Nice day. An oul bar of a song now, Cahal Kinsella, to raise me heart before I tear at the turf. G'wan, y'oul bags. Ho-ho, Tom. Have you the Gob with you? Work him hard. Keep down his temperature. Stop him rousing after the women. (You could nearly see Gob blushing.) Good day, Mister Murphy, grand day for the work, God bless it. We'll be all dead at Christmas. Cahal chuckled. An obscure blow under the belt. The Murphys let him pass without a word so he took up his song and sang it to the larks. It was like a royal procession. Cahal felt he would like to be like Peder. Let the world pass over your head. An independent clot of blood in the body parochial.

The sky was red and raw with the going of the sun, as if it was suffering from a burst appendix. Only then they straightened their tired backs and rubbed their bog-encrusted hands on the heather. Skeleton heather it was now, all stalk, the brush just beginning to grow like the fuzz on the face of a sixteen-year-old boy.

They tackled the jennet and they loaded some of last year's dried turf from the tight clamp near the road.

They started off home.

Cahal was leading the jennet when it bogged.

One minute its four hooves were pulling at the road and next minute it was up to its belly in the bog. It had hit a soft patch. The jennet reared and the harness clinked as it tore itself free. Almost free, but it went to its belly again. It was maybe Cahal's fault. He should have supported the weight of the cart by holding the shaft over the bad patch so that the jennet might have skipped it. It was too late now. The jennet was struggling and roaring trying to pull itself out of the bog. One leg out and then it sank again.

Cahal felt his shoulder being taken in a hand and then he was pulled and propelled. He heard Barney shouting at him, but he lost his footing and went slithering towards the drain on the side of the road. It was a fat drain, pregnant, with the placid water scummed over with green slime. He fell on his back and his head and shoulders went under it. It went into his eyes and pained them and it went into his open mouth and he nearly vomited straight away. His hands were clawing, digging into the ground that had no hold, that came away in his hand. Then he felt his legs caught in two hands and he was pulled out of it.

Barney hauled him to his feet and left him there, spluttering, his hands up to his face, rubbing at his eyes, dry vomiting tightening his stomach.

He cleared his eyes sufficiently to see Barney bending over the shafts and raising them in his hand, his shoulders hunched. He saw the cart come up and he saw the jennet come up with them. It was a terrible feat on the part of one man. The jennet sought harder ground and stood there, its slender grey legs shaking and dirty.

"What the hell are you doing? Why the hell didn't you lead the bloody beast on the right path? What kind of an eejit are you?"

No other word.

To say, I'm sorry I pushed you and humiliated you.

If Cahal had had the slean in his hand he would have split his head open.

His limbs were trembling. He felt the eyes at his back. He knew they were all standing up looking, that if he turned around they would all be pretending to be working. All these nice kindly people he had been loving five minutes ago.

"Go on, take him off and lead him home now and watch where he is putting his feet."

That was Barney, and then he swung away carrying the can, leaped over the drain on the far side and headed over the bog.

Cahal felt his face burning. Was it shame? He had felt the feeling before so it wasn't as bad as it might have been. He didn't look around. Later he might be able to face them and keep his face straight, and take their joking in good part. He had gone through all this before. Being humiliated before people. More people than now. Hundreds of boys. Standing round in a ring to watch your shame. There was nothing you could do then only hide your tears. Now you were too big for tears, but you had violent emotions swelling inside you.

He caught the jennet and clucked her on and held his hand under the shaft to take the weight of the load. He knew they were still standing up looking after him. He went on, the cart rocking to the holes, and floating after him there came the strains of a song. Not sung well, because Sonny Murphy hadn't a good singing voice. It was an old Irish song called *Fear na Móna*, "The Bogman". He heard a laugh or two.

He could see the figure of Barney getting smaller and smaller with distance. He thought how good it would be if he was a hawk as big as a man, how he would dart out of the sky and how he would sink his cruel beak into Barney's head, right into the matter that he used for a brain.

The words and strains of "The Bogman" floated after him and his ears burned, but they were as nothing to the way he was burning inside.

Chapter Six

They come over the hill like the trail of a snail
Pouring down in their torrents to rail and to wail;
They walk raw on their knees for to pray and to grieve –
When they wipen the porter froth off on a sleeve.
  Óri, oró! St Pathrick was grand –
  He shlaughtered the shlaves and the shnakes of our
    land.

CAHAL WALKED INTO it with his eyes open, because Barney couldn't read.

They got few letters, but sometimes As The Fella Says would prop his heavy Post Office bicycle against the white-washed wall outside and come into the kitchen shifting the bag on his back. He would God bless all here and sit on a chair waiting for a mug of tea and telling them all that was happening within a radius of twenty miles. He would talk and eat and philosophize. Like, if the weather was bad; As the fella says, it'll get worse before it gets betther. Or if you lost a cow; As the fella says, betther a cow than a corpse. A harmless soul he was, wearing navy-blue puttees on the legs of his Post Office uniform. Cahal met him once in the town in ordinary clothes and hardly knew him. If he had a letter for you he wouldn't give it up until he had exhausted all the possibilities of its delivery. Then he would go away.

Barney would take the letter and look at it. If it was an American letter he would open it to see if there were any dollar bills or Post Office orders in it. If there were none he would just throw it on the fire. If it contained money he would put that in his pocket and hand the letter to Cahal saying: Read that.

Cahal would read it. It would be from one of Barney's exiled children. Stiff letters, hoping you are well father and that all is going well with you and I met Sarah Ann in Boston and she is looking well and she married a Polish-American and he is looking well and they have two children and they are looking well and I am enclosing a few dollars even though times are hard with us. Things are not like they were and when you have to provide for a wife and children it's not so easy. Your son John. Of all the children that he had sired, Cahal only read letters from two of them.

They were vaporous people to Cahal. Nothing remained of them in the house, even the talk of them. There were no photographs. None had ever been taken. No rag dolls remaining from the girls; no broken toy soldiers from the boys. They had never had them. Nothing remained of them except in the imagination or in the queer mind of their father, who never spoke of them, had forgotten them the day they had won their freedom from him.

Barney couldn't write.

He would say: Write a letter. Cahal would get the watery bottle of ink from the dresser and the cheap writing-pad from the drawer of the dresser, with the stained white envelopes. The paper was porous like blotting paper, so that as you wrote a word it spread and you had to allow big spaces between the lines. The letters were always the same, delivered in the hard voice of Barney, who sat there with an arm round the chair, the old stained hat on his head. Dear John, I hope this finds you as it leaves me. Times are very hard. The rates are due on me. So is the annuity. Milk is making no price. The oats was thin this year. I don't know how I will be able to keep the place going. Your father.

Then he would rise and go out, and Cahal would trace up As the Fella Says, who would be drinking a mug of tea in

Cassidy's or Creel's and would give the letter and the coppers for the stamp.

The letter that decided Barney to go to the holy well came in May. In big round writing, four lines on one page. Dear Barney, In the matter we were speaking about last Tuesday on the green, could you come to Valley for the Holy Well. James Bright. There were eight spelling mistakes.

So they went to the Holy Well.

It was a break that Cahal was determined to enjoy. They were crucified in the house without a woman to manage. There was so much to be done outside. The cut turf to be saved, to be turned to the sun and footed to let the air go through it, and stooked after that and then stacked and clamped and drawn from the clamps load by load through the terrible bog road, with the horse and jennet straining and pulling and breaking their hearts. Every sod had to be handled. The jennet carted it to the good road outside the bog where the horse could not go on account of his greater weight and lesser agility. It had to be unloaded there on the side of the road and then loaded again into the horse cart which Barney drove, and then hauled home to the dunghill outside the stables, on top of which it was dumped and built up into a great clamp, sloping like the roof of a house, and cunningly sloped so that the rain would not lodge on it and it would remain dry for the coming months. In between all this, the fields had to be ploughed and turnips, mangolds and potatoes and oats prepared and sown. And how the hell could all that be done and you having to cook in the house as well, and feed the animals and scrape the pots, so that in the end of course they weren't eating anything except huge pots of potatoes that they put to boil and turned the pot out in the evening, piling the potatoes on the table and skinning mounds of them and eating them with a bit of butter and salt? If you had time to do the churning of the butter in the middle of everything else. And one day Barney had taken up a plate and smashed it on the concrete floor and shouted, "This can't go on," and somehow, Cahal had the impression that the letter from John Bright had something to do with this. He didn't think deeply about it. He was too excited at the thought of the break.

They left the house at six o'clock of a May morning.

It was a fine and clear morning with the early light just appearing. They were driving the horse cart because they had a long way to go, all of twenty miles. There was a plank laid across the sides of the cart and there was a bag of hay placed on the plank and they sat on this and if it tickled you behind for a while, it was softer than the wood. Barney was dressed up for Sunday. A bowler hat that bore its long years well, and a stiff collar and front attached to his shirt and held in by a dark waistcoat. Over that he wore the heavy bréidín coat, a dull brown, that was shaped like a swallow's tail. His trousers were the same. He looked well in this. He looked like a patriarch and a man of position. A sound man, you would say, if you stopped to see him passing by. Cahal sat beside him, his thick hands dangling on his knees. He had his navy blue suit on and the white shirt with no collar, and he could smell the polish off his boots.

Few of the houses were awake as they passed. The big doors were closed on the half-doors and the red blinds were pulled down on the windows, but as they turned from the village road on to the main road to the town they began to see many carts and traps heading the way they were going themselves. Sometimes fleet traps with lively ponies passed them. There were old men like Barney in them with their white fronts gleaming and their faces newly shaved or their beards trimmed. And their women were with them too, most of the old women dressed in black, with their shiny cloaks on them and the black bonnets on their heads. They didn't wear those because they were mourning, but because they were respectable. Even the women that didn't wear cloaks wore black coats. There were young girls too. They made Cahal sit up a bit in his seat to see so many fresh young girls. You got out of the habit of realizing there were other people in the world, besides the weary people of Caherlo.

Bright eyes and silk stockings if they were on bicycles. Pert hats and blue coats or pink coats, with scarves. They had left their mothers generations behind. Even the bicycles they rode were generations ahead of the traps, and Cahal thought it was nice to see the shape behind of a young girl on a bicycle. Some of them were thickly shaped but some of them were young and lissomely shaped, and he found himself enjoying this, enjoying the curve of a young breast that you could see under the arm that was holding the handlebars.

The land on either side of the road looked good. It was brown and scattered with green where the weeds were coming with the summer or the shoots of the plants were appearing. Stretching away in broken fields as far as the eye could see on either side, and then ahead they saw the spires of the town and the traffic on the road was thickening. Near the town a horse trap passed them by. A big smooth trap with rubber-shod wheels, and it wasn't until Cahal heard the shout of, "How's the Bogman?" that he looked at the Murphys. Very prosperous. Sitting up straight and clean as if they had all come out of the one box. Mark raised his hat to say, "Hello, Barney." Barney waved his hand holding the thick stick. Cahal said, "Hello Mrs Murphy," because she was the only one of them that he really liked. If you went into her house you felt welcome. She would have the kettle on the crook before you knew where you were. She wasn't tall and she wasn't fat. But her hair was grey and she had little to say. How could she?

He didn't mind them calling him the Bogman, he thought, as he watched the dust curling up behind the iron step of the trap. He was used to it now. Everyone had to have a name and that was as good as another. He hadn't quite forgotten the incident that led to it, and he didn't like Sonny any the better for it. The five Murphys were in the trap. On one side Mark and Mrs dressed in their best, and on the other side the Spits, and Sonny at the end, looking back at them, his teeth white in his face, indolently holding one side

- 76 -

of the trap and waving a hand. There was a lot in that wave. Inferior people in common carts. You could nearly tell how much the Murphys had in the bank from that wave.

They halted in the town. They tied the horse in the yard at the back of the big pub and they went inside and they drank a pint of porter. Barney took the money from a small purse which he carried in his trousers pocket. A small purse that looked lost in his big hand. The careful opening of it with his back turned and extracting a florin from it and laying it carefully on the counter. Then he surprised Cahal. He took two half-crowns out of the purse and handed them to him. "You will want a few shillings at the well," he said, and drank his pint.

Then they journeyed on.

It was about ten o'clock in the morning when they topped the hill that looked down into Valley. It was a grand sight. Cahal felt excitement stirring in him as he looked at it. They were on a hill, and on the far side of the valley was another hill, and left and right of Valley hills and roads came down into it like the four parts of a cross. The four roads were jampacked with vehicles and people all converging on the little place below. All sorts of carts and traps; all sorts of animals; bicycles and a very odd motor car that hadn't room to pass and could make nothing of its speed. Colourful long snails' trails of people. All under a misty blue sky. Every colour you could think of and the terribly verdant green of the fields in the valley bringing out the colours more clearly. On the left of the little village below, he could see the old round tower in the ancient churchyard where the well was. It was a perfect tower but that the tapering top was sliced off as if it had been done with a knife. He saw the old church that had been the saint's of long ago and the sun brave on the white canvas of a big tent in a field near the tower. The village was small. You just saw blue slates of the roofs as if you were a bird looking down on them. About six houses on each side of the road and on the right a new church with a blunt spire and the house of the priest set back from it and surrounded by dark green conifers.

They trundled down towards the valley.

Progress was slow. It was like being caught in a sluggish stream. The horse was throwing his head in the air. He was uncomfortable with carts in front and carts behind. All over was the murmur of voices. Men were talking over the heads of people in carts behind them to friends in carts a few times back. Shouting, "Ah, Patsy! Patsy, you old bastard, are you still alive? Begod I haven't seen you abroad since we lost the cow the night of the big wind." Barney seemed to know quite a few of them. His greetings were quiet and not effusive. It took them a solid hour to get into the village. They went through it and then pulled into a big field beyond the church. There were hundreds of carts and horses there. They took the cart off the horse and tied him to the wheel with the rope reins and threw him the hay they had been sitting on. Cahal wiped down the horse when he had untackled him and thrown the gear on the cart. The horse was sweating heavily. His pelt was gleaming from the sweat.

"You can go where you please," said Barney then. "I have some people to see. Later on I will catch up with you near the white tent above when I want you."

"All right," said Cahal. He patted the horse who was eating the hay greedily and then he stretched himself to take the cricks out of his back after the long sit. He had never seen so many people in his life before. Even in the town where the school was he had never seen so many people even on the fair days. He made his way out through the gate. It was cut into thick mud by the passage of so many wheels. It was nearly impossible to walk in the village street. The smell of the horses rising supreme over all, from their sweat and their dung. Two of the six houses in the village were pubs; the rest shops. You couldn't even see the entrance to them by this. There was no order about the people. They were just jammed in from house to house, and since they were countrymen and unused to the niceties of civilization they pushed and used their elbows if they wanted to get anywhere, and if they nearly knocked the eye out of you with the point of an ashplant it would never enter their heads to turn and say, "I'm frightfully sorry, my dear man." Cahal laughed at the thought and then turned back and made his way towards the well.

He had to use his own elbows and his thick shoulders to push his way towards it, but he got caught into the right stream eventually and was carried along. There was a terrible chattering. Little children shouting for lost parents, and women chittering and pulling out rosary beads from their pockets as they came near the stile. It was a narrow stile and the walls all around were high so that only the young climbed the walls and jumped over. Cahal felt he was a bit old for that so he waited for the stile and crunched his way through and breathed more freely in the wide field that led to the well. It was a rocky path, simple limestone pellets, rose-coloured, laid over it. From there he noticed some people sitting at the wall and taking off their boots and stockings, tying the laces of the boots and hanging them around their necks, and then they ventured timidly and with a little groaning on to the stones. Others of them went on their knees and started walking on their knees, their rosary beads slipping through their fingers as they tried to concentrate on their prayers and take the pain out of the stones.

Cahal wondered.

They are holy people, he thought, and I'm afraid I wouldn't be able to do that at all. The Stations of the Cross started just inside the stile. Small boxes holding a picture of each station and they preserved from the weather by a glass front. They were raised on posts and the whole lot painted green. He stood well away and watched them. It was mainly older people who walked on their knees. Some of the younger people ventured on the stones with their bare feet. They giggled a bit if they were girls, and divided their time between giggles and "Oh, stoppit, let ye, and let me pray".

Cahal went on.

The Stations went into another field where there were all old graves tumbled. Most of the names on the headstones you could not read at all, the centuries having wiped out the craft of the stonecutter's chisel. The rose-stone path went all around the graveyard. And it was jammed with people. People on their knees and people in their bare feet and others walking to each station and kneeling in front of it, their eyes blank as they tried to picture the scene they were commemorating. Isn't it a quare thing now to be here in an Irish field in the middle of the country and simple country people, their minds taken up with a deed that had happened thousands of years ago in a strange land that they couldn't even imagine?

At the end of the Stations there was the well.

Many centuries ago, those ruins over there were the home of a famous saint. It was a monastery of great learning. Where shaven-headed monks had delved and read until they had discovered the secrets of living and handed them on to others. When the Danes came in their great big-bosomed boats, pillaging and raping, the monks would gather the people from the village and all would retire into the round tower beyond. The door into it was nearly twenty foot off the ground, so that when the Danes reached them they would have the ladder pulled up and the door closed, and they would be very snug up there and could pour down terrible things on the heads of the raiders.

Cahal climbed up the mound of the tower and saw it rising above him. It was easy to imagine it now. The birds used it and there was moss on the stones, and the slitted windows were chipped and old.

The well was below the tower.

They had to approach the well slowly. It was a very holy well. St Patrick himself had made it. He had come to this part on his travels. He had topped the hill above and looked down and he had said: Now, be the grace a God, there's a smart spot below, a right place for a monastery if ever I saw one. So he came down there and found it was all right but that it was all pagans and no water at all. And the pagans didn't take to him at first. But he gathered them around him on this very spot and he said: So that ye can believe now that my God is the right God and not your man beyond, nothing else at all but the stump of an oul tree, I'll show ye, and he stamped on the ground three times and he invoked the name of his god, and clear water spouted from the spot like a fountain and all believed and he set to and built a monastery and left one of his men in charge of it, and it became very famous, until it was destroyed by the English.

You could imagine it all right, Cahal thought.

The people at the well were very sincere, and you could hear many tales of the terrible diseases that were cured by it. They approached the well on their knees, and in their hands they held a coin or some precious thing of their own, or better still a little bunch of new heather with the purple blossom on it. Then they raised their faces to the sky with their eyes closed tightly and they held the heather over the well, and you could see them invoking with all their might and then they opened their eyes and dropped their gift into the well and watched it fall and waited as if the miracle was to occur right away. Cahal was fascinated watching the faces. Old withered faces of women. What could they be wanting? Please take away from me the bleeding I have. Or, please get my daughter to write to me from America so that I will know nothing evil has befallen her. Old men, their fresh shaven faces shining. Give me the price of a heifer in place of the one I lost in the flood. Give me two more perches of good land so that I can keep me son at home. Young girls, their faces flushed! Send me the fare to America for God's sake before I have to marry and become old and worn watching the pigs. Or, please turn the thoughts of the young man I love to me so that we can be happy forever.

You could almost know who wished for gifts now and in the future.

If they wanted something now, they opened their eyes and held their breaths as if it was about to fall into their hands.

Then the light went out in their eyes and you could almost see the shrug of resignation and the thought; Ah, well, next year maybe with the help of God.

"Our Sheila was cured last year," he heard a woman beside him say. She was sitting on the grass putting on her boots and stockings. Long black stockings that she managed to fix without pulling up her long black skirt. Then around her stockinged foot she wrapped pieces of linen before inserting her feet into the thick hard leather boots. "She was four when the pig's pot turned over on her and scalded her. I nearly died. The poor lamb has a mark on her this day all down from her neck to her thigh. She never spoke a word. I had me two eyes worn out cryin' and me two knees flittered prayin', but it was no use. Say Dada, or Mama. You could be at her for hours, but she'd just look at you with her eyes wide open and she shakin' her head. It was more than the heart could bear I tell you. Then I brought her here. I made her go all the rounds on her little knees. And she dropped the heather into the well, and I thought it was no use and we came right up here and I was sittin' on this very spot puttin' on me boots when she said to me. Do you know what she said? "Daddy is drinkin' porter, Mama," she said. Honest to God. As true as I'm alive. I med a promise then that to the day of me death I would do the round of the Stations on me knees for her."

Cahal moved away.

What would I want if I wished at the well? I don't know. I don't seem to want anything. That must surely be wrong. Is there a single soul in the world that doesn't want something?

He climbed over the wall and went into the field of the tent.

It was a big tent and it was packed. Mostly with men. A strange smell in there. Of white-bottled sunshine, closed-in grass and porter. There were a few planks stretched on barrels as a counter and sweating men behind getting the porter out of barrels as fast as ever they could. Cahal squeezed up there and got a pint and a small grinder and a hunk of cheese. One and sixpence. He worked his way out of the throng and into the fresh air and went around the side of the big tent and sat there on a box for bottles with the pint glass between his knees.

The dry crusty bread tasted very nice with the porter. Crusty bread and cheese and porter. Three tangs.

He looked up as a shadow fell on him.

"Give 's a piece of bread," she demanded.

Surprised, he complied, breaking a piece off the nose of the grinder and handing it to her with a piece of cheese broken off by his fingers. The hand held out to him was small, shapely, and dirty. He looked from it up the length of the bare arm to the face bending down to him. A young woman with a deep brown face and black hair pulled so tightly back into a bun that it shone as if it was oiled. Her nose was small, her lips were thick and her eyes were black and curious.

"Thanks," she said, and squatted on the grass in front of him. He noticed then that she had a child with her, held carelessly under her left arm. A small dirty child about a year old; an almost naked male child. He could see the sex because the single garment it wore was rucked up from the press of its mother's arm. A truly black child with great big eyes and very sturdy limbs. "Dada," said the child. The mother chuckled. "He thinks you're the da," she said, leaving the bread on the grass and casually pulling open her brown blouse to expose a startling white breast which she shoved into the child's mouth. When the child had grasped the breast and she had pushed the nipple into its mouth, she reached down and took up the bread and proceeded to eat it, looking innocently up into Cahal's red face.

"I know you," she said.

"Do you now?" Cahal asked. He was confused. He had never been so near to the naked sight of a woman except once that didn't count. The sight of her brown face and the bold challenging eyes and the exceptional whiteness of her flesh inside the blouse, left him feeling odd. Wordless. Her feet were bare, and as she sat the red skirt she wore went up over her knees. She had dropped a basket beside her. It contained holy pictures, scapulars, rosary beads and bits of lace, and little statues of the Infant of Prague. So, she was a tinker. These free livers that you heard about. She was young too. Under the smoke of the campfires on her face and hands she would only be about twenty.

"Not that I know your name," she pointed out. "Just the look of you. I saw you sitting there on the box and I said, I know him, I said, only your name didn't come into my head. Would you like to buy a rosary beads?"

"No, thanks," said Cahal, "I have them."

"Or a holy picture, or a scapulars or a statue?" she went on automatically, looking closely at him, her head on one side like a sparrow. "No, I don't suppose you would. It's oney the old people that buy. When they think they are nearer the grave they do be buying their passports into heaven."

She laughed. Her teeth were small and very even and white. Her gums as red as the skirt she wore. Her ears were pierced with little gold ear-rings.

"I've seen you somewhere," she said then, thinking.

"What age is the child?" he asked.

"Him? Oh, he's a year or sompin'," she said carelessly.

"What's his name?" Cahal asked.

"Danno," she said. "Like his oul fella. Don't you know Danno?"

"No," said Cahal, "I don't."

"Then you must be from the north," she said. "Everybody in the south knows Danno. We know every road in the country so we do, and every village. We've been chased out of most of them," she added, giggling.

"That must make life interesting," said Cahal.

"Where you from?" she asked.

"Caherlo," said Cahal.

"Caherlo? Caherlo?" she wondered for a while, thinking,

and then a light came into her face and a smile to her lips. She dropped her heavy eyelashes over her eyes and glinted at him slyly from them. "Caherlo! Caherlo! Oh, we used to go to Caherlo. Times ago. We don't go now at all much. Danno keeps away now from Caherlo. Now I know."

"What do you know?" he asked her.

"Nothing," she said, "nothing at all. Besides Danno would clatther me. Would you like me to read your fortune?"

"How would you do that?" he asked.

"Give me your hand," she said, wiping the crumbs from her own on the grass. He stretched out his hand. She took it into hers. He felt the back of his hand warm in her palm. It made him feel odd. Gave him a sort of sinking feeling in his stomach. Her head was bent so that he could see the skin of her scalp in the parting of her hair.

"Misfortune, misfortune, misfortune," she said, dropping his hand. "That's all. Will you pay me now?"

"How much do I have to pay for all that information?" he wanted to know.

"Oh, a tanner will do," she said, "when you won't buy a rosary or nothin'."

He gave her sixpence.

"Thank you," she said. "I like you. I like country boys. I like your white shirts and your clean faces and your blue suits. Are you strong?"

"I don't know," said Cahal.

"Maybe I'll see you again," she said.

"I hope so," said Cahal. "You never know."

"When I saw you sitting there alone on the box and I thought I knew you I liked the look of you, that's why I came over. Were you lonely?"

"No," said Cahal. "I don't think I was lonely."

"Anyway, I liked you," she said. "Are you sure you wouldn't like a statue?"

"No," said Cahal. "Thank you very much."

"Nessa! Nessa!" they heard a voice roaring the other side of the tent. It was a deep rounded voice passing through a hoarse throat. She looked up. "That's me," she said. "I'm Nessa!"

The voice shouted again.

"You had better go," said Cahal.

"Let him go to hell," she said, tightening her lips. "Always on tap I am like the porter he drinks. What does he want now? I'll tell you. The money I made. I didn't make a lot, only a few shillings. I will hide the sixpence you gave me." She pulled up the skirt of her dress, turned it and inserted the sixpence into a little patchwork pocket. Her leg was very white and well shaped. Cahal dropped his eyes, feeling a tightening in his chest. "Nessa! Nessa!" the voice roared again, coming nearer.

She settled her skirt.

"That's Danno now for you," she said.

The bull voice roared its way around the side of the tent. She dropped her head, holding the breast into the mouth of the avidly sucking child. Cahal thought the child was terribly big to be feeding from his mother's breast. The child was nearly as big as a calf.

"There you are!" said the voice to the right of them. "Why didn' yeh come when I called y'? Hah? Hear me callin', didn't yeh?"

Cahal looked up. Nessa didn't. She seemed to be deaf. Danno looked very big from where Cahal saw him. A big bare-headed man with a mop of curly black hair that was raddled with grey. A big face with a powerful nose and a week's growth of grey-black whiskers. He wore a red bandanna handkerchief knotted around his muscular throat. His chest was bare and brown and matted with hair down to his leather belt. He was wearing a black green-moulded coat over his nakedness. His stomach was flat and his legs were long in the tattered corduroy trousers he wore. A powerful right hand was holding a thick ashplant.

He came closer to them.

"Why didn' y' answer me?" he demanded again.

"I had t' feed the child," she said sulkily, throwing a look of scorn at him. Cahal though the whites of her eyes were very white.

"You had to be smellin' around young men like a she-cat. Always instead a workin'. Who are you?" This was directed to Cahal, gruffly.

Cahal felt his neck going red.

"Mind your own business," he said, rising to his feet. Finding that Danno was still tall. A head and shoulders taller than he but not so broad. Who is he, a tinker to be talking to me like that?

"You keep away," said Danno. "You don't talk to Nessa, see. None of your business, see, or I'll tap your scarlet for you, see," pushing his face into Cahal's. Cahal flinched from the smell of porter and onions.

"I didn't talk to her," said Cahal. "She talked to me. I didn't talk to you either, and you talked to me. I don't like you, and I'll leave you before I lose me temper."

"A cock," said Danno, pulling back and doing a sort of prance on the grass. "A country cock, begod. That should be down on his knees doing the Stations instead a standin' up to his betters. Come on now, man, if it's a fight you want..."

He backed away and threw his coat off and down on the ground. The muscles rippled all over his big body. A brown body that could have done with a wash. He was shouting. His voice was nearly a scream. Cahal felt sweat under his arms. He saw that people were converging from many parts to the spot where they were. Danno was a showman. Drunk or sober. He waved his stick over his head and leaped about.

"The first king of Ireland," he shouted, "was me father. Finn McCool was a first cousin once removed. I have bet every man in the length and breadth of Ireland from Bloody Foreland to Haven's Cross. Come on now, the country cock, till I clip your feathers."

The men had come out from the tent and stood there grinning with glasses of porter in their hands. Cahal felt desperate. How did I get into this? What am I going to do?

Try to fight a tinker with a heavy ashplant in his hand? Why? He looked down at the girl. She was looking up at him. A grin in her eyes. She was an animal that girl. She would enjoy this. Did she always go around looking for young men, so that Danno could come along and beat them into pulp with his stick for her satisfaction?

He moved towards the dancing Danno.

"Here now," he said placatingly, "let's be sensible about this thing."

"Hear him now?" Danno asked his audience. "After violatin' the sanctity of me hearth and home, he wants to be sensible. Hear that, men? Did ye hear him?"

Cahal barely dodged the blow.

One minute Danno was appealing to the crowd and the next minute the stick was swinging in an arc for Cahal's head. It was very fast. He just ducked in time, sweating, reaching a hand for the stick, but it was pulled out of his hot fingers.

Danno stood facing him, his back to the crowd. Cahal saw Old Barney pushing his way through that crowd, and coming into the opening behind Danno. Then before Cahal could say or do anything he saw his grandfather raise his heavy blackthorn stick and bring it down on the head of Danno.

Danno dropped the stick from his own hand and clasped his head and fell to his knees. Old Barney raised his stick again and brought it down with a dull clump on the back of the crouching man. Then he raised his heavy hob-nailed boot and kicked him in the side. The crowd was very still. Behind him Cahal heard the girl Nessa screaming and as old Barney raised his stick again, Cahal ran to him and held it as it fell and pulling it out of his hand shoved the old man back with his arms.

"No, no," he shouted at him. "That's enough. He didn't mean any harm."

Barney was looking down at Danno. His nostrils were white.

"I told you," he said then, "I told you before never to meet me, or I would give it to you. I told you to keep away. Let me see you again and I'll finish you. Come on, you. We have people to see."

He said that to Cahal, taking the stick from him and walking through the silent crowds that opened to let him pass. Cahal looked at the girl who was standing now, her breast covered. The child was lying on the ground, kicking its limbs, its pudgy thumbs in its mouth. The girl was smiling away. She was pleased. She looked into Cahal's eyes boldly. Then he dropped his eyes to the man on the ground. He was crouching there holding his head and the blood was flowing scarlet over his brown fingers. Then Cahal turned and followed after his grandfather.

Chapter Seven

They will sell you a pig or a cow or a ram,
They will split you the price of a sow or a lamb,
They will pray for the world and the ending of strife –
And if you're not cautious they'll sell you a wife.
  Óri, óró! Saint Pathrick was grand –
  He shlaughtered the shlaves and the shnakes of our
  land.

HE FOLLOWED BARNEY out of the field and over the stile and into the street of the village. It was less crowded. Barney turned into the second shop on the right-hand side of the street, turning his head momentarily to see if he was coming after him. He was no longer white about the nostrils.

Cahal pushed his way in after him. It was a pub. Crowded with drinkers at the far end, and this end the man was trying to sell groceries. The brown ceiling was timbered and was blackened by the fumes of the oil lamps hanging from the ceiling.

There were funny smells in the place. The smell of sacked flour, and Indian meal and washing soda and salty bacon and porter and fresh baker's bread. He saw Barney turning in a door on the right off the shop so he followed him. There was a passage here. At the end he could see people milling around in the kitchen, but Barney turned into another door off the passage and he followed him. The passage was white-washed and smelled of damp and cats.

He found himself in a parlour, that was dimly lighted by a small window heavily curtained and blinded as if someone was dead in there. Barney was holding the door open for him. When he went in, he shut it.

"This is him," said Barney.

There was a piano with yellow keys and the top of it cluttered with photographs of people in outdated clothes. There were two hard armchairs and a couch covered in depressing red plush and a round table at which three people were sitting, a man and two women. The man had a pint glass of porter in front of him which had spilt some of itself on the glossy table, staining it. In front of the two women there were two glasses holding port wine.

The man rose heavily to his feet. He was a fat man, who seemed even fatter in his best suit of thick broadcloth, wearing a white starched front and collar with a stringy tie and an enormous gilt watchchain spanning his great stomach. Bald as a swede turnip with a big red and white face not unlike the same vegetable. He stretched a small fat hand. It could only encompass three of Cahal's fingers. He shook them hard.

"Well, well," he said. "We're glad to meet you and you made a great man, God bless you. Sit here." He pointed at the chair beside the lady on his left. Cahal sat into it, conscious of the lady looking closely at him. He didn't look at her, but he noticed the hand holding the wine-glass was thin and had long fingers and that there was a shine off her fingernails and freckles on the back of her hand and that it had a glittering ring on the second finger, and above the wrist there was a fur sleeve. Apart from that he could smell her. Nice smells like the woodbine tree or the lavender bush. But his eyes were full of the animal girl feeding her child, or lifting her skirt to hide a sixpence, or of Danno sitting dumbly on the grass with the blood pouring over his hands. What kind of an inhuman man was Barney at all?

"James Bright," he heard Barney say as he pulled up a chair to the table.

A young man with his sleeves rolled looked in at them and raised his eyebrows.

"Three pints and two more wines for the ladies," said Barney, reaching for his purse.

James Bright, Cahal thought: that's the man who can't spell, or did he get somebody else to write the letter for him?

"You never met my sister Julia," said James Bright, indicating the lady beside Cahal. He turned his head to look at her.

"How are you?" Cahal asked.

"I'm pleased to meet you," she said.

"Julia was the baby of the family," said James with a wheezing laugh at Cahal's look. She wasn't like her brother. She was thin. Her face was narrow and her eyes were bright. She had small ears and ear-rings sparkled in them. Her teeth as she smiled at him were white and even. Cahal had seen very few returned Americans as they were called, but she was one. She was wearing a small hat with a peacock's feather in it and a string of pearls on a slender neck and he could see the top of a blue dress under the blue coat with the fur on the collar and cuffs, white sort of fur like would be on a collie dog.

"Julia is back from America," James Bright went on as if sombody was asking him questions. "Makin' a fortune she was out there while the poor family here at home was toilin'."

"Ah, now, James," said Julia, "I wish you'd stop talking about fortunes. They are not as easy to pick up as some people imagine."

Cahal thought she had a pleasant voice. It was soft. It didn't rasp like her brother's. What was he doing here anyhow?

"We're thinking of bringing her into the family," said Barney. Great God, Cahal thought, so that's it. Barney is taking the plunge. "Well, isn't that nice now," he said. "I'm very pleased to hear that. We need someone in the house. Are you a good cook?"

They laughed. An air of tension seemed to have been raised from the atmosphere.

She put her hand on his where it was lying on the table, a momentary touch. Her fingers were soft.

"You're a very direct young man," she said.

"Cook?" asked James Bright. "For God's sake, man, she has the whole of us pantin' since the day she kem home. All day in the fields we think of nothin' but gettin' back to Julia's cookin'. I don't know what we'll do when she laves us. Isn't that right, Bridget?" digging the other lady with his elbow. She was a fat woman too, wrapped in a brown shawl, her greying hair pulled back tightly in a bun from her round wrinkled face.

"That's true, James," she said. "That's true. I don't know how you'll be content with your own wife's cookin' when she's gone from us."

"Yeer terrible flatterers," said Julia laughing. "I spent my whole time in America cooking, Mister Kinsella. Out in a big mansion in Westchester County outside New York. They cried when I said I was going home. But I had to come. No matter what they offered me, and they offered me the moon, I had to come. There's no place like home after all."

"I hope you'll like our place," said Cahal, thinking, well, she seems to be very nice – but feeling a bit sorry for her, thinking of her married to Barney. And Barney would be twice her age too. She'd be about thirty-five, he guessed. Wondering why she wouldn't have gone after a younger man. But then look at Barney. As straight as a whip and as virile as a two-year-old dog. Maybe the old devil would soften up with a young one like her. Besides Cahal could be nice to her.

"Well, that's great," he said. "It'll be a relief to have a woman in the house again."

"Well, we're very glad now that it's all fixed." This was James Bright, while Barney rose up and went to the door and roared "Tom! Tom! Hurry up with the drinks, will you?"

"Did you go around the Stations on your knees?" Julia wanted to know. Every time she moved, the flower fragrance came from her and the rustle of silk. All that didn't seem to go with Barney somehow. No matter. Let it lie. What business was it of his? Anything to take the house off his back. He had enough to do in the fields.

Tom came and they drank.

"Is it true that ye have the Brodels from Roscommon over there, Barney?" James Bright was asking.

"No, I didn't," said Cahal in answer to her. "I had nothing to pray for."

"Not even for a cook?" she asked, looking at him oddly.

"No," he said. "It never entered me head. So here we are with one now, so that proves that it's not good to pray for things. Maybe if you just wait for them, they fall into your lap."

She laughed, still with that strange look.

"That's right," said Barney. "New herd over with the big man. I haven't talked to him yet. He seems to be quiet."

"Faith," said Mrs Bright, "he has cause to be quiet, the dance that daughter of his led him."

Cahal listened.

"What's all that about?" Julia wanted to know.

"The Brodels," James Bright said. "He used to herd the big estate over near us. They left a few months ago. Himself and his daughter. Herself was dead the years. Good job too. She didn't have to wait and see."

"See what?" asked Barney.

"Oho," said James Bright, sinking his face in the big glass.

"She's a one," said Mrs Bright, nodding her head.

"Do you mean Máire Brodel?" Cahal asked.

"That's right," said Mrs Bright, her lips tight, "that's the one."

"What was wrong with her?" Julia asked.

"Oho!" said James, coming out of the glass and licking his lips. "Oho!"

"She dropped one," said Mrs Bright in a whisper, looking

around, then tightening her lips and nodding her head. Cahal felt his face blazing.

"Dropped what? Is it a baby?" Julia wanted to know.

James Bright said, "Oho!" again. Cahal felt he could have cracked the glass on his bald head. His thoughts were whirling.

"Are you sure it's the same Máire Brodel?" he wanted to know.

"Of course it is," said Mrs Bright. "Ther' couldn't be two of them."

"She's the one," said James. "Such terrible things. And that quiet man her father. We couldn't put up with it of course. They had to go. We went in a deputation to the big house. I was the spokesman. We can't have things like that in the village, we says. She'll have to go. Then we went to the Brodel place. We gev them a month to move. Poor Dick. He took it well, but the one!"

"Like a wildcat, she was," said Mrs Bright. "The things she said to Mister Bright you wouldn't believe. And she a tramp. It's easy known the bad drop was in her, I said. No shame."

"And now we have them," said Barney.

"It's not the same in a way," said James Bright. "The you-know died afterwards. No sign now. But watch out. Be careful. That's all I'm tellin' ye."

They talked more, but Cahal wasn't listening to them. Máire Brodel! The clean-stripped virgin by the side of the river. Making him feel as if there was something lacking in him. And she all the time with that. Well, that's a good one, that is. That's something to bring things out of you, all right. Wait'll he saw her. Not for that, he didn't give a damn if she had fifty babies, but putting it on him like that as if he was a mental defective.

He wanted to see her. To tackle her. How would her eyes look when he taxed her with this? It made him smile. He felt a bit superior now, a little bit like God would be who could see under all the exterior that men showed to the world.

They parted from the Brights.

"That'll be all right, so?"

"Of course it will," said Cahal. "We'll make her as welcome as spring grass after the cold winter. The house will be like a house again."

"Great talk, man, great talk," said James. "We'll fix the date."

The evening was drawing in as they went home. They talked little. Cahal was turning it all over in his mind. Once he laughed out loud, to the amazement of his grandfather who turned to him grunting. Cahal didn't explain himself.

Barney only said: "That went off well. She has two hundred and fifty pounds athin in the bank."

"That'll be a help to you," said Cahal.

He left Barney at the house, backed the horse and cart under the great tree near the little dairy, and then untackled him and rubbed him down with a piece of hay. Over from the road opposite their house they had a square field where they grew oats one year and potatoes the next year, and beyond that they had green fields that sloped away down to the wind of the river. He turned the horse loose in this field, with a slap, and the horse galloped away, kicking its heavy legs in the air, as if it was a colt, and then it threw itself on a dusty part of the field where the grass had been worn off and it bathed there in the dust, whinnying with ecstasy.

Cahal barred the gate. The sky was clear with stars and rosy all the way around. Why would I wait until tomorrow? he wondered then. Why shouldn't I go right now?

He set off along the road, and when he crossed the big bridge he turned down the road towards the river, through the gate where Peder had gone the first day he had come to Caherlo.

About a mile down this rough road, he saw the light shining from the Brodels' window.

The house was set on a hill, sheltered at the back by tall plane trees that had a mournful sigh with their big leaves. It looked down at the river and it was sheltered by a low stone wall that was whitewashed and gleamed. The house had a slate roof. There was smoke coming out of the chimney. He hesitated at the small wooden gate. Would he or wouldn't he? He had never met her father. He was a quiet man, they said, who always kept to himself.

A dog barked in the house at the scrape of his boot on a stone. The half-door was closed. The dog came bounding out over it in a graceful leap and ran down to the gate barking. It was small black and white collie.

"Nice fella," said Cahal, clicking his fingers at it. The dog backed away snarling and showing its teeth, and then the figure of a man blocked out the light in the door. "Here, Rex, Rex, down, boy," said the man, the dog immediately turned from its baiting and went back to the house wagging its tail.

"Good evening," said the man.

"Hello," said Cahal.

"Come in and warm yourself," said the man.

Cahal opened the gate and closed it after him and walked up the path. He smelled flowers on either side of him. He could see grass and flower-beds vaguely in the light of the up and coming moon. I'll bet that's her, he thought. She'd be the kind that would grow flowers.

The man had gone back to the fire. He was sitting on a chair, one foot was resting on his knee. He was scraping a brown pipe with a penknife. Cahal blinked a little in the bright light from the paraffin lamp. It was a very clean house. The dresser wasn't like their own, open. It was a dresser with glass doors, and the delf was shining behind it. The table under the window was covered with a flowered oilcloth. The chairs weren't coarse crudely built ones. They were better than that. They were scrubbed white. There was a picture of a woman over the mantelpiece. She was young and dressed in old-fashioned clothes, but her eyes were gay. She was very like Máire. That's her mother so, he thought.

The father was a tall tough-looking man, with long slender fingers. He wore an old hat on his head. His face was long and tanned and he wore a moustache. Fair the hairs in it were, except for a few very white ones. He had shaved too. His cheeks were tight and shining in the light of the lamp.

"Sit down, won't you?" he asked.

"I thought Miss Brodel might be here," said Cahal, looking at the closed door above the fireplace. Two doors, one there and one behind his head as he sat facing the fire.

"She's not," said the man. "She's away out."

"It's a nice night," said Cahal.

"It's all that," he agreed.

"This is the first time I came to see ye in yeer house," said Cahal.

The man considered this, blowing the scraped bits from his pipe. He had brown eyes with long fair lashes over them. He's almost like a collie himself, Cahal thought.

"You're welcome," he said after pondering it. Then he looked at Cahal. They were clear eyes that assimilated him in a few moments. Quiet eyes. Cahal shifted under the gaze. The man saw a powerful young man with a deep chest and black, black hair growing down on his forehead. It might have been the black eyebrows that made the eyes seem so alive, and so restless, with a shimmer of excitement in them. What was the excitement about? "You're Cahal Kinsella, I take it."

"That's right," said Cahal. The dog came to him and stuck a wet nose into his hanging hand. Cahal rubbed its head with his fingers. "Nice dog," he said. "That's a good dog you have?"

"He is," said Máire's father. "He's a good dog. It took me a time to train him. He thought you had to bite sheep as well as bark at them. He used to bite the tails of the cows too. He's all right now. He's a good dog." Cahal had a picture of this tall man with a crooked stick out in the great broad sloping fields with the dog by his heels, a pipe in his mouth, looking down at the white dots near the bog land.

"You know," he said, "I'd put you down for a shepherd straight away." The man laughed. His look at Cahal was more friendly. "That was sharp of you," he said. "I like sheep. They are good companions. They're a bit contrary, but you get to know them, and to be able to shepherd them. Not like humans. Humans will go back on you no matter how you train them."

Cahal felt his face going red, at the wonder if the man was talking about Máire not knowing that Cahal knew.

"They're quieter anyhow," he said quickly.

"Yes," said the man. "And they don't complain. You wash all their diseases away in a dip-hole. Will you have a sup of tay?"

"Ah, no," said Cahal.

"Of course you will, man," said the other, "isn't the kettle hoppin'?" It was, too. He got up and with slow measured movement took the brown earthenware teapot from the dresser and heated it with hot water and threw the water out over the half-door, saying: "Máire would murder me if she caught me at that." Then he came back and made the tea and got two mugs from the dresser, sugared and milked them and came down again to the fire. It was good tea.

"That's nice tea," said Cahal, feeling panic in him for the first time. Now he wanted to run away, to get out before she came back. He felt his body straining, waiting for the sound of her step on the path outside. The tea was scalding hot, so he couldn't get rid of it quickly.

"Do you like Caherlo?" Máire's father asked between sips.

"Oh, I do," said Cahal. "I like it fine. I don't see much wrong with it. Does it please you?"

"Aye," said the other judiciously. "I think it does. I like the big bogs. You can be real alone down on one of the big bogs. And the odd things you see down there. Now the last place we were had no big bog like here and it had no river. It was very fertile and it's a strange thing that nothing is more boring than eternal fertility."

Over behind the man, in the nook made by the fireplace and the wall, there was a sight of shelves with a lot of books on them. Cahal couldn't see the titles from here. He thought Máire's father talked well. He must have been a brave reader.

"It's spaces," said Cahal. "It's like over in the next county where they have the mountains. That's a right lonely spot too." Then he stiffened as he heard the steps outside. There were light steps and they were accompanied by heavy steps. Who's with her? Cahal felt his heart pounding dully. With a mixture of excitement and panic.

"Here she is now," said her father, unnecessarily.

Cahal didn't turn his head. He dug his lips into the mug. He heard the scrape of the half-door, and then he heard the feet and then he heard Sonny Murphy's voice saying, "Well, here's the Bogman with us and all." Cahal turned then and looked at her.

"What brought this great honour on our house tonight?" she asked.

"I just kem over to see your father," said Cahal. "I'll be going now." He rose to his feet, leaving the mug on the table, saying to her father, "Thanks for the tea. It was grand." The father's eyes were regarding him quizzically, like he would examine an ailing sheep maybe. "What's your hurry, Cahal?" he asked.

"Don't let us drive you away," said Sonny.

"Indeed yeer not," said Cahal, stretching. "I'm tired anyhow. We had a long day."

"Is it true ye were match-making?" Sonny wanted to know.

"You go and ask Barney," said Cahal.

What was she doing out with Sonny Murphy? Sonny had his Sunday clothes on too. And he looked well in them. A tall straight young man with prosperity written all over him. He stole a glance at her then. She was putting turf on the fire. She looked up at him. "Don't leave us as if we had a disease," she said. He had a close look at her face. That was it. It had maturity. There were two or three straight wrinkles grown in the corners of her eyes, and one on each side of her nose. Her face was flushed and the light of the fire behind her made her hair look wispy and radiant.

"Ye weren't the only ones that were match-making," said Sonny, sitting in the chair Cahal had heated for him, and letting his hand rest on her shoulder. "Maybe we ought to tell him what we were doing, Máire?"

It infuriated Cahal. Sent some sort of savage glow up from his stomach, to see Sonny there with a possessive hand on her, and she looking at him sideways out of her eyes, almost knowingly. If he had had the mug in his hand he would have smashed it on the floor. Like the unaccountable feeling that had come over him long ago when she had taunted him at the bridge and he had crushed his face on hers.

He felt his teeth scraping against one another.

He spoke through them.

"Before you match her," he said, "I'd ask her what happened in Roscommon."

Then he went out of the door. His legs were tight. He found it hard to push them with the feeling that was in him. He was conscious of the three of them stiffening in their positions, and then he was outside. The feeling took him to the gate and beyond, and then a great desolate emptiness took possession of him. He thought of her father. That was first. Like hitting the man a box in the face. He didn't mean to hurt him. It was to be all different to that. He was to get her by herself and bring it out and then things would have been cleared between them. But he didn't and now he felt ashamed, the rhyme at school beating in his head, keeping time with his faster feet,

Tell-tattle, tell-tattle,
Buy a penny rattle,
Hang it on the cow's tail,
When the cow begins to kick,
Out comes sugary stick.

He kicked at the stones in his path and when he reached

the bridge he looked down at the cool clean water and thought that by rights he ought to leap into it and that he might be clean afterwards.

Barney was sitting at the fire.

"Where were you?" he asked.

"I was out," said Cahal challengingly, his jaws tight. Barney didn't take it up. His mind was on something else.

"You liked Julia Bright?" he asked.

"Yes," said Cahal. "She smelled nice. She says she can cook. She has two hundred and fifty pounds in the bank like you told me."

"Well," said Barney, "what date will we set for yeer wedding?"

Cahal stared at him.

"What are you saying?" he asked.

"Well, you met her. You knew. You told them everything was fine. What the hell is wrong with you?" His face was going red.

"But I thought she was for you," said Cahal.

Barney allowed his jaw to drop.

"Are you cracked, you eejit?" he asked then. "What would I be doing with her?"

"I thought ..." Cahal tried to say, and then thought back and it all fitted in like a hand into a hand. He just took it all the wrong way. He tried to bring back the picture of Julia so that he could look at her in a different light. She was all right. She was what they wanted. What else could you get? Bring a woman in to Barney that had nothing but her body and the two of them would end up on the road. Besides he felt so small and mean now that it would be a wonder for anybody to look at him. Well, why not?

"Does she like me?" he asked.

"I suppose she does," said Barney. "If she didn't she wouldn't be willin'."

"Well, give me a night to think it over," said Cahal.

"Well, think it over fast," said Barney, going up to his room. "The sooner we get her in here the better, and we're lucky to get anyone like that at all for you, considering who you are." He went into his room and the door closed behind him.

Cahal looked at the fire and thought. I am nineteen. I have never been closer to a woman than the touch of a hand or the touch of a face, and that touch scorched me. He thought of Danno's Nessa feeding the big baby. And then he thought of Julia's hand. A small hand with freckles on the back of it and a shine on the nails. It was soft to the touch. What did it matter anyhow? What was wrong with her? She could cook, couldn't she, and she had two hundred and fifty pounds in the bank as Barney stated and you could buy a new mowing machine for that and a new plough and maybe another cow and they would be living on the fat of the land. Where was all the love business you read about in books long ago? He never saw any of it around Caherlo. They got married this way. This was the way. They were all right. Everybody was all right. Very few bastards could get a woman who had travelled over the world, and who smelled like woodbine and lavender bushes and could cook and had two hundred and fifty pounds in the bank.

All right.

He went to bed.

It was a big double bed with brass knobs on every corner of it.

He wondered what it would be like to have the body of a woman sleeping beside him. It made him shiver. He pulled the clothes up close to his chin, and said, I will not think about the mean thing I did today.

He finally slept.

Chapter Eight

The birds of the breezes;
The beasts from the byres;
The furzy-bush lovers;
The priests and the squires;
The toilers and tinkers
From village and green
Are bid to the joinin'
Of lovers' young dream.
*   Fáilte! Fáilte! the whole bloody lot of ye!*
*   Dance, diddle-diddle, for fiddle and fun.*

CAHAL WENT THROUGH it as if he was in a dream.
They rose at half past three in the morning and pol-ished their boots. They could eat nothing because they would be receiving, so they left the village when the moon was still high with a bright shine on their boots and their stomachs growling. They followed the winding of the Ree right in through the town and out of that again to Valley of the Holy Well where his fate had been sealed unbeknownst to him. And here the Ree flowed into another big river about three times its size and they went on past that to James Bright's village another good six miles.

They didn't go beyond the church. The horses and carts and traps were all there gathered outside the church.

Cahal felt light-headed as he went in.

Inside the altar rails he had to go. There were two prie-dieus there for them. He knelt on one side and she knelt on the other as the ceremony began. Times he wanted to laugh. He couldn't even see her. Just the side of her face, because she was wearing a veil from her hat that had spots on it. All he could see were her hands joined. They seemed very thin hands for all the jobs she would have to do. He saw her looking at him once or twice from behind the veil and he felt his neck going red. Why, he thought, I don't know this woman at all. If he said that to Barney what would Barney say? It was like a lucky dip really. That's all it amounted to. You put in your hand and you pulled out a packet and when you opened it, it might be a good prize or a bad one. It was all luck. But he felt a bit excited all the same.

He had seen her once more since the agreement was made. It had been in the same ill-lit public-house in Valley. She was wearing a different-coloured coat and dress under it. Once when the stuff brushed against his hand, he thought how fine and smooth it was, not like the coarse stuff they wore themselves that was like the rub of sandpaper. He hadn't as much talk the second time. What could you say in a case like that? Like the books? I love you, darling. I am thrilled that you are to be my bride. He wondered about courting. In the ordinary way. What happened to people who were supposed to be in love? Was it just animal? Did you do a bit tonight and another bit tomorrow night and gradually get on and on until you knew it all? And was it pleasant to have that slow growth of your consciousness? What about what they wrote about longing? You saw her tonight and if you didn't see her tomorrow night you thought that the world was coming to an end.

This had to be different. It had to be the pattern of the fields. The life of the rustic people. Did a cow after all get an introduction to her husband and a long period of time to get to know him before they became man and wife? These sort of things he thought about and they made him giggle. Because he hadn't a feeling for anybody, just a feeling for that Máire Brodel. That was nothing soft. It was anger and a little shame that she had made him feel small on two times.

So, welcome Julia.

The priest turned twice in the middle of the Mass to read a prayer over them. That was after they were married. Nothing frightening about it, except where you had to say I Do to the bit about forever and ever. A terrible empty feeling of panic had come over him then. To the end of his life. With a woman he didn't know. He felt like getting sick. His dream feeling became a sea of misty sort of vapour that was holding him tight. There was deep inside him a feeling that wanted to explode into action. But the sight of sober Barney, stolid and immovable like a tree in a field, quietened him down.

He thought he heard her sigh.

The ring he put on her finger was hot from the grasp of Gob Creel who handed it to him. Gob was frightened. His Adam's apple went up and down in his throat. Gob had cycled all the way to be his best man. He was the only one Cahal would have. If I can't choose the wife, he said, then I will choose the best man. That was a laugh. Gob didn't like it. He would do anything for Cahal, but it frightened him to be in the public eye. Cahal had to keep on assuring him and backing him up, and that was a good thing, because it kept Cahal himself from being panicked.

That was that.

They came out of the church, and apart from Gob who stayed near him, and Barney and James Bright and his wife whom he had met before, Cahal knew nobody else at all. It was odd to feel her holding on to his arm. He could feel a tremble in her and that made him feel better and a little sorry for her. After all she didn't know him either. He was only nineteen. Maybe he'd turn out completely different to what he was now. That couldn't be, but how would she know?

There was no confetti.

All the Brights. There seemed to be legions of them. People shaking Cahal by the hand, and saying, "Ah, so this is him? A fine man you got, Julia. I was watching the size of him athin in the church." The priest shook hands with them and came over to Bright's afterwards in his car. Cahal and Julia were brought over in Bright's trap. They sat side by side. He could feel her knee touching his and he noticed it was thin. Her hands were covered in white gloves. She kept pulling at the fingers of them. James Bright was happy. He flogged the horse with the whip and laughed. "Well, it's a great day, Julia, a great day surely." He didn't add that it was a day he thought he would never see, but here it was at last, and it was worth what it was costing him.

Bright's house was a two-storey slated house with a big yard and the yard was filled with horse and carts and ass and carts and ponies and jennets and bicycles and three motor cars. There was the big kitchen and the two rooms off the kitchen and they were both filled. Cahal didn't know a sinner. They were at the head of the table in the parlour. He saw Julia for the first time without her hat. Her head was small, and the hair was put close to her head and there were sort of regular waves in it. Brown waves, with a little grey here and there in them. Her face seemed too big somehow for her head. But it was a nice enough face he thought. She had a blue dress on her with white sort of stuff at the collar, and when she laughed her teeth were very even and white. Top and bottom. She had grand white teeth. Well, she's not a big buxom country wench anyhow, his mind said. She had very little in front, some of the young guests were saying, and some of the women in the kitchen, talking about her and assessing her chances, shook their heads and put the odds very high, and said that even if, her hips were as small as a young girl's and she'd roar the place down.

Cahal didn't know all this.

He took whiskey for the first time in his life.

It was pressed on him as a toast and he drank it and he barely stopped the fit of coughing that it engendered. But he loved the way it warmed his stomach and the gradual way it insinuated its way into his brain, so that it emboldened him and he could look Julia in the eyes. Her eyes were big and had long lashes over them. They were the best part of her. There were shadows beside her eyes and it made her look a bit mysterious, and she had a habit of looking out of the sides of them under her lashes.

Nobody made speeches.

They were too busy eating roast goose and boiled ham and jelly and cream and emptying big mugs of tea and drinking whiskey and porter and Sandeman's port, but the talk got louder, and besides they were all talking and laughing about people they themselves knew, and Cahal had no interest in them at all, and under cover of it all she talked to him.

"I hear you are a great one for songs," she said.

"I sing a little," said Cahal.

"Your own songs too," she said.

"Ah, oul things that I make up," said Cahal.

"Would you sing some of them for us today?" she asked.

"Ach," said Cahal, "I don't know. Sure I know nobody here at all."

"Maybe you would if I asked you nicely," she said then, looking at him that way from the sides of her eyes.

"If I have enough courage in me, I might," said Cahal.

She reached for the whiskey bottle and passed it to him.

"That's for courage," she said.

He filled his glass again.

"That and love is the things that give a man courage," she said.

She looked at him full in the face. Cahal felt his heart fluttering again.

"The trouble about all this," she said, "is that it doesn't give us a chance to get to know one another well. They don't leave you alone for a minute even."

"We have the long night going home," said Cahal.

"Aye," she said. "I liked you from the first minute you came in the door in the shop in Valley."

Cahal drank.

She embarrassed him. She shouldn't make this personal. It was a deal. She was all right, but the night frightened him. The long night home and then when they would be alone. Two strangers that were wedded forever. He felt his knees quaking with panic. He searched with his eyes wildly for Gob.

Julia felt complete, for the first time in her life. She couldn't believe, looking at the dark young man beside her, that she had found him for herself. A fine young man with heavy shoulders and powerful hands on which black hair was sprouting. She liked the youngness of him too. It would have been terrible if he had to be old and formed. As the long years went by she had been dreading that more and more. That she would end up with an aged man. She knew from the soft look of him that he was kindly, and from the glint that came into his eye at times that he wasn't stupid. He would be sensitive. And she knew the world. She had been abroad, and this nice simple young countryman would be a haven into which her ship had sailed after stormy seas. She had left her home for America in the first place because she was sensitive. She didn't like the dirt and bawdiness of country living. She had been educated by the nuns and had been taught that there is more to living than fields and animals and big feeding and heavy sleeping and sweat and sunburn and cows moaning. She had been taught about the better things and she had set out to find them. So they said she was odd. Julia Bright *was* odd. She was sexless because after a dance at the cross-roads, she screamed and screamed when a hot young man became curious in the field of the corn-stacks. Just because she let him take her there so that she could point out the position of the moon and could tell him the names of some of the stars she had learned.

He was shamed and sheepish when her screams were answered. She was escorted home in a welter of tears and hysteria, and the young man got an undeserved reputation after that for being a ram, that twenty years did nothing to abate, and all the mothers in seven baronies warned their daughters about having nothing to do with him, so that he had great trouble in procuring a wife for himself and in the end had to be satisfied with an old one with a bit of money and seven acres of land near the river, and many a time in his cups and out of them he cursed Julia Bright from a height.

So she sought the cultured lands.

She was protected there. They were people who had books in their libraries which they read, and the sons of the house were young college men who could talk about anything under the sun. And Julia was nice and young and sort of untouchable, and they allowed her to read their books and to talk about the stars and she dreamt that one of these nice young men would see her for what she was and say, Julia Bright, even though you are only my mother's maid, I wish to marry you for your mind. One of them did try, after two in the morning when he came in from a jag wearing a silly paper cap with his evening tie all awry, and she was forced to scream again as he loomed over her bed out of the night, and as he tried to shush her, his mother came running and his father came running, and that drunken young man got a terrible dressing-down and his pocket money was cut off, and he wasn't allowed to drive the Cadillac for six months, and Julia had to change her job, heavily compensated.

That was the last. She became a cook and a good one, and she read a lot and she found it very pleasant to be alone. She married in dreams. There was always an ideal man, but he never came her way, and one day out of the blue, the thought came to her of home, one lonely night when there was eight inches of snow over the county, and she listened to the sound of car chains clattering on concrete and airplanes thumping over her head and the high voices downstairs of the man of the house arguing with his wife about her bridge club; she thought back to the night of the crossroads dance and the young man in the cornfield and she pressed her hands on herself and said with her teeth tight, Oh, I wish he did! I wish he did! And a great nostalgia came over her for all the things that she had fled from, the heavy fields and the insensitive people, and she thought, I will go back home. I will get a man at home. I don't want to be alone. Barely to herself there that night did she admit that more than two score years had passed over her head. She got out and switched on the light and looked at herself in the long mirror, and she thought, Yes, there is still time. There is still time.

So she came home.

And Cahal was her reward.

Cahal, Cahal. I love the sound of the name. It is gentle and simple and beautiful. She knew he had no father or no name worth talking about. But that didn't matter. In a way it bound him to her. He would be her baby. She would enlighten his mind. She knew so many things. Gently, gently she would inject them into him. And thank God he was young, young. She was eager to be away and to start a new life.

Cahal sang, but mostly he played the melodeon for them. When they discovered his aptitude for it they gave him no rest. They put him in a corner and they plied him with drink and Cahal loved it. It put it all back on himself, his fingers dancing on the keys, crazy words coming into his head for the fast tunes, and he would throw back his head and laugh.

The Brights went mad. They danced and they sang and they nearly roared the roof off, and old James lorded it there in front of the fire with his face beaming. And fat Mrs Bright got talking with the ladies. Cahal did not like Mrs Bright. He thought of the avidity with which she had passed on the story of Máire the first day he met them.

Gob did his singing for them. Because Cahal asked him to, since in the end his fingers were nearly paralysed on the keys. Then he came close to Cahal again in the corner and pulled the cap down over his eyes. Cahal wondered about Gob. He would like to have married Bridie because he had a genuine feeling for her. Imagine that. That there could still be left in this queer world a solitary man who wanted to marry on account of a vaporous thing called love.

It was night-time when he went out with Gob to harness up the horse to take his bride home.

The horse shivered when he heard them coming and neighed to them. The horse is fed up with this wedding, Cahal thought. He rubbed his velvety nose for him, and said, "It's all right, boy, we're going home now."

They tackled him and backed him into the shafts.

They were one each side of him and Cahal looking over the horse's back saw Gob regarding him seriously.

"Do you like herself, Cahal?" he heard him ask.

Cahal was surprised.

"She's all right," he said.

"I hope ye'll be happy, Cahal," said Gob.

"Thanks," said Cahal. "We will. Don't worry. Wait'll we're putting yourself off, Gob. That'll be a night to remember."

"That'll be never," said Gob. "Bridie will never come home."

"And what will you do, Gob, if she never comes home?" Cahal asked him. He paused from his task and leant on the back of the horse. "If you never see Bridie again, what are you going to do? You'll have to marry someone. You can't take the house and the land when your father dies and let it die for want of a wife. Think of that, man. What will you do then?"

"Let it die," said Gob. "Let it rot. I wouldn't marry a woman that I never knew. Maybe you're different from me. I got to know Bridie. It takes me such a time to get to know anybody. I'd never get to know another. I'd put salt on the land and beg the country. I'd do that."

Cahal felt the sincerity of him in the night, even through the heavy fumes that were clouding his brain. He went over to him.

"So you are telling me something now, Gob. You are wondering what's wrong with me. There's nothing wrong with me. Nothing now. What do you want? A man wants a bloody cook in the house, someone to mix the swill in the pot for the pigs. That's all. What does the rest matter?"

"You don't think it matters. I think it matters," said Gob. His voice was rising. "I liked you. I don't know why I am brave now. You shouldn't have done this. You don't love this one. You saw her two times in your life. I wish I hadn't come with ye."

"What are you saying?" Cahal demanded belligerently.

"What I said," shouted Gob, finding it hard to get out the words. "A fella like you. That is young and can laugh and make up songs that sets people hummin'. I thought you'd never do a thing like this. Why did you do it?"

"What could I do?" Cahal demanded, wondering how all this had started or if it was just the whiskey. Feeling surprised, as if a gentle cow had turned on you with her horns. "We wanted a woman in the house, didn't we? What could I do?"

"Barney wanted a woman," said Gob. "Why didn't he take her? You didn't have to take her. You could have said no. That was all you had to say."

"Say no, is it?" asked Cahal. "And be thrown out on me head on the side of the road, is it? Why should I do that?"

"What do you care if he threw you out?" Gob asked. "Aren't you young? Couldn't you go and work for somebody else? Couldn't you take a melodeon even and earn enough playing at dances and fairs to make a living? Couldn't you have done anything else you liked, couldn't you, instead a sellin' yourself like a young bull to an oul wan like that for the sake of a few pounds in the bank?"

"Shut up!" Cahal roared at him. "Shut up!" He was over on top of him with his big fist raised in the air. He caught it with his mind before it fell, and then lowered it slowly, his chest heaving and sweat gathering thickly in the palm of his hand. "You shouldn't have said things like that, Gob. What did I do to you?"

Gob's face was strained in the light of the moon. It had

been red, and slowly the red ebbed out of it.

"Japers I'm sorry, Cahal," said Gob. "What's got into me? Maybe it's because I just wanted to be married. I don't know. I'm sorry, Cahal. You should ha' hit me." He took off his cap and threw it on the ground and dug his heel into it.

Cahal said nothing. He proceeded with the tackling of the horse. He heard them calling from the house. The sweat on him was beginning to grow cold and damp so that he shivered.

"You must have had bad drink," he said, and turned away.

He wasn't drunk any more.

It was like a mist clearing away from a valley on the blow of a fresh gale. What have I done? Like Gob said.

Gob came after him.

"Listen, Cahal, I didn't mean all that," he said almost pleadingly. "It was just something that came over me. I'd do the same myself in the morning. Honest to God I would."

Cahal turned to him.

"Oh no, you would not, Gob," he said, shaking his head. "You would never do that. But I'm different to you. I have been taught to obey. And there's other things. You have something soft in your mind. A picture of Bridie, that won't go away because she went away. Maybe if she hadn't gone away you might have ended up the same."

"I would," said Gob eagerly, "I would surely."

Cahal shouted at him.

"You would not! You would not, you thumpin' liar!" And then he put his hand on his shoulder, and said: "I'm sorry, Gob. There's something got into us. We better make for home."

"All right," said Gob, and turned away towards his bicycle that was lying amongst the others up against the gable of the house.

They got a good send-off from the Brights. The horse was impatient to be away and Barney had a job holding him in. Barney was sitting between them holding the reins. They were facing back. They were resting their feet on her trunk, a large blue trunk with glittering steel bindings that reflected the light. They kept waving back at the people bunched in front of the door until they were buried in the night and they could only hear the clop-clop of the horse's hooves.

The Brights were finally alone. The whole family stood there in the kitchen, almost ankle deep in the litter of the hooley, and James Bright said it for them.

"Well, thanks be to Christ," he said, "that we saw the end of her."

"Amen," said Mrs Bright.

One son said: "If I had another meal with the old hen, I'd ha' gone mad, I tell ye."

"Remember her," said a daughter. "Young girls oughtn't to talk with their mouths full. Young girls oughtn't to sit in front of the fire with their legs spread out."

Another son took up the litany: "Young men oughtn't to come into the nice clean kitchen with cow manure on their boots. Cow manure, you know."

Said a daughter: "Young girls go out late at night to dances and things happen to them. What would the Blessed Virgin think watching young girls coming home in the middle of the night?"

James Bright said: "Even me, a grown man."

They chanted it for him: "Grown men shouldn't sit down at the table with dirt in their nails. What goes on the hands goes into the stomach."

"For Christ's sake, do you remember the day of the fair that she called the Guards because Murty Thornton was hitting the sheep on the back with a stick."

"Or mother's cooking. About the cabbage and the potatoes and the bacon."

"Or the po-po in the kitchen when you were caught out at night."

They laughed remembering that. They could afford to laugh now.

"Open the door," said James Bright, "and let in the fresh

night air, and then we'll all kneel down and say the Rosary in thanksgiving to the Sacred Heart that took her off our hands at last."

"Amen!" they all joined in heartily.

The daughter said: "I'm sorry for that poor young man. It was a terrible thing to do. She's more than twice his age."

"To hell with him," said a brother, "isn't he a bastard? He ought to be lucky he got anybody at all. Nobody'd look at him. And didn't he get two hundred and fifty pounds with her?"

"All the same ..." said the girl.

"In the name of the Father and of the Son and of the Holy Ghost, Amen," said James Bright on his knees, blessing himself with the cross of the beads. "Thou, O Lord shalt open my lips."

"And my tongue shall announce Thy Praise," they chanted.

"Incline to my aid, O God."

"The Lord make haste to help us."

"And He did," said the son laughing. They all laughed.

"Shish," said James Bright, "remember yeer at yeer prayers."

The journey to Caherlo seemed very long to Cahal. Very long one way, and in another way it seemed to be very short. Nothing to hear but the clop of the hooves and the creaking of the cart wheels and Barney clicking at the horse with his tongue.

It was brilliant with stars. She pointed this out to Cahal.

"Do you know the name of that constellation?" she asked him.

"I do," said Cahal, "and that one and that one and that one and that one," pointing them out and naming them. "Once I had long lonely nights. I learned them."

She stayed quiet. He knew more about them than she did herself. It was a link nevertheless between them. "I love the stars. Imagine a young farmer knowing all about the stars. You're the first I've met."

- 116 -

"They only fill the eye," said Cahal, "they don't fill the stomach."

He had Gob's words with him. Why did things like that explode from Gob? Suppose he had been Gob and Gob had been he? Marrying a woman older than himself. He felt bleak. I'm only nineteen, he thought. There had been a Brother at school. "Thinking," he used to say, "begins at the age of thirty. Before that men only experience. After that they think about their experiences and that's thinking. It's around then that whatever education you have shows itself. It assumes a meaning. You apply it from thought." It sounded nonsense then, when they weren't allowed even an experience unless it was stolen under the watching eyes, the eternal watching eyes.

And the nearer they got to Caherlo, the stronger he began to think that what he had done was wrong. Maybe she was the woman for him. But when Barney said it, he should have replied, I will not, until I know what she's like. What did he do? He consented airily, for the sake of any woman in the house and a few hundred pounds, to sell his freedom. For the rest of his life. And what would happen when he was alone with her? He had never been alone with her. He had only in all his life been alone with one woman and she didn't know he was there when she was washing herself in the river. Oh, God, if only I had a drink, a long long drink of whiskey, maybe it would be easier to go through with.

It was the middle of the morning when they reached Caherlo. There was a pleasant surprise in store for them. The door of their house was open, and as soon as they turned in from the road, many willing hands took the horse from them and took him from the shafts, and unharnessed him and put him away, and inside the house the fire was roaring and the teacups were on the table and everything was bright. All of them were there. Peder Clancy was the first to shake them by the hands and to peer at Julia and say "Begod, it's a jewel you got for yourself, man, curse of Christ but it is." And even though she pulled back a little

Peder insisted on kissing her slap on the mouth with his moustache that had lately been dipped in porter. And Jamesey Jordan was there and Mary Cassidy who had done most of the work, and surprisingly Sonny Murphy and his father Mark and his mother and Gob's father Tom Creel.

It made Cahal feel good. They shook all by the hand, and they sat around and talked until they had drunk their tea and the delf had been washed up and then a sort of silence descended and they went away in a body. Their talk was loud as they left. And when Cahal saw them going he felt a terrible panic in his chest. He wanted to shout after them: Don't go! Don't go! Hold on! Don't leave me alone with this strange woman! I don't know what to do with her! Look, let me go with ye, men, and leave her here with old Barney!

Their exit was inexorable.

The three of them were left alone. And then Barney without a word knocked out his pipe and went up into his room and closed the door after him, and Cahal was left alone with Mrs Kinsella.

Outside the house Peder Clancy, Sonny Murphy and Tom Creel leaned against the gable end of Cassidy's house and looked back.

They saw the light go on in Barney's room. After a time they saw the light go on in the other room. After a long long time they saw the light go off in the kitchen. After another time they saw Barney's light go off. And they they saw the light in Cahal's room go off.

"She's old," said Sonny Murphy. There was glee in his voice.

"Gob told me," said Tom Creel. "There was tears in his eyes."

"Well, it was himself did it," said Sonny Murphy. "The smart man himself. He was always after me, about how hard we work, and why don't we take a day off and tomorrow is another day, and look where he is now.

"She has false teeth," said Peder judiciously. "I felt them stirrin' under me mouth."

"Now he's fixed anyhow," said Sonny Murphy. "Mr Cahal Kinsella's goose is cooked."

"It's a pity," said Tom Creel. "Oul Barney shouldn't have done it. Cahal is too young to have any sense. Barney shouldn't have put an old one like that on him."

"What does it matter about that?" said Peder. "The old sayin' still stands, You don't look at the mantelpiece when you are stirring the fire."

Sonny Murphy laughed.

He laughed very loud.

Cahal heard that laugh even in his agony.

Later he even heard what Peder Clancy had said.

The morning was stealing across the sky.

Chapter Nine

My love will be
The petals of a white rose
Crushed in the hand.
My love will be
The ripe pink apple blossoms
Falling on to sand.
My love will be a white dream
Of clouds mating in the sky,
And I –
Oh God, I will love my love.

HE CAME STUMBLING out of the house in the false dawn. His white blue-striped shirt was pushed into his trousers. His braces hung around his hips. His feet were bare.

The small stones in the yard leading up to the road pressed bruisingly into the soles of his feet. He welcomed the hurt of them. Over the stones, over the droppings of the hens and the ducks he walked. No birds sang. No cocks crowed. The light of the stars was cold and fading and the light of the rising sun was hazy. The trees on the road were dark masses, barely whispering. He crossed his arms and pressed his forehead into them, wiping away the sweat. It was cold sweat. His feet felt the ruts on the road and he turned away.

He was like a drunken man as he made his way down the lane into the blackness of the tall bushes. Once he stumbled and the thorns in the blackberry bushes tore at his raised arms, digging into the flesh and pulling free so that the blood welled and mixed with the black hairs. He didn't feel the pain of it. He caught his hair with his two broad hands and bent forward and shoved the hair back from his forehead and raised his face to the sky with his eyes closed.

Then he ran. A run from side to side, hitting his toes against the flint rocks peeping from the yellow soil unworn by the passage of the iron-shod wheels.

He had no destination. Just to get away from the house. That was all. It was the river that drew him. He had thought of it once in a searing pain, of the clean clear swift-flowing water of the river Ree. He had felt the cold cleanliness of it flowing over his tortured body.

He leaned with his back to the little bridge. He couldn't open his eyes. He kept his head down. Pressing his eyes closed brought red dots dancing in front of them. He tried to concentrate on the red dots. They gradually became black and then white and faded away. He opened his eyes to the pale horizon.

He wanted to blame everybody but himself. He was the chief villain but he couldn't see it that way at all.

He was a lonely boy with stars in his eyes and tunes in his head and a blinding optimism. Once here on this very bridge he had met the one that had the solving of him. She had infuriated him. He saw her eyes wide with anger and a sort of helpless desire to knife him so that his understanding would flow.

It was flowing now. Just the same as if a knife had been applied to his chest, twisted and pulled down to his navel, laying the whole of him open to the air. He had had his dreams. Now he knew he had had them. Starting from the make-belief of who his mother was and how he had come to be born. As he got older, he had built on the dream. He had seen the faces of girls in the sky, with their long hair floating out behind them on the cumulus clouds, with thin eyebrows and red cheeks and their breasts rising embryonically from the misty transparent chiffon cloud-cloth.

More material ones had been peeping from the pages of magazines, or glimpsed on the other side of the road as the long snake-line of boys went for the Sunday walk with their heavy boots knocking sparks from the footpaths and their coarse suits a uniform of the captivity. Young girls with gym frocks and white blouses and black stockings on their shaping legs. Their hair cut across the forehead in a fringe. Their hair different colours as it settled towards adolescence. The dreams there of one of those even, turning her head to look at the line of boys, staring at them with hotly embarrassed eyes, some of the coarser of them muttering bawdy things between their teeth and the others hard set to keep from laughing, and one of them would meet his eyes and say to her companion, Who is that black one? He is a fine boy. I will go and get him released and I will marry him.

It was as foolish as that.

And he married a witch that rode on the black insinuating rain-clouds. He had never been sensitive about the feel of snails in his hands as he thinned the turnips, or feeling the slimy length of a black earthworm turning in his fingers. Now he was suddenly conscious of those things. He merged them together and into his head came the thought of a broken finger-nail catching on a woollen sock, so that he pulled in his breath and went away from the bridge.

He leaped the low stone wall into the field.

The grass was kind to his feet. The tall weeds were caught between his toes so that he pulled them and left them behind him.

He went down to the river. Right down to the alder grove and there he threw himself at full length with his face buried in the short green grass.

If only he had known.

How could he have known what it was to be violated; to be feeling the way he felt now, that everything in the world that might have been sacred was torn up by the roots and left to wither in the light of knowledge. It should never have come this way. Oh God, it should never have come this way at all. Here where he was lying he had seen the body of a young woman. It hadn't filled him with lust or hatred or love. It had been like looking at good things. Like a diving duck, or a soaring bird, or the nest of the little field-mice barely as big as the tip of your nail, or the smell of grass that was hay when the blade of the mowing machine cut it down, or the sight of the zig-zagging snipe over the heather. All those things it had been. And now that too was changed. It was too much of a contrast.

He looked across the river at the other bank. She could be there, her figure wraithlike in the very early morning.

You drove me on to that, he shouted silently to her across the broad flow of the river. You. If I had never seen you washing in the flow of the river, this other might not have been the awfulness that it is. Every fold, every crease, every cream tint of her, he could see now as if it was etched on his eyeballs. And the other was the terrible withered feeling and fumbling in the dark of a room. It was autumn when all was dead, when the windfalls rotted under the apple trees, when the shorn meadows grew a stunted yellow grass, and the trees were stark and withered and their sap away to the earth whence it had come.

All my own fault. All my own fault. I needn't have done it. I needn't have been afraid of the big world outside Caherlo. What had he been afraid of? Not even phantoms. No man starved who had a body and two hands and feet. But he wanted to be sheltered. He couldn't face the thought of a night passed under the stars in a ditch by the side of the road. He had got so used to having the call come and answering it. The breakfast and dinner and supper and bed and lights out. You got used to that. You got used to being provided for. Your heart beat fast at the thought of you alone in the world. So Barney was his shelter. For three years, that had passed pleasantly.

But it was Barney who was really to blame.

It was Barney who turfed him in there in the first place

when there was no need for it. Because he was ashamed. Never thinking of the shame of the morsel he was putting into a locked cupboard. And then when the time came for him he opened the cupboard and took him out and asserted his mastery over him, and married him away. No choice. He had a choice if he had stopped to think about it. But Barney gave him none at all. So what should he do?

He got up and climbed back the way he had come.

The blood rose in his face. He thought of Barney in his bed, his long sinewy arms outside the blankets, his moustache rising and falling to his breath. I will go into the room and I will take his stringy throat between my hands and I will squeeze them until no life remains in him. I will hold him down with one hand and I will bash in his nose and his eyes and his teeth with my closed fist so that his whole face will be a mask of blood and death.

He found himself hitting one fist into the palm of his free hand.

It brought him to his own yard. He thought of the cruelty of him. The very first day he came he was cracking the ribs of the dog with his heavy stick. The time he had pushed him roughly into the bog. He saw him opening the skull of the tinker, and raising his heavy boot to kick him. But what he has done to me is worse than that. Those things are not lasting. They pass. What he has done to me is going to last the rest of my life. There is no escape from it. It is the same as if I had been maimed.

He stood outside Barney's door and the heat went away from him. Barney would be surprised. Nothing else. What had he done? He had done good deeds.

Because I am to blame, he said, as he stirred the red ashes of the fire into a blaze.

There's no use blaming Barney for my own stupidity. Something has happened to me. I am not the same. I will never be the same again. Every day and hour that passes I will be looking at the world with new eyes.

The thought of the one up in the room, sleeping, wondering what kept him so long from the bed. That didn't disturb him any more. Not at all. He felt his mouth hardening as he thought of her. She made the bed, he thought, and now she can lie in it. She is a cook. She can cook. Her thin freckled hands would get hard. The vomiting disgust that arose in him was no longer there. He just felt drawn and old. His mind was working in new channels. His dreams were destroyed so he would do without them.

Nobody can kill songs that grow in your brain. They can only kill the direction of them.

He threw open the front door to the cold dawn.

Chapter Ten

The waves on the meadow are dancing and green
When they fall to the kiss of the mowing machine.
Whirro-whirree, and the corncrakes fly;
The larks are indignant and flutthering high.

IT WAS A warm misty July day and the wind was rising
hotly, carrying waves of heat from where the river
wound like unmoving melted glass.

Cahal was tramping a haycock and he could see over the
meadows. The cock was nearly completed. It was tapering
in from the broad butt and he was finding it harder to keep
his balance. He was enveloped in the heat and the smell of
the hay. It was short hay. All the animals loved this hay that
was cut in the river meadows. The land wasn't very good on
account of the periodical flooding from the river, but it was
good enough to grow a short grass, with few weeds, some
heavily scented clover, and the bite of the grass must have
been tainted with the things that grow by a river and
nowhere else. He always knew in winter when this particular hay was pulled from the huge cock beside the house,
that he would be more welcome in the cattle stalls. They
nuzzled him when he came with his arms full of this hay.
The other long hay of the ripe meadows, redolent of the
thistle weeds and dock and the valiant nettle, they treated
casually.

It made tighter cocks too, and it felt good in the hands, a
sort of velvety feeling, that was absent in the other, which

would have hidden thistle thorns to stick into your cuticles or into the palm of your hand, and you would have great trouble getting them out afterwards, digging at them with the point of a needle.

The whole village was at the hay.

As he looked towards the river, he could see Jamsey and Spray, right over from him. They had the meadow right beside the river, and cut off from this one by a deep drain, with a plank bridge across it, that was covered in scraws for the wheels of their cart. They were not alone, he noticed. They had a girl with them using the rake. She had a dress on her, a sort of pink yoke, and her feet were bare like her arms and they were very brown. He could see the outline of her body as she used the rake, out, pull, and scoop. The sun was glinting off her hair. He knew her well. He didn't look very often. He had given up looking, as well as thinking, for the past year.

On his right the Murphys had the biggest meadow of all, and they were attacking it like ants. They had machines. They had a horse rake, which took a lot of the labour out of the hay. They were the only ones in the whole place like that. In the other fields, the people just quartered a field of the saved hay and with the two-pronged fork and the rake and with much sweat built it up in walls of hay that eventually surrounded the butt of the cock. Then one man would tramp and the other man would pitch until the cock was complete, and after that the whole area would have to be raked for the wisps left behind and directed to the site of the next cock.

The Kinsella field was prepared. There would be five cocks. The butts were built and the hay was gathered around them. The Murphys would have eleven cocks. They were all gathered and six of them were built. They had the most help anyhow. With the father and three strong sons and application of a high degree, as Cahal thought.

Barney was pitching to him. He would gather a great load of hay on to his fork. It would weigh a considerable amount, and with no apparent effort, he would raise it above his head and hurl it up at the tall figure of his grandson. Cahal would take the load of hay and spread it evenly, pressing with his arms or tramping with his feet. He wore only a light shirt that was open to let the breeze blow on his sweating chest. Sometimes he reached an arm to pull out offensively tickling wisps that went down his back. His head was bare and his skin was almost as black as his hair from the beating of the summer sun. The belt holding the corduroy trousers to his waist was becoming limp with the sweat of its own contriving.

On the left were the Creels, Gob and Tom. They were at about the same stage as the Kinsellas, with five butts and building on one. Gob was tramping and Tom was pitching, and when Gob had a minute he would straighten the crick in his bending back and wave an arm at Cahal.

Beyond them and near the river Mary Cassidy and her two children were doing great work on their smaller patch. Tommy was growing tall. He was out of school now, and he was beginning to look like a man of the house. He had even taken to smoking his dead father's pipe, when he thought his mother wasn't looking. He was built solid like his mother, and gave great promise of growing into a big man. But Jennie was like her father. Cahal didn't remember her father, but that's what they said. He had been a slender man. Too thin for the fields, they said of him, before he bent over one winter like the back of an s-hook, and had to walk like that for two years, coughing and choking, before he died. Tommy was tramping, Mrs Cassidy was pitching and Jennie was indolently raking.

One time, Cahal was thinking, I would have got great pleasure out of a day like this. But there had been many days like it now since he had come to Caherlo. The life seemed to have closed in on him. He had changed considerably. One time his laugh would ring out over the parish, and you would hear him singing and being encouraged at the gable end of Cassidy's house. But ever since his marriage he had become a silent man. He never went to hooleys to play for them, or to sing for them. His melodeon was in its box untouched over the mantel since the night he came home with her.

He would greet them on the road, and pass the few minutes and then he would go away. Begod, they said, that wife of his has a powerful attraction for him. We never see him any more. He had been walking for a year with his head down and two grim lines were growing at the side of his jaws. He took the hay from the fork of Barney and wondered idly how many words they had exchanged in a year. You could count them if you were particular. He looked down at the face below, a thin face with the moustache becoming whiter, heavy downward-trending lines beside his eyes, that were white lines if he relaxed his skin. What did he think about when he didn't talk, you might wonder. Cahal gave up wondering. He had avoided him for many weeks altogether for fear of what he might say or do, but that was gone now. He no longer wondered what Barney thought, because he had come to the conclusion that Barney didn't think at all. If a person remained silent long enough, people were inclined to think that they were very deep and were extraordinary people, who must be mulling over the secrets of the world. It was either that or the simpler solution, that they just had nothing to say. Cahal had decided that Barney Kinsella just had nothing to say, that his small brain just ticked over slowly. I must sleep now. I must eat another time. I must beat the dog. The season has come for the cutting of the turf or the hay. Just stupid.

He had to balance very precariously as the cock became topped. There was very little space under his big boots and the top wobbled dangerously. Barney stopped pitching and threw him up the rake, and he raked the cock down from his feet, so that all the lose hay fell gently to the ground and the tramped cock presented a waterproof front to the winds that might blow the rain, until the time came for them to cart it home to the haggard.

He remained there, balancing his body with the rake, while Barney bent and unrolled the hay rope they had twisted. He threw it to him and Cahal put his feet on the middle of it, while Barney stuffed one end of it into the cock near the butt. Then he went over the other side and Cahal threw him the other end and he stuffed that in. Then they put on another rope, so that the cock was quartered with the ropes of itself, and held down solidly against the winds that might blow it over later, if it was badly built or if the ropes were faulty.

He slid down then from the cock, and wiped away the sweat on his forehead with his arm.

Beside this meadow there was a long sloping green field going back to the road. He scanned this and saw her coming. She was half way down. He was hungry. He threw down the rake and seated himself with his back to the cock. Barney stood up too and looked, and when he saw her coming got down on one knee and trimmed the butt of the cock with his hands. It was well trimmed already.

Cahal lighted a cigarette and watched the blue smoke of it. He could hear the rustle of the river weeds from here. The wind was rising. That's not good, he thought. It will make it harder to build the cocks. There was a heron dropping slowly and awkwardly from the sky on to the river. Would it be nice to have wings and be able to fly? Maybe. Maybe that would become boring too, with time.

She came through the gateway into the meadow. She was carrying a big basket covered with a white cloth.

He regarded her coldly as she approached them. He tried to remember back to what she had been like the night she came home. He found it hard. There was very little resemblance in her now to the nicely turned-out lady that was Julia Bright. She was wearing big boots on her feet, an old pair of Cahal's that had got small for him. The thin legs looked odd going into them. Thin legs covered in coarse black. Like if you saw a bird wearing a pair of big boots. They made her walk slow. She was wearing an apron made out of a canvas bag and an old faded skirt under it. She had a blouse on that had once been a shirt, and around her head she wore a kerchief of coarse linen. Her face protruded from it like a hen with a shawl on its head.

Funny what such a short time had done to her. Nothing remained of her except the two lines of beautifully white teeth in her mouth, and the sunken eyes looked out apologetically at the world, from a little world of her own. Her sleeves were short and the skin was loose on her arms. Her nails were broken and her hands were thickened. Maybe I should feel pity for her, he thought, but he didn't. A cold hard feeling rose in his chest when she came near him, with her mild eyes, like a dog begging you to be nice to her.

"I'm here," she said, placing the basket down, and putting her hand to her side.

"It's about time for you," said Barney ungraciously. "What kept you?"

"Men!" she said in the sort of sedate voice she used. "You forget what has to be done in the house. The chickens. And the pot for the pigs. Pigs eat such a lot. I never knew pigs had such terrible appetites."

She got down on her knees and spread a white cloth in front of them. There was no need for the white cloth, Cahal was thinking, but she always did it, laying it out with a gesture, I have been used to better things. She took two pint bottles wrapped in cloths, holding the tea, and then the sandwiches.

They ate voraciously.

"I see that the Jordans have a girl helping them." She shaded her eyes with her hand to peer into the sun. "Who would she be now?"

Neither of them answered her.

"Oh, it's that one," she said then. "She's still here so. It's a wonder the Jordans would have her with them at all. Wouldn't you wonder now? I do admire the Murphys. The amount of work they get through in a few hours. They are very good boys. He's a lucky man to have them. Is it true that Sonny Murphy was going to marry that one, I'm told, and then he didn't. He threw her down. That was a lucky escape. You know that Jennie Cassidy is growing. Every week I see her she seems to be bigger. Jamesey Jordan, Jamesey Jordan. What is he having that poor old father of his out in the fields for? The poor man is tottering."

She talked on, sitting on the hay and resting her body on one hand. He hated the look of that hand with the flesh so loose on it. It screamed to heaven about her. Even Barney's hand was hardly as loose-fleshed as it. She talked on, and all the time her mind was only occupied with a small part of what she was seeing. The other was thinking of him although she wasn't looking at him. She was afraid of him, and yet she wasn't afraid of him. In time, she thought. In time he will come back to me. When he sees how good I am, and how much work I can do. Even he must see that now. We could have such talks. Such fun we could have.

She put her hand up to her breast when she thought of him bending over her the night after the night. The muscles tight in his jaw and his eyes glaring and sparking. She thought he was going to hit her and she felt like crying. She had never felt so alone, even in America. As if it was her fault. He didn't have to do it either. She told him that and he raised his hand and she thought he was going to hit her across the mouth with the back of it, and then he lowered it and she started saying like a parrot: "You can't blame me! You can't blame me!" "No," he said, "I don't suppose I can blame you." Then he had left her. "This is your room," he said, "and you can do what you like with it."

He opened the settle bed in the kitchen, rucked up the straw and slept there with his clothes on. She left him like that for four nights. When she saw he was determined, she got out spare sheets and blankets and each night when she had swept out Tom Creel's spits and raked the fire she would pull down the settle bed and make it. What did Barney think? She didn't know. Barney never said anything at all. The first morning he had come down and found Cahal sleeping there and had wakened him with a question on his tongue, Cahal had looked at him unblinkingly for a few moments and then Barney grunted and took his socks from the crook beside the fire.

He had never had a mother. She was working her fingers to the bone for him. She had never really known what it was like to be a farmer's wife. She knew now. She wasn't built for it. But she had forced herself to it. Until she went to bed in the early days with every bit of her body screaming in anguish. Pulling the big three-legged pot across the floor and crying as her little strength failed to lift its terrible weight on the crook. Trying again and again, and sitting on the little stool with the apron over her head, crying until one of them came in to put it on for her.

She thought she might have a child. After the just once. But she didn't, and now she knew she never would because it was too late. Even if he came back to her tomorrow it was too late. She was past it now, and all that too, leaving her weak and exhausted so that she often went to the big bridge wondering if she would have the courage to throw herself into the black water and knowing that she couldn't.

He will change, she thought. I'm sure he will change when he sees how good I am.

Barney took out his pipe and filled it slowly. She gathered the things and put them into the basket. It wouldn't be so unbearable if only they would talk. They talked so little.

"Will I wait and help ye with the hay?" she asked.

"You might as well," said Barney, cocking an eye at the sun. "I don't like that wind and the haze that's before it. We better get this finished tonight. There will be rain."

"So there ye are, men," they heard Peder Clancy roaring from behind them. He was coming through their field gate waving a stick, his coat over his arm and great patches of sweat under the arms of his shirt. "There ye are, men."

"Hello, Peder," said Cahal, "what brings you down here?"

"Dammit, didn't I come down with a bit of news to ye," said Peder, "and to give that Cassidy woman a hand with the hay and she having only the two childer with her." He stopped then and roared over at the Creels. "Hey, men, men, come here, I want ye!"

They rose from their positions where they had been eating.

"Is it us?" Gob shouted.

"Come on, the whole bloody lot of ye," said Peder.

The two Creels started to walk towards them.

"Hey, Jamesey, Jamesey, come here to me!" he shouted, "I want to tell ye something." Then he went out a bit and roared at the Murphys. The two boys were working and Sonny and his father were eating. He encouraged them over with more roars.

"It better be good news you have," said Cahal, "to be upsetting every meadow in the village."

"It's not good news," said Peder, sitting down with a grunt. "They're going to sell up Foxy Killeen."

"Is that so?" Barney asked.

"It's as true as God," said Peder. "Didn't I see the bills today with me own eyes, when I went into the auctioneer man to pay up for the hire of last year's conacre. Down in black it was on one of the small green posters."

"Did you hear that, Gob?" Cahal asked the young man who ran ahead of his father and threw himself on the ground. "They're goin' to sell up Bridie's oul fella."

Gob raised himself.

"What are you saying, man?" he asked.

"That's right," said Peder. "Seems he hasn't paid rates or annuities for the last twenty years, or only a couple of bob a year. He owes every shop in the town for something so that he can't get a crust athin there without hard cash. He's a done duck."

"Good God," said Cahal, thinking of Bridie the night before she went away saying: You'll look in on the old man, Cahal, won't you, and give them a hand and see that they're all right? Yes, I will, said Cahal and never went near them.

"That's bad," said Jamesey Jordan, squatting, his big broad face troubled.

"He was bound to come to that some day," said Sonny, pulling at a cigarette. "The way they lived you'd think they had forty acres instead of ten. He was too feckless."

"Ah, the poor man," said Mark Murphy. "It'll be hard on him to leave the place."

"The point is," said Peder, "what are we going to do?"

"What in the name of God can we do?" Gob asked. "We'll have to do something."

"I was thinking if we all got together," said Peder, "and kind of dug into our purses a bit that maybe we would tide him over."

There was a silence in the gathering then.

"What would it take to tide him over?" Barney asked.

"Well, maybe about a hundred pounds," said Peder.

Jamesey Jordan laughed. He had an odd laugh. He had strong white teeth. He never seemed properly shaved and looked fearsomely criminal with the big jowls, but he was a quiet inoffensive man. The only thing about him Cahal disliked was the spittle that poured in a continuous stream down the shank of his pipe. He laughed a little like a donkey, the hee-haw type of laugh.

"I'll give you the price of next week's tobacco, Peder," he said. "That's one shilling and twopence."

"Well, to tell you the truth," said Peder, "I haven't any actual hard cash mesel, but I was thinking of selling maybe twenty loads of turf and that'd be a few pounds."

"It's no use," said Barney. "Even if that happened, in a few years more he'd be in the same trouble again." He got to his feet. "I don't like the look of the weather. If we don't get it done we'll have the rain on top of us."

Peder watched him moving off with the pitchfork in his hand.

"You're a hard man, Barney," Peder shouted after him.

"I am not," said Barney, turning back. "I'm a practical man, Clancy. You let your head run away with you. You wouldn't get a hundred pounds from the whole village here, and what's the use of thinking it?"

"You knew Foxy well," said Peder.

"I knew his father, too," said Barney; "but that won't help anyone."

He turned then and went over towards the next butt.

"He's right," said Sonny Murphy. "What put a notion like that into your head, Peder? The heat must have got you."

"It seemed good to me at the time," said Peder. "Would you help at all, Mark Murphy?"

Mark Murphy looked startled. He had a pale complexion that never seemed to change no matter how long he was in the sun. Just a pale film of sweat over an ivory-coloured face.

"Peder! Peder!" said Mark. "Where in the name of God would I get a hundred pounds? It's hard to come by a hundred pounds. Think of all the years a man must work and slave and save to have a hundred pounds."

"Mebbe just once to give away a hundred pounds would be more exciting than saving it up," said Peder.

Cahal felt like laughing, looking at Mark. The thought of him being separated now even in thought from a hundred pounds was bringing a look of horror on his face.

"You're cracked, Peder," said Sonny, rising to his feet. "We're all sorry for oul Foxy but you know as well as the rest of us that he has this coming to him. It's a wonder it hasn't happened years ago. You keep after Cahal there. He's soft-hearted. He'll give you the shirt off his back. Isn't that right, Bogman?"

"If I had a hundred pounds he'd get it and welcome," said Cahal.

"Well, what about ..." Sonny started to say, until he noticed that Julia was sitting near the cock. "Oh, well. Come on, father. Barney is right. I think the weather is goin' to break."

Mark was apologetic.

"It's a hard world, Peder. A hard world. But Foxy will be all right. They'll take good care of him and the wife in the poorhouse."

He meant it kindly.

Cahal noticed Peder going a bit red.

"The sentimints does yeh credit, Mark," he said. "And when the time comes and you're very old, and one of your sons kicks you out into the night, I hope they'll be good to you in the poorhouse, too."

"Now, now, Peder," said Mark, "you mustn't take me up. I meant no wrong. It is a good place. Well, I'll be off. It looks like getting bad all right."

They watched him away.

"If that fella gev you the itch," said Peder, "he'd cut your nails to knock the good out of it."

"It was a good try, Peder," said Cahal. "You tried."

"Why does all the wrong people have the money?" Jamesey Jordan asked.

Barney was shouting.

"Come on, Cahal, until we get on with it. Bring the rake with you, woman."

Cahal paid no attention to him.

Julia caught up the rake, and waited for him.

"We better go with him," she said. "The weather is looking bad."

Cahal didn't answer.

"I"ll go over to him, and keep the man quiet. I think it's sad about Mister Foxy," she said. "It's a pity from what I was told that he wasted so much substance on drink. It's odd that his daughter couldn't send him enough to keep him out of the poorhouse. Men, men!" she added, and went away.

"In case you're wondering," said Cahal, "I didn't get the money she brought with her. Barney got that."

He saw the three of them looking at him startled. "You could have had it if I'd got it." They were embarrassed. They looked away. Jamesey rose to his feet. "I better get back," he said. "Well, isn't the oul fella a great oul lad! Isn't he now? The age of him and the way he can fork hay. Did ye ever see anything like it?"

It always surprised Cahal to see Jamesey with old Spray. He really loved the old man. There he was now picking away at the hay with trembling hands. He was like a scarecrow, with his green-moulded old frock coat and his odd bowler hat faintly green and the thin-shanked trousers that showed up too well the pitiful scarcity of flesh on his bones.

"He's a great oul divil," said Peder. "He's worth four min."

"Isn't he now?" said Jamesey. "He's as good as meself any day."

He believes that too, Cahal thought, that is the surprising thing.

Jamesey crossed the bridge over the big ditch.

"I don't know what possessed me," said Peder, "to put up a proposition like that. If I had the money meself, I'd give it to him. I thought mebbe that the milk a kindness might be flowing in the Murphy veins. Isn't that Máire Brodel over there with the Jordans?"

"It is," said Cahal.

"Well, well," said Peder, "she's keepin' herself to herself this weather too, no more than some others. What's come over you, Cahal Kinsella? You're like a duck that went back into the egg. Is that what marriage done to you? We hardly see you now at all."

"You're missing nothing," said Cahal. His voice was guarded. Peder looked at him and didn't probe any more.

He heaved himself to his feet.

"Poor oul Foxy," he said. "God knows I tried anyhow. Is there anything you can do at all, Gob? You had a soft spot for Bridie, didn't you?"

Gob was lying on his front chewing a wisp of hay.

"Leave him be. Leave the boy be," said his father. Tom had taken no part in the conversation. Because they all knew that Tom hadn't two hapence to rattle together. So it would have been superfluous.

Peder was a little aggrieved.

"I don't know what's come over the whole village here,"

he said. "Yeer all as touchy this weather as a carrying woman. Look at me for Christ's sake, will ye," he went on then, pointing at his trousers. "I haven't a decent stitch to me name. The backside outa me britches. It's me that'll end up in the poorhouse. Hi! Mary Cassidy! Mary Cassidy!" he roared, waving his stick. "I'm comin' over there to ye. I'll pulverize that hay for ye." The kids stopped working and waved to him. He looked at the glum faces of the young men. "Well, I'll see ye again, in better weather, I hope," and away he went.

"We may as well go back, Gob," said his father.

"I'll be after you now," said Gob. Tom went.

"Do you hear from Bridie?" Cahal asked.

"Now and again," said Gob.

"How is she?"

"She says everything is all right," said Gob.

"I see," said Cahal. "There's nothing we can do, Gob. I wonder does Bridie know what's happening."

"I suppose Foxy wrote her," said Gob. "I know one thing I can do."

"What's that?" Cahal asked.

"I can drive them to the poorhouse," said Gob, rising to his feet. "I'll be seeing you, Cahal." He went away then, his hands in his pockets and his head down.

Cahal felt very sorry for Gob. For the first time in a long time he really and truly felt sorry for someone as he watched his despondent body walking towards the ditch dividing the fields. On his own feet, he wondered frantically what he could do. There was nothing he could do. He got the wife and Barney took the money. That was a laugh. He had muttered to Barney just once about it. How do we pay the rates, Barney wanted to know? How do we pay for the flour and the salt bacon? How do we buy a young cow for that old one with her dugs drying up? Cahal left it at that.

He didn't like to think of Foxy and his wife in the poorhouse. Just the very thought of it had reduced them in the eyes of the people.

The wind became boisterous. It was very difficult to place a layer of hay. The wind got under it and blew it up with the consequence that the heaviest tramping was done on the side nearest to the wind, so that there was a danger of the cock becoming lop-sided and toppling. The mist that covered the sun was becoming thicker. It was white up high and then it graded down, becoming very grey and yellow near the horizon. Every figure in the meadow was a swift-moving one, if you had time to look around at them. They only spared a short look at the sky and then their movements became almost frantic. Julia had to use the rake on the cock to keep the layers of hay pressed down. Her arms were aching. She made dramatic grimaces of pain and endeavour with her face, so that Cahal looking down on her would notice how good she was. She felt good. Out there in the meadow. It made them a family.

They got four cocks done before the rain came. It came very gradually. A few drops. The wind was cold. It was no longer torpid. All the sweat had been sucked from their bodies. Every forkful that Barney pitched was robbed before it reached Cahal by the streaming wind. The wind seemed to be everywhere. It made the rushes by the river bend and scratch so that the noise of them was like a giant taffeta cloth being shaken. It got into every free wisp of grass and made it hum. It was an annoying wind.

The cock was nearly topped. Cahal had to keep one foot pressed on the windward side to stop it from being blown away, and had to bend awkwardly around with his body to scatter the hay on the other side. Once his foot slipped and a whole bale of hay was lifted into his face and around his body and blown away.

Barney was furious. He banged the cock with the fork.

"What are you doing, you bastard!" he said, his lips pulled back so that you could see all his teeth. "Come down from the cock if you are not able to make it and let Julia get up."

"Shut up!" said Cahal, pulling the hay from his face and neck.

"Who are you talking to! Who are you talking to! You useless son of a bitch," said Barney. He drew back the handle of the fork. "I could stick you," he said. "Look at what you've done. The bloody cock'll be over on its back in two minutes."

Cahal jumped from the cock to the ground. It was a long jump. He landed crouching. He was mad. It might have been the wind.

"Don't talk to me like that, you," he said. "I've taken enough from you! Too much I've taken. You hear. If you want to finish the cock now, you go up and do it yourself."

Barney went into action. He raised the fork high over his head and he brought it down. It should have landed on Cahal's head.

Julia whimpered, her hand over her mouth.

Cahal went close to the body of his grandfather as the fork fell. He hit him on the Adam's apple with his left fist and he took the handle of the fork in the palm of his right hand. Barney was standing up choking. Cahal raised his right hand and hit him on the side of his head with his open palm. The old man fell to the ground.

Cahal went to work on the fork. He raised it over his head and brought it down on the ground with all his strength. It broke in two. Then he caught the piece in his hand and flung it away. He bent and took up the broken piece attached to the fork and flung it after the other.

All the labour in the field had ended. He didn't know that they were all watching him. That they had been watching since his first leap from the cock. It was a terrible sight. The old man on the ground, and the young, terribly strong and black young man bending over him, and the hay-cock, released of Cahal's weight, was being stripped and raped and scattered before the wind.

"I've had enough of you," Cahal was shouting at him, his hands clenched. "I've had enough of your cruelty and your stupidity. If you ever raise a hand to me again, I'll cripple you. Do you hear that? If I ever see you hit a dog or a man again, I'll hit you. For every blow you strike I'll strike two. You have ruined my life for me. It's too late for me now to tell you this. I should have told you this before you shamed me. I should have turned on my heel the first day I came and you were beating the dog. I should have fled from you, you selfish old man, before you tied me up with a woman that could be my grandmother and ruined me forever, forever."

"Oh, Cahal, Cahal," he heard her saying from the background.

"Shut up, you," he said. "I'm not blaming you. It was his fault.

"Get up now," he said to Barney. Barney was sitting on the ground. One hand was rubbing his throat. His eyes were looking up. The whites were red-veined. His hat had fallen off. His close-cropped hair was scanty and was being flattened by the increasing rain. The white band around his forehead from the protecting hat made him look old, very old, and helpless. Cahal saw all this as his anger waned. It was the end of Barney. That he could feel sorry for him at the tail-end of his rage. Nobody had ever felt sorry for Barney in his whole life. It's doubtful if even he himself had felt sorry for himself.

Cahal bent down and took his arm and raised him to his feet. "We'll forget it now," he said, "and we will go to work." He got his own pitchfork and put it into the old man's hand. Then he ran out a bit and took a run at the cock and clambered up it, pulling with his arms, shoving with his legs.

He gained his balance and stood up.

They all saw him looking at them and they went back to work.

"Hurry, hurry, hurry," he said to the old man, "or the rain will have it destroyed on us."

The old man gathered slowly and pitched a forkful. Then he paused, hawked and coughed, and spat blood on to the ground.

"Go on," said Cahal to Julia. "Go out and rake in the free hay, woman."

She looked at him, frightened, and complied.

The old man coughed and hawked and spat again. This time his spit was clear, so he gathered more hay and pitched.

The wind rose high and the rain became stronger and stronger and the calm river was ruffled and tossed.

Chapter Eleven

Those naked rafthers, forlorn, unthatched;
That saggin' doorway, unhung, unlatched;
That peelin' plaster, now mouldy green,
Once sheltered laughter and Dan Killeen.

"IT'LL BE ALL right, agirl," said Foxy. "Whisht now. Don't cry."

She tried hard. She was sitting on the stool opposite him. They were bent over the fire. She was wearing her black bonnet and her short cloak and black woollen mittens on her hands, just as if she was ready to go to Mass. Her white hair was pulled back tightly into a bun. Her hair was scanty. You could see the pink tint of her scalp here and there. She was woefully thin, her cheek-bones standing out through the pale skin of her face. The tip of her nose was red from the crying.

"I'll try, Dan, I'll try now not to," she said then.

"Afther all," said Foxy, "it's improvin' ourselves we are in a way. I hear great tales altogether about it now. 'Tisn't the same at all as when we weren't runnin' it ourselves. We'll have a room of our own, they say, and they's big big fields that you walk around. And you get a plug a tobacco once in a while, and they'll let you walk down the road to the town. All in all it'll be like livin' in one of them hotels."

Foxy was all dressed up too. He had on his bowler hat and his frieze coat with the swallow-tails on it, and he was wearing a dicky without a tie. All his foxy-looking nose and the spread of his thin cheeks either side of it was red and indented.

"I know I'm foolish to be cryin' about it, Dan," she said, "but so long in our own place, and never out of it, that'll be hard kind of to get used to bein' in a place with a lot of strangers, and maybe people bossin' us about."

"Who'll boss us about?" Foxy demanded, banging his stick on the hearth. "Nobody'll say a word to us, I tell you, or if they do I'll lay them flat, so I will and we'll walk outa that place, so we will. Mark me well now."

"I could always depend on you, Dan," she said, and then she was sorry she said it, because his head dropped low, almost between his knees and he shook it from side to side.

"No you couldn't, Josie. No, you could never depend on oul Foxy. If you could have depended on oul Foxy we wouldn't be goin' now where we are goin'. The Killeens wouldn't be endin' up now, disgracin' seed and breed of them in the County Home. Ah, Josie agirl, what have I done to y'!" His gnarled hand came slowly up, pushing back the bowler hat as he rubbed his eyes.

"Dan," said Josie, firmly, "I don't know what you're talking about. Listen, Dan, if they had lined up the whole of Connacht for me when I was a young girl, every man in the province under the age of thirty, and put yourself in the middle of them, I would have picked you out."

"I don't know why I was like I was, Josie," he said. "Life just seemed to be slippin' by and I caught up with it and chased it, spendin' next year's money this year. Four and five generations of the Killeens kept this place, and it was a good place. It reared hundreds of people and it took me to lose it all on them."

"Dan, Dan," she said. "What's the use of talkin' like that now? Isn't it the will of God?"

"Bridie doesn't know, anyhow," he said. "Bridie mustn't know."

"No," she said, "Bridie must never know. She has her troubles."

"You think that she has. She writes shockin' cheerful letters, doesn't she now, Josie?"

"Aye, they are too cheerful, so they are."

They stiffened when they heard the wheels of the cart pulling off the road into their yard. They looked at one another with panic-stricken eyes, and then Foxy relaxed and rose haltingly from the stool.

"The curse a God on old age," he said. "It has me crippled." He walked over to the door and stood there as straight as he could, one hand firmly on the stick, the other back under his coat.

"Well, well, min, yeer welcome," he said. "Come on away in with ye and have a sup a tay. Josie girl, heat the pot."

"Ah, now, man, for the love a God," said Peder, pushing past him in the door, "what would we be wanting tay for? Aren't we oney after rising from the breakfasts? God bless you, Josie, you look as spry as a sparra, and if himself wasn' there with the stick in his hand, meself and yourself could have the pieceen coort on the sly."

"You can turn on your heel again, Peder Clancy, and go back the way you came," said Foxy, "if you won't drink a cup of tay."

"Who said I wouldn't drink a cup of tay?" Peder asked. "Did I say I wouldn't drink a sup a tay? Isn't me tongue hangin' out for a sup a tay?"

"You're welcome, Cahal Kinsella," said Foxy.

"God bless ye," said Cahal, coming in, feeling sad at the sight of the old man doing the host. He had been many times at the same door welcoming people in. "Isn't it a nice day, Mrs Killeen, after all the rain?" Keep things on an ordinary plane. Thank God for the weather.

She turned from making the tea. He dropped his eyes immediately from her face. The signs of tears on it were too recent.

"Indeed it's about time," she said. "It's been rainin' for a fortnight. We were afraid the river would be risin' and takin' the hay. I says to Dan last night, Well, at least you won't have to worry about the river takin' the hay."

"Man, but it's well for ye," said Peder, sitting at the table. She got five cups from the dresser and laid them out with the milk and sugar.

"I have no bread left," she said. "We et the last of the baking for breakfast."

"Well for ye," said Peder. "No more milkin', no more pludder, no more worry about where the next pinny is goin' to come from to pay for this and that and the other. Man, but yeer goin' to have a great time of it."

"Are you comin' in or what are yeh doin', Gob Creel?" Foxy was shouting.

"I'm comin'," they heard Gob say.

"Will I be putting yeer stuff on the cart?" Cahal asked.

"There it is," said Foxy, pointing to the plaited straw trunk in the middle of the floor. "After seventy years of work and toil Mr and Mrs Dan Killeen go off to the poorhouse with the whole of their house in a straw trunk. Jaysus, even a snail has more on his back!"

He kicked the trunk with his boot.

"I'll put it out," said Cahal, bending and lifting it. It was very heavy. "It'd be a hairy oul snail that'd try to carry this on his back, so it would," he said as he staggered his way with it to the door.

Foxy laughed. He slapped his thigh.

"Ah, God, it's true for you, it's true for you, man, in a way," he said.

"You're letting all the furniture go in the auction?" Peder asked.

"We are, to hell with it," said Foxy. "What's in it? A few oul beds and a few oul chairs and a dresser. Why wouldn't we? Herself put in the best of the china. She wanted that."

"I couldn't lave the china after me, Mister Clancy," she said. "I have to have the china. We bought it at the fair the year after we were married, the time we sold the heifer, the black one. He was bad-tempered. You remember him, Dan."

"Oh, I do," said Foxy. "That was a bad heifer. He had a

red roll in his eye. I was glad to be rid of him."

"So we have it all that time," she said. "And never a brack on it except one chip out of a saucer."

"That happened the night Bridie was born," said Foxy, sitting on the stool again. "I got the shakes in me hand that time."

"So," said Peder. "Yeer having the best end of it now. What's here left for any of us? Aren't we all too old now nearly for the world? What sort of life have I meself? Out in the bog and off the bog, everyday into the town with a load of turf, selling it for half nothing. What reward for labour is there in that, tell me? The devil the one bit."

"It's true for you, true for you, Peder," said she.

"'Tis, 'tis indeed," said Foxy. "It's just the sights you will miss, Peder, like looking out of here now and seeing the river between the trees, and going back over the bog behind the house. It's just things around you that'll be missed."

"Anyone can have them things for my money," said Peder. "Man, what is it? Only weather. When you want it to be fine it's pissin' on yeh and when yeh want it to be wet it's scorchin' the skin off yeh. Right. You don't have to worry any more about what the weather does to you. Isn't that in itself enough reason to be happy for leavin' it?"

"It's true for him, Dan," said Josie. "Every time we look at the river we have to think will it take the hay before we have time to get it in. Let ye pull over now and have the sup of tay."

Foxy came over to the table pulling his stool with him. He took off his hat and put it on the window-sill and crossed himself and said his grace and then sipped tentatively at the hot tea.

Cahal and Gob came in then.

"Pull over a chair, men," said Foxy.

"Thanks," said Gob. "Hello, Mrs Killeen."

"You're welcome, Gob," she said. "It's very dacent of you to drive us to the station."

Gob gulped and didn't answer her.

"You'll look after everythin', Cahal, won't you?" she asked.

"I will, ma'am," said Cahal. "I'll look after everything."

"Maybe we should have waited for the sale," said Foxy, "but we couldn't do it. It might be hard to bear. Ye understand that, men?"

"What would ye be doin' waitin'?' Peder asked. "Ye get out of the way and the best prices'll be paid for everything. At the heel of the hunt there will be a few pounds going into yeer fists, wait'll ye see."

"Devil a much," said Foxy. "Let's face it. There's too much owing."

There was a silence as they drank the tea. Cahal felt terrible. To be here like this and to be powerless to help them. The little lousy money that was between them and a completely radical change in living. At the end of their life they had to go to institutional living. Maybe it was better that way, he thought. Maybe it was better at the end than at the beginning. That's poor enough consolation.

"Who'll buy the place, do ye think?" Foxy asked. "I'd like someone nice to have it. Not somebody foreign that we wouldn't know."

"It looks as if the Murphys'll bid for it," said Cahal.

"Aye, it does," said Peder. "They're very sorry for ye. They say what a pity it is that the Killeen land might go to somebody outside the parish. So that ye won't suffer that as well as everything else, they'll bid for it."

"Well, I suppose they are part of the village," said Foxy.

"They are the village," said Peder. "Watch us all dying out, man, and in twenty years' time the whole of this village will have been bought in by the Murphys. You wait and see."

"They'll have no use for the house, then," said Foxy, looking around the kitchen.

"I wouldn't think," said Peder. "They only want the land. They'll fodder a few new beasts on it."

"We had good times in this house," said Foxy.

Cahal thought of the hooley to bid Bridie goodbye. The

kitchen packed from wall to wall. The sound of music, the smell of porter, old Foxy cuddling the half barrel and ladling it out with his eyes shining.

"I think we bether go," said Gob, "if we are to get the train."

There was a silence then.

"I better wash up the delf," said Josie after a time.

"I"ll do that, ma'am," said Cahal. "Leave that to me."

"All right, Cahal," she said. She rose, looking around the kitchen. It was a credit to her. The walls were blindingly white, the window panes blue-clean, and all her delf on the dresser was glittering. If you wanted you could eat your dinner off the concrete floor. Cahal was terrified she was going to cry again. She looked so helpless, an active old woman standing up, conscious for the first time in her life of her hands because there was nothing to do with them.

Foxy bustled. "Here what are we waiting for? The train will be gone on us. We might miss it. Suppose Gob's oul horse went lame on him."

"Just that," said Josie, pointing at the picture of the Sacred Heart over the fireplace. "I'll have to have Him. Didn't I nearly forget!"

Cahal stood on a stool and unhooked the picture for her.

"Thanks, Cahal," she said. "I can put it on top of the trunk."

"We're off now so," said Foxy, going out the door quickly. "Come on, woman, for the love of God. Isn't it awful the way min have to be waitin' for women?"

"Do ye know," said Josie, "this is the first time I'll ever have put a foot in a train. I've seen them at the station and we can tell the time by them whistling when the wind is right from here. A sad sort of whistle a train has in the distance."

"Never in a train," said Peder, "think of that now! Won't it be great times so going into yeer first one?"

He ushered her out, holding her arm, and helped her up on the cart. Gob sat in the middle and the three of them easily fitted on the hay-covered plank.

"Chk-chk," said Gob with his tongue at the horse and the horse turned out of the yard and clattered up on to the road.

"Goodbye, goodbye," said Foxy, waving his stick but not turning his head at all.

"Goodbye," said Cahal.

Peder ran after them out on to the road.

"Hey, Foxy," he shouted, "when ye get there tell them to keep a room hot for meself and the wife. We won't be long after ye."

They heard Foxy's thin chuckle and then the horse and cart turned a corner of the road and were gone, not before Cahal had seen Mrs Killeen's hands rising to her face and her back arching.

"The poor divils," said Peder then, "the poor oul divils."

"Yes," said Cahal, "and how many people in the whole world would care?"

"Well, now," said Peder. "You care, and I care and Gob cares and Bridie would care if they told her. She doesn't know?"

"No," said Cahal, making for the house. "All will be grand. They will write as if from home and As The Fella Says will get her letters to them sent on."

"They're shockin' proud," said Peder.

"What else have they left?" asked Cahal.

"What else have any of us left?" asked Peder. "Wouldn't I be goin' the very selfsame road meself if the childer I reared to emigrate weren't sendin' me enough to keep us out of the poorhouse? It's a quare life."

Cahal washed up the cups, and dried them off well and put them on the dresser. The dresser was lacking. There was something doomed about the look of the silent house.

"How much will the Murphys offer for the place, Peder?" Cahal asked.

"A hundred pounds," said Peder. "Ten pounds an acre."

"That much'll only clear the debts," said Cahal.

"That's right," said Peder. "Who else would want the place?"

"Supply and demand and no charity," said Cahal grimly. "Does the Murphys know what I told ye, that I got no money out of my wife?"

"'Tis hard to say," said Peder. "You said it loud enough. Maybe they don't. People don't talk about things like that."

"I'm different," said Cahal. "Maybe I'd raise the price a bit on them, if they don't know."

"You're different," said Peder. "Cahal, man, listen, you want to walk cautious in this village. I'm telling you. People have so little to do apart from workin' that they can be disturbed. They don't like things brought into the open."

"What's under you?" asked Cahal.

"Hard to say," said Peder. "The day you ... you ... you lowered Barney. You know. People didn't like that."

"All that's my business," said Cahal coldly.

"I know, man, I know," said Peder uncomfortably. "Be patient with me. Very few people liked him. That's true. He's too severe. Too dominant a man. But it's different to see him brought low under your very eyes, in a manner of speaking. You see what I mean."

"No," said Cahal.

"Let it ride, let it ride," said Peder with a sigh. "You are a hurt man, Cahal. I can see that. But don't start hittin' out in all directions. Sing, man."

"They're coming now," said Cahal, listening to the sound of a motor car.

They met them outside. Two young men. City suits on them and striped shirts and colourful ties. Well shaved, shoes shining, and very bored. It was such a small sale. They examined what was to be sold. Laughed and made jokes about the pitiful remnants of a lifetime. Inspected the one cow tied in the stall. You could hang your hat on her hipbones. One of them did.

Shortly the buyers came.

The three Murphys. The father stayed at home. He wouldn't like to see, he said, the end of poor Foxy. So Sonny go and the two boys. If they liked they could buy the old cow for charity's sake. They could feed her up and sell her at the next March fair. Five pounds would be a good price for her. Make it five pounds ten for pour oul Foxy. And he had one pitchfork that was in good order and the turf barrow had a new wheel and would come in useful. All right, father. And a hundred pounds for the whole lot. It was doing him a favour because who else would want to buy it, unless speculators came from the town, and what good would the ten acres be to them: it was too scattered?

Jamesey Jordan came and Tom Creel. They didn't want anything, but they'd buy something for Foxy's sake. Tom Creel said he'd take the table and two chairs, and Jamesey said he'd buy the harness of the ass. It was in good repair. Foxy was a good man like that with his hands. He was great at any work he could sit down to. They laughed at that, thinking of poor Foxy. Mary Cassidy was after the bed linen, the blankets and the hair mattress. Peder said he'd buy the dresser with the cups and mugs and Cahal would take the buckets and the utensils and any farm things that were going. There were very few actually. Foxy had already sold the plough and the harrow and the ass. In the end he was only digging and sowing potatoes in the small garden at the back of the house. A few strangers came from Ballybla way and over the road, and just before they were all set to begin a car pulled in from the town and a man alighted from it with a red face and a comfortable stomach, a battered hat on his head and a very good suit looking odd over heavy boots.

He greeted Peder.

"Hah, you old bastard, how are you and are you still alive?"

"I'll bury you," Peder greeted him, shaking him by the hand, "and your children."

"Then you'll wait a long time," the man said, coughing a terrible cigarette cough and putting his hand up to his chest. The first two fingers were the deep yellow colour like a fire leaves on parts of the whitewashed chimney. "I haven't got them yet."

"Yev none out of the blanket," said Peder, "but even thim I'll put down."

The man laughed.

They got the auction over very quickly. The young salesman was surprised at the prices things went. A little more than they were worth. He couldn't understand this. Foxy to him was just a name on a bit of paper.

The cow presented a little difficulty. Sonny said "Five pounds," and the man with the cigarette cough said "Six pounds," and Sonny tentatively said "Six pounds ten," and the man said "Eight pounds," and Sonny shut up with his lips tight.

The man laughed and coughed, and said, "I want her for the glue factory."

They started on the land. The young salesman gave them a speech about this. As if he felt he had to earn his money. Listening to him you'd think he was selling a slice of the garden of Eden. There were many chuckles and digging in ribs. He persisted to the end, and said "What am I bid?"

There was a pause then, and Sonny Murphy said "Eighty pounds," and they waited and it seemed that Sonny was going to get it for that when Cahal said "One hundred pounds" in a loud clear voice. He saw Sonny looking at him and he looked back at him with his eyes clear and a message in them: This is what I'm doing with her money. Sonny tightened his lips and said "One and ten." Cahal said "One and twenty." Sonny said "One and twenty-five" and Cahal said nothing. He looked a bit deflated, and then the man with the stained fingers who had a bout of coughing said "Two hundred." The Salesman said, "I beg your pardon," surprise in his voice. So the man repeated himself. Sonny looked at his two brothers and looked at the man. He was a cattle man obviously. If he knew Peder. He had the look of a cattle-jobber. You always knew. It was possible that he would take the land and feed some bullocks on it. Why did this have to happen?

"It's an odd thing," said Cahal then. "We don't like strangers buying land in Caherlo."

"It's a free country," the man said. "We can buy where we like."

"But will ye be able to hold it?" Cahal asked.

"We will," said the man.

"We'll see," said Cahal.

"Gentlemen! Gentlemen," said the salesman.

"Two hundred and five," said Sonny.

"And ten," said the man.

"And twenty," said Sonny.

The man thought for a moment. "All right," he said then, "you can have it. It's not worth any more." He had brought a boy with him in the car. He paid what he owed and then left the boy in charge of the cow to drive it into the town. Then he turned his car in the yard and was driving away when he made a mistake.

He waved his hand.

"So long, Cahal," he said, and chugged away in a plume of exhaust smoke.

The three Murphys were around Cahal, Sonny and Piddler and Dipper. Sonny was the tallest of them. The other two were short and stocky and were sandy-haired, with the pale skin of their father that gets red easily. Their skin was red now.

"You know him?" Sonny was asking.

"I do," said Cahal.

"You put him up to it," said Piddler.

"I put him up to nothing," said Cahal. "I was talking to the man in town last Saturday and told him the place was up. He wanted a place."

"You frigger!" said Dipper, bursting through them and aiming a blow at Cahal's face. Cahal didn't move. Peder caught his arm.

"Here, easy now, easy now, Dipper," he said.

"He did it deliberately," said Dipper. "He knew. He did it deliberately."

"What's wrong with you?" Cahal asked innocently. "Your father liked Foxy, didn't he? Your father was doing Foxy a

- 155 -

favour, wasn't he, buying his land? Won't he be pleased when you go home and tell him how charitable you were with his money? The land is worth more than what you paid for it. Everybody in Caherlo knows that. So what's wrong with you?"

"There's nothing wrong with us," said Sonny. "It's just the underhand way it was done. To think that a man could be so calculatin' like that to cheat his neighbours."

"The black divil," said Piddler, aiming a blow at him.

Sonny stopped him.

"Leave him alone," he said. "That's what he'd like. Wouldn't you like that too, Bogman?"

"I wouldn't mind," said Cahal, the muscles of his jaws tight, his arms bulged tensely against the cloth of his coat. He was laughing inside. He was thinking of the face of Mark Murphy when his sons went home to him with the good news. He was thinking of the face of Foxy when he was told the result of the sale. He was quite willing to tussle like dogs with the Murphys in the dust of the road. There was a smile on his face, and running through his head was a song about Mark.

"That'll do," said Sonny to his brothers. "It was a nice move, Kinsella. We'll go now. It isn't the first harm that you've done to us, since you came here, but it's going to be the last. I'm telling you that."

"You can talk to me any time at all you like," said Cahal. "I'll always be willing to talk to any of the Murphys."

"Come on," said Sonny and walked away. The two brothers followed him. The company watched them away, and then set about collecting the things they had bought and putting them on their carts. The auction man saw that the house was cleared and then he put a new padlock on the door and locked it and drove away.

Cahal was left alone with Peder Clancy.

"You've done a good day's work," said Peder. "Had you all that arranged beforehand?"

"I arranged nothing," said Cahal. "I thought it a shame

that those good acres should go so cheap. I told him about it. He said if he got it for two hundred it might be worth it. So he came. You know yourself it's a bargain for the land, and Foxy will have a bit in hand."

"Will he?" Peder asked. "I think he'll have to hand it all up to the people that keep him."

"Jay," said Cahal. "I never thought of that. Anyhow he'll get the benefit of it."

"I hope so," said Peder. "Maybe tomorrow I'll feel like laughing over it. It's a good joke on the Murphys. No doubt. But they won't like you, man. You know that. You could hurt them people anyway you like, in name or fame or farm, but great God, when you get them in the purse, it's a bad thing. They'll never forget it."

"To hell with them," said Cahal.

He put his stuff up on Peder's cart and they went home. Peder left him, shaking his head and looking at him wonderingly.

Cahal wrote a letter that night.

"Dear Bridie,
Today you will be glad to hear that your mother and father were carted off to the County Home. They don't want you to know. Now you know. They guess you are not doing well in America. Gob Creel is breaking his heart over you, and will without doubt get sick or mad if you don't come back. Come back for Christ's sake. Your going away did little good. Maybe your coming home might be different.
Your friend,
Cahal Kinsella."

Chapter Twelve

The River Ree winds quiet and slow
Where ash and rush and alder grow,
  Near willows weepin'
  And old men sleepin',
Or lovers lost in the afterglow.

IT HAD RAINED steadily for two weeks. In a land of rain this was not unusual. But the rain was odd for two reasons. It was almost unrelenting and it was the wrong time of the year for unrelenting rain. There had been a good fine spell sufficient for all the farmer's needs. When he had his hay cocked and his turf home and his fields weeded and his potatoes moulded, that was the time he wanted rain, but it didn't come, so that the bishop had to put into the Mass the special prayer for the right weather, but even at that the rain held off for a long time, until the earth all over was dry and parched and men raked their memories to find in them a time that the river had been so low.

The big river itself was low so you could almost see the roots of the reeds by the side of it, and all the little rivers leading into it were very low, so that the poor little trout had a hard job finding a pool to play in and thousands of them were destroyed by boys. Even the perpetually soaked bogs dried out, so that the bog streams draining them were low and the brown earth caked. The stalks in the oatfields were low and small.

It looked very bad. Most men started to think not of the

yield but of the destruction and counted up the things they would have to do without this year.

Then the rain came.

The earth was hard and it threw it off, so that it plied into the streams and the streams became pregnant. The wind blowing over the dry earth had uprooted many things and had borne them away until they came to rest in the gullies of the streams. They blocked the water so that it rose high, and groaned its way into the larger streams and from them into the rivers and finally into the big river that rose slowly and hard just the same as a bicycle tyre being pumped. The rivers never got rid of their loads, because the baked earth opened to the rain and soaked it up and kept soaking it until it became waterlogged and fed the residue to the complaining streams which passed it on, dirty and littered, to the grumbling rivers, and these in their turn carried it away faster and faster to the big river.

The big river was big but it was not big enough. Its bed was too small to carry the terrible load it was asked to bear, so up near Valley of the Holy Well, it rose and rose and lapped over the banks.

This happened up there in the dark night, and the first that the sleeping people knew of it was having their dreams disturbed by a nightmare of cattle lowing and sheep bleating pitifully. The sheep had no chance. They are foolish animals. When they awoke to feel the insidious water soaking into their heavy wool, they arose bleating and ran around in circles, and because they hadn't the sense to run in the right direction they ran towards the flow of the stream, and the farther they ran and bleated, the farther and the faster the water crept up around them, and sucked them towards the main flow, so that shortly their hoofs were free of the ground and they bleated and bleated until the water shut their mouths for them.

The cattle had better instincts. They moved away from the water around them, but the water crept very fast and slyly, and since most of the fields were surrounded with drains, and since the water covered the fields, some of the cattle couldn't distinguish between two inches of water over grass and five feet of water over a drain and they stepped into the drains and were carried away, their horns waving wildly and helplessly, lowing to the sky until the drain whirled them into the chuckling main flow and their weight carried them down. Others of the cattle sensed the danger of the drains so they made for the wooden gates into the fields and they put their heads over the top bar and they bellowed for rescue from the bottom of their lungs in the direction of the sleeping houses.

Cahal woke from a deep sleep, hearing the banging on the front door. He felt for his trousers and pulled them on.

There was a voice outside shouting, "Cahal! Cahal!"

He drew the bolts and opened the door. There was a chill grey look in the sky that heralded the wet morning.

"Get out quick, let ye," said the voice of Gob. "The river is risin'. It'll take the hay."

"Go to the Jordans," said Cahal. "They're the ones nearest the river."

"All right," said Gob and ran.

Cahal went to Barney's door and pounded on it.

"Hey! Hey!" he shouted.

He heard the sleepy voice muttering.

"Get up! Get up!" he shouted to him. "The river is risin'."

He went back to the fire and pulled his socks from the crook. He could barely distinguish them. He kicked at the ashes of the raked fire and sparks flew out of it. He got his socks on and pulled on his heavy boots over them, feeling for the leather thongs to tie them tight. The room door opened then and he had to look away from the blinding light of the candle that Julia carried.

She was dressed in a long white nightdress. Two thin plaits of hair hung one on either side of her neck. She had forgotten her teeth.

"What is it? What is it?" she asked. She found it hard to speak.

"The river is rising," said Cahal.

She remembered then that she was without her teeth, so she put her hand in front of her mouth, leaving the candle on the table and backing back into the room.

Cahal pulled on his braces and flung his short coat on his back, making for the front door. He shouted at the closed door of his grandfather: "I'll tackle the horse!" and then he ran into the air. It was raining but it wasn't heavy rain. It was tapering away. So well it might, he thought, as he ran. He unlocked the door of the stable and felt for the horse's winkers on the nail. He pulled them free and ran across the road, opening the heavy wooden gate into the oatfield and running through, feeling the long grass and the nodding stalks hitting at his clothes and wetting them, so that shortly their strokes soaked through his clothes and he felt them very cold on his warm skin.

The horse came to him the minute he opened the other gate. He was pleased to see him, and whinnied. He was frightened. The field he was in was the field that ran down to the river meadow. He nuzzled Cahal's arm as he put the winkers on him by feel. It was too dark to see. Cahal peered but could see nothing in the early light, just the dark outline of the bushes. But he heard cattle lowing and sheep bleating. It was the custom when the hay was saved and cocked to let some cattle or sheep into the meadows to graze the sweet after-grass.

They'll have to be got out of there, he thought.

"Come on, fella," he said then to the horse and trotted him back the way he had come.

When he got to the road, he could just make out the white of his own house, and the blank look of the doors and windows like a funny face on the moon. He took the horse to the stable and quickly went in and brought out the heavy tackling. He fitted the collar with practised fingers and tied the belly-band and then led him over towards the cart. Barney came out of the house then, pulling on his coat. He raised the shafts while Cahal backed the horse into them.

"Is it bad? Is it high?" Barney asked.

"I don't know," said Cahal. "I couldn't see."

As Barney finished the tackling he took the high sides off the cart and threw them down and put on the short low creels just over the wheels that they used to keep loads of hay from fouling them. They got up on the cart then and Barney clicked his tongue and the horse raced up on to the road. It was becoming easier to see now. They passed through the oatfield and into the next one. It sloped down and away at the bottom of it they could see a silver gleam.

"That's the boot drain," said Barney. "It's bloody high." He urged the horse, bending forward to beat him with the slack of the reins, but the wheels of the cart were digging into the soft ground and the horse had to strain hard to pull the cart along.

Cahal jumped down to open the wooden gate into the meadow. He crossed towards it and felt the water up around his boots. The drain was filled and overflowing. He threw the gate open and Barney drove the horse through. The horse jibbed when he felt the water around his hooves. Barney hit him with the reins again and he went galloping in sideways.

"It's very high," Cahal shouted then. "The Jordans' is flooded already."

You could see that now. The drain between the two fields was filled and flooded out. The Jordans' field was right beside the river, and of the four cocks of hay they had two were already surrounded by the rising waters. Their own five cocks were free for the moment but it wouldn't be long. At Jordans' gate Cahal could see the bulk of the two cows. They were bawling their heads off.

"I'll release the cattle," he shouted. "Let you get over to the far cock."

He ran across the meadow towards the gate. The cattle were very glad to see him. He had to wade the causeway. It was well flooded from the drains. He opened the gate. The cattle lowered their heads and sniffed suspiciously at the water in front of them. He had to get behind them and slap them hard on the rumps. "G'wan our that, ye bitches!" he shouted at them. "Do ye want to be drowned?" They fled across jumping awkwardly. He ran them across their own field then and chased them into the green grass of the field above. Their relief at being away from the water was almost pathetic. They ran with their tails lifted to the high ground and when they got there turned back and looked as if to say: Thank God we got out of that alive.

Cahal went over to Barney. He had drawn the cart close to the cock and already had flung the ropes off it. He tossed them away and took the pitchfork and climbed on to the cock. Cahal mounted the cart and as Barney pitched him the hay he folded it and placed a big doubled bit of it at each corner of the cart, filled in the middle and started from that to build up the rectangular load that a cart demands. He had time to see that the Murphys were abroad. They had a hay lorry. They would, he thought bitterly. It is easy to shift a cock of hay with a lorry. The tail of it is lowered. The ramp is smooth timber. There are two handles in front that you wind when you have tied a rope about the butt of the cock, and shortly the whole cock slides up on the lorry. The lorry is righted and the cock pulls away. No labour. So that the eleven cocks of the Murphys' meadow hay were as safe as if they were in a house.

It took them a good half-hour to load the cart with the cock. Then with the horse straining and pulling and Cahal using all his strength to turn the wheels they managed to get the cart out of the meadow and into the high ground of the upper field. They just had to upturn it all and leave it there. There was no time to build it again. But fortunately now that it had done its work the rain had stopped. The clouds were rising a little higher from the drowned world, but no gleam of the sun was permitted to come through them.

Everybody was in the fields by now. The two Jordans were in the far field. Jamesey was pitching from the far cock to the old man on the cart. It was pitiful. Cahal wanted to go over, but what could you do? There was their own hay.

He noticed that the water was already swirling about the ankles of the Jordans' horse, and that he was rising his hooves and champing. If they only had someone to hold the horse's head. Jamesey had to stop from the pitching at times and shout "Whoa! Whoa! Whoa up, will you!" Gob Creel and his father Tom were working quickly and methodically. One half of their meadow was very high and three of their cocks were on the high ground where the flood would be baulked, and they were moving the two cocks in danger up along with them. Mary Cassidy was in like case. They had only one cock to shift, but it was hard going for them with only an ass cart and two young ones.

When they came back after moving the second cock the water was swirling in their own meadow. The three remaining cocks were built on small hillocks so that as yet they were out of the grasp of the water. The Jordans' hay was in great danger. One cock near the bank of the river was bending over and falling. Soon the water would have got it and it would be swept away. The horse didn't like standing in the water. They were having great trouble with him.

Their own horse was very restive now too. His nostrils were distended. Cahal had to keep shouting at him to keep him quiet, but when they were halfway loaded Julia came into the meadow, pushing her big boots through the water. She stood at the horse's head and kept him quiet, patting his nose.

The fourth time they returned they had great difficulty. The water was lapping the butts of the remaining two cocks and the dry hay was greedily soaking it up, so that they woud lose a great portion of it now. It could have been worse. The horse didn't like it at all now. They had to beat him heavily to get him to go into the flooded field at all, and when they were manoeuvring him near the cock, he reared high, pulling the reins out of Julia's hand. She screamed and backed away from his front hooves. Cahal chucked the reins savagely and shouted at him, and then he had to come down from the cart and box the horse on the nostrils. He calmed down. He handed the reins again to Julia. "Keep him tight! Keep him tight!" he said. When he got back on the cart he saw that old Spray was now holding the horse's head, that Jamesey was loading the cart and that Máire Brodel was up on the cock, pitching the hay for him and doing it well and swiftly. It's a good job someone came to them, he thought. The old man will get rheumatism. The water he was standing in now was up to his knees. After the next cock, Cahal thought, we can take our cart in and help them.

It would frighten anyone now to look at the flood. It completely covered the fields and you could see the flooded ditches like streams in the placid waters of the meadows. The flood had spread this side of the river and the other, so that the whole place was like a lake. From his height on the hay, Cahal could see a drowned sheep floating in the stream of the river, and other things too, going at a very fast pace. It was the most peculiar sensation to be wading through a meadow with water lapping into your boots. They had little time to think. They got their fourth cock out and had to leave half of the fifth because it was spoiled. The Jordans had fared badly. Two cocks had been swept away. They had saved one and were in process of loading the other.

"We'll go in and help," said Cahal.

"All right," said Barney. Cahal thought he was going to refuse at first. He was looking tired. The breath was coming fast from his chest, and now that they had stopped working he was beginning to shiver. "Maybe you shouldn't come," Cahal suggested. "Maybe you should go into the house with her."

"No, I'll come," said Barney and got up on the cart with him.

"I'll have a meal ready for ye," Julia shouted after them.

They crossed their own meadow towards the Jordans' gate.

The horse jibbed in the centre of the field. Every step he moved brought the water higher and higher up towards his belly. Beating him was no good. Cahal jumped down and pulled at him and led him towards the gate. He patted him and talked nicely to him. The horse's eyes were wild. He calmed down then and moved slowly.

The only gauge Cahal had for entering the field was the two posts of the gate. The causeway was covered with nearly two foot of water. We will have to be quick getting out of here, he thought, or the carts will founder. The water was racing in the drains. He had to dig in his toes so that its flow would not sweep him off his feet. He got the horse through and manoeuvred the cart by the near side of the cock they were stripping. He jumped up beside the girl and used his fork to pitch to Barney.

"God bless ye!" was what Jamesey said. "Maybe we ought to leave it, Barney? Will we be able to get back at all?"

"Save as much as you can," said Barney. "Think of what the price of hay will be next spring after this."

Máire didn't talk. She kept pitching away. They were restricted on the cock. Cahal could feel the warmth of her coming from behind him. Her skirt was drenched and clung to her legs. Her feet were bare. He jumped down into the water and put the fork back behind his shoulder and dug it in, and exerting all his strength he moved a great reach of the hay on to Barney's cart. They soon reached the level of the water and they had to stop.

"We'll go now," said Jamesey. Cahal could feel the pull of the water around his legs. "You stay up, Barney," he said. "I'll lead him out. We'll go first," he said then, "and ye can follow after us."

"Good man! Good man! Good man!" oul Spray said to him. The old hands were glued to the reins of the horse. The water was up around his thighs. He was shivering. His face was blue and the skin hung limply from his face.

"Come on up, father," said Jamesey. "Get up!"

"No! No!' said the old man, "I'll lead her out, Jamesey. The poor thing won't go without me. Will you, agirl? Will you, agirl?"

The mare was extraordinarily quiet under his hands. She nuzzled against him.

"He has a great way with horses," Jamesey shouted after them. "Go on, father. Get her out now in the name of God."

"Come on, girl! Come on, girl!" said Spray. "Soon be home. Soon be home. Carrots you'll get and Indian male and the nice things. Up now, agirl. Up now."

Máire went to the other side of the mare.

"Get up on the cart, can't you?" she asked. "I can lead her out."

The mare reared, and reared again. "Whoa! Whoa!" said Spray. "Go away, girl. None a ye'll get her out of here except meself, I'm telling ye."

He calmed the mare.

"Lave him alone, Máire," said Jamesey. "He'll manage. Wait'll you see. He can do anything with horses."

The mare pulled. The cart had sunk its wheels into the ground. Máire caught the spokes of the wheel and turned. "Up, girl! Up, girl!" said Spray, and the mare lurched free and set off towards the gate. The water was well up to her belly. Máire could feel it wetting her up to the waist. She felt frightened for the old man. Suppose it sweeps him off his feet. She saw the cart ahead with Cahal leading the horse negotiate the gateposts and the causeway. The horse was jibbing, and she saw Cahal pulling at his mouth with the reins. Then he rushed through and was free of the causeway. Cahal stood aside, hit the horse on the flank and came wading back towards the gate.

The mare came quietly through. She was standing on the causeway when she felt the pull of the drain around her legs. Then she reared. "Whoa! Whoa!" Spray shouted but the mare was not to be calmed. She reared again and tugged her head high and then ran across the causeway, the heavy load lurching behind her, and in her sideways run Spray's hands were thrown free of the reins, he was forced back towards the edge, and Cahal saw him just vanishing as if he had been swallowed. Jamesey saw it too.

He shouted: "Father! Father!" and then he jumped from

his position on the hay right into the deep swilling water of the drain. The sight was implanted for a long time on Cahal's eyes. The disturbed water that had swallowed the old man with nothing left of him except an old green bowler hat that was being swept away on the top of the water and in the air big awkward Jamesey leaping and the hobnails of his boots gleaming.

"Get the mare! Get the mare!" Cahal shouted at Máire and went towards the drain. He saw Jamesey rising out of it. His cap was gone, his thin hair was flattened to his big ungainly head. He lashed the water with his hands. He shouted "Father!" in a frantic way and then he went down again. God, thought Cahal, he can't even swim. While he was thinking, Jamesey had been swept for three yards. Cahal raised himself as much as he could and threw himself into the drain. He could feel it sweeping him along and he helped it with a kick of his feet and a thresh from his arms. That was all he could do, and then he felt the body of Jamesey under him. He held him with one hand and tried to grasp the edge of the drain with the other. The edge was two foot under water. He had to hold his breath and put his head under too and scrabble for it with his clawing fingers. He dug them in deep to the roots of the round reeds and held on and pulled. He brought his head out of the water and kicked with his legs and won free of the pull of the drain. Then he sat on the edge and pulled Jamesey along with him. His head broke free. He had his eyes and his mouth closed. Cahal stood up and raised him. Jamesey came alive then. "Let me go! Let me go!" he shouted. "I'll have to get him! I'll have to get me father!"

"Stop it! Stop it, Jamesey!" Cahal shouted. "You'll drown, man! You'll drown, man!"

"Let me go! Let me go!" Jamesey said, raising his fist and bringing it down on Cahal's face. It was a hurtful blow from a hard fist, but he held on. "It's no use, Jamesey," he shouted. "It's no use. Nothing can save him. You'll only drown yourself."

"Let me go! Let me go! Let me go!" Jamesey shouted, using his fists and his heavy boots.

Cahal hit him.

"Will you be quiet!" he shouted, almost crying with vexation. "I'll go after him if you'll be quiet."

He felt figures beside him. It was Gob and his father.

"All right," said Tom Creel. "We'll hold him. He can't swim. He'll be kilt if he doesn't stop."

"Oh, me father," said Jamesey.

Cahal couldn't swim along the drain. He couldn't run along by the edge. It would be too slow. The river was a semicircle here and the drain was a diameter that joined the river further on in Murphy's field. He ran from the heavy water towards the edge where it was light. He climbed into the next field and ran free on the unencumbered grass. He ran along until he came to the next gap and then he ran into the flooded fields again, heaping to hillocks on the high ground which the water hadn't covered. In this way he made fast time. He could distinguish where the swirling outlet of the drain met the main flow of the river. He headed for there. He was in water up to his thighs when he came to it. But he thought he would be in time. If Jamesey hadn't held him back! He watched closely and he saw the black bulge well below the surface. He went in feet first just behind it and grabbed with his hands. He could feel the cloth under his fingers. He held tight with one hand and kicked his head free and grabbed with his other hand. It's now or never, he thought. If we are swept into the river that's the end.

There was somebody near him shouting. It was Sonny Murphy he saw. He was reaching a rake out to its full extent. Cahal freed his hand from the edge and made a grab at the rake. His fingers held it and Sonny hauled and he came out of the drag of the drain.

"Is he gone?" Sonny asked.

"I don't know," said Cahal, and lifted the old man into his arms. He was very light. It was like carrying a child. His head fell back. The thick clothes were stuck to his body. He was as thin as the rake that had pulled him out of the water. "Come on," said Cahal, and headed through the water for the dry fields beyond.

They were all running towards him and converging on the green field. Cahal reached it first. He placed the old man on the ground and felt for his heart. There was no stir from it. He was dead, Cahal knew. He thought he must have died at the shock of hitting the water, because there was little water in his lungs. Cahal turned him over and pressed. There was only a mouthful in him and after that nothing. He was just dead.

They kept trying.

He gave way to Jamesey. They stood there in a ring looking down at him bending over his father. Anyone could see he was dead. Jamesey was a sight. His heavy jaws had three-day-old bristles on them, and his big teeth were yellow from the tobacco. You could see them well because his lips were pulled back from them. Because he was crying. "Oh, Father, Father!" he'd say, bending down and putting his face against the dead face of the old man. You wouldn't recognize old Spray. You couldn't imagine he had been so thin and worn in life and be still alive. You couldn't imagine that anybody at all would have loved the sight of him. But Jamesey loved his father. He was really crying. You'd think his heart would break in two. They turned away. It was a terrible thing to see.

Jamesey bent after a while and put his two arms under him and raised him high and then walked up the long field towards the road, the flood water dripping from the two of them, and they saw as he went that he buried his ungainly head into the body of the old dead man.

Cahal turned to look at the flood with his jaw muscles tight.

The curse of God on it, he thought. The curse of God on it. The flood didn't mind. It swept along triumphantly, looking serene, undangerous in the placid way it gleamed and mocked under the lowering grey skies.

Chapter Thirteen

He wasn't that ould, I tell ye, men,
He was short of the hundred be one and ten.
He could hould his end up with slean or spade;
Ye should see him honing the mowing blade.
He had olden songs that med me cry
Of men and things in the byimby.
Ther's little he wanted but twist and bread,
His Rosary beads and the feather bed –
Och! God could have gave him a longer span,
He wasn't that short of just one oul man!

"IT'S A QUARE do," said Peder. "I had to come out for the air. I left the wife in there for me. She's raising the roof with her roars. She was always a great one for a wake."

They were standing at Cassidys' gable-end that backed on to the road. They were facing the small road to the bogs and they could see one window of the Jordans' house. The red blind was drawn and the light was making it look like a ruby stone.

"He's hurt bad," said Cahal.

"It's unnatural," said Peder, "the love he had for that oul man. I can't understand it. I was kind of glad when my old one passed over, to tell you the truth. He was shockin' cranky. The day before he died he went to attack me with the blackthorn stick. I had to take it away from him. He died cursin' enough to make you blush. He was a hearty oul devil. We missed him for a while, but oney like you'd miss an oul collie that you'd be used to stretched in front of the fire. Then we found it was great to be rid of him."

It was a pleasant night. The moon was riding high with innocent clouds passing across its face. You'd never think the sky would be capable of all the damage it had done. The whitewash of the houses was gleaming green. They were sitting on two flat stones, with their backs to the end of the house. It was a favourite place for the village men at night when the work was over. To sit here or stand here and chat and smoke until they went home to bed.

"I wouldn't know," said Cahal. "If I had an oul fella maybe I'd be like that about him too."

"You have an oul fella once removed," said Peder, chuckling.

"Oh, him," said Cahal, blowing the smoke of his cigarette into the air. "It's different with Jamesey. Jamesey really thought the sun shone out of Spray. The way he'd say, 'Look at him, will ye. He's a better man than meself.' And the poor old divil tottering on the verge of the grave. Did Jamesey never have a woman at all?"

"I don't think so," said Peder. "He had one sister that went to America. Jamesey was born late. His mother was a terrible tyrant, Lord have mercy on her. She used to smoke a pipe and she walked like a man. She clattered Jamesey a bit. I don't think any woman dared come near him. The old woman would have read them off the roads. Not that Jamesey is what you'd call a handsome man, God bless him. He's as plain as a duck's backside."

"That's not what matters," said Cahal. "He has the farm. He'd get plenty that'd marry him for that."

"Anyhow he never did," said Peder. "It's too late now, I think. He wouldn't know what to do with her if he got one. Spray was the apple of his eye. Jamesey used to slave for him, like a wife. To hear him talk you'd think the poor oul divil was the miracle a the ages, and all he could do was sit in the sun and tell everyone that passed the roads to spray their spuds." Peder laughed.

"Still he must really have felt for him," said Cahal. "He's takin' his death so hard. I haven't been in there yet. What is it like?"

"It's bad," said Peder. "It's shockin' to see a big eejit like Jamesey cryin'. He must ha' never cried in his life before. He was savin' up all the tears for now. Everyone new that goes in he cries for them. It's very sad. But it makes you want to laugh when you hear Jamesey and then go in and look at the poor oul fella laid out on the bed, just like a thin stick with a habit on him. You did a good job, Cahal. Everybody thinks so."

"Hum," said Cahal. "I might have got the oul man out in time if Jamesey hadn't jumped in. I'll never forget that, Peder. He really would have given his own life for him. That's why I say, he must be really hurt."

"I suppose you better go in," Peder said, "and get it over."

"I might as well," said Cahal, but he didn't move.

"Ho-ho," said Peder, "here's more mourners now, and not one of the five of them is capable of a single tear. Goodnight, Mark Murphy and Mrs Murphy, ma-am," he said then in a loud voice. "It's a sad night, a sad night."

The whole Murphy family were passing by. They were dressed in their Sunday clothes. Most people were, going to wakes.

"Goodnight, Peder, it is indeed," said Mark pausing. "Poor oul Aloysius. He'll be missed."

"God, Mark," said Peder, "we must be talkin' about different wakes. I thought ye were turning into Spray's."

"Oh, yes, yes," said Mark. "It doesn't seem respectable to be calling him out of his name now and the poor man dead."

"Well, God, I never knew that was his name," said Peder. "It's a queer country. You have to die before they find out your name." He laughed. "Isn't that good, Cahal?"

Mark peered.

"Is that who's with you?"

"It's me all right, Mark," said Cahal.

"I believe you owe your life to me son, Kinsella," said Mark. "If it was me I hope that I would have been as charitable as him, and as forgivin'."

"I'd have got out anyhow, Mister Murphy," said Cahal. "It's hard to kill a bad thing."

"We'll be goin' now," said Mark, and walked down the road towards the house, his wife waddling beside him.

The three Murphys leaned against the gable-end. They lighted cigarettes. The tips glowed in the semi-darkness.

"I wonder why I handed you that rake, Kinsella?" Sonny asked.

"I don't know," said Cahal. "When I saw who was in it I was expecting a blow on the head."

"It's a pity we can't live bits of our lives over," said Sonny.

"You'd have a lot to make up for," said Cahal.

"You don't keep very good company, Peder," said Sonny.

"Well, now, Sonny," said Peder, "if you like I'll go away from ye."

Sonny ignored that.

"You took to writin' songs again, Kinsella, I believe. They're singing what they call Bogman's Ballads athin in the town, and there's one called 'Saint Mark' that we don't like at all."

"You surprise me," said Cahal. "I never heard of that one."

"It could only have come from you," said Sonny. "There's also a cattle man in there who happened to be at Killeen's auction and he's tellin' everyone in town how the two of ye cooked up a scheme to rob the Murphys. You should at least have picked a man that would have kept his mouth shut."

"Thanks for the tip," said Cahal.

"You can go too far," said Sonny; "we can only take a certain amount. And after that we'll do something about it."

"You're welcome any time at all you like," said Cahal, rising up and standing facing him. "It must have really been a hard job for you to hand me that rake."

"You'll never know how hard it was," said Sonny. "It could never happen again." Then he turned and walked down the road and his brothers followed after him like shadows.

"Cahal, man," said Peder, "thim fellas mean business."

"It would liven life up a bit," said Cahal, "if they had the courage."

"I don't know," said Peder. "They could be bad bits of work. What was the song?"

"The song?" Cahal asked.

"About Saint Mark?" Peder asked.

"Oh, that," said Cahal. "I'm not saying it kem from me, mind. It's just a thing I heard sung around the town. Do you want to hear it?"

"No," said Peder. "What in the name of God am I askin' for?"

"All right," said Cahal.

He sang it nice and low.

Peder laughed. He started with a low laugh and then it became a chuckle and then he slapped his thigh and laughed louder.

It was then that the two came out of Cassidys' house.

"Is it you, Peder Clancy?" Jennie asked. "It's a nice thing to be roarin' laffin' and poor oul Spray dead down the road."

"God, I forgot," said Peder, covering his mouth with his hand.

"You shouldn't," said Jennie. "Hello, Cahal."

"Hello," said Cahal.

She leaned against the gable-end beside him, her hands behind her. She was nearly up to his shoulder. She had brown hair held back from her face with two slides and lively eyes. "What was Peder laughin' at?"

"I don't know," said Cahal. "He's sad because oul Spray is dead."

"I saw you leppin' into the drain. Jay, me heart stopped in me mouth," she said. "Were you all wet?"

"I wasn't dry," said Cahal.

"All the same, Cahal," said Peder, sobered now, "songs can be very dangerous things. They can hurt more than a weapon. You want to be careful."

"It's the privilege of the bard to be like that," said Cahal. "Long ago, man, one of them could come and live with you for a whole year and ruin you at the end of it."

"I can't see the Murphy's takin' you into their house for a year!" said Peder.

"What are ye talkin' about?" Jennie asked.

"Little girls shouldn't have such big ears," said Cahal, pulling the lobe of the ear near to him. It was as soft and silky as the udder of a cow.

"Ow," she said, rubbing it with her hand.

"Hey, Peder," said Tommy, "give 's a cut a yer tobacca."

"What?" ejaculated Peder.

"Give 's a bit a the plug," said Tommy, coming over and standing near him. "I ran out of it today." He had a huge pipe in his hand.

"Great God, what's comin' over the country," Peder asked, "with the childer smokin' pipes?"

"I'm not a childer," said Tommy. "Haven't I been smokin' now for two months? I can near put it down me nose, even though it's shockin' strong. Is it plug or twist you have?"

"Plug," said Peder, mesmerized into handing it over.

"Thanks," said Tommy taking it and producing a huge knife from his pocket. "I was passin' out for a pull. I can't smoke in front of the oul wan. She doesn't understand. Women!" He sighed.

"Listen to that fella," said Jennie. "He'd give you a pain. You'd think he was grown up or somethin'."

"You should be in bed, girl," said Tommy. "It's past your bedtime."

"Listen," said Jennie.

"Will th'oul wake be any good, Peder?" asked Tommy, leaning against the wall and cutting tobacco authoritatively into the palm of his hand. Peder was watching him fascinated.

"I hope so," said Peder.

"I hope they tap a half-barrel," said Tommy. "I could do with a pint."

Cahal laughed out loud.

"Holy God," said Peder. Tommy was barely as tall as his sister. He was wearing a pair of his dead father's trousers that had been cut down for him. The bottom was very slack, the waist wide.

"Well," Tommy said indignantly, "ye could slip me a few sips out a the glass when nobody is lookin'. Thanks, Peder, you saved me life. I was burstin' for a pull." He handed back the tobacco. Peder kept watching him. He scraped the bowl of the pipe with the blade of his knife, kneaded the tobacco and then stuffed it in and felt in his pockets. "God," he said, "I forgot me matches too."

"Here," said Peder. "Don't be short of anything."

"Thanks," said Tommy. He lit a match. The night was calm. The pipe looked very big in his mouth. He cupped his hands around the match. His small teeth had a hard job holding the pipe. It was funny to see him trying to suck it alight. Finally he succeeded. He handed back the matches. "Thanks, Peder," he said. "Watch this now, men!" He pulled the smoke in and then blew it down through his nose.

"See ..." he was about to say, when a terrible fit of coughing attacked him. He had to bend double. Peder got up and slapped him on the back.

"Great God," he said, "what kind of childer do they be rearin' nowadays?"

"He can't smoke at all," said Jennie. "He does be practising with turf-mould."

"You're a liar," said Tommy when he had recovered. "It's just that Peder's plug is not me own brand."

"Are you goin' to the wake, Cahal?" Jennie asked.

"I suppose so," said Cahal. He didn't know that he wanted to look at Jamesey, but there was no way out.

"Are you comin', Peder?" Tommy asked.

"I am," said Peder.

"I'll stroll down with yeh," said Tommy, putting his hands in his pockets and taking long strides. "Poor oul Spray. He was past his best but he'll be a loss to the community."

Peder laughed and went along with him, shaking his head.

Jennie slipped her hand into Cahal's and pulled him from the gable-end. "Come on, Cahal," she said. "We might as well go. This is oney me second wake. I don't want to miss it."

"All right, Jennie," he said, going along with her, feeling sad that the small hand lost in his own should be so hard and roughened with work.

"I think you were great," she prattled, "goin' into the wather after the old man. Jay, he must have been cold to the touch. Would you go into a drain afther me, Cahal?"

"I'd go into the river after you, Jennie," he said.

She pressed his arm.

"Oh, it's a great pity you didn't wait, Cahal," she said, "until I'm seventeen and you could ha' married me instead of Mrs Kinsella." She sighed. "We'd ha' med a great couple," she said.

Cahal laughed. That's what's wrong with the village, he thought. There isn't enough youth in it.

They squeezed their way into the Jordan kitchen. It was packed full just as if it was a hooley. You wouldn't know any different if the talk wasn't a bit subdued and if you couldn't hear Peder's wife moaning up in the room as if she had lost her whole family in the flood, and you could smell the dead man too, that subtle smell creeping down and permeating the stuffy kitchen. It was a rough kitchen. You could tell at once that a woman hadn't been living in it for many years. Máire Brodel had tried to do something with it, but she couldn't eradicate the carelessness of the long years. It was built on a big rock so that the floor of the kitchen sloped from the back. The black rafters were unboarded and the whitewash was yellow on top. The furniture was heavy and crude and had been painted over unskilfully until you would be hard put to it to know whether it had been painted in black or brown. Chairs could have been mended, tables could have been scrubbed, but people forgave them, Spray being so helpless and Jamesey having so much to do. They lived on bread and boiled eggs, the people said.

Everyone was there. Jamesey was over near the fire talking, using his big workworn hands in awkward gestures. His eyes were red. Barney was sitting over opposite him with his head bent and his elbows on his knees. Even Julia was there. She had resurrected her early clothes and they looked incongruous on her, when her face lacked paint and was rough and raw from the weather. Máire Brodel's father was filling glasses, slowly and competently and quietly.

Mark Murphy was this side near the door with his sons around him, and there were many other people, young and old, from Ballybla and from over the road.

"Sure, sure, sure, that's true," Mark was saying.

Tommy interrupted them. He left Peder's side and went right over to Jamesey, holding out his hand.

"We're sorry for your trouble, Jamesey," he said. "There's only a few of us left now."

Jamesey looked up and shook his hand and then he raised his head and his eyes met Cahal's. He rose, slowly.

"You're not welcome here," he said.

A heavy silence descended on the kitchen.

Cahal was shocked.

"What did you say?" he asked.

"I don't want you here," said Jamesey distinctly.

"Now, now, Jamesey," said Peder.

"You can g'out now," said Jamesey, "the way you came in. If it wasn't for you me father wouldn't be lying dead above in his bed. If you hadn't held on to me, I'd have got him out of the drain."

"Are you cracked, man?" asked Peder.

"It was his fault," said Jamesey. "He held on to me and dragged me out of there when I near had me hands on him. Let him go now and make a song about that."

What's the use? Cahal thought. You don't make a speech

against stupidity like that. He quelled his anger.

"All right, Jamesey," he said, and he turned on his heel and went out the door.

"Y'oul eejit, Jamesey," said Jennie. "If it wasn't for Cahal we'd be having two wakes instead of one."

"Jennie!" said her mother, who had come down from the room in the silence. "Shut up or go home to bed."

"I had me hands on him," said Jamesey. "I could feel him under me hands when he caught a hold of me and dragged me out. Nobody can tell me any different. If it wasn't for him, me father would be living now. I'm sorry, Barney Kinsella. I mane nothing against you or yours, but he'll never put a foot in this house again."

"You were born with a head like an ox, Jamesey," said Máire Brodel, who had come from the room to see the silence. "But you didn't have to be as stupid as one. Where did you get that idea? If it wasn't for him yourself and your father would be floating out on the river with the dead sheep. Everyone that was looking knows that. Who put that idea into your head?" She looked over at Sonny Murphy who was sitting on the table smoking a cigarette.

"I said nothin'," said Sonny.

"No, but you looked a lot," said Máire. "It's a nice thing, Jamesey, with your father lying in there, and you talking out here. If it wasn't for Cahal Kinsella you'd be laid out on the bed."

She went out the door in a fury, pushing past Jennie. The women in the kitchen were tight-lipped. They looked at one another. They might have said something, if Máire's father wasn't there or if she wasn't a distant relative of the Jordans.

"We'll gup and say the Rosary," said Peder, reaching in his pocket for his beads. "We'd be better fitted to be at that than misjudgin' our neighbours."

Máire had to stop outside the door to accustom her eyes to the darkness. She listened and heard the sound of his footsteps. They weren't sounding his road home but down towards the bog. She ran out into the road and looked. She could see the bulk of him as her eyes became accustomed to the moon-relieved darkness.

"Cahal!" she called. "Cahal Kinsella!"

He stood on the road and turned his head.

She walked up to him.

"Are you hurt?" she asked.

"I don't know," said Cahal. "The trouble is that I can see Jamesey's side of it."

"That's a good sign," she said.

He walked on. She went beside him.

"It must be a terrible thing to be thinkin' you're a hero," she said, "and then to be told that you're an almost murderer."

"It is," said Cahal. "What else could I ha' done? Don't you think Jamesey would have been drowned? You were there. You saw."

"He would," she said.

"Maybe I should ha' hit him," said Cahal, "even though his father was dead in the room."

"What good would that do?" she asked.

"It's what you want to do with people as stupid as him," said Cahal, "to hit sense into their thick heads."

"Jamesey'll get over it," she said.

"Did you notice that kitchen?" he asked. "I was afraid in that kitchen. They all seemed against me."

"You're imaginin' it," she said.

"I hope so," said Cahal. "Not that I give a damn, mind, I don't. I don't care if the whole bloody lot of them came after me with pitchforks."

They were silent then for a time, thinking.

They reached the small bridge and they stood there, resting their elbows on the rough coping stones.

"A village is a peculiar place," said Cahal. "You take Caherlo. What's in it? The six families. Five now, with Foxy gone. From Foxy's house to the big bridge over the river and down to here. About quarter of a mile either way. In there is the village. It's like a family. I suppose it's because life is so confined that they keep tracks on everything you do. Did you find that? That no matter what you do you seem to be doing it under their eyes?"

"I know what it is," said Máire. "I had to leave our village. You know that. You told me."

Cahal dropped his head in his hands.

"See," he said, "even you I hit."

"That's not it," she said. "It's what happened. What business was it of theirs? You should have seen them standing in the yard in front of the house telling my father he would have to go or put me. You couldn't believe it. It was night and you would look out and see the light shining on their faces. Nice quiet simple people that you thought you knew. Every one of them. And their lips were tight and virtue shining out of them. But they were terrible implacable. I told them what I thought of them. But I was afraid all the same. Sometimes I don't know if we did right to leave. Maybe we should have stayed and fought them. But then they might have done things to my father."

"Tell me something," said Cahal. "That night when I said that, in front of Sonny Murphy, were you and he really going to match?"

"I don't know," she said. "I think we were."

"Was it what I said, that bust it?" he asked.

She thought. Cahal went out of the kitchen, leaving it tense behind him. She knew her face was red. It was red with fury. He was the first man she had met who could make her feel like that. Then the fury left her and she looked at Sonny. He stood there looking at her speculatively, as he might have looked at a beast he was thinking of purchasing at a fair and had been told on the quiet that it had a defect, hidden, and not to buy it. She hadn't any particular care for Sonny. She had a yearning just to stay in the one place now forever, where her father was content with the collie and the sheep and poling for fish in the river in the evenings. Sonny was well set-up, and he wasn't coarse. He was just a nice simple hard-working farmer's son. And she didn't care.

"Now, Sonny," she said. "What happened in Roscommon?" Sonny asked. Her father had his back turned, he was replenishing the fire. "Why do you want to know?" she had asked, thinking then, why did Cahal Kinsella do this, and she knew he did it because he was hurt, and why was he hurt, he was hurt because he cared for her, and her face flamed then and her heart started to pound. "You better go, Sonny," she said, turning away. "What happened in Roscommon wouldn't suit you at all, and since you'll hear it soon enough from the villagers there's no use my telling you." And what happened? Sonny went away. Without another word. She was sure that he was relieved when he got outside. My God, that was a near thing.

"I don't think so," said Máire. "It wouldn't have happened anyhow. I don't think I could have taken Sonny in the end."

"You know the reason I did it?" he asked.

"No," she said.

"It was because ... It was because I wanted you," he said.

He moved one of his hands and touched her bare arm. Then he took his hand away. His head was down. He had to wink his eyes and hold his breath to conquer the suffocating feeling that rose in him. He was conscious of every bit of her, of the hair falling over her face and the line of her body leaning on the bridge. He could feel the heat from her arm seeping through the cloth of his coat. There was a silence between them that was no silence. It was all so clear.

"Why didn't you come back the next day?" she asked. Her voice was very low. She wasn't looking at him either. She had joined her hands and was rubbing her forehead on the backs of them. "I thought you would. I was waiting for you to come back."

"I was ashamed," said Cahal.

"Why did you marry your wife?" she asked.

"Because I never thought," he said. "You remember the last time you and me talked down here by this very bridge, and the things you said to me?"

"I think I do," she said. "I remember your face against mine. You had a fresh shave. You fell back against the bridge."

"You said that I would wake up some day," he said. "You didn't say what a terrible thing it is to wake up."

"Oh, Cahal," she said.

"It's a thing beyond belief," he said, "the things that men will do. The thing I did, in marrying that old woman. I did it airily, I tell you, like you'd take part in a good joke. And it's no joke at all."

"You shouldn't have hit Barney," she said. "When he went to hit you with the rake, you shouldn't have hit him."

"I don't care about Barney," he said. "Barney had it coming to him. He did a lot of things to me, Barney did. I saw him for a giant and after all he's just a dull ageing domineering old man."

"You see," she explained, "you are an outsider. That's the way they look at you even though they like you. They all wanted to see Barney brought low, but when you hit him in front of them it was like hitting themselves."

"What does that matter?" Cahal asked. "I'd throw them all into the river tomorrow morning if I could recall just five minutes in front of the priest in Valley. That the worst thing that was done to me. There's no going back on that."

"No," said Máire, "that's a final thing."

"So long as you know, Máire," he said, "even too late." He turned towards her. She faced him, with the moon shining on her. Her dark eyebrows were like black pencil marks. Her lips were slightly open. He could feel her breath on his chin. He stood close to her, looking into her eyes. Give me back the months, he thought, the stupid months. They lay like a sheet of thin impenetrable steel between them. You could swim a river or cross a bog or walk a thousand miles, but you couldn't go through this.

The voice spoke behind them.

"Oh, there you are, Cahal? And who's that with you?"

She had come silently because she was wearing her

American shoes. He could have turned around and hit her in the face. His fists clenched. His jaws tightened. He turned slowly towards her.

"Goodnight, Mrs Kinsella," said Máire. "It's me."

"Oh, so it is," said Julia. "I'm sure you should go back to the house, Miss Brodel. I'm sure they are looking for you."

"Go home," said Cahal.

She looked at him. He could see the whites of her eyes.

"Go on home," he said. "I'll be after you."

She fought.

"It's a bit odd," she said, "if people see me goin' home on my own and you down the road with an unmarried girl. Not that it means anything, but you know the way people talk."

"Go home," said Cahal. "I'll be home after you." She answered the cold anger in his voice.

"Yes," she said. "Don't be long. I'll have the stir-about on the fire."

They watched her turn away and walk slowly up the road.

"You see," said Cahal between his teeth. "If she was different. If she was a young woman as stupid as a cow, but she is a proper trap. She's old and she has the look about her of a pup that you try to protect. She can't be hurt, that old woman, and yet you can't do anything to hurt her. She's like a load they throw on your back and you can't drop it."

"Goodbye, Cahal," said Máire. "Things will work out."

"They will not," said Cahal. "Things will not work out. They have to be broken up, and I haven't the courage to break them. Give me time."

He caught her hand as she passed him and swung her around so that she was facing him. He could feel her breast heaving against his chest.

"Goodbye, Máire," he said and let her go.

She turned away and followed Julia up the road. Julia had stopped to watch.

Cahal leaped the ditch and walked towards the alder grove near the wind of the river.

Chapter Fourteen

The jobbers are buyin'; the farmers are cryin';
The sweet smell of hops is invadin' the air.
Ladies in britches are horse-leppin' ditches;
The eyes of the lassies are bright at the fair.
   Ó-hóró, tomorrow will be
   A mornin' of reckonin' and fiddle-de-dee,
   So laugh in the glitther
   And dance in the litther,
   Ye won't have a fair in Eternity.

HE WAS GLAD to leave the village behind him. Something bright was bubbling inside him until he passed Foxy's house. That was a soberer; to see the thatch completely gone and the black rafters reaching gauntly to the early morning sky. A little over a year had passed since it was closed and to look at now you wouldn't think a sinner had lived in it for a hundred years. What did Bridie think when she got his letter? He never knew. She still wrote to Gob, but so far she said nothing about coming home. He should have minded his own business. He had felt so sorry, and here after a year Foxy was barely a memory.

He clapped the ambling polly on the back.

"Go on! Go on!" he said, "after today you'll have a new master and I hope he'll be kind to you."

He felt sorry parting with her. She was a nice philosophical cow. Rarely upset. She took her life at ease, her visit to her husband and the birth of her calf and the seasons. She was placid and you got fond of her. Why could you get so fond of an oul cow? This one too seemed to have intelligence. She would often greet you in the winter. You'd swear there was a welcome in her eye. And yet she was a dumb animal with no brains or intelligence. He wondered if there was a cow heaven. He hoped so. They were a hell of a sight better and nicer than a lot of humans he knew. It was the first fair he had gone to on his own. Barney wasn't up to it. He didn't feel so good. Just as well. He preferred to be on his own. Sell the cow for not less than twenty-eight pounds, Barney told him, and buy a good young one for not more than nineteen. He'd have to get his friend the jobber to help him. He was bound to be there.

The cow ambled ahead and he followed, leading the horse who was pulling a full creel of turf. He would get eight shillings and sixpence for the turf, so that he could have a bite to eat and a few drinks. He thought of the labour that had gone to the cutting and the saving of that large load of turf. He thought of the reward for the labour. How many sods was that for a penny? Well, it didn't matter. Forget it. He would soon be like Peder, getting old and raggedy and driving to the town every second day with a load of turf to get the price of a few drinks.

What had he done in a year? Here it was around to the July fair. What had he done since last July? There was no very pleasant memories, just work and eat and sleep, and shut out from his mind his troubles. Sometimes they caught up with him, and when they did he would walk miles over the wet bogs until he was nearly exhausted, or if the weather was fine he would go into the wilds after the river and bring his fishing-pole and fish or strip himself off and go into the water. The house was a silent place, all except for her talking, talking, with nobody listening much, answering her in grunts. She was sweetly malicious. Everybody came under her tongue in the vague way she had. Well, let her go on. What life had she either any more than himself? If only she would leave him alone. Instead of plying him with little bits of this and that, specially cooked like she had learned in America. Dainty things that didn't suit his palate. He couldn't say, That was nice. Every inch he gave in to her found her coming nearer and nearer to him, until he thought he would suffocate. Times, when he had a terrible longing for Máire, remembering her as he had seen her the first time, until the memory of it nearly made him groan, that would lead him to other thoughts and in the dull glow of the fire or the light from the paraffin lamp he would look at her sitting opposite darning socks and would think, She is not so bad. She must be lonely. Maybe I ought to go back in the room with her. But then the thought would revolt him and he would rise and go out.

There were few people abroad. The houses were sleeping, with no trail of smoke seeking the summer sky. It was a fresh morning. The dew was heavy on the fields, and the rising sun was sucking it up in a sort of spiralling vapour that left knee-high mists in the meadows, so that the curious cattle looking out at you seemed to be walking on clouds.

He sang a song. A light one, that carried far on the air. The horse twitched his ears and even the imperturbable polly glanced back over her shoulder.

"Did you like that, Poll?" he asked. "It didn't offend you, did it?"

He laughed.

He knew that some of his songs were being sung in the towns. Men were laughing at the *Races of Caherlo*, and the Murphys were greeted with *Saint Mark* everywhere they went, until Mark had given up nodding at him whenever they met. Sonny still talked to him, between his teeth. He felt sorry about Sonny. He would have liked to have been friends with Sonny, if he was made different. Why should they be hurt by a song? Songs were made for laughing and humming. They had always gone on in rural Ireland, and it made it better to know the people that were named in them. If Máire was walking here beside him now, it would

- 188 -

be good. They would have good fun. They could feel that once the blinds were down there were no unwinking eyes watching them. He had talked to her not more than twice in the past year. Standing well away from her, in a prominent place, under their eyes, so that tales couldn't be spread. Talked about nothing, words on the lips, but just the talk of eyes and heaving chests and speeding pulses, that you couldn't control, but that were free from their eyes. She had had enough trouble.

It was high morning when he came close to the town. There was dust on the cow and his highly polished boots were white. He paused to rub them black again and he went on. There were herds of cattle being driven into the place. They were choking the roads. Carts couldn't pass them and impatient motor cars were honking furiously. He joined the procession with his single cow. He felt like laughing. The cow and himself and his cart of turf. Don't mind, Poll, he told her, you're worth fifty of them any day.

The town was guarded on this side by the river, and once you crossed the bridge you climbed the hill into the winding main street. There were ugly buildings on either side of the road. Some tall, some elegant, with an occasional thatched cottage, sandwiched between the tall buildings and looking completely out of place.

The shops were open and already even at this early hour there was a great smell of porter floating out on to the sidewalks, narrow sidewalks that were blocked here and there by erected creels, lifted from carts and confining screaming bonhams. The gutters were beginning to flow with the droppings of the animals. Just where the street took a wide turn before it went up to the Fair Green, he stopped beside a shop that had a wall beside it pierced with a red gate that was yawning and displaying the carts and released horses inside it.

"Stay here, you," he told the cow, throwing down a few bits of grass from the bag tied to the side of the cart. She bent obediently and ate some of it. He drove the horse into the yard, put some of the grass in front of him and tied the reins to a whitewashed pole. Then he left him and went in the side door to the shop. It was nicely filled. He pushed his way down and opened another door that went into the kitchen. There were two women in it. The young one was big and her face was red from bending over the fire. He spoke to the older lady who was washing dishes. "I have a load for you, ma'am," he said. "Do you want it?"

"Ah, Cahal," she said, "how are you, and what are you asking for it?"

"It's good turf, ma'am," he said. "It's mostly stone turf and grand brown cooking turf. I'll give it to you for ten shillings."

"Do you hear the scoundrel?" the woman asked the girl. "Ten shillings he wants for a load of turf and all I do is walk out in the street and I can get a load for seven and six."

"Not this turf," said Cahal. "You know where it comes from."

"It would want to come out of a goldmine." she said, "to be worth that."

"All right," said Cahal, "nine and six."

"Nine bob," she said.

"It's yours," said Cahal. "I have a cow to bring up. I'll be back again and unload it for you."

"All right," she said. "They'll pay you in the shop."

"Thanks," said Cahal and left them, thinking, Well I'm sixpence better off than I thought I would be anyhow.

He collected the cow outside the shop, and drove her towards the green. He had difficulty, not with the cow, but with other cows who hadn't her outlook. The road widened well near the green. It was a very big green sloping up towards another street of the town. The grass on it was very short and very green, because it was freely manured several times a year by the animals. There was great milling in it. All the animals lowing or trying to escape and being beaten back by blows on the face by the drovers. There were squealing pigs too and up at the far end there were a few horses. Intermingled with all those there were a few tents where dirty-faced men were roaring their lungs out enticing the farmers to risk their hard-earned money on roulette machines and odd games of chance. They weren't very busy now. There were a few lorries with their backs down to disclose a sort of shop, with barkers up on them selling off clothes at bargain prices, and others selling odd things like fifteen-jewelled watches for two and six, and bottles guaranteed to cure croup or cough, cancer or consumption, foot-and-mouth disease or piles in man or beast for one and three.

Cahal edged the cow well into the throng. He came to a free space where a man was talking to a friend. He was guarding three cows, who were well on, and staple.

"Would you keep an eye on this one for about half an hour for me?" he asked.

"To be sure, man," the other answered immediately. "Shove her in there with them."

"How is it?" Cahal asked.

"It's brisk enough," the man said. "But their prices are slow. They should pull up later."

"I'll be back soon," said Cahal.

He made his way to the shop. He manoeuvred the cart and piled the turf into the outhouse of the yard. He left the horse free then and gave him the rest of the bag of grass. He collected his nine shillings and put it into his purse along with the threepence halfpenny that was already there.

Then he went looking for his friend the jobber.

He wasn't on the green.

Cahal covered it well, all around and in the middle and the space around the jumping enclosure. Then he left the green and started looking into all the pubs on the opposite side.

He tracked him down. He couldn't see him where he found him but he could hear him. He was effing and blinding the Government. His face was red, his hat was on the back of his head, and his large stomach was barely fitting on the bar stool.

Ah, Cahal, the hard man. Come over and what are you having? Nothing but whiskey today. It's a sorrow and a shame for any man to drink porter on a day like this. Have you met Cahal Kinsella. Here, he sings songs. Divil a such songs. Your man here is after cheatin' me for the first time in me life. Honest. Seventeen bullocks I bought off him and I'll be lucky to make the price of a packet of fags off them. Listen, tell him about the auction. Wait'll you hear, man. Down I go. They were selling up some poor old bastard. That was bidding. What's his name. Murphy. He was mad, that fella. God, he'd ha' chewed iron and spit rust that day. Go on man, a little song. Nobody's listening.

Cahal was feeling good. The whiskey hit his stomach. There was no food to absorb it. They gave him a hand. Gradually all the boozers in the pub came around him. Asked for more. Listen, man, you should be on the radio. Man, but you have a powerful voice. Listen to some of the lugs they have on it. Gobble stroppers. God, I know him now. Here, aren't you the Bogman of Caherlo? That's right. What did I tell you? Listen, they're singin' your songs all over our place. Isn't that so, Jim? So it is, be Christ. Is he the Bogman? Here larrup it up there, Jim. Give the man a glass of the best from me. It's no use protesting, man. Is it trying to insult me you are?

He must have been there an hour. He must have drunk nearly a bottle of whiskey. His head was churning. He'd laugh at the drop of a hat. He got spun out of songs. You'll come over to our place. You will, by God. Hop a bike. It's oney ten miles. You play the melodeon too. I heard that. You can make it hum, they tell me. Don't forget to come now. We'll be expectin' you. Divil a such songs. Where did you get them? Is it true you got them out of your head? Man, dear, you'll be famoust. What are yeh doin' diggin bogs? Out with you on the roads with your melodeon. You'll make a mint, man. Wouldn't he, Joe? Here, give the man another glass. Wait'll I tell them at home that I met you. You know what you'll do. Scribble down a few of them on a bit of paper and send them to me. You'll do that? For the love of God. Here it is. Peter Daly, Castledowney. You won't forget. Man, I'll haunt you.

The jobber? You want to sell a cow. I don't want cows only if they're castrated. You heard what I said, Joe. Isn't that something? Don't want cows except they're castrated. No, son, I'm after bullocks this weather. Beef to the heels. Mullingar heifers. I'll sell your cow for you. You want a two-year-old instead? Right. God, if I can't sell a cow in this man's town for how much? for twenty-eight pounds, I'm not worth me livin'. Goodbye, men. See ye later. We'll be back. This is going to be the quickest sell in the history of the fair.

He had trouble getting away. They all wanted to shake him by the hand. Even though they had pint glasses in one hand and ashplants in the other. They got in the way. Cahal felt as if he was walking on air. He was sure he was cross-eyed. He was damn certain he was cross-eyed. He had to pull his lower lids down to straighten out his eyes. Great God, how did I get into this? Why didn't I just sell me cow and go home? The air was hot outside. The risen sun was beating off the pavements. Everywhere you went you walked into dung. Everytime a car passed it raddled the people with clouds of dust. A cloud of dust was hanging over the green. The shouting was louder. The crowds were greater. He walked carefully across the road as if it was a river and he was walking the water. He giggled.

Where's this oul bitch of a cow? This cow is not an oul bitch. This is a nice cow. This cow is a friendly cow. I'd rather sell me own mother than this cow. T'only friend I had in the whole world, this cow. Talk to her. Tell her everything. Sometimes nobody else to talk to. I wish I had the money and I'd buy this cow for myself. Sing to her. Make up songs for her. Down in the bog pasture. Comin' home on the winter evening. Like the driven clouds of heaven, wavin' weary to and fro, to and fro, silken fronds do bear the cotton on the bogs of Caherlo. Here pipe down.

You know, man, you can't hold your drink. You'll have them handin' out pennies in a minute. Sorry, my friend. Sorry, my friend. Don't sell the cow. Here, where is she? Over here. This way. Scuse me please.

The minder was aggrieved. Here, man, isn't it half an hour you said? I have me own sold and the stomach fallin' out of me, and I wasn't bad enough to leave your oul cow. Look, I'm sorry. I was held up. Will you come and have a drink with us? Come and ate with us. You deserve that. Can't you forgive me, man? I'm right sorry.

I have a cow, the jobber starts roaring.

He has a powerful voice. It rises over the noises of the fair. He gets a ring around him. Very quickly. Cahal remembers standing there with his arm around the neck of the polly. Shaking his head, trying to squeeze some sense into it. Talking to the oul cow. Maybe he wasn't talking. Maybe it was only in his mind the things he was saying to her. Goodbye, Polly. Don't forget me. I'll miss you, you complacent oul divil you. You suffer with the strain once a year when you calve. That's all you know. You don't know the pain it is to be me. A sort of flame in me, eating and burning away inside me. Things I can't say because I haven't the ways of saying them. Things I can't do because I haven't the courage to do them. You know Máire, Poll. She's something. The whole feckin' world I'd give to be with her on the banks of the Ree in a starry night and she goin' bathin' again down be the alder bushes. Or to raise me hand and silence the old bitch that Barney willed on me. To be free from meself, Poll, that's all. To throw off the shackles of respectability and be free. Maybe some day. Some day. And you know what? I'm goin' after you, Poll, old girl. I'll collect you. You were the first I whispered at. You know all my secrets, Poll. You know me, Poll. Don't forget me.

Are you mad? the jobber is asking. Twenty-five pounds for that cow and she having a stomach on her that'll live on a handful of grass every two months and an udder on her that'd feed a flock of calves from here to Meath. Get out of me way before I spit on you. We'll take thirty-five quid for this cow and the man that gets her'll be saying novenas in thanksgivin' and doin' Lough Derg four times a year for the benefits ourselves and God is bestowing on him. Four gallons of milk a day, as true as God. They don't know what to do with her. She's too prolific, I tell you. She's the greatest cow since Maeve's bull.

He sold the cow for twenty-eight pounds ten shillings. The new man drove her away. He raised a big stick and hit her a blow on the hip. Here, you bastard! The jobber caught him by the arms before he hit him. Be nice to that cow, you son of a bitch, or I'll folly you. You hear. I'll smadder you if you bate that cow. Do you hear. All right man, all right. No offence. No offence. I didn't only touch her. He watched the cow out through the throng. She went off a different road to the one she had come. She looked back once over her shoulder and she mooed at him. Goodbye, Polly, old girl. Goodbye, old girl. Jaysys, he's cryin', said the jobber to the minder. I was fond of that oul cow. Too much whiskey he has, says the minder. Look, we better go and eat. Then we'll buy the springer.

His brain was as clear as a pane of glass, but his movements were behind. He could taste the bacon and eggs they ate. He was afraid there was gravy on his chin. He found it hard to wipe his chin with the palm of his hand. He couldn't find it. They drank again. Cahal spent four shillings of his nine and threepence halfpenny giving them a treat. Then they bought the young cow. She wasn't a quiet young one. She was gamey. They got her for eighteen pounds ten, so Cahal could go home with a pound more than he was supposed to. He bundled the money in his inside pocket and clipped it with a big safety pin. You never know. Some of these fellows would steal the milk out of your tea.

He parted from the jobber. He was afraid he would be sick if he drank any more. He had the spare pound in his purse now too. He left the young cow in the yard with the horse, a piece of rope around her neck and she tied to the wheel of the cart. That'll hold you. He didn't want to go home yet. The day was young. He wanted fresh air. It was hard to find. He found himself in the jumping enclosure. Hurdles and ditches and men and women on horseback, leppin' them. An old gouger beside him. Jay, look at the ones. In britches. Big ahs. They should be ashamed. At home havin' kids they should be. Bowler hats on them and white things around their necks and fawn-coloured trousers with narrow legs. Faces like horses. One young woman hadn't a face like a horse. She had long fair hair under the bowler hat. Cahal desired her. Her backside was slim in the britches, the waisted coat uplifted her breasts. She was haughty-looking. She jumped well. Took the plaudits, and then she came to the water jump. The horse jibbed. She went over his head. She landed in the water. She lost her bowler hat and her dignity. She went around the jump and she hit the horse in the face with the short whip she had. Oooh! said everybody. Hah, you mean-streaked bitch, the gouger shouted, his hands cupping his mouth. Boo! said the people in the mean seats with Cahal. If she had had a gun she would have shot them. Another big one went by. Every time the horse jumped she rose in the saddle bent forward. God, there's a waste land, says the gouger. She lost her seat at a hurdle. Everybody held their breath, waiting for the bump. Ugh! said everybody as she landed. Instinctively they felt behind them. That'll loosen her up, said the gouger. Hey, ma'am, give it Sloan's Linimint, he shouted. They laughed. She got to her feet. She limped back. She tried not to put her hand back, but she had to in the end. Cahal giggled.

He was there some time and still the effects weren't worn away. He was feeling that he would like to vomit. The sun was very hot. But it would quieten. It was coming on to the evening.

Outside the crowds on the green were thinning away. Most of the cattle were gone. Here and there small disconsolate boys herded a few cattle, looking anxiously towards the pubs where their parents would be. There was a crowd farther down gathered in a ring around. There seemed to be a horse in there and from the centre of the ring you could hear a great voice booming. Where have I heard that voice before? Cahal asked his befuddled head. He walked slowly towards the scene. He pushed his way towards the edges. He knew before he saw that he was listening to Danno. His coat was on the ground. He was in his bare chest and there was a red scarf tied around his bronzed throat. His hair was a great tangle of grey-black curls, sweaty and falling over his forehead. He was holding a thick stick, banging it on the ground and roaring. The muscles and tendons rippled all over him, although he was a bit thick at the waist.

"There's a horse," Danno was roaring. "There's the finest horse that ever was seen at a fair." There was a young boy of about five, holding the reins of the horse. He was small and black-haired and the clothes he wore were too big for him. He was standing there, a small brown dirty hand holding the reins and he grinning. God, Cahal thought, is that the little lad that I saw sucking his mother? That day came back to him so clearly. He searched the crowd with his eyes. There was no sign of her. Danno was a little drunk. As he swung around he'd have to take a step too many. "He's the greatest horse that ever put a hoof on the green grass of Ireland," Danno was shouting.

"Where did you steal him, Danno?" an anonymous voice from the crowd shouts. Danno circles them roaring. "Who said that? Who said that? If he has the courage of a mouse let him step forward and I'll pull the thirty-six feet of guts outa him." He circled them menacingly. They hid their grins behind thick hands. "Don't mind him, Danno," said another, "on with you." "If I ever find him," Danno roars, "I'll cripple him. The father of this horse was the stallion of Mahomet of Arabia," he roared, "and his mother was Caitlin ni Houlihaun. Who wants the best horse the world has ever seen? He's as fast as a bullet from a gun and as strong as two railway engines. He's a horse fit for a giant, I tell ye. He can carry more on his back than a ship at sea or four horses under a dray. Stand back, let ye, and look at him. Danno, prance the baste."

The little boy ran around the ring with the horse. Cahal thought the horse looked tired. He was a dappled grey horse and he had a bend in his back. "Which of ye wants him now?" Danno demanded. "Which of ye wants me darlin'?" A tall countryman pushed his way in to the horse. He had a heavy bréidín coat on him, and the bottoms of his trousers and his boots were caked with dung. He rubbed his chin and walked around the horse and then bent and examined his fetlocks. "Sound in wind and limb," Danno assured him. "He's as strong as a Connemara policeman. He has legs on him like oak trees." The man took the horse's head in his hands and shoved back his lips to look at his teeth. "Ivory you're lookin' at," Danno said. "Every one as sound as the womb of a virgin. Every tooth in his head could bite a bar of iron. He'll be alive to work for the children of your grandchildren. He's the greatest two-year-old horse that was ever bred."

The countryman straightened up and looked at Danno. "The horse is five years of age," he said. Danno danced. "Do you hear him, God?" he asked the sky. "Did you hear what the gawk said about me nag? Do you doubt me word, you Thomas you? Were you there like me the day he was born, were you?" He pushed his face closer to the other's. The man drew back from what was obviously a foetid breath. "It's a five-year-old horse," he said then, "and I'll give you eleven pounds for him." "You'll what?" Danno asked. "Say that again to me." "He's five years of age," said the man, "and I'll give you more than he's worth. I'll give you eleven pounds for him."

Danno raised his heavy stick and would have brought it down with force if some men hadn't converged on him from the crowd and held it and him in their grasp. "Let me at him! Let me at him," Danno was roaring.

Cahal felt a hand plucking his sleeve.

"Will you buy a scapular?" a voice asked, and he turned and found himself looking into the eyes of Nessa.

He remembered that look in her eyes so well. Just as if he had seen it yesterday. She was wearing a man's coloured shirt open at the neck and a striped skirt. Her feet were bare. "No," said Cahal, "I don't want a scapular." "Give's sixpence so," she said, holding out her hand. It was as small and as dirty as ever. He could see that by screwing his eyes. "No baby," said Cahal. "No baby today." "No," she said. "I remember you well. You thought I wouldn't remember you. I did. Will you give me a drink?" "What kind of drink?" asked Cahal. "Anythin'?" she said, shrugging her shoulders. "I will," said Cahal. "Come on," she said, taking his arm. "You're a bit drunk. Did you drink much?" "I am not drunk," said Cahal. "I am sick, not drunk." "Come on," she said, pulling at him. She was laughing. "What about Danno?" Cahal asked. "And your child in there. He might be murdered." "Him," she said. "Let his oul fella look after him."

They left the throng and crossed the green and went into a public-house. Cahal remembered that well. Remembered pushing in. It wasn't terribly crowded, and she opened the swing door of a snug. There was a wooden seat in it. It was shiny so that he was slipping off it and had to brace his feet hard against the wooden floor. She rapped at the little opening and a glass window went up and she said, "Two glasses," and then said, "Where's your money?" Cahal laughed and said, "Here it is," feeling for his purse and opening it and taking out the pound. "Bring me some biscuits too," she shouted at the barman and Cahal gave him the pound and got change and put it back into his purse and put the purse into his pocket. "Here's luck to you," said Nessa, and raised her head and the drink was gone. Her hair was gleaming blackly in the reflected light. It was a dark pub. The light was switched on. "Give's a cigarette," said Nessa. He handed her the packet and she took one and gave him one and took matches out of his pocket and lighted her cigarette and lighted his, and he drank the whiskey and the movement of his body then proceeded to be a few seconds after his brain.

She put her arm through his. She was very close to him. He could feel the softness of her breast against his arm. Felt the tightening of the muscles. "I never forgot you," she said.

Danno, Danno, what happened Danno, the time Barney hit him? Oh, only four stitches he got. He hit me too. He said it was my fault. Sure, it wasn't my fault. It wasn't your fault. He's very cruel to me. Why did Barney hit him? How did Barney know him? She pulled away. She laughed. That's a laugh, she said. I don't know. He wouldn't tell me. Why don't ye come and camp near our bridge like the other tinkers? We're not tinkers. Well, trickeys then. We're not trickeys. We're respectable people. Stand us another drink. Rap the little window. Two more. You've changed since I saw you before. You got stouter. Look at that big muscle on your arm. Could you bate Danno? I could bate Danno if I had to; if there was any reason for me to bate Danno. See your face changed too. You're not too old. Look at that line down be your nose and another one on the other side. He felt her finger tracing it on his face. Felt cold shivers in his stomach. I like you. Felt her mouth on his own. She was standing up over him, between his knees, cupping his face in her hands. He couldn't smell whiskey off her breath. You got marrried too, I hear that. She's old, isn't she? Is she any good? Leave me alone. He flung her away. Feeling peevish and excited. She shouldn't have brought the old one into it. The window opened, the two glasses appeared. He paid. All right, if you don't want me to. Sitting back sulkily, with inches between them. He could feel the movements of her body. She raised her feet and looked at them. They were brown and dusty and stained where water had fallen on the dust.

You sing. Sing me a song then. I know all about you. I know everything you do. We hear everything that's going. If you only knew all the things we hear. He sang a song. Very low. He was feeling sad. One of the terrible sad songs that came into his head sometimes on the bog. She tucked her legs under her on the seat and came closer to him so that her chin was resting on his shoulder. He put his arm around her. It encompassed her so that his hand was on her breast. The door opened then. He heard the voice first calling his name. He didn't free his hand. Her hands were on his shoulder, her chin resting on them. Gob came in the door. He wouldn't care if God Almighty came in the door. He stopped his song. He saw the brightness on Gob's face going out like a cloud that passes over the sun. Hi, Gob, he said. Come in and have a drink and tell us the story. You know Nessa. Isn't she nice? Nessa was nice to me, Gob, when nobody else in the world was nice. I heard your voice, he heard Gob say. I wanted to tell you something. It'll do again. Don't go 'way, Gob, for the love of God. Stop, man, when I tell you. What is it? Go on, tell me what it is? Gob looked at him with hostility. Bridie is coming home, he said. That's all I wanted to tell you. Then he closed the door and was gone.

Here Gob, Gob, Cahal was calling ... come back ... come back. Here, let me out, he said to her, and rose and went into the shop. There was no sight of Gob. He went up the far end to look for him, to ask questions about him. It was as well he did. At that moment Danno came into the shop roaring. "Nessa! Nessa! Where are you?" he shouted. "It's no use hidin' from me. Young Danno saw you slinkin' into the shop with a man. Come out before I cripple you."

Nessa came out of the snug.

"Young Danno was blind in one eye," she said. "He saw me comin' in on me own for a glass a lemonade."

Danno was nonplussed. He swept past her and into the snug. He sniffed it. He didn't look under the seat where she had hidden the glasses.

"Now, smart one," he said. "I've a good mind to clatter you. Wait'll I lay me hands on that little bee of yours."

"Now, now," said the proprietor, coming and leaning over

the counter. "None of that language here. You get out of here, Danno, or I'll call the Guards."

"Ah, go and hump yourself," said Danno and went out. Nessa stuck her tongue out. "Goodbye," she said then as she followed Danno. Cahal knew the goodbye was for him. It was a little mocking.

He waited a time and went into the street. There was no sign of Gob. How did Gob know he was there? Oh yes. He was singing a song. Gob would have heard that.

He staggered down the street to the shop where he had left his horse and his cow.

He collected them. He was the last. The sun was dying and the lights were shining on the carnival at the green. As he passed he heard the men shouting the odds. There were girls walking around eyeing people. You could see the lights gleaming in their eyes. A great tent was stuck up farther away. There were lights on in that too. Now and again greatly exaggerated shadows of people dancing were outlined on the canvas. Even in the near dark you could see the mess the place was in, all the papers on the once-clean grass and the orange peelings and the cigarette packs and the leavings of cow and man. A tremendous litter basket. He drove on and on. He had to be careful of the young cow. She wanted to go side roads. Back to where she came from. Sometimes he had to chase her and corner her and beat her back to the right road, cursing, his mind in a fevered state.

He had to stop near the railway station. The level-crossing gates were closed. There was a milling crowd down there as they loaded the cattle on the wagons. Men cursing and sticks rising and falling under the feeble gleams of the gaslight. There was an old man near the conflux. He had sheets of green-coloured ballads in his hand. He was singing hoarsely. A long tattered coat on him that reached to his boots that were gaping and showing his dirty toes. A red cloth around his neck. Every few seconds he would raise a finger and rub his nose, and all the time he was pouring out his song. Cahal had been listening to him for some time before he recognized the words. The man was singing *The Races of Caherlo*.

"Here," Cahal called. "Come here."

The old man closed on the cart, still singing.

"Have you that written down?" Cahal asked.

The man nodded, still singing and twitching his shoulders as if he was being plagued with fleas.

"Give me a few copies," said Cahal. He felt for his purse. It wasn't in the first pocket or the second pocket or any pocket. He thought bemusedly, What could have happened to me purse? And then he thought of Nessa, so close to him, so loving. "Well, the bitch," he said out loud, and then he laughed. God, there was a one for you. He found a lone sixpence somewhere in a corner after feeling first to make sure that the cattle money was still pinned to his inside pocket. The man handed over three sheets. Cahal went over under the flickering light to read them. There it was on top, written big, *The Races of Caherlo*. He read the words. They were distorted. It wasn't all of his words. The verses had been changed, he supposed, passing from mouth to mouth.

"Well, now," he said. "Imagine that!" It was a very queer thing to see the words of his head printed on a ballad sheet.

The crossing gates opened and he went ahead.

The sound of the rag-tag of the fair followed him far into the country.

Chapter Fifteen

The thatch is tight against the might
Of Winter's bitther battle;
The hay is high in the haggard, boy,
To fodder hungry cattle.
The oats are stacked; the pits are packed
To feed us full and plenty:
You should not sigh in the night-time, boy,
For it's only the heart that's empty.

IT WAS THE following autumn that Bridie came home.

Cahal was looking forward to her homecoming. He remembered well the first time he came to Caherlo. She was like a great big friendly breeze. This particular day too he felt that he could do with a friend. They were pulling home the Cassidys' hay. It was the custom in the harvest time to help in communion. To reap the harvest was too much for one family. It would take a long time. So on a certain day the whole village would do one family's hay and then move on to the next family. It was generally a happy time. You were away from your own house for the day and eating in somebody else's house. That was a change however small. Men were very good-natured, and you could laugh, and each family spread themselves to put up the very best of the food for the day.

Mary Cassidy had about ten cocks of hay to bring home. Five from the river meadow and three from the mearing and two from the reclaimed bog meadow. All the cocks were carted to the small sheltered garden behind the house and built into one huge garden cock, that, when it settled down, would be thatched tight with ripe rushes from the banks of the river. They had drawn Murphys' hay and Creels' and Kinsellas' and today they were building Mary Cassidy's. The Murphys were using the lorry so the work was fast. The butt of the huge cock was laid on planks and shaped sods of turf, that raised it from the soiling touch of the earth, and allowed the air to circulate under it. With five cocks of hay pitched on it the cock was higher than the roof of the house. So then it was too high for direct pitching, and a ladder was placed against the side of the cock, and a man stood on that facing out and took the pitch-fork full of hay from the man on the ground and stretched it up to the two men on top who were shaping and tramping the cock. Cahal was on the ladder. He had always liked this period of drawing the hay. The disturbed hay had a different smell entirely from the raw saved hay of the summer. It was mellowed. It was the smell of autumn, of full-ripened things, and now and again a faint reminder of a smell that brought back the uncut meadows under the sun and the smell of bees and honey and the foolish flittering of the corncrake when the mowing machine came nearer and nearer to its nest.

The whole village was helping, but Cahal felt that the whole village was not for him. For a time he had liked this annual getting together of everybody. Now it meant that he had to be days and days with people who no longer seemed to like him. He didn't want to do it, but custom made it a necessity. He was happier just going his own road and meeting them and nodding to them. Saying, A brave day, or, A soft day, and that was all. Jamesey Jordan was more embarrassed than anything else with him. He had got over the death of his father, but he had a sort of ashamed look when he met Cahal's eyes, so that they had very little to talk about. One look at Gob's face and he saw the pub in the town and Nessa close to him so that he could smell her and still get a sort of sinking feeling in his stomach when he thought about her.

So he rarely saw the people. He had become more and more like Peder. When he had finished his work, he would load a creel of turf and bring it to town and get the few shillings for it and maybe meet Peder in there or the jobber and they would have a few drinks and come home. So that you didn't have to meet anybody and life didn't seem so futile then. Tommy and Jennie were the only two he didn't mind. Jennie seemed to have taken a fancy to him. She could make him laugh at things. That was because they were young and he could look at them and think, Well, imagine, I was like that one time, a few centuries ago.

They topped the cock and raked it down and Gob went away to clean himself up and borrow the Murphys' trap to go and meet the train. She was coming to live with the Creels. Where else could she go?

Cahal didn't eat in the Cassidys' house when the work was done. He went home, resisting the blandishments of Jennie, the commands of Tommy, the frowns of Mary Cassidy who thought he was casting aspersions on her food. He left them all there, and he could think that they would be the easier for his absence, and went home to his own house.

She wasn't prepared for him, but she made him welcome.

"Why didn't you wait?" she asked.

"No why," he said, stripping his coat off and rolling his sleeves and pouring hot water into the tin basin.

"Is your grandfather coming?" she wanted to know.

"No," said Cahal, blurring the word as he rubbed the soap on his face. She poured water into the black saucepan and put two brown eggs to the boil.

"You wouldn't get much in Mary Cassidy's place," she said. "She is a very sloppy cook. I can't understand why these women won't learn how to cook a simple meal. You'd think it was for the pigs they were cooking all the time, the way they destroy the cabbage."

She looked at him as he dried his face with the towel. The black hair was thick on his head and growing down well on his neck, sprouting from his chest and heavy on his thick arms. His jaws were big and bulging. If I didn't know him, she thought, I would be afraid of him, he looks so black and sort of villainous. She sighed. She resented him now. Even if he wouldn't be a proper husband to her like God had bade him, he shouldn't make her look so small in front of all the people. She was sure they were all talking about her behind the back of their hands. Did the whole village know that he didn't even sleep with her, she wondered? Were they too stupid to see what he had reduced her to? She was a lady the day she came to Caherlo, and look at her now; her hands as raw as beef, and the bones showing through her from the amount of work she had to do. The terror it had been to her to accustom her body to the feel of rough woollen things and canvas aprons, and to have heavy woollen socks on her feet and the soiled linen wrapped around to take the torture from the big boots. And she was so alone, and so helpless. There was nobody to say for her, not even her own brother. She had seen him once since she was married. She had poured down her sufferings on his head. It was all his fault. He knew what he was marrying her into. His face was red. He stamped his boots on the ground. Goddam it, she was so mad for a man that she grabbed the first thing God gev her. Didn't she know what it was to be a farmer's wife? What about her own mother? And when the tirade passed and she hinted would he ever let her come back and stay with them, just to teach her husband a lesson, so that he would come after her when they found how much she meant to them, her brother hit the ceiling. He told her he'd tell the priest the wicked things she was talking about. For betther or worse, me girl, he said. For betther or worse. You med the bed. Now lie in it. She couldn't tell him how she would have to lie alone in it, having nothing ever beside her but hot phantoms of her own making.

"Maybe you'd take me to town with you a few times when you are going," she said.

Cahal looked at her.

"You can go to town whenever you like," he said. "The jennet and cart is always there."

"I'd like to go with you," she said. "People are remarkin' about you goin' to the town on your own. And what you do be doin' in there. Singin' for trickeys. You shouldn't do things like that. What'll everybody say? Won't it be bad enough to have them talkin' about us this way, than to have you giving them more things to chew on?"

"Let them chew," said Cahal.

He sat at the table by the window, waiting for her to hand him his tea and eggs. He rested his heavy chin in his hand and looked out the window. The same view. The white-washed wall and the red corrugated roof of the stable. The big plane tree towering over the road; the chickens pecking at bits in the yard and the ducks exploring the channel of water made by the draining of the manure heap. You could get to look on that, he thought, with different eyes. If in here was different, out there would be different. Was he to be like a motor for evermore, just ticking out his life, with no seeming purpose in it? He could be gay in town when he had a few drinks and congenial company, but it was unreal because it was an explosion arising from this. This would have to be fixed. But how? For ever and ever. Because he was caught in the quarter-mile like he told Máire one time. He rubbed his hair with his heavy hands. It could be so nice, if only he hadn't been cheated.

"You could be a bit nicer," she said, pouring tea from the brown pot. "If it was only for the appearance of things. You don't know what I have to put up with. You'd never stop and think of me. I wandered into this without knowing. I didn't think I was going to become a sort of slave for two men, that wouldn't open their mouths to me from one end of the day to the other. Don't you think you have punished me enough now in the years we have been married?"

He got up and took his coat from the settle bed and started putting it on as he went out the half door. She went after him calling, "Cahal! Cahal!" He didn't turn back to her. His teeth were clenched. She'll madden me some day beyond endurance.

He turned right and walked the road to the big bridge.

He stood there looking into the water. By the side of the bridge there was a deep grass verge where the tinkers came and camped. You could see the long marks they left and the odd bits of rags that were left behind them to become discoloured by the weather.

He waited on the bridge for a half an hour before he saw the trap coming, in the distance the horse kicking up a cloud of dust. What would the time have done to a simple soul like Bridie? Would it have turned her out like the other old woman behind him in the house? He'd soon know.

Gob stopped the trap. His face was as bright as a new shilling. There was a great gleam in his eyes. Gob is all right anyhow, he thought, and was glad.

"Hello, Bridie," he said.

She had lost weight. She wore a hat and a coat, but it was hard to recognize her because her face had become small, it seemed to him. The structure of the fine fat face was there but the flesh was loose on it. He thought a stranger was looking at him from deep eyes.

"Hello, Cahal," she said. "You shouldn't have sent that letter. If you had to write a letter like that, you could have wrote it before, not afther when it was too late."

"That was bad about the letter," said Gob. "I never knew about the letther. Bridie only told me now."

Cahal stepped back. He waved his hand.

"Pass on, stranger," he said.

He hit the horse with the flat of his hand. It reared and ran. Gob's face was red as he tried to pull him up. Bridie's face was white. "You are the end of a dream, Bridie Killeen," he shouted after them. "You went to the land of the free and you came back a slave. Goodbye."

He was furious. He jumped the wall beside the river and ran. It had to be like this, he thought. This was the way it had to be if only you stopped to think it out. What was the use of stopping and talkin' to them? He could. He could spend an hour with them and show them the way and have them again with friendliness coming into their eyes. He didn't know that he wanted friendliness to come into anybody's eyes. Only one.

Her father was dipping sheep down by the river. Cahal halted to watch him. He worked very slowly and neatly with the dog. The sheep were penned in a small grove and kept there by the dog. The man would walk up to one with his crook and get a sheep by the leg. He would catch a handful of the thick wool on its neck and its back and turn it towards the river incline. Then he would walk into the river until the sheep was almost submerged. He would rub it well. He was up to his thighs in water so that when he came out and freed the sheep his trousers and boots were dripping.

He saw Cahal on the hillock.

"Are you afraid of getting pneumonia?" Cahal asked.

He laughed. "No," he said. "It's just a short while and then it will be over. It does me good as well as the sheep. We haven't seen you for a long time. Are you well?"

"Yes," said Cahal. "I'm as well as can be expected."

"You don't sound cheerful," he remarked.

"No," said Cahal.

"It's a odd thing," he said. "Times when the work is over. When the hay is drawn and the oats is stacked and everything is ready for winter, country men become depressed. Why is that?"

"They get time to look at their neighbours," said Cahal, "and they can't bear the sight of them."

"Is that the way it is with you?" he asked.

"I don't know," said Cahal. He sat on the grass, leaning on his elbow. The sky was studded with clouds behind his head. Máire's father thought his eyes were very restless. He was chewing a blade of grass.

"That's not it," said Brodel. "They have worked very hard and then it comes to an end and all they have to do is chores, and they are bored. You know something – if I met you in the ordinary way and didn't know you at all, I would say, This man is not a farmer."

"Do you think that?" Cahal asked. "What would you take me for?"

He smiled. He shook his head.

"You'd be insulted if I told you," he said.

"Not me," said Cahal. "I have a Caherlo skin on me now."

"Maybe you were born at the wrong time," he said then. "You should have been born in earlier years. You might have been better off."

"What do you do," Cahal asked, "when you feel that men don't like you? That you are on a hill all by yourself. And you don't want to be there at all and it doesn't seem to be your fault that you are there?"

"I don't know," he said. "I have been a bit that way all my life, but that's the way I wanted to be."

"That's right," said Cahal. "You prefer sheep."

"That's right," he said. "I have very simple wants. I like to be with sheep and I like to be on great ranges like this, where you are small in a valley and men can't get near you. I like a fire at night and something to read, and rarely a bit of chat. But you're not like that, are you?"

"No," said Cahal. "I'm not like that. I like movement. I like people. I want them to like me. I like music. I like towns, but I don't want to live in towns. I like a whole of lot of things like that, but more than anything else in life I like your daughter Máire."

He saw him stiffening. I might as well part from him now as well as the others, Cahal thought, wondering have I a cruel streak in me after all, that I shoot a thing like that at a quiet inoffensive man? He felt himself calmly watching the reactions of the other. Brodel went and hooked out another sheep and brought it into the river and dipped it well, the sheep bleating miserably. Then he freed it and came back to Cahal. Had he expected me to go away? Cahal wondered.

"This is a small community," Brodel said then. "There's no policeman around the corner. There's no priest within six miles. It has to protect itself. It has primitive ways of protection. One sinner can upset the complete living of a small community. I'm just telling you this. What you do is your own business. If you want to fight them you can. But if you really like her the way you think, you will leave her alone. We have had one community down on us. We don't want another. Because this time I have come to a place I want and like. I won't leave it. You understand that?"

"If things had been different," Cahal asked. "If I had been a young man without a wife, and if I had told you these things, would you have welcomed me?"

"I told you what I am like," Máire's father said. "I would never offer violence to the wishes of anybody, even my own daughter. I didn't in the past. I wouldn't if the case was the way you said."

"You wouldn't give a damn, eh?" asked Cahal. "Well, just suppose that you were different, what would you think of me as a husband for your daughter?"

"I think I might be afraid of you," he answered slowly, "because I don't know what you are."

"I don't know myself," said Cahal, "and that's worse, and I don't know what I want. But maybe soon I will."

He rose to his feet. He smiled.

"You took that well," he said. "Maybe you don't think I'm too bad after all. In the whole place there are only two men with free minds. One is yourself and the other is Peder Clancy. Goodbye now. I'm goin' up to see Máire. You needn't fear."

"I don't," Brodel smiled back at him. "I don't fear that, but I fear the eyes that are watching you. Every time will be counted and it will be all added up and written down and some day it might be produced as evidence. That's what I'm afraid of."

Cahal left him.

She was churning in the kitchen when he came in.

"God bless the work," he said, going over and taking the dasher out of her hands and pumping it up and down in the wooden churn.

- 212 -

"Hello, Cahal," she said.

"You tell me something," he said, grunting between words as the dasher went up and down. "Why can I look at you with big men's boots on your feet and a canvas apron around your waist, and feel me heart thumpin' quicker than this dasher, and when I see another woman the same way I am squeezed dry of liking and love and sympathy?"

She laughed, pushing the hair back from her face.

"Because you are cracked," she said.

"Give me a sup of tea, girl, will you, for God's sake?" he said then. "I haven't had a bite since midday."

She put the kettle on the crook over the fire.

Why is this house so bright, he wondered, and our house so dark. It had the same number of windows, the same door, the same direction and exposure, and yet the whitewash seemed whiter, the fire seemed brighter and the delf shinier.

"I had to leave in a hurry," he said. "The house, I mean. I had to leave before I hit her. I barely could stop my arm from rising and bringing my fist across her face." His teeth were clenched, the muscles on his jaws were bulging.

"Cahal," she said, "don't talk like that."

"Well, it's true," he said. "It was an overwhelming desire, I tell you, and the only reason I didn't hit her was because I knew that if I once did that, I was chained to her forever. Isn't that a quare thing to say?"

"You can get rid of it on the churning," she said.

"Máire," he asked, "is there no place at all in the world for us? Would you have the courage to come out the door with me now dressed as you are and the two of us to take the high road and never come back, just go on and on?"

"To where?" she asked.

"That's it," said Cahal. "To nowhere."

"That should be done now," she said, looking at the little pieces of butter that were dashed up the hole in the top of the churn. She took it from him and raised the lid. "Yes," she said, looking in, "it will do." She rolled the churn away to the corner of the kitchen. He saw down at the table, his head on his hands.

"I feel a great restlessness," he said. "Something inside me that wants to burst."

"I hear you go on a burst in town," she said.

"Everything you do or say or think goes back," he said. "That's what sickens you. Listen, Máire, whatever you hear about me, I do it all for you or because of you."

"Don't saddle me with your sins," she said.

She poured out the tea. He caught her hand above the wrist. He rubbed the skin softly between his fingers, watching the light fair hairs on her arm. She stopped pouring the tea. His hand stopped moving on her arm. A long, long time seemed to pass. He dropped her arm. They didn't speak. She cut bread for him. It was cake bread she had made herself.

She sat well away from him, on the other side of the table.

He studied her. She looked back into his eyes. Her skin was very clear. It was tanned well, but it still seemed to shine from behind the tan. The whites of her eyes were clear and startlingly white when she opened them wide.

"We are two unfortunate people," he said.

"We are unfortunate through our own faults," she said.

"Máire," he asked then, "did you really love your man ... you know?"

"I thought so," said Máire, "until now."

He shut up.

"I shouldn't have come up, I suppose," he said. "It's really harder to bear than the thought." He rose from the table. "I'll go."

She didn't stop him. He was waiting for her to stop him, but she let him go. When he was outside the door she stretched her arms along the table and rested her head on them. Her copper hair was gleaming. She was breathing hard.

I haven't the courage anyhow, he thought, so what's the use?

He went the long way home.

Chapter Sixteen

Oh, God in heaven, He gave's light,
He made 's black and he made 's white,
But the curse of the Divil was on Him the night
He invented the tin-thumpin' tinkers.

IT WAS SPRING and he was poling for fish at the bend of the river.

It was a nice place. It was a deepish pool with a sandy bottom and the fish often waited there to see what the flow of the river would bring in to them. There were trees at his back and all around him so that he was in a sheltered place. The grass was very green in here and he was sitting on the bank with his legs dangling over the water. Because it was Sunday he had his new blue suit on and his newest boots that creaked protestingly every time he walked. They would get over that. His fishing-tackle was very simple. It was a young ash tree cut down with a piece of fishing-line tied on to the end of it. There was a hook at the end of the line with four of the fattest black-headed worms wriggling on it that you ever saw on your life. They were held in the stream by the cork of a porter bottle through which the line ran.

The fishing wasn't very good, but he didn't mind. It was Sunday, so he had plenty of time to spare. This had been his Sunday to stay at home and mind the house while Julia and Barney went off to Mass. It happened that way. Each Sunday one would stay at home and mind the house while the other two drove off to Mass. It always suited him. He liked being alone in the house these Sundays. Sundays in the country was mainly the smell of boot-polish and scented soap. People had to be respectable going to Mass in the town, well shaved and clean clothes and boots shining. They would all have breakfast, and then when he had seen them away he would wash up the breakfast dishes; they always had a fry for breakfast on Sunday, thick slices of salty bacon and eggs and fried scallions. Very nice and tasty. After that he would feed the roaring pigs from the big pot, throw handfuls of Indian meal to the hens and ducks, drive the cattle down to the bog pasture; put on the spuds for the dinner and the bacon and cabbage simmering and all would be right. Then he would sit there for a while with his melodeon and he would stretch his legs and play a few tunes for himself with variations. Traditional folk-song tunes that he knew, and as he played them new words for them would come into his head and he would fit them, laughing sometimes if it was a funny line that clicked into his head. Or sad sometimes when he thought. This was the only time he played any more, when he was alone in the house, and the other house-minders of the village would listen to the lively airs coming from Kinsella's and they would frown a little, thinking, It's hardly seemly in a way to be playing lively things like that and Holy Mass on in town, or they would think, There's the Bogman at it again. I wonder who he's makin' songs about now.

The other two would come home then. He would have the dinner prepared so that all she had to do was to turn it out on the plates while he put the jennet and the horse away. Then they would eat, and he would go out. To the river like now, for fish. An odd trout of good size or a prickly perch or a fat bream would fall to his wriggling worms, and they would prove very palatable for the tea. But mainly he liked the solitude of this part of the river, when he could lie on his back and watch the clouds in the blue sky or the black rain-clouds gathering. He could see great pictures up there and he could fulfil wishes like looking into the flames of the turf fire. He couldn't see the bridge from here at all and only a little bit of the road where it wound, so he was quite alone.

He often had thoughts with his eyes closed, of feeling a hand on his face and sensing the warm feeling on his skin that comes from the nearness of a woman. She would cover his eyes and he would have to guess Who is it? Máire, he would say, and she would bend over him and kiss him slowly, and she would pour out all the things he wanted to hear her say with her eyes soft for him, and he would hold her and tell her in a flood all the things that were raping the insides of him, and they would walk by the river with arms around one another and walk and walk, not caring who saw them, but always they would stop at the railway station, because his thoughts couldn't take them on a train. His life was circumscribed. There was a circle around the big town where he was at school, and a long gleaming railway line linking that with another circle around the town that provisioned Caherlo, and there you were in a tight circle that you couldn't break out of.

He thought he was still dreaming when he felt the two hands going over his eyes and his face enveloped in the warm feeling that could only come from the body of a woman. He put up his hands and felt two small hands over his eyes. He pulled them away and sat up.

"Well, you thief!" he said.

There was Nessa kneeling beside him and sitting back on her legs, her white teeth smiling at him.

"Hello!" she said.

"You're a thief," he said.

"I brought you back your purse," she said, digging into a pocket in her skirt. "It fell out of your pocket the night I met you and then Danno came before I could give it back to you, and there was a little biteen of money in it, but I spent that when we were short. I wouldn't have spent it at all, if we had met you in time."

He took the purse. It was indeed empty.

"That's a long speech for you," he said. "What are you doing here?"

"We kem last night," she said. "We're campin' up at the bridge. Are you pleased to see me?"

Cahal laughed.

"Well, God bless us," he said. "You're a cool one and no mistake. Was it a nice thing to do, to rob a man like that?"

"Oh, but I didn't," she said, her eyes wide. "The purse fell outa yer pocket. What are you doin'?"

"I'm fishing," said Cahal.

"You don't seem to be doing very well," she said.

"How in the name of God did you come on me?" he asked.

"I'm down settin' rabbit snares," she said. "Danno and the boy are gone off sellin' tin cans. I was over there in the field behind. They's lovely rabbit holes over there. Then I saw a man. I kem over. Then I saw it was you."

She was wearing a white striped shirt. It was open at the neck. Her face was shining. It was a sort of ivory colour, the remains of last year's sun. He thought she looked very clean. Even her hands were clean for once. She saw him looking at her.

"I washed in the river this mornin'," she said. "Every time we come to a river, we go washin'."

"And what brought you to Caherlo?" he asked.

"Oh, things," she said, smiling and looking at him out of the sides of her eyes. "Things. And I persuaded Danno that he should come back. Maybe I wanted to see you."

"That's enough of that now," said Cahal. "It's not a fair day now and me drunk in a pub and me sense astray. Besides I've only fourpence ha'penny on me, so it wouldn't be profitable."

"I like you," she said, rubbing her fingers on the lapel of his coat. "Danno didn't want to come. He's afraid of Misther Kinsella."

"I hope Misther Kinsella doesn't come up against him," said Cahal, "or he'll be gettin' some more stitches in."

"I don't think so," said Nessa. "They say Misther Kinsella got very old in the few years ever since his grandson hit him in the meadow."

"Where did you hear that?" he demanded.

"Oh, we hear everything," said Nessa. "Didn't Misther Kinsella get very old?"

Cahal thought. He leaned back on the grass to think. Think of Barney when you came when he was beating the dog. Think of Barney when he came back from Mass this morning. It took him a long time to get down from the cart, and the breath was short in his throat, and then Cahal remembered that he had reached a hand himself to help Barney down. He could feel a thin arm now in his fingers. His hand had nearly been able to span that arm. Yes, indeed Mister Kinsella had got old.

"If Danno goes near Misther Kinsella," he said, "I'll see that he gets the stitches."

She bent over him.

"You've quare eyes," she said.

"What's wrong with me eyes?" Cahal asked. Her face was very near his own. He could feel the touch of her breast against his chest. She put up a small finger and flicked his eyelashes. "Them are so black," she said. "You could have quare lights in your eyes if you lit them."

Cahal said: "Nessa, go away, will you?"

But he didn't raise an arm to push her away.

"I liked you from the first minute I saw you," she said, twisting the brass stud of his shirt around and around, so that he could feel her fingers against the flesh of his neck. He remembered the first time he saw her. "I washed me hair too," she said then inconsequentially. She raised a hand behind her to the bun, pulled, and her hair fell in long straight folds around her. "Feel that," she said, and she rubbed the strands of it across his face.

"God," said Cahal, "the divil is in you." He sat up holding her upper arms. They were substantial. They were soft. She fell back. He bent over her. Her lips were parted. Her eyes had no curiosity, no mockery, no seriousness. He bent down and placed his face against hers. It was cool to the touch. He kissed her and her arms rose up around his neck. Her hair looked very black against the green grass.

Your eyes are like stars on a frosty evening. Your hair is like the silken touch of bog cotton. Your breath is as sweet as heather honey. If only you weren't who you are. If only you were someone else. But you are songs in a way. You are the only incarnation of youthful dreams, not the white dreams of the clouds in the sky but the hot cloudless baking skies of summer, everything about you and around you heated by the burning beams.

The cork on the line behaved queerly. It wobbled and then it went under and it came up again and then it went under again and a strain came on the line that was holding it and the strain was translated to the pole that was left discarded on the grass near the edge of the bank. The pole gradually moved towards the water under the strain and then it halted for a moment at the brink and toppled over.

Julia was reading the paper for the old man. She was sitting on one side and he was sitting on the other side of the fire. She liked reading the paper for him. Cahal used to do it. They always bought the paper when they went to Mass on Sundays, and after dinner somebody had to read it aloud. It was very dull. It was about fairs and people that would interest nobody else in the world but the little parochial public for whom it was written. Father Murphy has been appointed P.P. of such a place. This hooliganism will have to stop, said the Justice, as he fined Martin Foley ten shillings for being drunk and disorderly in the green last Wednesday. It's a poor thing if in a Christian country a decent woman can't have an evenin' walk without being hooted at. The price of turf is again falling. The price of hay is up seven pounds a ton, owing to the bad summer. The Deputy addressed an overflowing meeting from a lorry in Valley. He said that the Government were doing nothing about the flooding of the area. Millions of pounds were being lost every year. Next time the people knew what to do with the Government. The County rates will be increased by one and eightpence in the pound.

She enjoyed reading. It made her feel that she was necessary. It gave her a feeling of superiority over the old man. Imagine not being able to read! But he knew figures. He had a little book that he totted up for the milk account. They sold milk to an institution in the town. He could add and subtract a column of figures while you would be looking around you.

He smoked his pipe and listened. He would grunt disapproval of this or comment shortly on that. He said bad words about the Deputy. She didn't notice that he was getting all that old. Because the years had caught up with herself, maybe. Anyhow when Danno came in the door with the new milk-cans on his arm he had a look at the old man before the eyes turned red with anger. Begod, it's true, his thought went. He's as old as an old horse. He saw the hollows in the neck and the temples, and the tightness of the skin about the cheekbones. The collar of the shirt wasn't fitting about his neck.

"God bless the house," said Danno, boldly opening the half-door and coming in. Julia halted her reading. She was looking at the old man. At the red that came into his eyes. He got to his feet. One time he would have been towering on them. He wasn't now. He had to spread the legs well to support his body, and they were bent under the weight of that.

"Get out! Get out!" he said in a choking way, the big bones of his hands clenched and failing to tighten the loose skin around the knuckles. The force of the way he said the words pushed some spittle on to his white straggly moustache.

"I will not get out," said Danno, coming well into the kitchen. "I've been waitin' a long time, Barney Kinsella, to be able to come into your house and not be sent chasin' out of it again with the blood floodin' out of me."

Barney turned and took the thick stick from its resting-place near the settle bed. He gripped it tightly and came across the kitchen, the stick raised in his hand. He brought it down. The blow was very feeble. Danno caught the stick in his hand and pulled. It easily came away. Then the body of the old man fell against him. Danno caught him by the shoulder and backed him into his chair. "It's no use, you see," said Danno, "you haven't the strength in you."

Julia was frightened.

She could smell Danno from here. He was very tall and grizzled-looking but strength flowed from him, and the smell of smoke and dust from his clothes. A small boy appeared around the door and sidled in. He caught her eyes on his and grinned. His hair was over his eyes and cut away around his head. It gave him an odd tribal look.

"I don't want to do anything to you," said Danno. "I just want to talk to you. It's a terrible thing that I have to wait nearly thirty years for you to get old enough so that I could talk to you." He sat on a chair out from them and left his cans on the ground.

"You never would listen to me, would you, you obstinate old bastard? Why? Because I'm a travellin' man. What's that got to do with it? If you'd let me talk to you I would have told you. I loved your daughter Nan. There, that's true. Maybe I'm a bad man. Maybe I drink and am rowdy and whip a few small things that I need. Well, does that make me a pagan, does it? I would have married your daughter if you'd let me. You hear that. I would have even settled down on a piece of land with your daughter if you'd let me. Did you know that? I tried to tell you that before you turned the dog on me and ran me out of Caherlo so that I haven't dared to show me nose in the place again."

"Go on now, go on now! Go away!" muttered Barney.

"I'd ha' even gone to church or chapel for your daughter Nan," said Danno, "but you send her out of the country before the child is cold out of her. You shouldn't have done that. I wanted to be a good man too. We were young that time. We were only twenty, the pair of us. We were young and well set-up and your daughter Nan was one of the most beautiful girls on the face of Ireland. I know. I have travelled all over it since, man, and I've never seen the like of her. Would you marry a tinker, ma'am?" he asked suddenly, turning to Julia.

"Why can't you go away and leave him alone," she said. "Can't you see you're not doing him any good? Them things are all past."

"No, they are not all past, ma'am," said Danno. "No matter where I've been I've never forgotten. I could have been different. I was a good man when I was young and knew Nan Kinsella. I wouldn't have been a tinker. It was him there that made me one, because he drove me away and drove her away. Why wouldn't I want a settled home like anybody else? Is men tinkers because they want to be or because they has to be? I don't know. But you married a tinker and you ought to know."

"What are you saying?" she asked, rising to her feet.

"What do you think I'm saying?" he asked her. "I'm telling you that you married a tinker. You married my son, ma'am, that I never laid an eye on since the day he was born until he's too big to be any use to a father. A great big drunken lout he'll turn out to be, you see, because that old man there, first he creased me, and then he creased his own daughter and then he creased the son. You ought to know that. And look at him now. A shrivelled wrinkled old man with one foot in the grave and you look at him and you wonder how a man like him could have done such damage to so many people, all because he was a proud set-up old fellow, that didn't want dirt thrown on his name, as if he had a name that mattered."

"You can't be right," she said. "Cahal is not your son."

"Take a look at me!" he demanded. He stood up. "Go on, take a good look at me! Who is he like? Is he like me or is he like him? Go on now! See for yourself."

The black hair, the deep sunken eyes, the big jaws and the blackness of him. He was an old soiled dirty edition of Cahal if you looked closely enough. She sat down again.

"Yeh," said Danno. "I wait this long. All these years I wait to walk in here and talk to the old one. And it's no use now. Because the time in between is too long. Long nights on the hillsides I twisted and groaned when I thought about her. She hadn't the courage to run out on him. She was afraid of me, that the tinker strain would bring her into the by-roads of the country, sleeping be the side of the ditches. But it wouldn't – do you hear that? There's nothin' I couldn't have done if I wanted to. I could have owned this country if I set me mind to it, and I would have for her. When I think of the things. And then there was nothing left but to come some day when he was too ould and feeble to hit and to tell him these things, and here I am tellin' him and what use is it now? It's no use. What good does it do? It doesn't do any good. Because it's all boiled away, so it is, like a rabbit that's left on a fire too long so that the meat of him is sodden and useless, like him, like the whole bloody lot of us. And it could have been different maybe. Come on, son, to hell out of here." He clipped young Danno a blow on the head with his fingers.

He turned at the door.

"'Shaw!" he said with a spit of disgust. "I shouldn't have come. What does it matter? Isn't it thirty years too late? Look at him. There's nothing left of him. He's nearly a dead man. And what is terrible is that there was never any need to be afraid of him. He should have been faced. Any man that would face him would have won."

He went to the door. He walked on to the main road.

The old man had his head in his hands. "I don't feel well," he said. "I think I'll go up and lie down." He made his way to his own room, helping himself with a hand on the back of a chair, and the settle bed, and the side table holding the cans of water near his room. Then he was gone. I married a trickey, Julia thought. A feeling of glee rose in her. She laughed softly. Think of that, she thought. The mighty Cahal with his top-lofty thoughts and his strivings and he's nothing but a tinker's get. Look what I've married into, she thought. I brought them clean pure blood and they spurn me. Him. Wait'll I see him. Wait'll I tell him. Wait'll I tell the whole of Caherlo. Who will the laugh be on then, I wonder? Who will they be laughing at then behind their hands? She went to the back of the door and got her head-shawl and put it on. She walked fast. Mary Cassidy's was near. She would be the first.

Danno didn't see the young trees sprouting by the side of the road. All the bushes, all the trees, even the young grass was peeping greenly from everywhere, the fresh young green of spring, the touch of the virginal green of the world that would go a little old, a little discoloured as the days passed by, so that it would never be as freshly green again for another year, but would mature and be lustreless, losing its colour to the coming blossoms, that would ripen and fall and become withered and yellowed and old. Danno was thinking, What did I make out of that? Wasn't that a dead loss? Who was Nan Kinsella? Was she real with him or was she just a dream in his mind? Why had he held on to the memory of her for so long? Was it because she was the only decent thing he could remember over his lifetime? There had been other young country girls willing to fall for the black beauty of him when he was young and had a leg like an ash tree. Why should she have remained with him? She was gentle. She was sensitive. She was a shrinking violet that when she flowered flowered like an orchid. Phantasies she had in her. Little stories, and a sort of peculiar charm that Danno had never met, so that in all his coarse virility he felt humble that she should have seen him and become loving to him.

It was just that he had lost something that might have changed things for him. He wondered would it. If she had, would he have sat down on a small farm for the rest of his life, content to look at her and work for her and fill her quiver? Was he ever any good at all? The curse of hell on it!

He crossed the bridge. The camp was empty. The fire was out. He cursed again. Where is she? Where is that whore? Why hasn't she the dinner on? The horse was grazing in the field by the river. She did that anyhow. She let him in there. Where would she be? He threw down the cans and caught up a stick and jumped the wall by the river. He went along the right bank. He didn't call. He came to the wind, his eyes searching.

He went another bit. He stopped and called: "Nessa! Nessa!" He thought he saw a movement on the opposite bank of the river, near the wind of the river, near the grove of trees.

"I see you! I see you!" he roared.

Cahal sat up. One minute she had been with him and the next minute she had gone, like a shadow, into the shelter of the trees. He got to his knees. Right across from him, he saw Danno, his legs spread, the stick being waved in his hand. Cahal stood up.

"What are you shouting about?" he asked.

"You black bastard!" Danno shouted across to him. "She was with you there. I know she was with you there."

"You're a liar," said Cahal to him, feeling that it was possible she could have got away unseen.

"I saw you! I saw you!" Danno was screaming. Cahal could see the tendons standing out on the side of his neck. His face was red and his eyes were bloodshot. He could see all that with the sun shining full on him. "A nice thing, you pagan, that you make a cuckoo out of your own father."

Cahal felt as if he had been hit.

"What are you saying?" he asked. His voice travelled even though it was low. There was terrible force behind it.

Danno noticed the crack in him. He laughed. "That fixed you, you ungrateful bastard," he said. "That's right. Look across at your father. Take a good look at your father. Now you know. Now Barney knows. Now the whole world knows because I told them."

"You're a liar," Cahal found himself screaming.

- 226 -

"No!" said Danno. "You black divil. Take a good look at me, boy. Take a good look at your long-lost father."

"You're a liar! You're a liar!" roared Cahal. He was trembling with fury. He bent down. He searched around. He found a large stone. He tightened his fist around it and aimed it at the figure on the opposite bank. "You're a goddam liar!" he screamed and flung the stone. It was a big stone. It was only terrible angry strength that sent it so far. Danno dodged it easily and jeered.

"Now, now, now," he taunted, "who'll be a show in Caherlo? Who's the black bastard of Danno the Tinker?"

"Hello, Danno," said Nessa, coming up beside him. "Were you callin' me?"

Danno's mouth dropped open as he looked at her. If she was on this bank how could she have been on the other? She didn't cross by the bridge because she came from the side away from the bridge.

Cahal saw the two of them there. He was seeing them through a mist of anger and a sort of panic that was flooding over him. If this was true – but it couldn't be true. But if it was? What then?

"What were you roarin' for, Danno?" Nessa asked. Her hair was wet. She was squeezing it with her hands. "I was down beyant washin' me hair when I heard you calling." The river wasn't fordable. Her clothes were dry. He didn't notice the water dripping from her body under the long skirt.

"You weren't over ther' at all?" he asked.

"How could I be there when I'm here, Danno?" she asked.

"Great God!" said Danno.

"Here, you," he roared across the river. "I'm sorry, boy. I didn't mane what I said. It's all a mistake. I was oney cursin' you."

"Did you tell him at last that he was your son?" Nessa asked in a loud clear voice.

"Shut up," said Danno. He hit her across the face with the

back of his hand. She fell down. She looked up at him, like a cat, her lips drawn back from her teeth.

"If you only knew! If you only knew!" she bit out at him.

"If I only knew what?" he asked. "Answer me!"

"Nothin'," said Nessa. "Nothin' at all."

Cahal was calling.

"Did she know what you told me, Danno?" he was asking. "Did that one know?"

Danno was sorry now for all the trouble he was causing.

"If there was anything to know, she knew it," said Danno.

"The curse of God on you, Nessa, do you hear that?" Cahal called. Was it possible for God to make a woman without a soul? He turned away. He stopped then. Behind him there were two figures standing. They were the two young Murphys. Away to his right, there was another figure standing. That was Tom Creel and where he stood now he could see the bridge. He could see Jamesey Jordan leaning on the stones and spitting into the water. How long had all these eyes been there? What had they seen? What had they heard?

Cahal stumbled away from the grove, where he could cut across the road and down to the empty loneliness of the boglands.

Chapter Seventeen

The Canon drives up in a fearful state
And he dins his horn at Peder's gate;
  "Come here, you pagan,
  And give 's a rason
For missin' your Men's Retrate."

"Dear Canon," says Peder, "don't give me blame.
Me boots is in flitters, me clothes the same,
  Lackin' in riches
  The back a me britches
Won't let me to Church for the naked shame."

"Christ's feet were bare and He walked far –
From the round of the earth to a glittherin' star!"
  "That's true," says Peder
  With no more blether.
"And He didn't get there in a mothorin' car."

CAHAL WOKE UP sweating. He sat up feeling his heart pounding with terror. It was dreams. But at the tail-end of the dream he could have sworn he heard somebody calling. He listened now. There was nothing to be heard except the monotonous clicking of the clock beetle in the mortar of the fireplace. He raised his hand and wiped the sweat away. It was some time before the terror left him and he could lie back again. The settle bed wasn't comfortable, but he was used to it. In the day it would fold up into a wooden box that you could sit on. In the night it was let down to form a big rectangular coffin, so that you were enclosed. There was nothing between him and the boards except fresh straw packed into a canvas sack. It was changed at times when the straw became stale.

There! What's that now? It was a faint voice calling, "Cahal! Cahal!" It was coming from Barney's room.

The night was pitch black. There were no sparks from the raked fire. The blind was drawn on the night outside. He felt his way out of the bed. The stone floor was cold to his feet. He knew where the oil-lamp rested. It was on the window. He had blown it out himself. There was a box of matches on the window-sill. He got the lamp lighted. He shivered with the cold. He pulled on his trousers that were thrown on the back of the chair. He went to the closed door of the room. He listened. He heard a faint moaning. He lifted the latch and went in.

Barney was out of the bed. His naked legs, terribly thin, trailed on the floor. His arms were on the bed. He was trying to pull himself up on to it, but was failing. His face was buried in the bedclothes. There was a candle lighted on the chair beside the bed, and the old tin trunk that he kept under the bed was yawning open. Cahal left the lamp by the candle and bent and lifted him. He was as light as a feather. He put him in between the sheets and pulled the bedclothes up around him. His eyes were open. They turned to look at his grandson. He made movements with his mouth, but they didn't seem to get beyond his throat. His eyes were wild with endeavour.

"What is it, Barney? What's wrong with you?" Cahal asked.

He felt sorrow. He would have done anything at all for Barney at that moment. And he would have if the mouth hadn't closed and the Adam's apple run up and down his neck and he died, there in front of his eyes. Cahal couldn't believe it at first. He shook him. He called softly. It was no use. It isn't possible for a person to die like a snuffed candle. But it was.

Cahal stood up, and looked down appalled at the thin dead figure under the clothes. He wanted to leave the room and close the door and wait for the light of the morning. His feet took him part of the way and then his mind brought him back. Barney Kinsella is dead. You wouldn't think that face with the white bristles on it, the sunken cheeks, the bones standing out, a face drained of strength and thought, was indeed Barney Kinsella. To be sure, he put his hand inside the shirt. There was no movement under the sticking-out ribs. Barney is dead all right.

It was a bare room. It smelled musty because although there was a fireplace no fire was ever lighted in it. There had been a fire in it in the winter months long ago when Barney's wife was bearing her children. It was a big double bed with a feather mattress. The brass knobs gleamed dully in the light now. The light didn't get into the shadows. There was one big holy picture over the dead fireplace. There was nothing else on the walls. No picture of Barney as a young man with a light in his eye and tall collar. No picture of the happy husband with a beaming young wife in a black bonnet; no picture of a proud father surrounded by children dressed in Lord Fauntleroy suits.

He looked into the open tin trunk. It contained very little. There was a purse which he opened. It contained five pounds in notes. There was a box with notebooks in it. There were simple books with columns of figures on one side and some on the other. They were made up to date. What came in and what had to go out. A large M was milk. It was all there meticulously, how much Barney had made from the milk, and the oats of last season set off against the bags of flour it had taken to feed them. There was outlay for bacon and meat and sugar and tea and a few other things. They were all to be guessed at. Just large letters as if Barney had asked someone how do you spell Bacon, and on being told had laboriously drawn or copied a B.

There were bills from the tailor, to suits for Mister Kinsella and Cahal Kinsella. Boots. Demands for rates. Land annuities. It was all as clear as a bell. What was clear was that Barney owed around one hundred pounds to various people, and unless there was some more money somewhere there was only five pounds to meet it. No post-office book, no bank book. There was nothing else in the box, except the stone with which he sharpened the scythe. There was a green silk tie rolled and put away, two white handkerchiefs with initials B.K. in the corner, and a bundle of letters, not tied, just left there. He looked at the envelope. They were written by an unformed hand and addressed to Mister Barney Kinsella, c/o the Post Office.

Cahal opened the letter and read it. He read the others as well. There were about twenty letters in all; the ones at the bottom were yellowing already.

Goodbye, he thought then, to the money that came with me wife Julia. Goodbye to any hope except by the sweat of my brow of paying off the bills he has left behind him. Goodbye to the farm unless I can work night and day selling and sowing to make up for the load on it. He sat on the bed and looked at the dead man. It had to be something like that. Under the cold eyes, the gruff voice, the deliberate cruelty, he had been vulnerable, of all things to the daughter that had injured him the most. All the letters were signed, "your loving daughter, Nan". From an address in New York with a fabulous street number and a number of a house, in the thousands. They were niggling little letters, grudging gratitude for what he had already sent her and begging for more. She was married, the children were sick, her husband was out of work. He seemed to be the same way all the time. She had reasons. That it was the Depression. That the foreman was cruel to him. That he was sick. That she was sick, that they were all sick, and no letter that didn't fail to complain, "Why, oh why, Father, did you drive me away from home?" She never once asked, he noted wryly, how things were faring with her little son, or what had become of him. She wanted Barney to write to her. It seemed so terrible just to get those Postal Orders, with not a line in them

- 232 -

for her. Couldn't he get somebody to say a word for him, to let her know how things were going? No line. He just got the address written to her, probably by the assistant in the Post Office, stuck in the order and sent it away.

Cahal looked at him.

So that was the hard man, he thought. He was as weak as water when it came to her. Why? Because he had really loved her or because he felt he might have been wrong not to keep her at home to get over her shame? Great God, who would have suspected Barney of that weakness? And even from her letters you could tell that she wasn't much good. He thought of the other letters Barney got from his children. They were all right. They weren't well off but they sent him something now and again. He had little respect for them. But here was her ladyship draining him of every little he possessed, and the subtle way he hid it all, with her writing to him at the Post Office and he sending her money from there. Who read her letters to him? Did he have to go out on the street and find somebody and say, Read this, will you? He must have had somebody when all her appeals were answered, including Cahal's dowry, the only reason he had married. He had to grin, even there, looking at his dead grandfather.

I'm sorry about the day on the haycock, Barney, he told him quietly. You and I had worked out a system of living together. I even liked you in the early years. I like you now too, because you were a weak man after all, and because you could let a heart run away with a hard head. Great God, what did he get out of life at all? Marry and work and kids who go away. If you thought now, Barney couldn't have been such a tyrant or he would have kept some of them at home, or was he such a tyrant that they had all to flee from him? Is that what is to become of me? Only I'll have no kids. And I would like kids. I'd like to go to town and bring home a bag of sticky sweets in my pocket, so that they would be waiting and wondering what time they would see me, and they'd be back at the bridge watching for the sight of my cart.

He took the letters with him to the kitchen. He raked out the fire and blew on the red coals until they blazed and he put on a few sods of turf until he had a good fire and then he burned the letters one by one, until there was nothing left of them. Then he went back and took two pennies from his pocket and he closed the open eyes with his fingers and he put the two pennies on them, and when he had all that done he went to the door of her room and he knocked until she wakened and when she said, "What is it? What is it?" he said, "Would you come down now? I think oul Barney is dead."

Then he went back up to him.

He was leaving the graveyard when the young priest tapped him on the shoulder.

It was outside the gates. All the horses and jennets were tied to the railings. All the village was there; he had to grant them that, even though they had made a point of giving their sympathy to Julia who accepted it. He had held Máire's hand in his own. She didn't say anything, looked into his eyes. He hadn't seen her for a long time. Wondered if she had heard about Nessa and the bridge, a long time ago now, and about Danno. If she did, it didn't matter. Her eyes were clear. Her father said in his soft voice that he was sorry too.

"Will you call in to the Canon on your way down, Kinsella?" the young priest said. It wasn't a question. It was an order. The young priest didn't stop to think about this himself. All he knew was when the Canon wanted anybody to come to him, they came.

The Canon wasn't at the funeral. He was very old now, they said, anyhow, and then Barney Kinsella was not a well-known man except to the village and its surroundings.

"What does he want to see me for?" Cahal asked.

"I don't know," said the priest. "He just told me to tell you."

"Right," said Cahal, and the young priest got into his car and went away.

"I wonder what he wants to see you for?" Julia asked as he got on the plank beside her.

"I don't know," said Cahal, shrugging his shoulders and flicking at the horse with the whip.

"I hope it's not more trouble," she said. "We have had our share of troubles now. We should be left alone."

"Gup our that," said Cahal to the horse.

"They all came to the funeral anyhow. Did you see my brother?"

"I did," said Cahal.

"He's heard queer things too, over in Valley," she said. "Our name is going over the whole country."

"See," said Cahal, "you married into fame as well."

"It isn't the kind of fame I'm wantin'," she said with her lips tight.

"I won't be long," he said, when they came to the Canon's gate. It was a nice two-storey house set well back, with railings and a broad path up to it, with shrubs that were dead now in the winter except for a few evergreens.

"Shouldn't I come in with you?" she wondered.

"You should not," said Cahal, putting the reins into her hands. "You can hold the horse."

He jumped down and went up the driveway. There was a glass porch on the front of the house with two steps up to it. There were flowers in pots inside that were doing nicely even in the winter. He rang a bell on the door. The other door inside opened and an old lady with white hair came out to him. "Well?" she inquired.

"I'm Kinsella," said Cahal. "They tell me the Canon wants to me."

"Oh, yes," she said, stepping back. "Come on in. Isn't it very cold?"

"It is," said Cahal.

"This way," she said.

There was a hallway carpeted, and a stand with a black coat and a hat on it and an umbrella. The stair in front was painted white with a red carpet looking startlingly red mounting it. The four doors off the hall were painted white too. There was a picture of Christ being taken down from the Cross. It was a good picture. It was very stark. It looked very real. She went in the door on the left and closed it behind her. Cahal felt awkward standing there. He was conscious of his hobnails biting gleefully into the carpet. He had the whip in his hand. What could he do with it? Nothing. He couldn't put it into his pocket. That made him smile so he was smiling when she said, "This way," and passed her by to go into the room.

There was a very bright coal fire and the Canon was sitting in a deep chair facing Cahal when he went in. It was a nice room. There was a highly polished table and a sort of sideboard with gleaming glass things on it and a big thick carpet. It was a man's room. There was a pipe-rack over the fireplace.

The Canon had one of the severest faces Cahal had ever seen. His hair was pure white, and what was left of it was standing up on his pink scalp. His face was pink too. There were pouches under his eyes and his eyebrows were shaggy and drooping over the blue eyes, shrewd eyes, Cahal saw, that wouldn't miss a thing. His mouth was drawn down at the corners and his jowls were hanging. He looked fearsome.

The Canon, for his part, saw a tall, very black-looking country boy who was no longer a boy but a man, with black hair uncovered and falling over his forehead, a deep furrow between his eyes and lines bisecting his strong jaws. Odd eyes, the Canon thought, very odd eyes.

"You're a black-lookin' devil," said the Canon. "Sit down."

Cahal sat on the chair opposite him. He found himself sinking back into it, so pulled himself up to sit on its edge. He had the whip dangling from his big hands.

"I thought you were shockin' fearsome-lookin'," said Cahal.

This diverted the Canon.

"Did you?" he said. "Well, I can be fierce when I like."

Cahal said nothing. He looked back into the shrewd peeping blue eyes, very cold blue, like the sky on a frosty night. He didn't look down or away.

"I hear things," said the Canon.

"I'm sure you do," said Cahal. The Canon's hands were joined across his stomach.

"I have been nearly fifty years in charge of this parish, young man, and I have been in every bit of it, and when I thought of Caherlo at all I thought of a small schattered village near the bridge. Your grandfather is dead. I knew him. I said Mass out in that house of yeers once."

Cahal didn't comment. Let him get on with it.

"Humph," said the Canon. "Well, in all that fifty years, I never heard the name of Caherlo mentioned so often as in the last few years and when I thrack it down I find at the end of it the reason. You know the reason?" He barked this.

"No," said Cahal.

"You," said the Canon and rubbed his hand down his mouth. Cahal saw that the flesh was very loose on the hand. He must be eighty or ninety, he thought, if he is a day.

"Why me?" Cahal asked. "I'm only a small farmer in Caherlo."

"Well, for a small farmer," said Canon, "you create a hell of a lot of fuss."

"How do you mean?" Cahal asked.

"There's no use pullin' your eyes down at me," said the Canon. "I've seen enough fellas pullin' their eyes down at me, and it never stopped me yet from sayin' what I have to say. Why did you make up that song about me and Peder Clancy?"

"I don't know," said Cahal. "It's a good song. It just came into me head."

"Well, it's not a true song," shouted the Canon, banging the arm of the chair. "Peder Clancy never said a thing to me about a motherin' car and besides that I don't talk with turf in me mouth like the Canon in the song. I was always noted for the purity of me spoken English. You hear that?"

"I do," said Cahal, laughing in his belly.

"Did Peder Clancy tell you the story that way?" the Canon asked.

"Maybe he didn't," said Cahal. "Maybe I only made it up."

"I know well he did," said the Canon. "It's just the sort of story he would tell. But there was no endin' to it. I just asked him why he wasn't goin' in to the retrate, or told him he'd betther or I'd turn him into a drake. That's that. You never heard that from him. But he's the hero when the story is tould, and I'm the what do they call it, the sucker. Is that right?"

"It's only a song, Canon," said Cahal. "It won't hurt anyone. It's a laugh. What's wrong with that? Everyone knows you. Everyone seems to like you."

"They betther," said the Canon. "It's too late now to call back the song. Every idler in the whole parish is at it. So pass it by. I'm too near the grave now anyhow to do anything about it. There's worse things I hear. How many million people in the world, man? Tell me that?"

"I don't know," said Cahal.

"There's a lot," said the Canon. "And why do you want to set yourself above them?"

"I do not," said Cahal.

"I hear tales from that village that'd curl me hair," said the Canon, "if I was young enough to suffer for them. I hear a lot about you. Is it true that you are a loose liver, tell me that?"

"No," said Cahal, "I won't tell you. You have enough tellin' you. I'll be goin' now, Canon, if that's all you want." He stood up. His jaws were tight.

"Sensitive too," said the Canon, sneering. "Sit down, man, I'm not that bad. I don't believe everything I hear. If I did there wouldn't be room in hell for all the people of my parish. Sit down."

Cahal sat.

"I know your trouble," said the Canon. "First you are a bastard and second you were married off to a sister of James Bright of Valley and she could be your mother. Is that right?"

"Your information is brutally true," said Cahal, his teeth on edge.

"Right," said the Canon, "That's at the back of you. We won't argue about marriages. Most of them are that way and a lot of them turn out for the best, but not yours, hah?"

"Not mine," said Cahal.

"Right," said the Canon. "Now if I was in your boots I'd be tempted to hammer hell out of the woman in the first place and to eye every young girl that goes the road in the second place. You can do neither. Because you are a member of the Catholic Church and what God puts together no man can pull asunder. You can't break your own chains. Hear that? Do you want me to put it that way?"

"That says it," said Cahal. "No redress."

"God will give you that," said the Canon. "He doesn't miss much. But listen, do you think you are the only person in the world who has been badly treated?"

"No," said Cahal. "But I have a bitther interest in meself, not in other people."

"You'll have to get rid of that," said the Canon. "Everyone in this world has a load to carry and yours is not the worst. You'll have to bear it temperately. Because why? Because there are men in your village who don't like you and they will pull you down, and then you'll go writin' bitther songs like the rest of them how the Church hounded you. Isn't that true?"

"No," said Cahal, "I don't think so. I can fight my own corner."

"That's what I'm afraid of," said the Canon. "Now listen. You have a bit of brains. I can see that. Accept your lot, man. What else can you do?"

"Nothing," said Cahal. "Nothing else, is there?"

"There are lots of things," said the Canon, "but the hardest of them is what you have to do. To settle down and be a small man when you want to be a big one. That's your destiny, me man, to be a small farmer in a little village."

"With grandchildren around me knee," said Cahal.

"I know," said the Canon, "I know. You have a hard row to hoe, man. But can't you look on it with charity? You'll be a betther man at the end of it be accepting than be making your name a byword. Where will that get you?"

"It might get me freedom," said Cahal.

"It might get you the semblance of freedom," said the Canon. "But you are not free. You can never be free. Isn't it betther to accept that now and make up your mind to it? Listen, man, I know those villages. Haven't I been giving them sermons and listening to their confessions all me life? Leave them alone. Become a part of them or they'll vomit you out, and then where will you be?"

"Nobody will vomit me out," said Cahal.

"All right," said the Canon. "I have told you. Don't give them any more to talk about for the love of God. They have you on their minds now and everything you do will be blown up. You look a decent young man to me, and maybe an unusual one. Try and be good, will you?"

"I will, Canon," said Cahal, "but the trouble about me is that when I try to be good, people see badness in the good things."

"That's what I'm tellin' you," said the Canon. "Well, that's that."

Cahal stood up.

"There's only one more thing I'm askin' you," said the Canon.

"What's that?" asked Cahal.

"Write me out a copy of that song," said the Canon. He winked and chuckled. Cahal laughed. "I'll do that," he said.

"God bless you, boy," said the Canon. "Be good! Be good!"

He took up a book that was by the side of his chair.

Cahal went out. The Canon heard the door closing. I

wonder, he thought. He's a queer young man. There's a curse of the divil on these marriages. I hope he'll be all right. But dammit I do spake good pure English!

There was another cart outside the door.

Peder was standing at the head of the horse. When Cahal closed the gate he came over to him.

"What did he want? What did your man want with you, Cahal?" he asked.

Cahal debated with himself and then told the truth.

"He'd heard the song, Peder," he said.

Peder wiped a handkerchief on his brow.

"God, I knew it," he said, "I knew it would come to his ears. What did he say about it? What did he say about me?"

"Well," said Cahal, "he said that he talked pure English and that you never said anything about the motherin' car."

"God, Cahal," said Peder, "you should never have med up that song. Why did I ever tell you that story? It was only a story. I never thought it'd go past you. You shouldn't have med up that song."

"He should not," said Julia from her eminence on the cart. "It's a disgrace. They have the whole place laughin' at the Canon."

"Don't be stupid," said Cahal.

"Well, it wasn't fair to me," said Peder. "I thought betther of you, Cahal Kinsella."

"Arrah don't be cracked, Peder," said Cahal impatiently. "It's only an oul song for a laugh and you'll be more famous than the man that made it."

"I don't want to be famous," said Peder. "I don't want to be famous that way. Holy God, I can't go into town now but I have the children pointin' me out on the street, and they roaring it afther me. That wasn't a thoughtful thing to do, Cahal. Think of the way it laves me. A sort of pagan. That I'm up against the Church and the Canon. You shouldn't have done it."

"What's got into you, Peder?" Cahal asked. "There was a time when you could see a joke too."

"This is no joke for me," said Peder. "It might be a joke for you, but I don't feel like laffin'. I've gone all me life with men respectin' me. I have them pointin' me out now and laffin' at me behind me back, all on account of a few lines in a song that you need never have done."

"Have it your own way, Peder," said Cahal, angry and getting up on the cart. "And to hell with you."

"All right," said Peder. "All right. I'll have it me own way. But I won't forget it in a hurry. It was a hand of an inemy that did it to me. It couldn't be the mind of a friend."

"Gup our that," said Cahal to the horse, flicking it with the reins. It passed Peder by. His face was red. Cahal kept his face averted.

"I won't forget. I won't forget!" Peder shouted after the cart. Then he debated with himself, plucked up his courage and went into the Canon's house, ringing the bell, wiping his face with his red handkerchief, making up plausible speeches in his mind and finally gaining entrance to provide the Canon with a lively and amusing interlude in the even tenor of his old age.

Chapter Eighteen

Come all ye neighbours far and near,
The great machine is pantin' here,
They's yellow stacks of oats to thrash
Before the winds of winter lash.
Come laughin' girls and brawny men
From Ballybla, from Grove, and Glen.
We'll labour first and then we'll glee,
The day is short, the night is free.

THEY WAITED.

Cahal and the machine man waited in the oat-field; Julia waited in the house with her white linen apron around her. The tables were set with the white cloths. The stacks of food were prepared and ready to go into the pots that were boiling on the fire. Nothing was wanting except the people. It was nine o'clock in the morning, and they were leaving it a bit late. By now the yard outside the door should have been filled with carts released from animals and bicycles white with dust. The oatfield opposite the house should have been filled with the chug of the tractor engine turning the belt on the big yellow threshing machine.

Every year, at threshing time, the threshing man came with his machine, and each year he would start with a different house, so that every house would have a first time over the years. This year it was Cahal's turn to be first. It was the custom for all to come and give a hand with the threshing and each day for the labour force to move on to the next place. It was like the drawing of the hay again, a grand bout of communal labour. There were two large stacks of oats in the field. There should have been men ripping at them now and throwing the sheaves to more men on top of the ugly thresher who would feed the sheaves into the maw of the machine, that would gather them in greedily, crop them in its craw, and other men would be holding the necks of the bags to the flow of grain at the back and other men in front gathering the discarded straw and building it into awkward straw cocks.

The man was tinkering at the tractor with an oily rag. He was a heavy young man with powerful arms that were brown and stained with grease. The cap on his head was the same. Cahal was leaning against the stack smoking a cigarette, and not believing that they were going to do this to him. Whatever happened he had always given them his labour in his turn even if he had felt uncomfortable; he had worked all the harder for that reason. He felt sweat under his arms now and on his forehead. He would have to have help for the threshing. It couldn't be done by one man alone. They couldn't be going to do that to him.

"What's up?" the machine man asked, coming over rubbing his hands on the cloth.

"I don't know," said Cahal. "Maybe they'll be here soon."

"They should all be here now," said the man. "They always are. It'll take us two days if they don't show up soon. Is there trouble about?" He was a bit worried.

"Nothing that'll interfere with you," said Cahal.

"I don't like it," the man said. "These things are nothing to do with me. Maybe we ought to call it off and I'll go on to the next place. Maybe they might come back to you later."

"You're getting paid," said Cahal. "You'll thrash this oats even if I have to do it all be meself."

The machine man didn't like the jut of his jaw.

"All right, man, all right," he said. "It's quare all the same."

He went back to his engine.

Julia came out of the house. She shaded her eyes against the late October sun. She walked across to the road. She looked both ways. There was nobody stirring. She could see smoke rising from the chimneys of the Cassidys and the Creels and Jordans. Very odd, she thought. They are up all right. She went into the field.

"What's wrong with everybody?" she asked. "Where could everybody be?"

"They might be all a bit lazy,"said Cahal, hoping.

"It looks to me," said Julia, "as if everybody was boycotting us."

She regarded him closely as she said it. His jaws were tight. There was anger in his screwed-up eyes. She was very glad. Even if it meant that all the food he had bought would be wasted; all her cleaning of the place from top to bottom; her days spent mixing the white-wash and putting the right amount of penny blue in it, so that it glittered behind her in the sun, very white, and the thatch very yellow and the window-panes blue with cleanliness, and the white lace curtains on the windows behind. It was a lot of labour but she was content to be at the loss of it, if nobody showed up. That'll teach him, she was thinking, the illegitimate tinker.

"Could you feed the thresher?" he asked her abruptly, "if I pitched to you?"

"Oh, no," she said, fluttering, looking at the big high machine. "Gup there on top of that thing. I'd be afraid of me life. I couldn't stand it."

"If I had only known they might do this," he said, "I could have hired some men to help us."

"It's a terrible insult to me," she said. "Think of all I had to do to prepare for them. Would I go over the road and ask some of them if they are coming? Gob Creel used to be a great friend of yours."

"You will not," he said. "Hey, you over there, I suppose you couldn't give a hand?"

"Not me," said the machine man, "I have to look after the

engine. If anythin' happens that we don't do nothin', whether or which."

"I see," said Cahal. He wanted to go out on the road and walk past their houses and stand outside each one and roar in at them what he thought of them. Their skulking. There seemed to be a terrible silence over the village. The swallows were gone away and the other birds were brooding and silent. There was no wind to stir the leaves on the trees. Let him get out of this one, Julia was thinking, her hands held in front of her, her eyes downcast in case he would see the way she was laughing with them. Now he might know what it was to be alone with himself. Let him get now what he gave to her all this time. The silence, the insulting abruptness of him to her, who was miles above him, and had lowered herself to the mud of the country to be married to him. She knew that the village wasn't against her. The village was very sorry for her. They knew the way she was treated. She had taken care to tell them. To drop a hint here and a word there. She never ever said that he hit her. But one time he was going to. She was bracing herself for the clout in the face. She had raised an arm to try and ward it off, but it had never fallen. The things I have to put up with, none of you will ever know. I lie awake at night, trembling in the bed in case he'll come in to me. He does be very savage at times. Not that he ever hit me, really, but the look over her shoulder was enough to throw doubt on that. She had hoped that when Barney died leaving a load of debt on the place, he would have to sell it and go away, go away to hell out of her life, so that her brother James would have to have her back whether he liked to or not. But he hadn't done that. He rose early and worked late. He cut twice as much turf and grew more stuff in his fields. He went every day, sometimes twice on the one day, selling turf in the town. He had cleared his way, and she was sorry.

She had only one joy in the struggle which he carried on, that at any given moment she could have said, Well, if you like I will give you the money to clear off the bills. Because she had it. She had three hundred and fifty pounds seventeen shillings in the Post Office. He was so stupid. She sold eggs at the market every fortnight, and she sold the pats of butter, and she would kill off an odd old hen and sell her too, when she had reared young chickens. He was too stupid to ask her to account for that. He never thought of it. She bought a piece of bacon and a pound of beef for dinner on Sunday and she bought the tea and sugar and he thought all of that egg money was used up on it, so that with every shilling that she put away, with every pound that grew into five, she knew a delicious excitement. It made her so happy, because she could look at him enigmatically, with that look in her eye. Every week is bringing me nearer and nearer.

"Maybe they will come yet," said Cahal, and he went slowly out of the gate and stood looking at the road.

We won't go over, the Murphys decided. They felt no uneasiness about it. Think of what that fella has done to us! Do we have to make a list of it?

"The best thing that could happen this country," said Mark, "is for him to get out of it altogether."

"I never liked him," said Sonny. "I knew the first day I saw him even when he was young that there was bad blood in him. He was too black to be wholesome."

"He's not entitled to Barney Kinsella's place at all. Did ye know that?" Mark asked. "Well, I know now. It's earlier we should have known that. Not to let near two years pass over our head. I wint in to the solicitor in the town. He could be turfed out of that place tomorrow morning. He has no title."

"How do you mean, Mark?" his wife asked.

"He's a bastard, isn't he?" Mark asked, "and in Irish law a bastard is a bastard and isn't entitled to the dust offa the road. He has no claim to the place at all. That place belongs, lock stock and barrel, to Barney Kinsella's eldest son in America. I'm gettin' me man to write to him offerin' to act for him."

"Did Barney not lave the place to the Bogman?" Sonny asked.

"He did not," said Mark. "There was no will at all. It's just a matter of possession, that's all. The place belongs to the eldest son, and I doubt very much if he'll want it. He never got on with Barney and he left for America whin he was nineteen, so he's not goin' to come back and claim it. So me man'll get in touch with him and offer him a fair price for the place in my name, a good round sum, say four hundred pounds, and I'm sure he'll sell."

"That would be nice," said Sonny. "It's good land and it's near all adjoinin' our own. We'd have no spreadin'. It could be worked easy."

"Maybe you're gettin' too much land, Mark," Mrs Murphy dared to say.

Her husband and her children looked at her as if she was mad.

"Hould yer tongue, woman," said Mark. "Are you gone cracked?"

"No," she said. "But maybe we're takin' too much on ourselves."

"For God's sake," said her husband. "Talk about somethin' you understand."

"I might be gettin' married, Ma," said Sonny. "And I could move into the Kinsella place. That'd be handy now, wouldn't it?"

"I suppose it would," she said. "But I do be afeard we have too much."

"Have sense for God's sake," her husband said. "Thim small farms don't pay for themselves. The whole village of Caherlo is only a good-sized farm really. It's against rason to have it split up among so many."

"Maybe so," she said, "but every one of them reared nearly fifteen childer apiece in the old days, and not one of them went hungry."

"And not one of them stayed at home," said Sonny. "How could they? Hadn't they all to go away? Well, they's none of us goin' away. So they's not."

"I know," she said, "I know, but it seems queer of ye not

to help a neighbour. It's always been done. People didn't get on before in the village but they went and helped when the time came."

Mark was mad. They thought he was going to hit her and they might have condoned the blow.

"They were real neighbours," he shouted at her. "Honest people. They weren't illegitimate drunken trickeys with no woman safe from them and no honest man safe from a dirty singing tongue."

"He gets all the women," said the thinnest of the Spits. "Maybe Ma fell for him too."

"Shut your mouth, boy," she said, rising and hitting him a blow on the face. "How dare you! If I stand up for the man it's because I like him and I don't think he's as black as yeer paintin' him. That's all. He was a nice boy. What chance had he ever? That's all." Then she went up into the bedroom with her face red and banged the door behind her.

"She's gettin' old," said Mark. "You shouldn't be talkin' to your mother like that."

"He got around even her," said Sonny. "He used to be in here long ago makin' her laugh."

"He can laugh now," said the hit Spit. "When he's trying to do six men's jobs with two pairs of hands."

They laughed at that. It was very funny.

"I think we'll go around be the river meadows," said Sonny, "and take a peep at him to see how he's gettin' on."

"Be cautious now, be cautious," said Mark. "He's as good as done now anyhow. He'll get notice to quit inside two months. Wait'll you see. We have him nicely tied up. Ah, well, thank God for a great day. Ye better get into the haggard and get the stacks prepared for the thresher. He'll be our way tomorrow."

Bridie knew that Gob was uneasy about it. He would get up from his chair at the fire and walk to the door and look out. He couldn't see anything from there, but he would look all the same. Then he would come back and sit down again, so that it was a relief when she had the breakfast prepared and put it on the table to him and called the old man down from the room. He was getting very old. He had to stay longer in the bed of a morning. Bridie was never impatient with him. Nobody could ever say that. He missed his visit every night to the Kinsellas. He didn't go since Barney died. There was no welcome for him. Julia didn't like all his spits on the floor. Cahal had nothing to talk to him about. So when Barney went he took a little bit of Tom Creel's living away with him. The nights seemed very long to him without the ramble to Kinsella's and the spasmodic conversations about things that they had talked about hundreds and hundreds of times. Bridie was a good girl. She had changed the appearance of their house for the better. There was no doubt about that. You could eat off the floor now and everything was shining.

"Bless us, O Lord, and these Thy gifts," he said, blessing himself and saying the grace. The moustache on either side of his split lip was white and the turned-up part of his lip was red so that it gave him a false look of being younger than he was.

"Eat your breakfast, Gob, for God's sake," said Bridie, sitting in to the table.

Gob pulled his thoughts back to them.

"Oh, yes, yes," he said.

"If you want to go out and help him," said Bridie, angrily stirring her tea, "there's nobody stoppin' you." She was sorry for being sharp.

"No, no," said Gob. He forgave her her sharpness. Her face was drawn and there were purple lines about her eyes. She would have the baby in two months' time. That should have cheered him. He often lay awake at night thinking about it, and when she would be in good humour she would let him put his hard hand where he could feel it kicking inside her. That was great.

"Well, don't be so restless so," she said.

"Leave him alone," said Tom. "Leave him alone, girl. I don't wonder that everybody in the village couldn't feel a bit ashamed. I'm a long time in it and it's the first time it's ever been known for to renage on a man on the day of the threshin'."

"Well it's not just us," said Bridie. "Everybody was agreed on it."

"I know that," said Tom. "It's a strange thing that there wasn't a single voice raised against it."

"Well, what could I do?" Gob asked. "Cahal pulled away from the lot of us long ago. He wasn't the same man. It was hard to talk to him. I tried to talk to him, I tell you, to show the way things were goin'. But he has everybody's back up so he has. We're not the only ones."

"If it was oney for the sake of his dead grandfather," said Tom, "the people should have helped him, even if they hate the sight of him. What has he done when it's all added up? Isn't he only his own worst enemy?"

"Now, Tom Creel," said Bridie firmly, "you don't be dotin'. Cahal Kinsella is a very bad influence in the place. Hasn't he the name of everybody in the village being hawked around the country in bawdy songs? What kind of a life does he give that poor wife of his?"

"I tould him the day he married her," said Gob, "that he was doin' wrong."

"Well, he shouldn't have married her," said Bridie. "Nobody was forcin' him to. Now that he married her he should make the best of it, not roarin' drunk in the town and being around with bad women. I liked him when he was small. He was a nice young fella. Nobody would ever think that a few years could make such a change in him."

She had a picture of him the night that she was hooleying before her departure for America. He was a clean-cut young man then. She was a soft thing anyhow. She had learned the hard way. For a few moments she had a picture of the big soft, sloppy girl she had been. Was she happier then, even that way? Maybe she was, but that was a long time ago. She was very young and terribly impressionable. Perhaps an odd creature like Cahal Kinsella would have appealed to her then. She might have taken the cruel letter her wrote as if it was kindly meant. Poor Gob was too kind to tell her. Every time she went and saw them now in the Home, getting older and older and more withered, she somehow thought of that letter. It might be unfair to think that it was all the fault of the letter that Foxy and her mother were where they were, but the two things seemed to be irretrievably mixed. She wished now that the two old people would die. She hated the visits to them. The red rheumy eyes, and all they could talk about was that they had to separate. They had thought it would be different or they wouldn't have gone at all. Thought that there would have been a nice little room of their own where they could have been together until the end. But it wasn't that way. They had to spend the long wide-awake nights of age apart from each other in wards like if they were in a hospital, and it was too late to see the other old people as anything but strangers.

"It would be betther for all if he went away," said Gob, as if he had been mulling it over and had finally come to the answer.

"He'll have to go," said Bridie.

"It must be a great thing to be God," said Tom Creel.

"Now, Father," said Gob.

"Well, isn't it true for me?" he asked. "Who is God? Isn't everyone in the village this mornin' God Almighty? What about if Cahal Kinsella is a bit odd? That's not for people like us to judge. That's something he'll have to answer to God about. What's it got to do with ye?"

"Look, Tom Creel," said Bridie, "you don't understand. You're too old. You can't be hurt be the things he does. But we can. Your life is nearly over in the village but ours is just beginning."

"Ah, hell with ye," said the old man, helping himself to his feet with his old hands tight on the chair back. "There's one man in the village that's goin' to live like we always lived. I'm goin' out to that field with me old bones and I'm goin' to help him. There ye are now."

"Father, you can't do that," said Gob rising.

"And who's goin' to stop me?" the old man asked fiercely, his thorn stick raised a bit in the air. "There's nobody goin' to stop me. I won't be much use, but I'll go to me grave when the time comes and I will have done the decent thing until I reach it. That's all."

"Now, Father," said Gob.

"Let him go," said Bridie.

Gob subsided in his chair.

The old man went out of the door. He walked very slowly. His back was terribly bent. His stick was a grim necessity. It took him quite a time to walk from the door of the house to the road.

"But, Ma, why can't I go?" Jennie asked. "He never did anything to me. I like Cahal Kinsella. I don't care what anybody says."

"Shut up, Jennie," said her mother, "or I'll clatther you."

"You have no sense," said her brother Tommy, lighting his pipe at the fire after his hearty breakfast. "You talk much to that fella and we all know the way you'll end up." He had grown. The pipe was part of his mouth. His hands were broad and the veins were beginning to bulge the young clear skin of them.

"I think yeer all jealous of him, that's what I think," said Jennie, "just because he's good-looking and because he can make songs and because he lives a bit like men and won't bury himself like a corpse down here until he gets old and withered and dies away like the rest of ye."

"Now, Jennie, that's enough," said her mother.

"Because ye have no laugh in ye," said Jennie, "and can't take a joke on yeerselves. That's why. And it's none of his fault either that he's married off to an oul wan that could be his grandmother. What else could he do? If it was me I'd coort anything in the country with a skirt on it afther one look at that dried-up oul withered hag his grandfather palmed off on him."

"I told you," said her mother, raising a strong right hand and hitting her across the mouth. The flesh on the arm was firm and the tendons stood out on it. "If I catch you talkin' to him ever again you're for it. Remember that. I'll take the switch to your arse the next time. Remember that."

"You still can't shut me up," said Jennie, feeling her tender mouth with her fingers. "I can think anyhow, and nobody'll ever make me think that he isn't a nice man and that he's being persecuted be the lot of you."

"I'll go after you in a minute now," said Tommy, "and really hit you, and just in case you'd have any notions –" He went up and closed the big door on the half-door and shut the bolt on it.

"Wash the dishes," said her mother. "You'd be betther employed than standin' up for that tramp."

"What do you really think of him, father?" Máire asked.

He took his time. That's what she liked about him, the careful way he listened and thought and then talked.

"I find him hard, Máire," he said. "You meet a man and you talk to him a few times and you exchange odd ideas, and you get a fairly good idea of what he is made up of, all the commonplace ingredients with the little spiced mixture that the Lord adds to all men by way of amusing Himself or amusing the rest of His creatures. He put a lot of spice into Cahal Kinsella."

"But how has he managed to annoy a whole countryside in a few years, tell me that? Is it so long ago that we met him? I remember. A big black young man with no harm at all in him, you would say. Like a black heifer in a field that raises his head and looks at you with inquisitive eyes. Cahal never set out to make them mad at him. It's all silly and stupid and maybe a little bit frightening."

"It's very simple," said her father, "and that's the trouble. It's simple things that kill men in small villages. A cow breaking a fence and cropping a little worthless grass. A remark passed in a pub over a glass of stout. Men have died violently because their chickens stole the tops off a few oats. It's the simple things. Because a village is like a family in a house. They get on one another's nerves over small things. There's very little dramatic in it and since we are all dramatic we have to create drama from the little things. Or life would be colourless and deadly too. You see, in a city they can go to restaurants and picture-places and they can escape into odd worlds as far away from their ways of living as a palm tree is away from a Caherlo ash tree. That gives them a lift out of the ordinary. The only lift to a drab life they have here is a row with a neighbour that will be carried on for a year or maybe more. The excitement they get from sharpening a claspknife on a stone and tellin' their wives how they are going to do for their enemy at the next meeting."

"Cahal is too honest," said Máire. "He plays his life in the open air."

"You can't do that," said Máire's father. "That hurts them. Cahal is too highly coloured for Caherlo. That's his trouble. He should never have come to Caherlo. He would be better off tramping the roads with his exotic father."

"Was that what was wrong with him, I wonder, the blood of his father in him."

"I don't think so," he said. "Cahal is two people. A man who is dying to be just a nice farmer with a white house and broad fields and a nice wife and children around him. And then he's a man who wants to sing and make people's eyes shine with a tune on a melodeon. His first dream has been shattered."

"Yes," said Máire. "That was a terrible thing to be done to any man."

"It was his own fault," said Máire's father. "He didn't have to."

"He was used to obeying, father," said Máire. "He had been obeying all his life. It was instinct in him. That's what I didn't understand until it was too late. What's going to happen to him?"

"I think he's in a dangerous way," he said slowly. "He's

not obeying any more. He's going to make up now for all the obeying he has done by fighting. He'll defy every man by song and by example. He doesn't care. He has found what was wrong. Freedom is a heady wine, so it is, and if you drink too much of it it will go to your head."

"How can you say he is free when he is so tied down?" she said.

"It's inside," said her father.

"They won't help him today," she said. "I know that they are all going to boycott him."

"It doesn't matter," he said. "He'll trash his oats if he has to use a flail."

"Well," she said, rising, "I have made up my mind. I'm going over to help him."

He was a bit startled. She noticed it.

"What is it, father?" she asked. "Are you afraid?"

"They have left us alone," her father said. "We have sneaked our way in and we have lain low. I like it here, Máire. I don't want to go on from it. I don't care what happens, I'm not going to go from here."

"And will it endanger you if I go over to lift a few sheaves of oats for Cahal?" she asked. Her head was on one side.

"You will be taking sides," he said. "That's dangerous."

"I don't care," she said. "I have been fighting Cahal Kinsella since the first day I saw him, and fighting myself along with him. I can still fight myself but I won't fight him, not any more. I'm going over to help him thresh, even if I have to hold one side of the flail. You know, father, I think it was a mistake for us to leave the other place. I think we should have stayed and fought them out. I think it is a mistake to run away. I'm not going to run away now from him if he is going to fight them."

"Whatever happens, Máire," he said, "I won't leave here. You understand that."

"Poor father," she said. "I have been a terrible burden on you. Where did I get my nature? It wasn't from you."

"You got your nature from God," he said. "You make

what you like of it after that. I have mine. Maybe I should have had more spice in my mixture and you less in yours. That's what it all amounts to."

"I'm sorry, father," she said. "I won't ever hurt you again that way. But I have to follow my own nose a bit too."

So Cahal, standing at the gate, about to turn away, saw a figure on a bicycle at the turn of the road. He paused and stood there with his hands on his hips, hoping. He saw her coming nearer and nearer. She was wearing a light frock. The breeze created by her bicycle was lifting her copper-coloured hair. She didn't wave at him. She was humming a song. She knew the words too. They had seeped out for the sake of scandal, the words of the song call *Máire Rua*. Her eyes were bright when she got off the bicycle in front of him. Her teeth were gleaming in a smile for him. She looked into his eyes. He read a lot in them. Even though we haven't met for a long time I know all about you. I know all that you have been up to. But maybe I know the reasons behind it all even if they bewilder you. Cahal's heart rose up and he grinned at her.

"Well, Mister Kinsella," she said. "I've come for the threshing."

"God bless you," said Cahal, "and the day is fine."

"Well, we better get on with it," she said. "We have only the short day."

"That's right," said Cahal, "the short long day."

They were about to turn in the gate, to face into the stiffened body of Julia, her lips tightened over her teeth, her nails biting into the palms of her clenched hands, shame and bitterness flooding her breast, when they heard a call from behind them. They turned.

They saw old Tom Creel hobbling on to the road outside the Creels'. He waved the stick. "Hey there! Wait there!" he shouted. "God bless the work. I'm comin' in for the threshin'. I'm betther than any two min in the village of Caherlo."

Máire left her bicycle resting against the hedge outside the gate. She looked at Cahal. They laughed. Cahal slapped his hand on a thigh.

"More power, Tom Creel," he cired. "Three cheers for freedom."

He had to help the old man into the field with one hand under his elbow. He felt very good.

"You are as welcome as God," he said.

They went towards the threshing machine.

Chapter Nineteen

When the moon falls from the sky
And grass grows grey,
I will forget you.
When the sun shines in the night
And no priests pray,
I will truly forget you.
　　When blackberries grow on the crab-apple tree
　　And sparrow-hawks nest in the hive of the bee;
　　When light becomes loam
　　And loam turns to foam,
　　Then I will forget you, my darling.
　　Then I will forget you, my darling.

IT WAS THE happiest threshing that Cahal had known.

It was as if the spirit of opposition had speeded all their pulses. Even Tom Creel straightened his back a little and boasted and laughed in a cracked voice. Cahal was up on the stack. Máire had climbed up on the top of the thresher and stood there tall and straight with her hands on her hips waiting for the thresher to begin its work. Of the three of them, only Julia was sour. She had to go to the front of the thresher near the engine and scrabble the threshed straw as it came from the machine and pile it back. Tom Creel stood ready holding the neck of the long sack to the grain chute.

The engine sputtered into life and sent a plume of dirty black smoke into the clean air. Then it settled down and the black plume became thinly blue and the chug of it was even. He pulled a lever and the belt started to turn and a slow rumbling started in the belly of the thresher as it creaked heavy-footed into action.

Cahal threw Máire the first sheaves. She bent down and fed them into the hole at her feet. The thresher swallowed them, chewed them and spat them out and settled down to its remorseless task.

The sound of the engine and the thresher travelled far on the still air. They heard it in Cassidys' and Jamesey Jordan heard it and Bridie and Gob and the Murphys, and if Peder Clancy had ears sharp enough he could have heard it, too, down in Ballybla. They mightn't like to hear it but it was there, a sort of rude return for their conniving.

Of course it will be slow, Cahal was thinking, but it will be done. It will take a few hours longer but the sacks will be filled. He wanted to laugh, so he laughed, and Máire flung back the hair that was falling over her face and looked at him and laughed too. They were almost on a level, he on the top of the stack, walking around, picking the tied sheaves from under his feet and pitching them accurately into her waiting arms.

"See what can happen," he shouted above the noise. "One man can defeat tyranny. One old man and a girl can utterly defeat tyranny and wipe it out if they have the heart. Isn't that a great thing, Máire Brodel? All you want in the world is one individual to stand up and say 'I disagree' and you have defeated it."

She winked at him.

I love Máire Brodel. That is a terrible inescapable fact. He told her so with his eyes and his body. His shirt was tight on his big chest and the belt at his waist was gleaming. She was a big girl too, full-breasted and flat-stomached and the thin dress pressed against her body and he could see the firm shape of her thighs. What in the hell ever happened to me? Why didn't I do? If only. The curse of God on if only. I should have seen and been strong the very first moment, and fought then and had her. None of this would have happened. There would have been no need maybe to have to go to town to find life in one or two pubs with the people who drank with him and loudly applauded a new song. Nessa would never have meant anything at all to him. Nor anybody else. It was a fever that was in his veins. Like a fire that could be quenched with porter or the feel of a soft arm in the palm of his hand. He loved Caherlo. He loved everybody in Caherlo. He didn't want them to look at him with sour faces and dour looks. He loved all of them. He didn't want to hurt them. He never had really. It was the terrible way they had all been brought up, the niggling puritanical soul-destroying education that had been handed out to them like meal fed to chickens. Well, they would see.

I am disgraced, Julia thought, I am disgraced forever. She was biting her lip, pinching back bitter tears that wanted to flow from her eyes. To have that one there, up on top of the machine for all the world to see. Flaunting her in front of the eyes of the world. The way he had looked at her, the way she had looked at him. She was flooded in shame. Oh God, what had happened her at all that she had seen the young Cahal and thought that he would be nice and quiet and malleable? She wanted to walk away from the field and go into the house and bang the door after her, but she was afraid. Because sometimes he made her genuinely afraid, when he had some drink taken and he looked at her silently with brooding eyes and a vein throbbing in his forehead. A bitter look, that stripped her bare and left her feeling helpless and hopeless, conscious of her old body and her destroyed hands and the terrible clothes she had to wear and the big boots on her feet. At times like that the money she had scraped and scrimped out of him seemed not sufficient compensation for the fear she had. She would walk away now and he would say after her in a cold voice, Where are you going? She could say, I won't stay here with that bad woman and you making eyes at one another. Isn't it enough that you hide your shame in the town without flaunting them in my face, an honest woman? He would say: Come back here and pile the straw. And the way he would say it would be enough to make her knees weak and a little flutter come in her chest and her mouth go dry.

"She's coming', she's comin'," old Tom was shouting as the yellow grain poured into his bag. In an intermittent flow and then in a stream. He upped the sack and the grain settled in the bottom it. It started to fill it high so that he had to hold the bulge of it with his bent knees.

I will have to go down to him, Cahal was thinking, when the bag is nearly full or it might fall on him and suffocate him. It was a big long bag. It would be nearly as tall as the body of the old man.

The sweat poured from them. Each one of them was doing the job of two men. The machine was inexorable. It had to be fed. If the stream became slow it protested grindingly, so that the water came from their teeth. Máire thought it was hard work. She got to her knees and sat on her legs in order to feed the sheaves in. She had few moments to wipe back the hair from her face or to rub the sweat of her forehead. But she was rejoicing inside. Because she had done the right thing after all. She had her reward in the look of his face when he welcomed her at the gate. That look. So complete, a confession and asking for forgiveness before it was necessary. She had nothing to forgive. She knew what was driving him. It was harvest time, wasn't it? She felt it in herself; she could see it in his eyes when he looked at her. When this is done, she thought, there will have to be a solution. We can't go on this way. Despite the world and Caherlo there will have to be a solution. Life is too short. Life is too sweet. Age is as inexorable as the threshing machine. It catches up with you. So you will have to cheat it before it's too late. Who will be hurt? A few people. But that will be the price you have to pay for grabbing a little of life.

"Hold it, Máire," Cahal shouted, jumping down from the stack to go to the assistance of Tom Creel who was struggling with the unmanageably full bag of oats. "Turn off the engine for a minute," he shouted to the machine man. "Here, let me help you, Tom," he said, catching the neck of the bag and hoisting it.

If only God would strike him dead, Julia was saying.

Máire got from her knees. The backs of her legs were stiff. She stood up. The front of her dress was long. She stood on the hem. It made her topple forward. As she toppled a little she put out her hand to save herself. Her hand and arm went into the hole at her feet.

The scream rose higher than the sky. It rose over the chug of the engine, the terrible grinding of the machine. It ran from the field into the sky and dispersed itself against the clouds and passed over the village like a smoke-cloud from a burning home. It caused all work to stop, all thought. Even the cattle feeding in the surrounding fields raised their heads as the scream ripped over them.

"Máire! Máire!" Cahal shouted, petrified. He dropped the bag. The oats spilled on the ground in a golden stream. He scrambled up the back of the machine. She was screaming, screaming, screaming. "Turn it off! Turn it off! Turn it off!" he was shouting. It had been done already. The machine stopped but her screams were only the clearer, only the more piercing. They chilled him. He felt himself going white. "Máire! Máire!" he shouted pulling at her body. Her right arm was inserted. Her mouth was open. There was scream after scream coming out of it. Oh, Christ! He had often killed a chicken. It fluttered in your hands. Panic has the effect you want. It terrifies you. You don't know what to do. Your stomach drains away. He raised his big hand in a clenched first and he hit her on the exposed jaw. It was a terrible blow. The screaming stopped like a jump stopped in mid-air. The silence it left was worse than the other. "Reverse the engine! Reverse the engine!" He shouted at the man who was gaping up at him with his mouth dropped. "Reverse the engine, you bastard, or I'll kill you!" The man sprang to the engine. "Oh, Máire, Máire," he said pulling her body up to him, nuzzling her face with his own. He heard the engine starting slowly, slowly. The belt went around, the grinding started inside it and he pulled her arm free.

It was a mass of blood. Oh, God above!

He took her body in his arms. He leaped from the top of the thresher to the ground, bending his knees to take the shock.

He went to the pile of straw. He laid her there. Julia was standing with the fork in her hand. She was wearing her white apron. He put out a hand and put it around the band of the apron. He pulled. The apron came away in his hand. He tore a strip off it. It came easily. He could have torn concrete then. He bound her bare pulped arm above the elbow. He drew it tight, tight, to that the blood would stop. Then he tore the rest of the apron into long strips. He bound it around her poor arm.

All the time he was babbling. Oh, Máire, Máire, what have I done to you, what have I done to you? You are the beginning and the end of life for me. You are the only thing that matters. You are better than the birds and the breeze and the hay in the meadows, or the songs in my head or music or heaven or hell or God. He took her up and he squeezed her against his chest. He put her from him and put his hand on her hair.

He knew what would have to be done.

"Cover her! Cover her! Cover her!" he shouted at them and he ran out of the gate.

Her bicycle was there. He mounted it and pedalled. How many miles to the house of your man? The only man near that had a telephone. Only he, there was nothing else to do. He would have to get there. Doctors had cars, had cars. They could come in a few minutes from the town. They would have to. If he could he would have got off at every house on the way and he would have gone in the closed doors and he would have struck around him blindly, furiously, with a stick or a stone or a knife. He would have killed some of them with his bare hands. See what they did. To a man what matter? He could take anything from them. But they did this to her, to a girl that never hurt any of them at all. Why had he put her up on the top of the thresher? He shouldn't have put her there at all. Why didn't he think? Why didn't he know? If it was himself he could bear it. They could put hooks into his whole body and pull him apart and he wouldn't mind. Oh God, to hear her screaming. His eyes saw nothing on the road. His mind didn't know where he was going except by instinct. It didn't take him long. His shirt was dripping with sweat and blood when he threw the bicycle into the yard. He went into the house. The door was open. There was a maid in a white apron. White aprons. White aprons. Get me the doctor in the town, for Christ's sake, for God's sake, for the love of heaven. She was dumb. He was such a sight. He shouted at her. He shouted at her again. His eyes were wild. She woke up. She went to the phone. She twisted the handle. She called and called. It was two hundred years. She got the hospital. Oh, hurry, hurry, hurry. A doctor is on the way. There is one here. He will come, the ambulance will follow.

He went back. The breath was short in his chest. He had to rip his shirt down the front – so that the buttons flew – in order to get air to be able to breathe.

He saw her father away on the sloping hill. The dog was with him. The sheep were like white balls flung away haphazardly by a child. What will he say to me? Her father? He couldn't get off the bike now. He couldn't tell him now. It would be miles and miles to go. She might be dead when he got there.

No, no, no. Don't say that. Don't think that. He had no breath left. He thought he was going to die, he could get so little air into him. Never again, never again. If You save her I will never sin again. I will be good and quiet and nobody in the world will ever hear another word about me. Only don't.

He threw the bicycle. He went into the field. He stretched

beside her on the mound of straw. She was moaning. She was moving her head from side to side. Under the tan of the summer her face was as white as the feather of a sea-bird. Her hair seemed brutally red. There were beads of sweat on her lip. The three were standing around her. They seemed to be petrified. They seemed to be afraid to move from their standing. "Get blankets! Get coats! you stupid bitch!" he shouted at Julia. "Cover her up! Cover her up!" He ran into the house himself. He dragged the bucket of spring water from the table. He grabbed the towel from the back of the door. He knelt beside her in the straw. He wiped her face with the cold water. She was moving and groaning. Her eyes fluttered open and looked up at him. That was all. She shut them again and she moaned. There was nothing in them. He read things in them. He read terrible things in them. He talked to her. The two men standing there turned away. It was a shocking thing to see him bending over her, pouring out things and words and incoherent syllables that should never have been heard in the light of day.

Julia came. He covered her with the blankets. Julia didn't stay. She went into the Cassidys' house. They were standing there. Waiting. Wondering. "What happened? What happened? For the love of Almighty God, who was screaming?" "Oh, don't talk to me, for pity's sake don't talk to me." At the fire sitting on the chair. Her hand up to her breast. She told them. She couldn't help it. It came into her eyes, into her voice, the triumph of the just, the punishment of the wicked. It was there triumphant, as if angels from heaven were bellowing it with heavy trumpets.

The doctor came. He still had his white coat on. He pumped something into her. Her moaning died away. Her head fell on one side.

The ambulance came. She was in it and away before they had time to think.

Cahal stood there on the road looking after it.

Gob who came on to the road to look after the ambulance at that moment turned and saw the figure standing at the gate. A terrible figure. His black hair was wild. The whites of his eyes were awful in the dark face. His chest was bared. His shirt was hanging from him, soaked in sweat, blotched with blood that was merging with the sweat.

He didn't say anything to Gob. He just looked. Gob felt his knees trembling. He wanted to talk to him, to say something. But he couldn't.

Cahal turned away. He went into his house. He opened the door of Barney's room that was now his since the death of the old man.

He threw himself on the bed.

He wanted to die.

Chapter Twenty

The summery birds are o'er the sea,
The trees are blake an' poorly,
The fires burn bright
In the early night,
And old men's bones are sorely.
But as for me
My heart flows free
Like the feather from a wild goose falling,
Oh me shirt is clean
And me boots do gleam,
For on my love I'm calling.

HE SHAVED HIMSELF carefully in the kitchen, peering at the small broken mirror hanging beside the door. He smelled nicely from the scented soap they used on Sundays before going to Mass. He put on a clean shirt and took his suit, smelling strongly of mothballs, from the big dark cupboard in Barney's room. Then he came to the kitchen again and polished his boots. They were his Sunday boots so they weren't terribly dirty and he got a good shine on them. Then he tried to tidy his hair with the comb and water, but it failed him so he left it alone hanging over his forehead.

Julia was coming in the door as he was going out. Her eyes roved over his cleanliness.

"Where are you going?" she asked.

"Over the road, over the road," he said, passing her by.

She turned to look after him. Where can he be going on a Saturday after dinner and he all got up like that? It wasn't to town unless he was getting a lift in from somebody. He didn't tackle the horse or the jennet. He just walked up on to the road, his arms swinging.

His feet moved to the rhythm of a song that was in his head. He pursed his lips and whistled softly though them. He didn't look to the right or the left. He passed the Creels' house and the Murphys'. He knew they saw him pass by but it didn't disturb him. Even a chicken couldn't pass the road that people didn't take notice of it. The roads were so lonely. Strange things passing by were unusual. A motor car could cause talk for a whole day, as to who could it be and what are they doing about here? Was it Land Commission men, or men about the bog, or engineers or just passers-by who had lost their road, or what? There wasn't hardly one of them could meet his eyes, since the threshing. Because, he supposed, they had a conscience, and what had happened could be placed on each one of them. They were really to blame. Not, he thought, that that would soften them or make them feel differently about him. It would have a contrary effect, because they would have to howl down the conscience, and ease its pricking with something else. What better way to do it than to say that God had smitten the unjust? They could be pious about that. They could go into the churches and thank God for his munificent mercy that He had reached out from heaven and punished the sinners in their midst. Strange are the ways of God. Take warning from them.

He was indifferent now about what they thought and what they did. He had only one ambition, and it was to leave them, because it was the only answer. But would it be possible? He wouldn't go alone.

None of them knew that she was coming home today. Because her father was such a silent man. None of them could get in under him. He was a hard man to put questions to, and none of them had the nerve to go up and put the question direct to him.

But she was coming today. She was coming in at the station above. In half an hour he should hear the whistle of the train away in the distance. And her father would be there waiting for her with the black and white collie at his heels. What would she look like? What had they done to her in the far, far place they had taken her to mend her up? He didn't know. He could think of a lot of ways she might have changed, that brought sweat on his chest. He had too much imagination. That was his trouble. If he had less he wouldn't be unhappy at Caherlo. Things would have come easily to him if he had been a bit more stupid.

Anyhow, he was happy. He could be that way for an hour or two yet until he got a look at her face and had seen her eyes.

She wouldn't expect to see him when she came in the door of her own house, so the first look would be naked and readable.

He walked down by the river as if he was going somewhere else. There was nobody to be seen, but for the last few years he had been conscious of eyes everywhere. He expected them to be glinting from bushes; to be even behind a skulking cloud in the sky; to rise with the smoke from the chimney-stacks.

He cut away from the river when he got to the big grove of trees that gave that parish its name. It was easy going from here. He was well covered by the gently rising uplands above the river, and the trees built as windbreaks all around your man's fertile acres.

It was a nice day. It was a bit chilly, but the winter was away from them yet, the tips of the grass shoots were yellow, the gorse was fading and the heather's brilliant purple was dying. A field of ferns was a mixture of green and gold as the autumn ate at the under fronds. But it was good weather.

The key of the house was under the stone. He lifted it and opened the door and went in. He left the door open so that the easy sunlight could flood it. The father had kept it very neat and tidy. He would be like that. There was an old blue coat belonging to her hanging on one of the wooden pegs beside the horse-collar. He rubbed it down with his fingers. He held it to his face and a vision of her came in front of his eyes from the fragrance of her that the coat still held, mixed up with the smell of the smoke from the turf fires and the oil from the sheep.

The fire was raked. He pulled it out. He stirred it into a bright blaze, getting down on his knees and blowing at it. He fed it with turf from the basket in the cranny beside the fireplace. He looked around. No cake. He supposed that they would buy a loaf in town and bring it with them.

He grinned and took off his coat and rolled his sleeves. They would have a cake. He would make one. It would be a prize cake. It would be golden on top like honey. He laughed. He found an enamel basin. He took cupfuls of flour from the flour bag. Cream of tartar, bread soda, he found in the press, and he was glad to see that her father had done a bit of churning. The buttermilk was there in the big earthenware jar. He tasted it. It was not too sour. It would do fine. He shoved in a piece of butter for luck. He mixed it up. He kneaded it in his strong hands. Then he heard the whistle of the train, very faint, like a boy blowing a whistle in a nearby field. He had to stop and drop his head for a moment, his heart pounded so heavily. She would be off the train now and on her way home, sitting beside her father in the pony trap he had borrowed from your man. What could have been her thoughts about him in the nearly two months she had been away? Well, forget it and get on with the cake. He had the three-legged oven heating upright against the fire. It was well heated. He rubbed a bit of butter around it inside and it sizzled and then he shook a little flour over that. He pulled out the triangle and put hot coals from the fire under it, placed the oven on that, and then when he had cut a cross with a knife in the top of his cake he took it in his two hands and placed it gently in the oven. He admired it for a moment, before he put the lid on the oven and put more hot coals on top of the lid. That will shake them now, he thought.

He found a white tablecloth and covered the oilcloth with it and took down three cups and saucers and plates from the dresser. Maybe I won't be staying, he thought then, but there's no harm in putting them down anyhow. It looked nice when he had it all done, but then he had nothing more to do except sit near the fire and watch the cake. He had to put fresh hot coals under and over it as the other ones blackened and cooled and disintegrated into black or white ashes. A few times he had to lift the lid with the tongs to see how it was doing, and to stick a clean knife down into it to judge it. It was doing nicely. It should be done and cooled before they came.

He stood at the door and looked out.

There was a good view from here. You could see the river glinting on the left as it wound out of the grove. He could see the top of the bridge and barely make out the smoke rising from the village. All the houses there like his own were surrounded by trees. They were hidden. Maybe that's what's wrong with them. Maybe they should be open to clean breezes. Maybe that might blow the cobwebs out of their minds.

He became restless. He didn't want to think too much. His mind had a habit of darting into queer upsetting places. Would I have been happy and settled down if it was Máire Brodel I had married instead of the one? He tried to picture it that way. Máire at home instead of her. And children around. He liked children. He wouldn't know what to do with one of his own. He spent a little time in town with his small bags of sweets talking to children on the green. But they were town children. They weren't the same. But they made you feel. They made you feel bad. Could he settle down? Why not? He had been here now how many years? He was almost thirty. Great God in heaven, he had been here going on fourteen years. So many things had happened.

He took the cake out of the oven. It was beautifully done. That's not any proof that the inside of it is good. But no matter. He went outside and stood it on the windowsill in the cool air. Then he went into the henhouse around the corner. The hen who was sitting didn't like him there. She cackled indignantly at him. He whooshed her out. She left, walking carefully like a great lady, her head high, and protesting all the time. There were five eggs in the nest. The one she had been sitting on was soft. He took it up in his fingers. Marvellous the things the Lord can do. The other shells were as hard a rock. This was soft and pliable like rubber. He left it down. That was why she didn't like leaving. He had disturbed her hardening of it. He brought the four fresh eggs into the house, put water into the black saucepan and put it ready by the fire. The kettle was singing. Everything was ready.

Then he heard the wheels of the trap very near.

The wheels were rubber-tyred so it was hard to hear them, but he heard the slight creak of the axles in the ruts. His hearing was very keen now. He put the four eggs in the saucepan and put it to boil on the fire, and then he stood up straight, his eyes on the doorway. He couldn't move from where he was. He was as well anchored as if there were weights tied to his boots. He heard the voices. Soft. No words he could make out. He had to swallow several times to get his throat clear. Then the doorway was darkened and she had walked into the middle of the kitchen so that the light from the window fell on her.

He had told himself before that his eyes mustn't drop to her right arm. Not first. They didn't, but not because he had told himself that. It was just that he wanted to see her first.

She was wearing a dark blue coat open in front so that he could see a coloured dress underneath and she had shoes and stockings. Her hair was uncovered, and it framed her face in bronze waves. Why can't I settle on the real colour of her hair? Her face was very pale, like as if it had been purged, so that her eyes were big in her face beside the cheek-bones that were appearing where they had been well covered the last time he had seen her. So look into her eyes.

She did an odd thing. She started to laugh. My God, is she hysterical? Has something happened to her? She bent forward laughing. She would have put her two hands on her thighs laughing like that before, but now she could only put one. She brought the other forward in the movement but there was no hand in it, just halfway up her arm something pushed out the cloth of the sleeve.

"You're awful funny-lookin'," she said then in explanation of the laugh.

Cahal's heart started to beat again. Her eyes were all right, weren't they?

She saw the man standing there by the fire, like a boy expecting to be beaten for a bad deed. His shirt sleeves were rolled and there was flour all over him, on his arms, spattered on his blue trousers and dulling the gleam of his polished boots. He even had a bit on his nose that seemed to alter the shape of his whole face.

"I med a cake," said Cahal.

"Did you?" she asked. "Isn't that grand now? Hello."

She came close to him. How did Cahal think to take her left hand instead of her right? It seemed very fragile.

"Did they give you a bad time, Máire?" he asked.

"It's all over now," she said, "all over now. You have grey in your hair. Did you know that?"

"No," said Cahal. "It doesn't matter. When I was waiting here for ye, I was thinkin'. I'm all but thirty. Did you know that?"

"You're a proper old man," she said. She turned as her father came in the door. "Look who's here, father," she said. "And he has a cake baked."

"And the table laid and the eggs in the saucepan and the kettle boilin'," said Cahal. "Now for ye." He felt as light-hearted as a spring lamb. Everything was all right. Imagine that!

"You'd make a great wife for somebody, Cahal," said her father. He doesn't mind me coming, Cahal thought. The collie came in waggling his tail and Cahal bent to pat him. He had lovely long silky hair. The dog licked his hand.

"We'll have to pass judgement on the cake," her father said then. "It was a kind thought to have the kettle boilin' for us."

"Sometimes my thoughts are good," said Cahal. "Sometimes they are unfortunate. Did ye see anybody and ye comin'?"

"We did," said Máire. She took off her coat and hung it on the wooden peg. She did it with ease. There were long sleeves on her dress buttoned at the wrist. Having her coat off made her seem very thin and her hand seemed irretrievably gone. I'll make up to her for it, he told himself fervently. Somehow I'll make up to her for it.

He had the tea made. He went outside and got the cake. He cut it into slices. It looked all right inside. The slices were thick.

"You have a heavy hand with a knife," said Máire.

They sat in at the table. They tasted his bread.

"Not bad," said Máire, "not bad at all, Cahal."

He had buttered the slice for her. He had remembered to have the teacup on the left side. He put the egg in the eggcup and said: "Wait'll we see if it's done." That got over the fact that he was slicing the egg for her. She could sugar and put milk in the tea herself.

Oddly there was no awkwardness between them. Just the father was silent. He was suffering a lot, Cahal thought.

He was. He hated to see anything maimed. He loved his daughter. Because he was silent it was a thing hidden deeply in him. He could never have come out with it. He should feel resentment against Cahal. He didn't because he knew that there was no use in that. There was no pity in the eyes of Cahal. If there had been he would have put him out of the house even though he was a quiet man. He wondered if even Cahal noticed her hand after the first look. Cahal did. It was burned in on his eyes.

"We had fun there," said Máire, "me trying to learn to do things with my left hand. It was a great pity you weren't born a *citóg*, they said, and you'd have no bother. It's wonderful how you learn. I can do nearly anything with my left hand. I remember reading books when I was young, all about sailors. There would be peg-leg men and then there would be one-armed men that had left their arm in a shark's belly. And they would have great big hooks on their arms and they would be trying to hook the hero with it. It always gave me the shivers. You know, it's not a bad idea at all."

"There's a lot in it," said Cahal. "It could be handier than a hand sometimes maybe."

She laughed. "It's a good job," she said, "I'm not young and foolish, or it might have ruined me chances."

"If you don't mind," said her father, rising and putting on his hat, "I'll leave the pony and trap back to your man."

Cahal noticed that even he was calling him *your man* now, and grinned.

"I won't be here when you come back," said Cahal. "I have to get back and milk the cows."

"Oh," said her father. "All right. God bless ye."

He went out.

Cahal poured her another cup of tea.

"Will I butter a slice for you?" he asked.

"Do," she said. "I'll be able to manage better later on."

He did it.

"He's more sad about my arm, you know, than I am," she said.

"I'm your arm," said Cahal.

"It's true what they say," she said, "you feel pain in your fingers and they not there."

"Do you?" Cahal asked.

"Aye," she said, "and you go to do things with your hand when you're not thinking and then find that you're not doing it at all. It makes you laugh. When I saw them on the station I went up and patted the dog's head. And I thought I felt him with my two hands."

You'd think the dog knew she was talking about him. He was stretched in front of the fire, crouched, with his eyes opening and closing from the heat like an old man dozing. He looked around at her and wagged his tail on the floor.

"Didn't I?" she asked.

"How do you feel, Máire?" Cahal asked.

"I feel very tired, Cahal," she said. "I can't understand it. I was never sick in my life, except once," she added thoughtfully, "but that was natural. It was over soon. Now I'm not sick but I get weary after a few hours. I want to sleep and sleep. Like something inside me wasn't working."

"I'll wash up the dishes before I go," said Cahal. He rose and poured water into the basin and started to wash the cups. "You know I don't feel sorry for you, don't you?" he asked.

"You ought to," she said, "it was your oats."

"I've been thinking while you were away," he went on. "I'm going to leave Caherlo."

She turned towards him, resting her left hand on the chair and leaning her chin on it.

"Yes," said Cahal.

"And where are you going to go?" she asked.

"I don't know," said Cahal. "One time when I came here I wanted to get on the road of the silver birches. It was the only place in the whole world I knew. I came, and the best thing that might have happened me was to have missed the road and to have gone on and on, only for one thing."

"And what's that?" she asked.

"I wouldn't have met you," he said. He got on one knee in front of her so that their faces were on a level.

"Maybe that was bad for you, Cahal," she said.

"No," he said. "It was bad for you."

"All right," she said, "so it was bad for me."

"So I go. I can stick a pin in a map and end up there. The land is broad. It's full of fields, full of farms. I will work here and work there and I will have seen the whole country."

"And what then?" she asked, reaching her white fingers and pushing back the hair from his forehead, gently.

"That depends," he said. "I either find a rut to lie in, or I take after me honoured father, and become a tinker."

She laughed.

"I'd love to see you tinkering," she said.

"What do you think about my father?"

"He's a wild man be all accounts," she said, "but in my opinion he's a better father than not to have one at all."

Cahal laughed. He was drying the cup in his hand. He looked odd on one knee with his hands drying cups.

"It's no wonder I love you," he said.

"I think that's the first time you ever came out straight with it," she said.

"It took a bit of doing now, too," said Cahal.

"So now I know," she said.

"As if you didn't before," he said.

"So you go away," she said. "And what happens to me? Will you send me coloured postcards?"

"You could come with me," said Cahal, and stopped drying the cups. He didn't look at her.

"When do we go?" she asked.

He started drying the cups.

"In the spring," he said.

"Why the spring?" she asked.

"I want to leave the place with all the crops sown and ready. But principally the spring because be that time you should have got over things. You could do with a bit of meat on you."

She laughed.

"We must fatten me up for the spring. And what about your wife?"

"She's all right," said Cahal. "She can have the farm. She can do what she likes with it, and besides she has nearly four hundred pounds in the Post Office."

"Where did she get that?" Máire asked.

"She thinks she's very clever. She sells eggs and butter and vegetables and puts it away. She thinks I don't know. But I do know. I must remember to tell her that before I leave."

"What about my father?" she asked.

"He's the one I'm worried about," said Cahal.

"Yes," said Máire. "He's the one to worry about."

"The spring is a long way away yet," said Cahal.

"It is," said Máire, "a long way. Couldn't we go at Christmas?"

"Máire," he said. "You'll have to not be light about this. This is very serious. I've given this a lot of thought. Maybe by the spring you might have changed your mind, hah?"

"I might too," said Máire.

"Then we betther go at Christmas," said Cahal.

They both laughed. Their pulses were jumping. So much behind the light talk. So much that they couldn't say, or do, not now. Just the feel of her hand on his forehead. The look of her eyes, the clearness of her skin. It almost wiped out the sight of her lying back on the straw, moaning and her hair violently red surrounding her white face. The nights he had lain awake seeing that, groaning into the pillow, wishing that it was his own suffering. He could have said, I only kissed you once in my life, Máire Brodel, down by the bridge when you were angry with me. Here are two single people who have never had their arms about one another. He wanted to rise now and take her into his arms, and tell her he would never let her go, that he would go on the floor and let her put her foot on his neck, that until his dying day he would look after her and mind her and never let her out of his sight. Oh, lots and lots of things he could have said and done, if this was the way it was to be, if they didn't have to be different because they were crossed.

"I thought a lot too, Cahal," she said, "lying on my bed. I thought a lot about you, but I never once wished that things hadn't happened the way they did. Only one thing, that you should have married the wrong woman. That's all."

"Maybe I look quiet and calm now," said Cahal, "but if you only knew there is a fire burning inside me."

"Aye," said Máire, "some of the smoke is coming out your eyes."

He rose to his feet.

"I'll finish the washing," he said, and he did.

He put on his coat.

"I'll go now," he said.

"I'll see you to the gate," she said.

She put her hand on his arm. They walked out to the gate. It was late. The days were getting short. There was a band of scarlet all around the horizon.

"Goodbye, Cahal," she said then. "I'll see you in the spring."

"In the spring," said Cahal, and took her bad arm in his hand. He could feel where it ended. He moved the cloth of her sleeve with his fingers. "You won't ever miss it," he said, "after the spring."

He walked away from her. He pulled air into his lungs. It was a long time since he had felt so happy. He changed that thought. It was a long time since he had felt happy. But he was happy now. That a decision was made. He could whistle now. He could play the melodeon. He could even meet his neighbours on the road and smile at them, instead of wanting to cut their throats. It was all so simple when you thought it out. The solution was all the time there under your nose. All you wanted was the courage to face it, to be willing to break out of the circle that hemmed you in.

He would break it now.

Nothing could stop him.

They would carve a little happiness from what remained to them from a begrudging world.

Chapter Twenty-One

The day I will be married, oh, the sky it will be blue
And buds they will be burstin' on the blackthorn and the
  yew,
The birds they will be singin', and the wather gently flow
By the bushes by the briars beside the banks of Caherlo.
That day I will be airy like a butterfly on the run,
With me toes I'll pluck the daisies and I'll hop and skip and
  hum,
I will bind me hair with bluebells and I'll meet him when I
  go
By the bushes by the briars beside the banks of Caherlo.

HE SHOOED THE cows into the far bog pasture. They were kept there by a ditch all around the place that could do with a bit of clearing. There was a narrow causeway over the ditch, and two upright poles hammered into the soft ground. Wire loops nailed to those held ash poles that barred the cows from running out of the place, the pickings in it were so coarse and poor.

"Ye'll have to put up with it," he told them laughing as they looked reproachfully at him from the other side. They sniffed disdainfully and moved away. The pasture was right on the edge of the bog. Some earlier Kinsella had reclaimed it, by ditching and fencing and sowing a little clover, when he had gone to the trouble of burning and uprooting the gorse and heather and ferns that the place was crowded with.

Cahal leaned against the post and lit a cigarette. It was a very calm evening. The chill of the late autumn was on it. Sounds were travelling far. He could hear the bog brook gurgling in its bed a bit away from him, that was the same brook that passed under the little humped bridge away out to his left. He could see the road winding greyly.

Then he saw the girl leaving the road and crossing into the fields. She was a long way away. She seemed very small from here. She was swinging a can in her hand and it was reflecting the sun. He could see her legs twinkling as she ran, kicking at the grass. She ran erratically. She would stop and bend down looking at something on the ground – what? A flower? An insect? It took her some time to get the place where she could see him. Then she saw him and paused for a moment and came on, one hand behind her back, holding the arm of the hand that held the can.

Jennie is growing up, he thought then as he made her out. She had a frock on, a blue cotton one with white dots all over it. Her brown hair was cropped close around her head, so that she would have looked like an effeminate boy if she wasn't wearing a frock.

He waited to see what she would do. He didn't look at her in case she might have been embarrassed. He looked up at the sky, blowing thin blue smoke at it.

Jennie saw him all right. He was in his shirt sleeves, with the arms rolled. He had an old waistcoat over that. He's very black, she thought. Hasn't he terrible strong hairy arms!

She stopped.

"Hello, Cahal," she said.

"Hello," said Cahal. "It's a nice evenin', Jennie."

"What are you doin'?" she asked.

"Nothin'," said Cahal.

"Do you know where I'm off to?" she asked, coming close, her legs spread, her two hands on the handle of the can and she swinging it in and out, in and out.

"Where are you off to?" he obliged her.

"Back pickin' frohans, I'm goin'," she said.

"Isn't it a bit late for them?" he asked.

"No," she said. "It's betther now, when the ferns are a bit withered. You see them easier."

"That's so," said Cahal.

She dug her bare toe into the soft bog, then she looked up at him.

"Would you like to come and help me?" she asked.

"I mightn't be good company, Jennie," he said. "It wouldn't be good if you were seen with me. What would the people say?"

"I'm not askin' the people," said Jennie. "I'm askin' you. Do you want to come pickin' frohans, or don't you?"

"All right," said Cahal, laughing and coming out to her. "We'll go pickin' frohans."

He walked slowly beside her. Her head was up to his shoulder. She had filled out a lot. She was a little woman, compactly built, and yet a child.

"Do you think I've nothing else to do but to be out pickin' frohans?" he teased her. "Why haven't you a young man to be out with you?"

"I wanted to be alone," she said, with a sigh.

"And what am I doin' here so?" he asked.

"Ah, you're different," she said. "You're a lonely one too."

"Am I now?" he asked.

"Well, nobody talks to you," she said. "Any more. My mother has me warned not be seen talkin' to you."

"She's a wise woman, Jennie," he said. "But it's not that nobody talks to me, but that I don't talk to nobody. You know, Jennie, sometimes my voice gets rusty from lack of use."

"Is that why you go into the town oilin' it?" she asked.

"That's right," said Cahal. "But I don't oil it any more."

"They have a terrible down on you," she said. "To hear them talkin' you must have a cloven hoof for a foot."

"I might have too," said Cahal.

"You don't really care what they think about you, Cahal,

do you?" She stopped still to put that question to him.

"Well, Jennie," he said, "I'm human too. Every human likes people to like him and not think badly about him."

"Well, I don't think badly about you," said Jennie. "I think there's nobody like you."

"Thanks, Jennie," he said gravely. "That's cheerful for me."

She walked on again. The track they were on was very rough. It was only a cow walk. It was bisected here and there by natural drains going towards the brook.

"You see," said Jennie, "I have a problem too. That's why I like you, Cahal. I think you are kind of free. You do what you like."

"Not really, Jennie," he said then gently. "Nobody can really do what they like."

"No, but," said Jennie, "they can try to and you try to. If I am like you I will want to have courage. If I'm like them I will do what they want me to do – not what I want to do meself."

"I see," said Cahal.

"I'll never forgive me mother for that day of the threshin'. That day I wanted to go out and help you despite. They locked the door on me, and she hit me and she'd have given me more. Tommy has grown terrible. As a young boy he had a funny way of being a man. Now he's a man he's not funny any more."

"I see," said Cahal. She was furrowing her smooth forehead with the concentrating she was putting into her talk.

"If I had gone out that day," she said, "I would have been another help, and that thing would never have happened to Máire Brodel. That was a terrible thing, Cahal. I cried all night that night so I did."

"It wasn't a nice thing, Jennie," said Cahal.

"And then they say it was her own fault, and a penance from God and a punishment for sin, and I don't think so at all, I think it was their fault and that when they die God will be up there waiting for them, and He'll say, 'Well, well, if it isn't the villagers of Caherlo. And now, min, let us have a little chat about the day ye crippled Máire Brodel.' I think that's what'll happen."

Cahal would have liked to have thrown his arms about her and squeezed her. The serious air of her too. He didn't answer.

"You're cracked about Máire, aren't you, Cahal?" she asked, standing facing him.

He looked at her.

"Yes, Jennie," he said. "I'm cracked about Máire Brodel."

"Now, see," she said, as if she was addressing an audience. There was none to hear her except the startled snipe or the big hare that fled away in front of them. "Here we are now," she said then, leaping a drain on the right-hand side and going into a great patch of ferns. They stretched for a half mile nearly into the bog. The ground was fairly dry. The ferns are great lads for salving a bog. Where they grow they pull the earth tight and hold it firmly with long roots.

Jennie's mind could only accomplish one thought at a time. Now she was intent on the frohans.

The berries were hard to find until you caught the knack of finding them. They were hidden coyly under the ferns. You had to raise the ferns and then look for the light purple glint of them, snuggling away. Cahal ate the first few he found. They squelched in his mouth. They were tasty. Jennie caught him at it. "I didn't bring you to eat them," she said, "but to put them in the can." Cahal laughed. "All right, Jennie," he said, "no more eating." It made him feel very lighthearted. Jennie's youth was almost contagious. How heavy could you feel when you were thirty and your mind was weighted with many things! Jennie was very quick finding the berries. Cahal was slower. His fingers were too thick, she told him, and his eyes were too slow. Maybe his mind wasn't on his work. They laughed, and Cahal felt it was good after all to be alive; that the world wasn't all that weighty. It took them about an hour to fill the can and then they sat down in a cleared space while Cahal smoked a cigarette. She asked him for one. He gave it to her. She held it as if it was a stick of dynamite that would explode any moment and when she blew a puff through her nose and started to sneeze and cough he took it away from her. She lay back with her arms under her head.

"Always," she said, looking at the sky, "I had pictures of when I would be grown up like now, what would happen to me. What kind of pictures had you, Cahal?"

"Probably the same as yourself, Jennie," he said. "Pictures in the sky."

"You see them in the fire," said Jennie. "I always saw the one that would come courtin' afther me. He was very tall and he had blue eyes and fair hair that was straight, and he would always wear a collar and tie and have a crease in the front of his trousers, and he'd have lovely manners. But he wouldn't be a softie. Just gentle, and maybe sometimes we would be down by the river and he would read things to me from books."

"The Lord save 's," said Cahal, "what kind of a fella would that be?"

"I'm givin' you a bad picture of him," said Jennie. "He'd have a sense of humour too, you know. His eyes'd crinkle up at the corners and he'd be cracked about me, and he'd run around a bit when I ordered him. I'd be in the house and I'd be pretendin' that I'd be goin' out to meet him. In the spring it would be, when everything is new and I'd meet him down by the river." She sighed.

"Maybe you will too," said Cahal. "If you wish things long enough you'll get them."

"Did you ever dream that you'd get Mrs Kinsella?" she asked.

"No," said Cahal. "Something happened the dream there."

"Well," said Jennie, "I didn't dream that I'd get Sonny Murphy either."

Cahal sat up.

"What did you say?" he asked.

She sat up resting her body on her hand.

"That's what I wanted to tell you," she said. "It's all fixed. Me and Sonny. Didn't you know that?"

"No," said Cahal, "I didn't know that."

"Well, that's the way it is," said Jennie. "It's a good match. We have very little. Sonny will have everything. He's goin' to build a new house maybe, he says. He's goin' to live in your house when they throw you out. Did you know that?"

"I know about the house," said Cahal.

"Isn't it well for me?" Jennie asked. "He's a nice man. He's nearly twice me age, but that doesn't matter. He has red hair and his teeth are white and he doesn't sweat too much, and I'll have great times. I'll be the lady of Caherlo, so I will, and I'll have about fifteen children, one every year until I'm old and wizened and have only two teeth in me head."

Cahal felt something rising in him. The pattern all over again. There were so few arguments against it, except a nebulous emotion called love. Love, what the hell is that, man? Isn't he the finest she could get this side of the county? What girl wouldn't give her two eyes for the chance? They would even tell you in the church that these things were for the best. Very few of them ever turned out badly. It might turn out for the best for morons who were unable to think, but how could you know what the long years would bring to the minds of the people who entered on a thing like that the same as animals being serviced? But not Jennie. He looked at her. She was looking back squarely into his eyes. Waiting for his reactions. She was a bright little thing, Jennie was. She was too bright to be broken on the wheel of tradition.

"Do you love Sonny Murphy, Jennie?" he asked. "Do you know what love means, do you?"

"How could I know what love means?" Jennie asked. "One time for a time I thought I was in love with you, because you could sing songs and people thought a lot of you and you could go nowhere but they had heard of the Bogman. But I don't love you, Cahal Kinsella. I like you, which is more important. But I don't feel anything at all for Sonny Murphy. If I didn't see him for the rest of me life I wouldn't miss him. But he has good prospects. Any one that marries him will be well off. There's that, isn't there?"

He got to his knees.

"It's not right, Jennie," he said. "You can't do it."

"What am I going to do, so?" Jennie asked.

"What do you want to do?" he demanded.

"I don't want to marry Sonny Murphy," said Jennie. "To hell with Sonny Murphy. But what can I do? I'm here. I have few things of my own. I have this dress and two more and school books and ribbons in a box and my Sunday shoes and my bicycle. What am I going to do?"

"You can do anything you like," shouted Cahal, "but don't let them drag you into a thing like that. If you had feeling for him I wouldn't give a damn, but you'll have to fight."

"There's no use fightin'," said Jennie. "They'd wear me down."

"Then go away," said Cahal. "Fly. Hop on your bicycle and don't look over your shoulder. Get away."

"That's your advice is it?" Jennie asked. "You didn't do that yourself and you were worse off than me."

"Yes," said Cahal. "But you could look at me, Jennie. So maybe I was an example. If there was somebody else I could have seen first maybe I wouldn't have been a fool. Listen, is there a single soul on the face of Ireland that you know?"

"I have some sort of a relative of me father's lives in Dublin," said Jennie. "He sends me mother a few shillings now and then."

"Well, there you are," said Cahal. "Go on your bicycle and reach the train and get on the train and go to Dublin and walk into this man's house and say 'I have come to live with you, they wanted to marry me off but I wouldn't do it. And so here I am.' He can throw you out. Right. Let him.

You can go and sleep somewhere and you can look for work. You can do something. Only fight free for the love of Christ. I'll give you money. I don't know what I have. A few pounds at home. I'll give it to you, but go, Jennie. Go, go. Maybe when you're away you'll find out that you love Sonny Murphy, but until that is sure get out. Don't let them tie you."

"I'll never love Sonny Murphy," said Jennie. "Sonny Murphy would only want a wife that would be a big stupid complacent cow. Sonny Murphy will beat his wife. Nobody can tell me any different. I don't want any part of Sonny Murphy. I will do what you say, Cahal. I knew if I could get to talk to you there would be a way out. This is the way. I'll take it within the week. You won't see Jennie Cassidy's tail for dust once I get on the bicycle. And I will pay you back what you give me. Sometime."

"That's good," said Cahal, smiling. "I will probably want it."

He reached his hand and took her chin in his fingers. Her skin was as soft as the white fuzz on the bog cotton. The little jaw was determined. She was the epitome of determined youth.

"Oh God, Jennie," he said, "if only I was like you when I was your age too. The world would be different. It'd be a greater place to live in. And all you want when you are young is courage, but old people don't expect young people to have courage. You will be all right, wait'll you see. Whatever happens you will only be good things. Wait'll you see."

He bent forward and rested his hard jaw against the smoothness of her cheek.

Then the man shouted.

"Jennie! Jennie Cassidy! Come home our that!"

Cahal turned his head.

He rose to his feet when he saw the angry Sonny Murphy charging across the ferns. His face was red; his fists were clenched.

He came close to them. Cahal stood tall in front of him. Jennie stood beside him, calmly.

Sonny reached for her with his hand.

"You were warned," he said. "Your mother warned you. You weren't to go near him. I saw you from the field above. It was a good job I saw you. Come on!"

Cahal hit his arm down.

"Stand a bit away, Murphy," he said.

"I've no talk to you," said Sonny. "Isn't it enough that you've done all you've done? There was only one thing left to do, to destroy the one young girl in the village."

"Because you're a bloody fool, Murphy," said Cahal, "I won't go after you with me hands and pull you to pieces. But don't try me too far."

His eyes deterred Sonny. He shifted his own from them to Jennie.

"Are you comin' now?" he demanded.

"We're not married yet, Sonny Murphy," said Jennie. "Until we are I go where I like and I walk where I please and I'll talk to whoever I want to."

"You go with him again," said Sonny, "and you'll find nobody about here that will marry you."

"That would be grand," said Jennie. "That would please me."

He looked at her for a moment.

"Well, come on now," he said. "We'll forget this."

"There's something else, Sonny," said Cahal.

He reached into his pocket for the letter that had come this morning. It was an important letter. It was the only letter that had ever come with his name on it that wasn't a bill or demand for rates.

"See this, Sonny," said Cahal. "It's a letter I got this mornin'. You'll not guess who it's from, but I'll tell you. It's from Barney's eldest son in America. And do you know what it says? Well, I'll tell you. It says he had a letter from solicitors in the town, saying that Barney had made no will and that the place was occupied by a bastard and that therefore the farm belonged to him and that a Mister Mark Murphy of Caherlo was able and willing to tender the sum of four hundred pounds for the place, lock, stock and barrel, and that he should take it. Did you know about that, Sonny?"

Sonny looked at him.

"Yes," he said. "I knew it. Why not? You're finished around here and you know it. You'll be put. You have no right to the place. That's all."

"I hadn't then but I have now," said Cahal. "Barney's eldest son thinks that the place shouldn't pass out of the family even though he says he had little happiness in it, so he has written a letter back to the solicitor telling him that he is assigning the farm to me for ever and ever as long as I live or the heirs of me body. What do you think of that, Sonny?"

"He can't do that," said Sonny. "It's not legal."

"Oh yes it is," said Cahal. "So you can go back now and tell that to your oul fella and let him spit it into the ashes of the fire. He will have to get another plan, I'm telling you, Sonny. So that you'll know and anything that you try now will have to be done to my face and not behind my back. You'll have to come into the open, Sonny. So, Jennie, do you want to come to the road with me or are you staying with your bridegroom?"

"I'll be up after you," said Jennie, thinking.

"Goodbye, Sonny," said Cahal. "You don't know how near you came to having your face busted open. You haven't enough sense to know how near you came." He turned then and he walked away.

Sonny turned on Jennie.

He vented his anger on her. He caught her arm in his hand and shook her.

"Why do you do it?" he shouted. "Do you want the whole of the village to be saying that he tumbled you? What'll your mother say? Is that the way to behave and we on the point of being married?"

Jennie shook her hand free.

"Leave me alone, Sonny Murphy," she said, standing away from him, sparks coming out of her eyes. "If you come near me again I'll hit you with the can. Who do you think I am? Do you think you can treat me like I was a slut?"

He reached her in a jump and wound his strong arms around her.

He held her close.

"I know what you are," he said. "You're going to be Mrs Sonny Murphy and you know that. And you'll be Mrs Sonny Murphy. You think of me, Jennie. I think you're a grand girl. There isn't another girl anywhere that I like as well as you." The feeling of her in his arms excited him. He rubbed his face on hers. There were bristles on his chin. They hurt her. She tried to free herself. He was too powerful. He crushed her lips with his bristled mouth. Red bristles. He's like a pig, Jennie thought, turning her face this way and that.

Then he let her go.

"Come home," he said. "I'll see you to your door, and then I have to attend to something else."

He stood up and looked after the figure of Cahal walking slowly across the bog towards the road.

Jennie stood behind him, breathing hard, wondering if she would hit him on the head with the can of berries. If only she had her shoes on she might have kicked him, but her mind was working too. Give them no idea, she thought, no idea, and then when you are far away you can think of Misther Sonny Murphy and you can laugh.

"We'll fix Misther Cahal Kinsella," said Sonny between his teeth.

Chapter Twenty-Two

Oh God in heaven, we humbly pray:
Protect our crops by night and day;
Smite our detracthors hip and thigh
And guard our bastes from the warble fly.
If You take our neighbours give them hell;
If they leave relations make them sell,
Put in their hearts a holy fear
So the auction price won't come too dear.
Grant our cattle, Lord, more room to spread,
If strange ones trespass strike them dead.
Bring down the price of things we buy,
Let our own prices gup sky high.
You know us, Lord, we won't say more,
From dint of prayer our knees are sore,
Reward a friend and roast a foe –
                    Mark Murphy, Sons, of Caherlo.

"Y OU'LL HAVE TO bring the girl into it," said Mark emphatically, standing at the door to see him off.

"Is ther' no other way?" Sonny wanted to know. "Afther all I'm goin' to marry her and I don't want them to be pointin' the finger at her afterwards."

"Nobody will point the finger at her," said Mark. "We'll see to that. But it's the oney way now. Who'd ha' thought that Barney's son would do a thing like that to us?"

"They were all a queer crowd," said Sonny. "He got a bit

of his nature from both sides."

"Well, off with you now," said Mark. "I'll wait up for you to see what they say."

"All right," said Sonny, and walked off.

Mark stood a few moments at the door. He was in his shirt sleeves. His stomach was stretching the band of his trousers. He scratched it with his two hands as he turned in. He was yawning a little.

"Thank God," he said to his wife, "it's a grand night. This 'd be a great world oney for some of the people that God puts in it."

Sonny went by the bridge.

He was running over in his mind what he would say. It was bad enough in all truth but he'd have to be a bit more upset about it. There would be a good gatherin' in Peder's anyhow. They were playin' for a goose. He should, of course, have taken Kinsella by the scruff of the neck today when he found him with her, and he should have kicked him. But he didn't. The Bogman was a mean-lookin' man, and who knew but he'd have a knife in his pocket, and since he was the son of the father, who knew but that he'd use it? It wasn't that he was afraid of him. He tried to picture what Caherlo would be like with him out of it. It would be a very good place. Since the day he came, Sonny had been wary of meeting him at all, on the road, in a house, at a hooley, in the town. There was always a sneer in his smile for him, and he had a blunt way of being funny that he thought was funny that wasn't funny at all. Sometimes Sonny wondered at the red-hot fury that boiled up in him when he thought of him. If they were smaller men they would have been disgraced forever by the things he wrote about them in songs. It was about time that honest men should do away with a jeerer like him.

The worst thing he had done to him was over Máire Brodel. He had liked Máire Brodel, very much, very much indeed. If he had married her and had found out about her afterwards, he wouldn't have minded too much, because she stirred the sort of things in him that no other girl had ever done. But the Bogman blasted that one. He had been shocked and had gone away to think and when he had thought and gone to see her again, it was too late. Pity for her, he thought. If he had gone back, she wouldn't be goin' around the country now like a lamed hen with one of its wings cut off. But Jennie would be nice. He always felt tight when he thought of Jennie. She was nice and young and she'd be soft in your hands and under you, and she would never be like the other one. She was so tall and you didn't have to bend to look into her eyes. Well!

He went the short way, cutting in on the cart-track past the bridge.

The moon was up. It was as bright as day nearly. You could see miles in front of you. He had to pass the Brodels' house and he walked softy. But the dog sniffed him out and barked. He passed the house quickly. There was a light in the window, and then as he turned the corner towards the river, he came full on her. She was walking towards him. The moon was shining on her. He could see where it had happened to her. It made him suck in his breath as he paused. Only for a second and then he went on. It was the first time he had met her. He saw it happen from the bushes that surrounded the oatfield, where his brothers and himself had lain, watching. It wasn't a nice sight, sure enough, but it was her own fault. She had all that comin' to her. Woe to the scandal-giver, and besides, she should have treated him better.

Her eyes were clear on him, the moon had turned her hair sort of black and green. Sonny felt a flush starting in his face, couldn't help it. Let her talk if she would. It was none of their faults. She picked her day and she picked her man, making little of herself in the eyes of the world and in the eyes of God.

"Goodnight, Sonny," she said.

He muttered a goodnight. He couldn't face her, he had to look away.

"What brings you down our side of the world?" she asked.

"Down to Peder's," he said. "We're twenty-fivin' for a goose."

"Oh," she said.

He ran over a few phrases in his mind. I'm sorry about your trouble. It's a pity you lost your hand. He couldn't get them out. He shuffled his feet on the dust of the track.

"Goodnight," she said then, passing him; "I hope you'll win a goose."

He went on.

She can't be, he told himself, feeling sweat on his palms. She will have to go. How could we be meetin' her on the road and havin' her look at us as if it was our fault that she lost her hand? She wouldn't be good for children. It'd bring up the whole story, when anybody'd ask. What's wrong with that Máire Brodel, where'd she lose her hand? and the tale'd have to be told when the whole thing would be best forgotten.

Máire turned on the road and looked after him. She felt worried. She didn't know why. Sonny Murphy was harmless. But was he so harmless when he wasn't on his own? Who or what had organized the stay away from Cahal's threshing? It wouldn't have happened that every one in the village would get the idea inspired on the same morning: we mustn't go back and help Cahal Kinsella.

She spoke to her father about it. He was reading a book by the fire, patting the back of the dog who had run in to him after barking at the figure on the road.

"I just met Sonny Murphy on the track," she said. "He was goin' down to Peder Clancy."

"What's wrong with that?" he asked.

"I don't know," she said. "Just something. It gave me a shiver. They are really the ones who are up against Cahal."

"They have cause to be," said her father calmly. "He's made them a laughing-stock in four counties with the songs he med up about them."

"He's made songs about lots of people," she said. "There's no harm in that."

"There's no harm in the songs, but there might be harm in the minds of the men that don't like them," said her father.

"There was a time when I thought all this place was peaceful and placid and stupid and benevolent," she said. "I don't think that I like it much any more. I don't think I'd mind leaving it."

He looked at her back. She was at the door. She was holding her maimed arm behind her with her left hand. He winced a little and looked away.

"I like it," he said.

She turned to him.

"You still like it, despite?" she asked.

"Yes," he said, "I do."

"There's no chance of shifting you so?" she asked.

"No chance at all," he said.

"Oh, well," said Máire, and made up the fire.

Peder's kitchen was crowded. The table was out in the middle of the floor and there were about ten of them gathered around it with a smaller number playing.

Sonny knew them all. The Caherlo men including his two brothers and Jennie's brother – not so good – Gob Creel and Jamesey Jordan and several young men from Glen and Ballybla.

Peder was at the head of the table. The hat was at the back of his head. He played the game very slowly. He was wearing old steel-framed spectacles and scrutinized the value of the cards over the tops of them. Then he would hold the cards to his breast and look at the ones already played and put down a card with a resounding thump, saying, Bate that now, digging the rib of a neighbour, and laughing. They nearly wore out their knuckles hitting the table with their good cards.

Peder looked up, when Sonny came in.

"Welcome, welcome, welcome, Sonny Murphy," he said. "Pull up a chair. I have the goose in me pocket."

Sonny went over and stood with his back to the fire. He waited until the hand was played.

"I was over in the fields today," he said in a loud voice. He got their attention. "I was looking over the bog towards the fern patches and I saw the top of a girl and a man in there. They were picking frohans. You know the place."

"Yes, we know the place," said Peder, turned towards him. "Go on!"

"It was Jennie Cassidy," he said. "You know Jennie and me is matched, don't ye? Well, I went down and went into the bog. It took me some time. I didn't see them then, they were gone. I went there as fast as I could, but it's a soft boggy road to travel. I got in there then. He was lying with her in a space and he was bending over her. He had been kissin' her. I don't know what more. I think I got there in time. There it is!"

Their faces were blank with surprise. That's the way to do it. Short and sweet.

Tommy was on his feet. His face was red.

"Jaysus," said Tommy, "I'll kill him so I will! I'll kill him!"

"Shut up," said Sonny. "This is gone past the place where boys can handle it. It's for us now."

"Are you sure?" Gob Creel asked. "Are you sure it wasn't all innocent?"

"Is it innocent for a one like him that we all know about to be lying with a young girl in the ferns?" Sonny asked.

"You saw him at her?" Peder asked. "Are you sure, man? We'll have to be sure."

"I saw him kissing her," said Sonny. "He had his hand on her face when I got to them."

"God, this is the end," said Peder. He scattered the cards on the table with a sweep of his hand. "Let him do what he likes with the dirt in the town but let him not come back here with young girls like that. Does her mother know?"

"I didn't tell her," said Sonny. "I told nowan, until now."

"I'll knife him," said Tommy. "I'll tell her mother, begod. She can take the stick to her."

"Shut up," said Sonny. "She's oney a young girl. She doesn't know any different. Well, now. What are we goin' to do?"

"He'll have to go, that's what now," said Peder rising. "We'll g'over and tell him tonight. We'll give him one week to be packed up and gone out of here and if he isn't gone we'll put him."

"It's too aisy," said Tommy. "He should be bet."

"I'll go over to him now," said Peder. "Will you come with me, Sonny? And you too, Gob? That will be the best."

"No," said Gob. "I won't go. Ye can go."

They looked at him. He was uneasy under their glances.

"Well, he was a friend one time," said Gob. "Let it go at that."

"All right," said Peder. "You can come, Jamesey."

"I will," said Jamesey. "It is a terrible thing. I think he should be whipped."

"Right," said Peder, "let the rest of ye wait. We'll be back."

They left a charged silence behind them in the kitchen.

They talked very little. They went the road by the humped bridge.

"It was over there," said Sonny, nodding his head towards the bog.

"Just to be sure," said Peder, "when we're passing the Cassidys' you go in and bring the girl out to us."

"No," said Sonny, "lave her out of it. She has enough done to her. Lave her be. I saw it meself, I tell you."

"Call her out all the same," said Peder. "This is a terrible serious thing."

They stood on the road. Sonny went in the door and came out with the girl walking beside him.

"Mrs Cassidy was gone to bed," he said.

"Good," said Peder.

"What's up with you, Peder?" Jennie asked. "You have a hard face on you. What's wrong with you?"

"Did Cahal Kinsella interfere with you below in the ferns today?" Peder asked.

"I see," said Jennie. "Sonny Murphy has a big mouth."

"Is it true or isn't it?" Peder asked.

"You can be sure whatever he told you is lies," said Jennie. "There isn't one of the Murphys has a straight tongue in his head. Cahal Kinsella did nothing at all to me. I met him and asked him to come pickin' frohans with me. He came and that's all."

"And what was he doing to you when I came on ye? Ye weren't pickin' frohans then," shouted Sonny at her. "He had his hand on you, didn't he, and he was kissin' you and only God knows what went on before I came."

"You're a liar, a liar, a liar," said Jennie. "You only want to hurt him, that's all. You'd do anything at all to hurt him because he is bright and you haven't the brains of a bullock. Don't believe him, Peder, it's all lies."

"Did he touch you, Jennie?" Peder asked.

"You can't tell a thing like that," said Jennie. "If I said he had his hand on me face, what can't ye make out of that? He never kissed me. He had his face in front of me. That's what that fella saw. That's what he's making trouble about."

"Bring her into the house, Jamesey," said Peder grimly, "and keep her there. The fella has an evil spell thrown on you there's no doubt. But you'll be the last. On my solemn oath you'll be the last."

"You stupid eejit, Peder," said Jennie at him. "You're as bad as that Sonny Murphy. You have something up your nose for Cahal, too. You're not willing to listen to any good on him. You want him out of the way, just because every one in the country is talkin' about yourself and the Canon."

"Take her into the house, Jamesey," said Peder.

"Come on, girl," said Jamesey, taking her arm. "In we go."

"Let me alone! Let me alone," shouted Jennie, struggling in his hold. She was no match for Jamesey. He was kind but he had a terrible hold on her.

"Now we'll see, Misther Kinsella," said Peder.

They turned off the road in towards the Kinsella house.

There was a light in the window. As they approached the door they heard the strains of music coming out to meet them. The soft sounds of a melodeon. The big door was closed. Peder rapped on it with his stick. They heard a voice say, "Come in!" They went in. They saw him over on the settle bed. He was sitting there with one leg up leaning back against it and the most diverting tunes were coming out of the melodeon. He didn't stop playing.

"We have something to say to you," said Peder. Cahal looked up at him.

"Say on," he said, not easing the music at all. There was no sign of Julia. She must be up in the bed. Just as well.

"We're givin' you one week to clear out of Caherlo, Kinsella," said Peder.

That stopped the music. Cahal sat up, still holding the melodeon in his hands.

"Say that again, Peder," said Cahal.

"We're givin' you one week to clear out of Caherlo," said Peder.

"I see," said Cahal. "And what's the idea now, Peder?"

"You know," said Peder. "We don't have to tell you."

"Oh, but you do," said Cahal. "I still don't know. Is it because I wrote a song about you and the Canon or is it because I wrote a song about the Murphys, or is it because Mark Murphy has no other way of gettin' his hands on the land than to run me out? It could be any of those, Peder."

"Damn well you know it's none of those," shouted Peder. There was a vein swelling on his neck. "We're tired of you here. We put up with a lot from you. You've done a lot of hurtful things to us. You've made the name of the place a by-word in the whole county. We don't mind you makin' a show of us. We don't mind the kind of life you lead in town or out of town, but when you start layin' your dirty hands on Jennie Cassidy we've had enough of you. Is that clear?"

"That's clear," said Cahal. "You're a silly old man, Peder. You know that. Your brain is blinded be a few lines of a song. You used to be good fun, Peder, and a great man, and to look at you one would have thought you were as free as the air. There was a time I thought you were as free as the air, but not now."

"We've told you now," said Sonny. "You have a week."

"What happened to you, Peder?" Cahal asked. "You used to be the life of a hooley all round. You had lovely yarns, Peder, that'd make a cat laugh. You don't make anybody laugh any more. Is all the fun and love gone out of life for you altogether? Are you so blind that you'll listen to a concocted story from an enemy like Sonny Murphy and believe it all, just because you want to believe? Do I look like a man that'd go interfering with a nice young girl like Jennie Cassidy? Have you lost your sight too, Peder?"

"I've lost nothing," said Peder. "Sonny saw you. And the girl herself practically told us. Even if you were oney kissin' her, that's too much. You are a married man with a bad name."

"All right, Peder," said Cahal. "I can see there's no use. You're dead. Right. Well, it might surprise ye to know that I had made up my mind before ye came that I was going to leave. I meant to send invitations around to the whole of the three villages so that ye could rejoice. Now ye have come like this and I'll tell ye something, I have no intention of leaving Caherlo. None at all. Before ye came in that door, I was practically gone. Now I stay. I'll stay until I'm an oul man of ninety, and be the great God, before I die I'll have educated the lot of ye into something resemblin' human beings, so I will. Take that back now, Peder, and brew over it."

He sat back and started running his fingers over the melodeon. The tinking tunes came tauntingly from it.

"We told you, don't forget that," said Peder. "We warned you, don't forget that. We mean to see the end of you."

Cahal didn't answer him. His head was bent over the melodeon. He did it because otherwise he might have sprung at them. His hands were trembling.

They went out. They closed the door after them. They

walked up the road. The music came mockingly louder after them, a few bars of Peder's song followed by *Saint Mark*. It made Peder increase his pace. There were sparks coming out of his boots.

"By God," Peder was saying, "by the Great God!"

Sonny walked innocently beside him.

Julia came down from the room. Her face was frightened.

"What is it?" she asked. "What did they want?"

"Nothing, nothing, nothing," said Cahal. "They are corpses. They smell to heaven. Go back to bed, woman."

The music rose higher and higher as he got from the settle and pulled the melodeon out to its fullest extent. Then he closed it to with a snap, released his hand from the leather band and flung it on the table. He went out the door. His fists were clenched. He stood there. He looked. There was no sign of them.

The moon in the sky was grinning at him through the trees.

Chapter Twenty-Three

The soft breeze will blow where the wather hens play,
The rushes will sigh at the turn of the day,
The heron will call and the curlew cry
By the free roamin' Ree in the evenan.
*   Óri-ó, I will be*
* Far away but I will see*
The wings of the swallows caressin' the Ree
* When I've closen me eyes in the evenan.*

CAHAL WAS COMING from the haggard with a huge armful of hay when he heard the voice in the kitchen.

He halted for a moment and then went on. The stables were cleaned out. He piled the hay into the stalls and threw a few cabbages on top of it. Then he rubbed his hands on his trousers and looked at the sky. It might rain. There were large clouds piling up over the river.

He walked into the house.

Danno with the cans on his arms turned to face him. Julia's face was red and outraged.

Danno raised his free hand in a sort of salute. A diffident one.

"Hello," he said. "Like the bad penny I am." He tried to laugh. Cahal noticed he was missing a lot of teeth since he saw him last. His face had fallen in with the loss of them. It didn't look as big nor as powerful.

"Hello," said Cahal equably. Danno sighed with relief.

"I was just tellin' herself," he said, "that I'm on me way from the fair in Clare and I'm goin' holin' up in Leitrim."

"Sit down," said Cahal. "Have a sup of tay."

Danno was amazed. He let his mouth hang open. Julia stiffened.

"Thanks, thanks," said Danno, sitting back on the settle bed.

"Make the tay, Julia," said Cahal quietly. "I could do with a sup meself." He sat at the table under the window. He looked over at his father. He wanted to laugh. Here's a situation. How should he feel? Like kicking out the rest of the tinker's teeth? Danno had more clothes on him. He had a shirt and a scarf and a waistcoat and another ragged short coat over that. His hat was well soiled. He could have done with a shave. He had two weeks on him at least and they were almost all white bristles. The hands were still powerful, he noticed, and muscles throbbed under the tight clothes of his trousers. Danno was finding it hard to find something to say. It must have been a new experience for him.

"Do you camp out for the winter?" Cahal asked, to help him.

"No, no," said Danno, shaking himself. "We have an oul doss above in Mohill. Stay there until the spring we do, and then we start them fairs again. There's oney meself now."

"Lost your family?" Cahal asked.

"Yes," said Danno. He drew his brows down. "That last wan. She was no good, that wan. She was waste, waste. I lost her up in Donegal."

"What happened?"

"What do y' think happened? She met a fella up there. He was an Orange tinker, the bastard, from Down. He was a pretty big man. I'm not as good on the pins as I was. I can still fight two min or three if I have to and you put a black-thorn stick in me hand. But this fella was shockin' big. Oh, a powerful big bull of a fella. He got behind me too when I wasn't lookin'. I was four weeks in the hospital above there.

When I kem out she was gone. Do you remember the little fella we had?"

"I do," said Cahal, "that was young Danno."

"Aye, young Danno, young Danno," said Danno. "I liked that little fella. He was good company. God, you should ha' seen him drainin' a porter glass. He was a good little man with a horse too. A good little fella. I liked him. Well, she took him as well. Haven't laid an eye on him from that day to this."

"All alone, so," said Cahal.

"That's right," said Danno, "all alone. That's a nice do at the end of me trip and all of them I launched, hah?" He chuckled.

"You must have a fair-sized family," said Cahal, grinning.

"Shush, man," said Danno, putting up his hand to hide his grin. It was a habit he'd got into since he had lost his teeth. Some of them he lost fighting, and some of them had been pulled for him by a comrade with a horse pliers. He was vain. He always knew he was a sight with the black hair and the white teeth. So it was instinctive with him to have that little vanity. Sometimes he forgot, when he was tired or didn't care any more. He was a betther-lookin' man than this Cahal fella. He was indeed. He had a well-shaped face; he hadn't the big bulge in the jaws like him. It was kind of him all the same to give him a sup of tay. It wouldn't be Barney that would be in it. Woo! That Barney. He'd frighten the guts out of you, so he would. He didn't like the old woman though. She looked at him like he was a bad smell. Gob's, where'd Cahal got her? He hadn't his father's taste anyhow, that was one thing. Danno liked them young and got them that way too. Hard now though, there was so many young bulls goin' the road.

"Pull over a chair," said Cahal, "the tay is made."

Danno left his cans on the ground, and took a chair over to the table. He dropped his hat beside him on the floor. His hair wasn't all black now, but it was still thick. He sucked at the hot tea from the mug. He broke off a piece of cake and put it into his mouth. He had to wet it well with the tea before he could masticate it.

"What will you do now, Danno, for the rest of your time?" Cahal asked after a while.

"Do? Do?" asked Danno. He shrugged his shoulders. "The same as always."

"And what happens you at the end?" Cahal asked. "A dog goes smelling along by the road and finds you dead in the ditch?"

"What matther? What matther?" Danno rubbed it away. "You have the sky over you. Dead doesn't matther."

"No ambition, even yet?" Cahal laughed.

"Hump it!" said Danno, "what does it matther? I had a good life. I'll have a good life yet." He ate ravenously.

"Are you back at the bridge?" Cahal asked.

"Um. Um," said Danno, eating. "Goin' away in the mornin'."

Julia sighed. Thank God for that. What strange fit was on him that he didn't kick that dirty divil out the door. People would hear about this, you'd see. It was so humiliating that it gave you a pain in your stomach. She would put that mug away high on the shelf so that nobody would ever use it again.

"Do you want anything?" Cahal asked Danno.

"Few things," said Danno. "Egg or two maybe. A bag of hay for the horse. A graneen of flour. Nothin' else. Nothin' else. An oul coat, maybe. It's goin' to be a hard winter. Did ye know that? Be well stocked up, man. It's goin' to be the hardest winter for a long time."

Cahal rose from the table. He took one of the cans and half filled it with flour from the bag in the nook. He put eggs on top of the flour from the dish in the dresser. Then he poured milk into the other can. "That'll keep you goin' for a while," he said. "I'll get you some hay on the way out."

"Thanks, man, thanks, man," said Danno. "You're a gint. Thanks for the tay, ma'am. It was grand." He rose to his feet. He collected the cans and followed Cahal into the yard. Cahal went into the haggard and pulled hay from the huge garden cock. He stuffed an old sack full and brought it out. Danno hoisted it on his shoulder.

"You're a dacent man," he said. "I won't forget. Or maybe I will forget but what matther? I have the good notion of you now, anyhow."

"That's good enough," said Cahal. "Goodbye, Danno."

Danno rubbed the toe of a boot on the gravel.

"I'm sorry, man, for all that happened," he said. "I really liked your mother. That was true. I tould that to oul Barney the day I kem to see him. You never think of the harm you bring on other people. Love is a curshe, man, honest to Christ it is. It causes more damage. Don't be talkin'. It's a pity we don't have times over again, but that wouldn't do. Well, good man, thanks for the stuff. You know what I'm tryin' to say?"

"I think so, Danno," said Cahal. "It doesn't matter. It's all fixed up some other place anyhow before we have anything to do with it."

"Well, so," said Danno. "You needn't think, man, that I'll be plaguing you agin. Never agin. This is the last of me you'll see."

"Have it your way," said Cahal.

"I was just passin'," said Danno, "goin' this road like, and I thought I'd drop in. It's quare you have to become ould before you're sorry for all the fun you have." He chuckled again. Then he moved up towards the road. "Goodbye, man, and don't think too hard of me." He threw that over his shoulders and then passed on his way. He still had powerful shoulders. There was still plenty of meat on them but they were permanently bent. He could imagine the enjoyment Nessa got out of seeing him being beaten. Well, maybe he had it coming to him. He sighed and went back into the house.

He washed himself in the basin and put on his clean clothes. She didn't say anything. Even if she disapproved. After that he went the road to the meadow and collected the two cows and brought them back, tied the chains on their necks and milked them. They were glad of the shelter. The evenings were turning very cold.

She had the supper ready when he went in. Potatoes mashed and mixed with butter and a few pieces of onions and milk. Cally. Very nice it was.

He sat at the fire and watched her washing up the dishes. What was wrong with him this evening, he wondered? He found himself feeling sorry for her. She was looking her age. The skin of her face was very coarse and was dragging. She was very thin. She might be hardy, but she was very thin. Her bones were barely covered. He remembered back to the day he had seen her first. The nice clothes, the soft hand and the nice smell of scent from her. God, how could time have done this to her? If you saw a picture of her the way she was that day, you would never believe it. He rose abruptly and went up to his own room. He pulled the letter from Barney's trunk and brought it down to the kitchen. He got the pen and ink from the mantelpiece. He wrote what he wanted to write on the back of it.

She was finished the washing now. She was sitting on the stool at the fire darning one of his heavy woollen socks. He was leaning on the table looking at her. She felt his gaze. It took her a long time. Then she looked up. She thought his eyes were kindly, and then thought she must be wishful thinking again. He spoke.

"It's been a poor do, Julia," he said.

"You shouldn't have kept him in here and fed him," she answered. "You know what they'll say now."

"I don't mean Danno," he said. "I mean me and you." What's the use of that, he thought? It's too old. The skin over it is too hard and too dried and shrunken. You can never get in through all that.

It left her without a word. What could she say? When she saw him at all it was through a cloud of inertia.

"Look," he said. "You know Barney's son has left me the place legally. This is his letter."

"What about it?" she asked.

"Well, on the back of it," he said, "I have written that I want you to get it in case anything happens to me."

"I don't know what you mean," she said. "What do you mean? What could happen to you?"

"Nothing, nothing," said Cahal, sorry already for his endeavour. "Just you never know. So I have written here that it's yours and I'll get two people to put their writing to it and it'll be all legal. Just that. I wanted to tell you that."

"You're actin' strange," she said.

"Maybe so," said Cahal, rising and going over to the settle bed. He reached for the melodeon and loosened it. "I just wanted you to know, that's all." How could anyone climb back over the years? What was the good of climbing back over the years? It got you no place, no place at all. It wasn't really her fault, all the wrongs and the rights. It was all written down in a cynical book somewhere. But she had suffered it. Or had she? Sometimes he thought she wasn't sensitive enough to feel anything. More times he didn't know. Let it lie now. It can never be squared. She didn't know that they would have callers tonight. It was easy to keep that from her. None of the others would tell her and he didn't tell her. Let it pass over her head. That's why he had dressed himself in his best clothes and shaved himself. If they had the courage to come, he wanted to be decked up when he told them what he thought about them. This night would go down in the history of Caherlo if he didn't go down in the history himself. There were so many things coiling up in him that he wanted to get off his chest, and they were presenting him with a large-sized opportunity to get them off his chest. He wouldn't even think about what he'd tell them. It'd flow out of him when the time came.

The music he played was lively and soft.

He played for a long time. Until the daylight faded outside and the dark clouds grew and covered the moon. They didn't cover it all the time. He knew that from the reflection on the white stable wall he could see through the open door. Sometimes it darkened almost from sight and then it emerged greenly white again. Julia got tired. She lighted the lamp and closed the big door and pulled the blind. Then she lighted her own candle and went to her room. No pleasantries. Goodnight, darling. Sweet dreams. It was affter ten o'clock. They were leaving it very late, weren't they? They were leaving it so late that it must mean their courage wasn't equal to the blowing of their big mouths.

He dropped the melodeon and he raked the fire.

It became very silent near eleven. He found himself walking the length of the kitchen and back. There was sweat on the palms of his hands. He went back to his room. He was sitting on the bed about to untie the laces of his boots when he heard the loud thump at the front door.

It made his heart beat fast. He swallowed. He tried to collect his thoughts. He was helped by another bang on the door. That angered him. He went down to the kitchen. It was in darkness. He had blown out the lamp. He pulled the bolt on the door. He was remembering Peder's tale long, long ago about the night he answered the door in his shirt. What had happened to those days of the stories? What had happened to Peder?

He opened the door and stepped out.

The moon was just being swallowed, but he had time enough to see the half-circle of forms in front of him. They couldn't come alone. They had to get help. These would be men from Glen and Grove and some of Peder's neighbours in Ballybla. He stood there in front of them. His hands were up on his hips. He was drawing breaths of air into his lungs.

"Well," he began, and got no further because a stone struck him on the side of the head. He staggered out towards them with his hand up to the wound. He was dazed. He was terribly surprised. I wanted to talk to them. I wanted to educate them. There was no time for talk, no time for education. They closed in on him. In the feeble light he saw the thin neck and teeth. "Gob," said Cahal, and then he was on his knees from the blow of the stick. A kick in the side sent him flat on his face. He was bewildered there. There's something wrong with this. It shouldn't be like this. He felt terror then. He had misjudged them. Because he knew them. There was Gob and Peder and big Jamesey Jordan. They wouldn't do this. Not to a dog. But they would. A boot crunched into his jaw and another one into his ribs. The blood was dripping into the gravel from the cut on his head. He would have dropped into insensibility but for the muttered sentence he heard in the midst of the pain. Somebody, a disembodied voice that said: Now we will go back and deal with the hoor Brodel. He pulled his thoughts into his head. He pulled up his knees to protect his sides. He pushed his arms over his head to protect them and then in a burst of passion he was on his feet, knowing exactly what he had to do. He butted forward with his head and struck out with his two hands and then he jerked to his left and threw his whole weight against the dark figures there. They exploded back from him and he ran. Not on to the road, but to his left towards his own haggard. He had closed the gate coming out with Danno's hay. Why did I do that? It didn't matter. He was over the gate in a vault and into the haggard and turned left and was over the wooden gate into the kitchen garden. He ran down by the cabbages. He couldn't see but he knew every inch of the garden. There was a hedge at the end of it leading into the common fields. It was a hedge of woodbine trees and hawthorn. They were young ones. He dived in through them. He went through because he could hear the commotion in the garden behind him. He landed heavily on his face on the far side of the hedge. He paused a few moments for breath and then he got up and ran. There were drills of potatoes under his feet. He could smell the rotten stalks of them. The ground was very uneven. The moon was hidden. There was no light. He had to guess. He stumbled and fell, stumbled and fell many times, driven on by the sound of them raping the hedge behind him, and then he was in his own plot and his feet became confident and he ran along the mearing and turned down towards the hedge guarding the common from the river meadows.

It was a high jump from there, but the moon came out and he could see it. He landed, but heard the shouts from behind him. At least they were shouting. It was the terrible silence that had been so bad.

He knew what he had to do now. He went down towards the river. He leaped the brook that came from the humped bridge and ran along on the wind on the right of the river. The moon was well out now. He could see them moving on the road to his right and he could hear them behind him. He ran closely, conserving his breath as much as he could, trying not to think, saying there is only one thing at a time to be done. He reached the great wind of the river where it turned towards the road and ran along it. It came too near the road. He could see them out there closing up to him. The river wound again, going away from the road. They ran from the road across the fields towards him. He could see the sticks in their hands, waving. He came to the planks across the river. It had narrowed here after its second twist. There were two heavy planks bridging it, to save the great walk around from the big road to the bog road. He ran across the planks and when he got to the other side he went on his knees and tugged at the ends of them with his hands. They were buried deep in the grass from the weight of the years. He got his fingers under them. The rotted piece came away in his hand. He tried again. He managed to lift it. He levered himself to his feet staggering and when he had got to his feet he swung with his arm and the plank went into the river. The river took it, swallowed it, regurgitated it, and carried it away. Then he bent to the second one. He got that too and the river took it. The figures on the other bank paused and then flung. He dodged a stick. It sailed over his head. He bent then and scooped water up with his hand. He drenched his face with it. It wiped off the blood that was seeping into his eye. He ignored them. He stood up. He shook his head. Then he turned his back on them and set off up the rounding hill, heading in a jog trot for her house. He had at least ten minutes on them. They would have to go around by the big bridge. They could swim the river. He didn't think they would swim the river.

There was no light in her house.

He banged at the door insistently. Banged again, looking around. He could see down to the bridge, but the moon was gone again. A light came on in the room on his right. That was her father. A light came on in her room. That would be her. Her father came to the door. He raised the candle in his hand. "My God!" he said when he saw him.

Cahal went in. He went over to a chair and sat in it deliberately. He drew air into his lungs. Breathed hard.

"We have very little time," he said then. "Tell her to dress. We'll have to go."

Cahal would remember her father for a long time. He didn't answer. He went straight to her door and he opened it and shouted up: "Get dressed, Máire."

"You won't come?" said Cahal.

"I'm staying here," he said grimly.

"What about your man?" Cahal asked. "Can they get at him?"

"No," said her father. "One time they drove his cattle. Another time they cut the tails off his bullocks. He will never forgive them for that. No, I'm staying here." He went up to his own room. He came back with a shotgun. He rammed two cartridges into it. "The first one over their heads," he said, "the next one into their teeth. You can stay here if you like. We'll keep them until they cool off, or until somebody gets the police."

"No," said Cahal. "You haven't been with them. They'd tear the house down. They have me afraid. Did you know that? How can it be possible to be afraid of simple men like them?"

"They're not simple," said her father. "They're in a mob. The darkness of the night is around them. They have power in them."

She came down from the room.

Her hair was disordered. There was sleep in her eyes.

She looked at Cahal.

"Oh, Cahal," she said.

"It's all right," he said. "It's not much. We better hurry. They'll come around by the bridge."

"We never knew," she said. "We never had a suspicion."

"I didn't either," said Cahal. He got her coat from the peg. He held it for her. She shoved her arms into it.

"We'll go now so," said Cahal.

"Goodbye, father," said Máire. "We will write to you."

For some reason then the three of them laughed. Was it hysteria? Cahal didn't think so.

"Be careful, father," she said.

"I'm finished being careful," her father said. "I'm goin' to hit back now. I'm not movin' from here."

"All right," she said.

He opened the door. They went into the night. Cahal caught her left hand in his. It was warm yet from the sleep.

They turned up behind the house and ran into the long, long sheepfield, cutting across it diagonally. It would bring them near the cross-roads. The moon seemed to have gone forever.

"Did they hurt you? Did they hurt you?" she asked.

"Not much," said Cahal. "It's them. Just ordinary men to be like that. Thought I could talk to them. Quietly. Maybe not peaceably. Got no chance." They were well across the fields when they heard the shot from behind. They stood up. They listened. There was no other shot. Cahal laughed.

"Is it funny?" Máire asked.

"No," said Cahal. "It's not funny. Runnin' away is not funny."

"And stayin' is murder," said Máire.

"It might be as well," said Cahal. "Isn't it a terrible thing that we have to be kicked into freedom?"

"What's that?" she asked.

"That's what they're doing," said Cahal. "They're kicking

us into freedom. I bet they don't know that. I bet, if they knew that, they would be beggin' us with tears in their eyes to stop. Isn't it so? Isn't it so? It all happened like that. What are we going to do? How will we not hurt other people? Now we don't have to worry. It's all taken away from us. The decisions. The world is wide. There is a lot of it. And a lot to be seen. Think of that. And the two of us together for always seein' the world. Imagine that, Máire? Does that make you feel good, Máire?"

"Doing what?" Máire asked. "You playing the melodeon and singing at fairs and me holding the beggin' mug in my maimed hand?"

"That's it," Cahal laughed. "That's the spirit, Máire. Now you see. The poor eejits: if only they knew."

"We'll know nothing," said Máire, "if they catch up with us."

They turned and ran. Her long legs covered the ground well. When she stumbled his hand held her up. Sometimes he had to raise a hand and brush the blood away from his eyes. But he felt good. It had to take a blood-letting to get rid of indecisiveness. Imagine that. Now he was like a bird. He could run fifty miles if there was freedom at the end of it. Behind them was the loneliness and the suffering. Before them was all that they should have taken years ago. Like an apple you could eat into. No inhibitions. No people. No one to decry.

They climbed the wall into the road. Máire was breathless. After all, it wasn't so long ago since she had been lying on a hospital bed. She leaned against the wall, her hand up to her breast.

"Máire! Máire! Are you all right?" he begged her. He had his hands on her shoulders.

"I'll be all right in a minute," she said, bending down, her hand on her knee, drawing breath into her. She was afraid she was going to faint. There was whirling in her head.

Cahal heard the boots pounding on the flints of the road. Fury welled in him. He'd have to kill somebody if they caught up with them. But that'd be no good. If they laid their hands on her. He took two heavy stones from the wall. He stood facing the pounding feet. "Máire! Máire!" he shouted back over his shoulder. "Tell me when you're all right and we'll go."

"We'll go now," she said. He threw away one stone and took her hand. She was not all right. Her running was slow. He had to shift an arm about her waist. She had her head back, pulling air into her lungs. The hair prickled on the back of his neck as he heard the pound of the boots coming nearer. He waited for a blow on his head. He was thinking wouldn't it be better to stop and face them, and rage into them with a stone in each fist. Then he heard the furious clattering of a horse's hooves. And a voice bellowing. Shouting. He could hear the thumping of the stick on the horse's back. It came nearer and nearer. He could almost hear the boots scattering; then he turned. He halted her. The moon came out. He saw Danno standing in the tinker's cart. The horse was rearing and galloping at intervals. Danno's stick was rising and falling, sometimes on the horse, sometimes on the figures that were near the cart. Then it was through the ring and he was waving at Cahal. "Here! Here! Here!" he was shouting.

He stopped the horse beside them.

Cahal reached for Máire and threw her up into the cart.

"What's goin' on? What's goin' on?" Danno was shouting. "Floggers tumble me outa me bed. Throw down me camp. Kick me pots. Hit me on the head."

"Give Máire the reins," Cahal shouted. "Come down from the cart." He could see blood on Danno's forehead. "Down with you. Down with you."

Máire took the reins kneeling and held the quivering horse. Danno jumped down beside Cahal, the stick swinging in his hand. Cahal collected another stone from the wall by the side of the road. They couldn't even leave the poor tinker alone; root and branch, root and branch, they would say.

"If they come near us we'll kill some of them," said Cahal between his teeth. "If I go down, get aboard and take her out of here." Then he shouted back down the road where the figures were black, indistinguishable even in the scudding light of the moon. "Come on into the open now," he shouted. "There's two men here. Can ye face two men? Come on into the open and show yeer faces."

"Ye lousy bowsers," Danno shouted. "Ye could have left me till the mornin'. I'm an oul man. But I can bate five of ye put together. Come on and get it now, ye skulkin' scoundrels." He danced a bit on the road. Like Cahal had remembered him selling a horse, threatening himself at a holy well a hundred years ago.

They had thinned out, Cahal thought. It was only the young that could keep up the chase. They didn't approach any closer. No sound came from them. They just stood, dark unmoving shadows in the shelter of the walls. The lust is gone, Cahal could feel. The drunken bout is over. Tomorrow they will wake up with a bad taste in their mouths. Well, let them go.

He shouted again.

"Goodbye, Gob," he shouted. "Goodbye, Jamesey. Goodbye, Peder Clancy. Don't forget me. The day ye are at yeer own auctions and the Murphys are buying yer little pieces of farms, let ye not forget me. When yeer dead in yeer graves and the whole of Caherlo is Murphyfield, let ye not forget me. Go back and think who is making ye do all this. How was it all worked. And then start thinking of the Murphys. And no matter where I go, ye hear, a song will reach back to ye from me. Ye won't forget me, by God, ye won't forget me!"

"Come on," said Danno. "If they won't come to us, we'll go after them. They're licked now. Come on and we'll knock the dust out of them."

"No," said Cahal. "We'll be gone."

He got up on the cart. Danno climbed up too, after shouting an obscene taunt back at them. He took the reins and the horse ran on. Cahal had his arms around Máire. "It's all over now, Máire," he said.

"No," she said, "it's only beginning now."

They came to the cross-roads.

"Stop here," Cahal shouted at Danno.

Danno pulled up the horse.

"Why? Why? Why, man?" he asked.

"Because you're going to Leitrim," he said. "This is where the roads part for us."

"Yeer not comin' with me?" Danno asked. "I know the roads. The roads is very lonely."

"Not for us, Danno," said Cahal.

"I see," said Danno, squatting on the edge of the cart and sighing. He helped Máire down.

"Thanks, Danno," he said. "We might meet again. We might not."

"The world is very wide," said Danno. "And very small."

"We are only starting it," said Cahal.

"God bless ye," said Danno. Then he clucked at the horse with his tongue and the horse went on slowly. They stood there until there was nothing but the sound of the cart to be heard. Then they turned up the road towards the silver birches. The moon was out. They could see it gleaming on the thin trunks of the trees ahead of them. Cahal tucked her good left hand into his own and started to walk towards them.

"We have no clothes, no meat, no money," he said.

"No shoes, or stockings, or wedding dresses," said Máire.

"What have we really?" Cahal asked.

"I have you," she said.

"If there was a trunk of gold and a thousand acres of land on me right hand and you on me left, I would take you," said Cahal.

"You can sing," she said. "You can make songs."

"Haven't we the whole world in front of us?" he asked.

"Not tinkers?" she inquired.

"No," said Cahal, "not tinkers; wandering lovers, that's

what we are. You know, the day I came here, I could think of nothing but the avenue of the silver birches. I thought when I got there I would be home. That was the way I felt. I got there, and I felt that way, and here we're coming up on them for the last time, and when we leave them, I don't feel like we will be leavin' home. I should never have come into them. I only came into them for one reason. You know why?"

"Why?" she asked.

"To take you out of it," said Cahal. "That was the reason for the whole trip."

"It took a long time," said Máire, "a long, long time."

"I'll make up for it," said Cahal, "on me oath I will; there will never be a tear out of you any more that won't come from a laugh. Wait'll you see."

They didn't talk as they went under the avenue of the silver birches. It swallowed them up in deep darkness. At the other end if it, the moon shone on the long grey road.

It seemed to be beckoning, inviting, exciting, as it stretched away to the very edges of the world.